SHIP of the DAMNED

SHIP

OF THE

James F. David

DAMNED

A Tom Doherty Associates Book

New York

SHIP OF THE DAMNED

Copyright © 2000 by James F. David

A Forge Book
Published by Tom Doherty Associates, LLC
175 Fifth Avenue
New York, NY 10010

www.tor.com

Forge® is a registered trademark of Tom Doherty Associates, LLC.

BOOK DESIGN BY AMANDA DEWEY

Library of Congress Cataloging-in-Publication Data

David, James F.
    Ship of the damned / James F. David—1st ed.
        p. cm.
    "A Tom Doherty Associates book."
    ISBN 0-312-87203-8
    1. Teleportation—Fiction. 2. Dreams—Fiction. 3.
    Ships—Fiction. I. Title.
  PS3554.A9155 S55   2000
  813'.54—dc 21

                                        00-024486

First Edition: August 2000

Printed in the United States of America

0 9 8 7 6 5 4 3 2 1

Thanks to my editor, Bob Gleason, and my agent, Carol McCleary, for their continued enthusiasm for my projects. I appreciate their suggestions and encouragement.

Gale and Abby, thanks for reading and re-reading my manuscript. Is it really true the story gets better every time you read it? Katie, you're next in line to be your dad's reader, and then, Bethany, it's your turn.

This book is for the readers of *Fragments* who weren't ready to say goodbye to Ralph.

Dramatis Personae

SHIRLEY ANDREWS—Mother of Anita.

ANITA ANDREWS—Seven-year-old dreamer.

DR. BIRNBAUM—Ralph's guardian and parapsychologist, who is confined to a wheelchair.

LEN CHAIKIN—Engineer who built the mind-melding computer.

JOHN COBB—A Special with the ability to generate and conduct electricity.

KARLA COMPTON—Field agent with the Office of Special Projects.

ROBERT DALY—Sixty-year-old trustee of the Kellum Foundation.

ROGER DAWSON—Sailor from the USS *Norfolk*; transmitter of the dream.

ROBIN EVANS—Scarred survivor of an earlier incursion into Pot of Gold; agent with the Office of Special Projects.

ELIZABETH FOXWORTH—Social worker; collaborator of Wes Martin.

GERTIE—A Special with psychokinetic abilities.

NATHAN JETT—Field agent with the Office of Special Projects; team leader.

JASON JETT—Nathan Jett's twin brother.

WANDA JOHNSON—Seventy-six-year-old chain smoker and one of the dreamers.

DR. WALTER KELLUM—Colleague of Albert Einstein; pioneer researcher in television, radio, and resonant magnetic fields.

MONICA KIM—Korean-American social worker who first brings the dreamers to Dr. Martin.

DR. LEE—Director of the secret government facility code-named "Rainbow."

DR. WES MARTIN—Experimental neuropsychologist, developer of the mind-melding software.

LAYTON MCNAB—Chief petty officer, whose psi ability allows him to manipulate the minds of others; calls himself "Prophet" and is cult leader of the Crazies.

SHAMITA PATEL—Indian-American engineer, designer of the hardware for the mind-melding computer.

JIM PETERS—Field agent with the Office of Special Projects.

RALPH—Retarded adult male, with a unique spatial ability and immunity to some psi powers.

ROBERTO—Civilian inside Pot of Gold, and one of Kellum's people.

JERRY RUST—A Special with pyrokinetic abilities (the ability to create heat and fire).

BILLY THOMPSON—African-American field agent with the Office of Special Projects.

MARGI WINSTON—Thirty-year-old dreamer.

OSCAR WOOLMAN—Director of the Office of Special Projects.

Preface

The Philadelphia Experiment

On July 22, 1943, scientists working for the U.S. Navy conducted an experiment that had remarkable and far reaching results, and which continues to generate controversy to this day. The goal of the original experiment was to develop electronic camouflage that would render U.S. warships invisible to enemy radar and even invisible to the human eye. Scientists recruited for the project included some of the world's finest, including Albert Einstein and Nikola Tesla. Based on extrapolations from Einstein's unified field theory, these researchers believed that by pulsing magnetic-field generators at certain frequencies, they could cause the fields to resonate, thus generating a magnetic field so intense that it would bend light and radar around a ship, making it invisible. Code-named "Project Rainbow," the electronic camouflage project succeeded far beyond expectations, and according to witnesses, the Navy released a force they couldn't control.

The destroyer DE 173, USS Eldridge and its crew were selected for the experiment and the ship was fitted with two large 75KVA degaussers (magnetic-field generators) which had been modified for the experiment. These were mounted in place of the forward gun turrets. In addition there were four large magnetic coils and three thousand 6L6 power amplifier tubes. The various pieces of equipment were connected with circuits designed for synchronizing and modulating the magnetic fields. The goal was to adjust the modulations (pulses) until the two magnetic fields resonated, thus exponentially magnifying the combined power of the two fields.

At 0900 hours on July 22, 1943, in the Philadelphia Naval Shipyard, the equipment aboard the USS Eldridge was powered up and the experiment began. At first nothing appeared to be happening, but slowly those on the ship began to feel the build-up of electric charge. The crew had been issued rubber boots and sou'westers to insulate them against severe electric shock. Slowly a green mist formed and the sky darkened. From the outside the ship appeared to be enveloped in a greenish fog spreading one hundred yards in all directions. Then the fog and the ship disappeared. A few seconds later the ship was back, and the experiment ended.

The Navy had succeeded in rendering the DE 173 invisible, but there were deleterious effects on the crew. Many of the men acted as if they were drunk, speaking with slurred speech and staggering. Some were extremely giddy, others were disoriented, and some complained of double vision. Most were nauseous and a few lost consciousness. Despite the effects on the crew, the Navy was excited by the first test of the equipment and ordered continuation of the research.

The second experiment took place on October 28, 1943, at 0715 hours. The equipment aboard the USS Eldridge had been modified to increase its power and adjustments made in the frequency of the modulation. When the equipment was powered up there was again the gradual build-up of an electric charge, and again the ship was slowly enveloped in a green fog which spread out around it. This time, though, just as the ship became invisible, there was a blue flash. Simultaneously, witnesses aboard the SS Andrew Fusureth, which was anchored in the Norfolk, Virginia harbor, reported seeing the USS Eldridge suddenly appear. The Eldridge, which displaced more than 1500 tons, had been instantly teleported from one state to another. Then, just as suddenly, the ship was back in the Philadelphia Naval Shipyard.

This time the effects on the crew were even more powerful. Some members were insane, many were unconscious or violently sick, some were dead, and some were missing. Most horrifying of all was the fact that some of the crew had fused with the metal of the ship, and arms and legs protruded from decks and bulkheads. There appeared to be delayed effects from the experiment, too; one Philadelphia newspaper carried accounts of a bar brawl in which some of the seamen from the USS Eldridge became transparent while others walked through walls and vanished.

Surviving members of the USS Eldridge's crew reported that during the experiment, time seemed to slow down, or for some, come to a standstill, and that while they were inside the green fog they felt sluggish. Their movements were labored and they felt like they were pushing their way through molasses. After the experiment the crew continued to experience time distortions, and would occasionally "freeze," or become stuck in time. (During a freeze the frozen person doesn't experience the passage of time and remains motionless like a statue, letting time flow around him.) Men who were frozen like this were unresponsive and seemingly unaware of their surroundings. Then, just as suddenly as the freeze had gripped them, the frozen men would thaw and rejoin the time flow, continuing as if nothing had happened.

While the U.S. Government admits that research was conducted at the Philadelphia Naval Shipyard in the 1940s, it denies that any ships were rendered invisible or that any crew members suffered from the experiments. Curiously, the Navy does confirm that there were experiments using high-frequency generators and that these experiments did create coronas, thus confirming parts of the story. Despite the government's denials, or perhaps because of them, many people believe that the Philadelphia Experiment did take place and, like the Roswell, New Mexico UFO crash and the CIA's MK-Ultra mind-control experiments, has been covered up by the U.S. Government. Because each of these events has been mythologized in its own complex way, separating fact from fiction is difficult. However, each of these legends seems to be built on the foundation of real events.

While the core of the Philadelphia Experiment story remains the same in most accounts, details of the experiment vary depending on the source. Some sources claim that there was only one experiment in the Philadelphia Naval Shipyard, which took place in July, with the October experiment taking place at sea. There are reports claiming that the ship wasn't teleported to Norfolk, but instead to another dimension where the crew encountered aliens. Another variation has the ship appearing in Norfolk three years after it disappeared from Philadelphia, and not instantly.

While not all parts of the story can be confirmed, some of the details can. There was a destroyer escort commissioned the Eldridge, and the DE 173 is listed in *Jane's Fighting Ships* and other ship registries. The Eldridge survived World War II and was sold to Greece in 1951 and renamed the Léon (there is a web page devoted to the ship). Albert Einstein was indeed a consultant to the Bureau of Ordnance between May 31, 1943, and June 30, 1944, the period during which the experiments supposedly took place. There are eyewitnesses who say they saw a ship disappear at sea, including the ship's master of the SS Andrew Fusureth, and there are newspaper accounts of the bar brawl that supposedly included crew members of the USS Eldridge.

For the purposes of my novel I assumed that two experiments took place, and that the second experiment never really ended. I have the first experiment taking place on the Eldridge and the other on the cruiser Norfolk. The CA 137, Norfolk, was designed to be a Baltimore class cruiser and was to be built at the Philadelphia Naval Shipyard at about the time of the experiment. Records show that construction of the CA 137 was cancelled in December 1945. I moved the second Philadelphia Experiment to the cruiser Norfolk in order to get more space for the action, and because I was struck by the coincidence between the ship's name and the location to which the Eldridge was supposedly transported. I admit to wondering briefly whether the details from the eyewitnesses might have become confused over the years; perhaps, in fact, the Eldridge wasn't transported to Norfolk, Virginia, but rather the cruiser Norfolk was transported somewhere in space and time. Could it be that construction of the Norfolk had proceeded in Philadelphia and that the experimental electronic camouflage equipment was moved to this larger ship for sea trials? The existence of two experimental ships might help explain why there is confusion over the number of experiments conducted and their location. It could be that the Eldridge was the ship that disappeared from the Philadelphia Shipyard, and the Norfolk the ship that eyewitnesses saw disappear in a green fog from the middle of the ocean. Certainly, listing construction of the Norfolk as "cancelled" would be the simplest way to cover up the loss of the ship. Then again, perhaps this is just the kind of speculation that gets passed around and confused for fact, and ends up as part of an urban legend.

If you would like more information about the Philadelphia Experiment there are books, web pages, and a movie devoted to it. Perhaps the easiest way to begin your search is to access an Internet search engine and type in the key words "Philadelphia Experiment."

PROLOGUE

Dr. Lee huddled in the belly of the plane, hands deep in the pockets of his parka, his briefcase at his feet. His wire-rimmed glasses needed straightening, but when he pulled his hand from his pocket it shook so badly he feared he would knock his glasses from his face.

"Want some coffee?" a crewman shouted over the roar of the twin jet engines.

Dr. Lee shook his head, refusing the coffee, knowing he could never hold it steady enough to drink until he was safe on the ground again. With preparation, meditation, and willpower, Dr. Lee could tolerate commercial airlines, but just barely. The flight in the Grumman C2-A was nothing like the comfortable Boeing 767 that had taken him to Philadelphia. The C2-A was known as the Carrier Onboard Delivery jet, or C.O.D. Capable of landing and taking off on carrier decks, the C.O.D. shuttled cargo. Dr. Lee was part of today's cargo, along with a jet engine, toilet paper, and cases of fruit cocktail.

The loud whine of the engines wore on Dr. Lee's nerves, and the vibrations resonated through his bones. The C.O.D.'s interior was spartan, with little to cushion his small frame. The two-hour flight to the Nimitz was an eternity to Dr. Lee; he was checking his watch for the hundredth time when a crewman approached, leaning close to his ear.

"We're almost there. The captain wants you to come forward."

Dr. Lee nodded, fumbling to work the latch on his harness and failing, the crewman finally reaching over and deftly releasing it. Using one hand-hold after another Dr. Lee worked his way to the flight deck, where a set of earphones was placed on his head and a microphone pulled in front of his lips. Stepping forward, he leaned between the seats. The pilot spoke from the left seat, pointing through the windscreen.

"The Nimitz is dead ahead."

There were two ships visible, but the aircraft carrier Nimitz dwarfed its companion. Nearly four times the size of the other ship, the Nimitz was nearly beyond his comprehension. Even from this distance Dr. Lee could see dozens of aircraft parked on the ship's vast, flat surface, the only vertical structure being the flight control tower on the starboard side. At the forward end of the deck, "68" was painted in giant numbers. Flanking the Nimitz was a cruiser that would have been impressive in its own right, but like the pretty friend of the beautiful homecoming queen, it paled in comparison. Despite working for Navy intelligence, Dr. Lee knew little about aircraft carriers, but he knew the Nimitz and its cruiser were at the center of a battle group that would include another cruiser, destroyers, and frigates, and somewhere hidden in the deep, miles ahead of the flotilla, two hunter-killer submarines.

Proud of his ship, the pilot fished for compliments.

"Ever seen anything like her?"

"Nothing in the water," Dr. Lee admitted.

"Nothing like her on land either," the pilot said.

The pilot was distressingly young, lacking Dr. Lee's gray hair. Dr. Lee thought he looked about twenty-five, but he preferred to imagine him as a young-looking thirty.

"That deck's nearly five acres, and that makes her as big as a shopping mall," the pilot continued. "She carries ninety aircraft, counting our C.O.D., and about 6000 crew. That's about the same as the town I grew up in—Gillette, Wyoming; ever been there?"

"No," Dr. Lee said.

"Didn't think so," the pilot said. "Someday I'll find someone who has."

"No you won't," Dr. Lee heard over the earphones.

The copilot turned and smiled, and Dr. Lee saw he was younger than the pilot. Dr. Lee gripped the back of the pilot's seat to steady himself.

Once composed, he studied the Nimitz, not seeing her as the most powerful war machine on the planet, but as a mass of conducting metal.

"How much steel?" Dr. Lee asked.

"Fully loaded the Nimitz displaces more than ninety thousand tons. I'd guess eighty percent of that is steel," the pilot said, looking at Dr. Lee. "That's a funny kind of question. I've shuttled a lot of visitors to the Nimitz before—congressmen, senators, reporters—and I've been asked a lot of questions, but never that one. Does what happened have something to do with her steel? She's been sailing since '71 so you'd think any problem would have turned up before now."

Dr. Lee wasn't good at lying. Now he chose his words carefully so he wouldn't raise further suspicions.

"I was just curious. Were you on board when it happened?" he asked.

"Yeah," the pilot said. "I was having coffee in the mess with some of the MIDRATS—that's the midnight watch—when someone came in saying there was something strange up on deck. We'd been at sea for three months and anything that breaks the monotony is a godsend. It was night so we got a good look at it. There was a green glow just off the bow and a couple of hundred feet in the air. Someone said it was the northern lights, but I've seen the northern lights and they look nothing like this. It was the strangest damn thing I've ever seen. A kind of green mist hanging in the air—looked a lot like the fog on a radar screen."

"Tell him about your hair," the copilot urged.

"Yeah, that was something. I was due for a cut, so my hair was pushing regulation. It stood straight on end in all directions. I was charged with static like I'd never been. I knew better than to touch anything metal, but some of the others didn't. I saw a three-inch blue spark shoot between one man's hand and the hatch. I'll tell you we stayed the hell away from metal after that!"

"Did the Nimitz sail into the green light?" Dr. Lee asked.

"No. The air around us was crackling like green wood in a hot fire, but just when we were about to pass under it the light disappeared."

"Were there problems with communication?" Dr. Lee asked, smiling and straightening his glasses again.

Both the smile and the work with his glasses were nervous habits. He was calmer now, the hand tremors controllable. Working on the problem was distracting him from the fact that he was a thousand feet in the air in a fragile craft, piloted by children.

"Some communication problems?" the pilot said. "We had broad band

disruption running from infrared through radar. At first we thought someone had triggered the jamming array on one of the Prowlers. The F-14
pilots flying patrol weren't affected, except for loss of contact with flight
control for a few minutes."

"Were any of the other ships in the battle group affected?" Dr. Lee
asked.

"Not to the same degree. The South Carolina was closest to the Nimitz
and had some of the same electromagnetic interference, but not nearly as
bad."

Dr. Lee nodded, noting that the effect was localized around the
Nimitz.

"How many tons is the South Carolina?"

"You're asking about steel again, aren't you? The South Carolina is a
nuclear-powered cruiser displacing fourteen thousand tons."

"I understand another carrier was affected too?" Dr. Lee probed.

"The John F. Kennedy," the pilot said. "It happened about a year and a
half ago in the same latitude. It's basically the same story except this time
the green glow was coming up from the ocean and it was flickering."

"Not as much interference, either," the copilot added.

"That's right, the interference wasn't anywhere near as bad," the pilot
said, picking up the story. "Kennedy flight control never lost contact with
its planes."

"Tell me about the first time Nimitz encountered the phenomenon,"
Dr. Lee said.

"It was daylight that time, so it was harder to see. It came at the Nimitz
from the stern but never managed to catch up to the ship. She does thirty
knots. Pretty impressive for something as big as the Empire State Building!"

"Yes, very impressive," Dr. Lee said.

In response to a call from the Nimitz, the pilot turned away briefly,
speaking to the ship, repeating and acknowledging instructions.

"We're next after they recover a Tomcat," the pilot said. "Now, what's
all this interest you have in steel?"

"Just a theory," Dr. Lee answered, making up a story on the spot. "If the
Nimitz and the rest of the battle group align themselves in a particular
configuration, and the atmospheric conditions are just right, a flow of electrons might occur from ship to ship, creating an ionizing effect causing
water vapor in the atmosphere to glow."

The pilot looked him in the eye, then turned to his copilot.

"That sounds reasonable," the pilot said sarcastically.

"Exactly what we were saying just before you came up here," the copilot said, then rolled his eyes for the pilot's amusement.

Dr. Lee was tempted to tell them what he really suspected, knowing they would find it even less believable.

"Here comes the Tomcat," the pilot said.

Dr. Lee could see a speck in the distance lining itself up with the carrier. While the Nimitz was massive, he realized the deck must look like a postage stamp in the ocean to the approaching pilot. When he remembered that his plane would have to land on the same postage stamp, his hands resumed trembling.

"There's a bank of lights called the Meatball on the starboard side of the ship," the pilot explained. "It helps the pilot stay on his flight path. If he's dead on he'll clear the stern by fifteen feet and catch the number three arresting wire."

"Ten bucks says he catches the two wire," the copilot said.

"I'll take the three wire," the pilot said.

"Since that green glow always seems to show up in the same latitude and longitude," the pilot continued, "and only when there's a carrier group in the vicinity, they moved our departure date up a few days so we could cruise the area and try to figure out what's going on. I guess that's why you're here."

Dr. Lee knew Navy and NASA ships had combed the area after the Kennedy first encountered the strange effect, but had found nothing. Dr. Lee also knew that all the research ships combined wouldn't have half the steel of the Nimitz.

"You some kind of radar expert or something?" the pilot asked.

"I'm a physicist," Dr. Lee said.

"Didn't I hear you were with Naval Intelligence?"

"A branch. The Office of Special Projects. We do research."

The F-14 Tomcat was lined up at the proper angle now, approaching and descending toward the carrier, its twin tails distinguishable.

"What kind of research?" the pilot probed.

"This and that," Dr. Lee said vaguely.

Suddenly a blast of static filled Dr. Lee's head and he clawed the headphones from his ears. The pilot and copilot pulled their headphones off too, leaving them hanging from their necks.

"Damn, it's back," the copilot shouted, pointing to the carrier.

Dr. Lee saw that the ocean under the Nimitz was glowing. Slowly, a sheet of green light lifted from the sea and began to envelop the ship. The

F-14 pilot pulled up, nearly to the deck, trying to avoid the green glow rapidly spreading up the sides of the carrier.

"Pull up, pull up!" the C.O.D. pilot shouted.

The nose of the Tomcat came up and the plane climbed, rolling left, afterburners on. As it passed over the Nimitz, the afterburners suddenly flamed out and the plane rapidly lost altitude.

"He's lost his engines," the copilot said.

"Eject!" the pilot shouted.

With little or no control, the Tomcat completed a roll just as it hit the sea with an enormous splash. Pieces of the plane flew in all directions as the bulk of the Tomcat dove deep, never to be seen again.

The Nimitz was nearly enveloped in the green glow. When the tip of its radio mast was swallowed by the mysterious mist, the glow suddenly disappeared. Where the sea had been dominated by the majestic mass of the USS Nimitz, there was now nothing but the gray Atlantic Ocean. Six thousand crew, ninety aircraft, a ninety-thousand-ton supercarrier and its nuclear weapons had just vanished.

BREAKOUT

Six months earlier
Bemidji, Minnesota, February 3, 1:12 A.M.

Half frozen and shoes soaked through, Bobby Wilson climbed over a snow-bank to a sidewalk someone had shoveled clean. Wearing white bell-bottoms, no hat or gloves, and a stolen coat too small to zip, he was underdressed for the subfreezing conditions and hugged himself, shivering violently. Bobby muttered as he walked, cussing himself for not finding someone to escape with.

"What were you thinking, Bobby boy?" he said out loud. "You should have waited for someone."

He could have gone searching for shipmates to escape with, but doors to the outside world were rare and had a way of disappearing just as suddenly as they appeared. When he stumbled across a way to get home he took the chance.

"Okay, so you had to risk it, Bobby boy, but at least you should have thought about weather," he told himself.

There wasn't any weather where Bobby had come from; no seasons, not even night and day. It had been so long since he had felt hot or cold, he'd forgotten how miserable weather could make you. Rubbing his arms vigorously, he walked faster, his joints stiff from his long trek through the frozen night. His legs responded sluggishly, his feet and toes numb. Snow started to fall again, the flakes catching on his eyelashes, melting and blurring his vision.

Coming to a skating rink, he paused. The windows were dark, the doors locked. He peered over the fence at the outside rink, remembering his childhood.

"You were a pretty good skater in your day, Bobby boy," he muttered. Bobby being just twenty years old, his "day" was only a few years ago, right before he joined the Navy to fight the Nazis and the Japs. He'd played a lot of sports then, baseball having been his favorite. The baseball thought set off a chain reaction of memories: playing stickball in the street; hitting a game-winning double in high school; and watching the Brooklyn Dodgers with his father, holding a Red Hot in one hand and an orange Nehi in the other.

Bobby looked up, trying to see through the swirling snowflakes to the gray clouds that delivered them. He had seen the clouds when he first emerged, and it had been intoxicating, transfixing him to that spot in the woods. It had been so long since he'd seen clouds or sky, or anything celestial. Like a blind man given his sight through surgery, Bobby had seen the clouds above him again as if for the first time.

Bobby shivered violently, his teeth chattering. He was freezing to death and needed to warm himself, but it was risky. If anyone saw what he could do, they might call the police, or the others the Professor had warned them about. The houses bordering the skating rink were dark, except for an occasional porch light. He decided to risk it. Closing his eyes, he held his hands out, palms facing each other, and thought about a campfire—a big one like at boy scout camp when he was ten. The air between Bobby's hands warmed as he concentrated on the image of that great log fire. There were memories of singing, too—silly camp songs—but he ignored those, focussing his mind on the fire, feeling the heat on his face just as he had that night so many years ago. Opening his eyes he saw there was a ball of light between his hands, radiating warm air. Now spreading his hands wide he watched the ball expand, enveloping him in the warm glow. The snow on his head melted into cold water that ran down onto his face and into his collar, triggering more shivering. A few seconds later the shaking subsided and he felt better. After three more warmings, Bobby felt something new— he was hungry. He hadn't felt hunger in years, and now thought of the hot dog again.

"Lots of mustard," he said. "So much mustard you can hardly see the dog. That's the way Bobby boy likes them."

The warming temporarily chased the cold away, but it also melted the snow into his clothes, and soon the cold seeped into his body again. He had to keep moving. There were lights in the distance, probably from a business district, and he trudged on, keeping on the sidewalks, thanking the home owners who had shoveled their paths clear, cursing those who hadn't.

"Thank you, Mr. Jones," he said to the sleeping owner of a yellow house. "Thank you, Mrs. Harris," he said to the imagined resident of the house next door. Then, climbing through the thick snow in front of the next home, he said, "Too cheap to give the kid next door six bits to shovel your walk, Mr. Smith?"

There was a car in "Mr. Smith's" driveway and Bobby stopped again, staring. Cars were so different here—now—and he had trouble passing them without gawking like a tourist. This one was as sleek as a torpedo, with a long sloping windshield and more glass than three of his Studebakers put together. So smooth was the exterior, it was hard to tell where the steel stopped and the glass began. Brushing the snow from the side he read "Taurus" written in chrome and thought it a funny name for such a spectacular machine. Bobby had heard that cars had changed, and he knew there were other marvels too—airplanes without propellers which carried hundreds of people, rockets that could fly to the moon, and machines that could do math as fast as lighting. He wanted to see all that too, but mostly he wanted to drive one of these cars. Mr. Smith's Taurus was built like a race car; he just knew it had to fly down the open highway. He shivered again, the chill seeping deeper. Reluctantly he moved on.

Three more blocks of talking to himself and he came to a school. It would have a phone, he knew, but he would have to break in to get to it and that could bring the police, or the others. He walked on to the bright glow of city center, but there were no phone booths and that puzzled him. In the cities that he knew there were phone booths on every other corner. A car passed and he resisted gawking, turning to the wall instead, hiding his face. Another block, and another car crossed behind him. He walked faster now, worried they would find him. He didn't know who to trust in this world anymore, not after what had been done to him and the others.

"No, Bobby boy, you don't trust no one you ain't related to," he said.

Another block, and he saw a big building labeled "Kroger." He turned toward it, searching the parking lot—no phone booth. He went to the glass front of the great building, walking its length, looking inside. It was a grocery store; he was amazed at the vast stock. When he reached the entrance at one end he found a phone mounted on the outside of the building. There was no booth and he wondered briefly about the lack of privacy. He picked up the receiver, then stopped—there was no dial, just squares with letters and numbers. There was a slot in the bottom of the phone and instructions telling him to put a card in the slot. He was confused by the instructions, but comforted by the familiar coin slot at the top. Then he saw that a call cost twenty-five cents.

"Two-bits? I want to make a call, not buy the company."

He fished a quarter out of his pocket with a frozen hand. Studying the squares, he pushed the one marked "O" "OPER." Car lights crawled across the wall toward him just as he heard an operator's voice on the line.

"I want to call Chicago, Illinois. Person-to-person to Mrs. Lucy Wilson," Bobby said.

A black car came slowly along the front of the Kroger. Dropping the receiver, he backed to the edge of the building and into a snow pile shoveled from the store entrance. The car stopped and two men got out, wearing beige overcoats and stocking caps but no gloves. When they saw the dangling receiver their hands were in their coats and out with guns in the blink of an eye. Bobby shrank back, indecisive: *fight or run?* He peeked again; they were walking toward his hiding place, the car following. The Kroger had a small roof overhang that created a trough in the thick snow along the wall of the building. He ran through the trough, feet crunching the frozen snow. Suddenly, a bullet whined off the wall, passing just over his right shoulder. He jumped left but the snow was deep and he fell face first. Another bullet passed over his head, smacking into something in the distance. He looked ahead—the car was there now, disgorging two men, flashlights probing the darkness. Rolling over, he turned on the two men behind him, pictured the scout camp fire in his mind and focussed his special ability on the lead man. The man's overcoat burst into flame.

Panicking, the burning man ran, fanning the flames with every step. The second man dove sideways, firing blindly. One bullet smashed a window in the black car; the men near the car took cover behind it. Cursing, one ordered the others to hold their fire. Focussing inward, Bobby let the power flow, heat currents swirling around him, melting the snow and then turning it to steam. The snow hissed as it changed from solid to gas. Pushing outward, he sent fog in all directions. Running toward the street, he tumbled over the snow cleared from the sidewalk then threw himself over the mound on the other side into the street. The fog he'd created was dissipating, and he could see the car again, the men emerging from behind it, searching for him with their flashlights. He lay in the street, shivering with fear and cold, concentrating—thinking of his childhood and the coal—fired furnace in the basement of his home.

"Stoke up that fire, Bobby boy," he said softly.

The fire in his mind roared to life, flames hungrily consuming the coal. In his mind he opened the grate exposing the red-hot core. Using that image, he stood and sent a fireball streaking toward the car. A side window imploded, the interior of the car bursting into flame, the men near it fleeing for their lives. As the fireball lit up the block, they spotted him and sent bullets whining past his head. He ducked too late; a slug buried itself in his shoulder. Left arm useless now, legs nearly frozen, he struggled to his feet, pushing in all directions with his mind, snow vaporizing all around him.

Under cover of the steam, Bobby stumbled across the street to one of the houses and climbed the steps to a screened porch. The storm door was unlocked and he crawled in. There was a porch swing and two chairs, but nothing else. His shoulder was soaked in blood now, and he was weakening. Voices sounded outside. Risking a peek, he pulled himself just high enough to see through the screen. They were in the street searching with flashlights. He looked both ways and saw there were lights in other houses now. Down the block a door opened and a man in a bathrobe came out looking at the burning car.

Bobby looked again at the front door behind him. There were no lights—the house might be empty. He crawled to the door and twisted the handle, pushing. It was locked. Then he heard the thumping of feet and a dog at the other side, barking. Turning, he smashed the far end of the porch with a fireball, then ran hunched over as bullets ripped through the screens, perforating the front wall of the house and shattering the picture window. Diving through the still burning hole, he landed in the snow, slipping twice as he tried to stand. Then he ran between the houses toward the backyard. There was a separate garage in the back of the house and he ran for it.

When he was nearly to the garage, bullets ripped through Bobby's legs, severing muscle and tendon. He went down hard; his face was buried in the snow, his legs were useless. He rolled, striking out wildly with his power until someone screamed. More bullets whizzed past and then his guts were on fire—he was shot again. *Fire*, he thought, and struck out; the garage wall burst into flame. Then a bullet pierced his neck, tearing through his carotid artery. He was bleeding profusely, turning the snow pink, then a vivid red. Bobby clutched at his neck, trying in vain to stem the blood flow.

"It's not fair," he said, his voice liquid from blood seeping into his voice box. "I didn't do nothing."

Men were approaching, guns drawn. He reached into his mind for his power, but it was gone and his vision was going as well. He could barely distinguish the men who had killed him. He lay on his back, perfectly still, eyes open, knowing they were holding their fire because they thought he was already dead. Playing possum he stared into the darkness, snow swirling down to his face. He wanted to see the clouds one more time, but could see only a few feet away. Instead, he thought of the car in Mr. Smith's driveway and pictured himself behind the wheel, driving flat out on the highway. Movement next to him brought him back.

"I never got to drive a car," Bobby said suddenly, startling the men around him.

Then a bullet pierced his skull, exploding out the other side. Bobby Wilson's last thought was of the sleek car with the strange name, "Taurus."

An hour later, a black van pulled up at the Kroger. A man in an overcoat got out and pried open the change box of the phone, spilling out the contents. By flashlight he pushed the coins around until he found the only one without a copper center. Holding the coin close to the beam of light he read the date: 1940. Turning off the flashlight, he dropped the coin into his pocket and climbed back into the van.

SPECIAL PROJECTS

Washington, D.C.

Remodelled four times since World War II, the five-story brick building with old-fashioned double-hung windows still looked run down. Mounted in a quarter of the windows were air conditioners that blocked what little light the windows afforded. The interior was a monotonous institutional green, with halls so narrow they felt like tunnels. Wood trim around the doors provided the only break in the monotony. The top third of the doors was opaque glass, the panes stencilled with the names of obscure branches of government. At the end of the corridor was an elevator, its steel doors painted the same institutional green. Chipped and scratched, the elevator doors shuddered as they slowly opened.

Nathan Jett rode the elevator to the fifth floor, where his department occupied half of the office space. The OSS had used the same space during World War II. When the OSS had been reorganized into the CIA, certain ongoing operations had been consolidated into one branch. Only one of the original operations continued, the one that employed Jett. On paper it was a subdepartment of a small branch of Naval Intelligence. In terms of function, it put the cork back in the bottle whenever the genie escaped.

Jett had been with the Office of Special Projects for four years now. Recruited out of the FBI, he knew he had been selected because he was "emotionally underreactive," had scored low on morality scales (M scores) and high on authoritarianism scales (A scores). The low M score meant he was unconventional, not amoral, so to find his moral center the psychologists had probed using moral dilemmas.

"You're an eighth-grader and you see a friend steal money from the teacher's purse," he remembered a psychologist saying. "He tells you it's to buy medicine for his mother. After school you see your friend buying ice cream with the money. The next day the teacher demands to know who stole her money or the whole class will be punished. Would you tell?"

"What's the punishment?" Jett had asked.

"Would that make a difference?"

"Yes."

"The class would have to miss a field trip to the zoo."

"Then I wouldn't tell."

"Why?" the psychologist probed.

"It wasn't much money, since it only bought ice cream. The teacher could afford to lose that much and I don't like zoos."

"But your friend lied to you—"

"I'd beat the hell out of him!"

Jett's individualized morality meant he didn't rely on others to judge right or wrong, or to mete out punishment. He did accept authority, but didn't wholly trust it, especially where his self-interest was involved.

His low M score was typical of agents like Jett, as was his high A score. The efficiency of hierarchical authority structures was appealing to people like Jett, who preferred a one-person, one-voice management style. A natural leader, Jett was promoted quickly.

There was no paper-and-pencil test for Jett's other distinguishing characteristic—"low emotional reactivity." Jett had a flattened affect, which meant he couldn't experience the full range of human emotions. Fear, panic, and terror were virtually unknown to him, but so were ecstasy, joy, and love. Only in life-threatening situations did Jett's autonomic nervous system pump enough adrenaline to give him a rush. Even then, the anxiety he felt when facing a Special was about that experienced by an average person giving a high-school speech. Jett's flattened affect, a high tolerance for his own pain, and unlimited tolerance for the pain of others, set him apart from the man on the street. Was he pathological? No. But he was well suited to carry out his government's necessary dirty work.

With a rattle and a clang the doors of the old elevator opened to another green tunnel, most of its doors unlabeled. Ten doors down he came to one with "Office of Special Projects" stencilled on the opaque glass. His agency hid in plain sight, and was listed in the phone book; its budget was a line item in the federal budget. But like an iceberg where two-thirds of the bulk is under the water line, the agency's black-bag budget was far greater. Research was the office's public function, and the walls were lined with reference works—statistical indexes, encyclopedias, almanacs, and guides to periodicals. Most of the data, however, was on CD-ROM now, and there was a "jukebox" containing fifteen hundred CDs that could be accessed from any workstation. Networked computers sat on every desk, gathering information on demand from libraries, universities, databases, and intelligence agencies.

As an official branch of the Navy, the office was listed in the Washington, D.C., phone book under "Navy Department of the—" Anyone who cared to look could tell it was an intelligence agency by the prefix. All the intelligence branches carried the "669" prefix. Office of Naval Intelligence was 669-3001, Coast Guard Intelligence was 669-4546, and the Marine Corps Intelligence Activity was 669-4343. Listed among the numerous other Naval offices was the Office of Special Projects, 669-3101.

Jett passed through the outer office to another complex, this time pausing by a desk and making small talk with the man stationed there. Though the man looked like a recent college graduate—young, eager, and friendly—he was actually an agent using a magnetic field to scan Jett and make sure he was carrying only authorized weapons. With a last smile and a cheery "Have a good day," Jett was admitted to the inner office.

This complex looked like the first one; he passed through, acknowledging greetings with his usual reserve, knowing people were curious about the outcome of his last mission. Woolman's office door was closed, but through the vertical glass panel next to it he saw a man sitting opposite Woolman. Jett recognized the middle-aged man as the next link in the chain of command. CIA chiefs were rare visitors to the Office of Special Projects. Jett waited at a discreet distance from the door, surreptitiously watching the CIA section chief. The man was composed, but intense. Woolman did most of the talking, the CIA chief listening, nodding his head occasionally. Finally, they exchanged a few last words, Woolman doing most of the nodding now. Then the CIA chief left, ignoring Jett.

Jett didn't wait to be invited in. Woolman expected agents to report promptly whenever they dealt with a Special. Jett closed the door as he entered, taking the chair vacated by the CIA chief. Oscar Woolman typed on his computer with his back to Jett. Jett waited patiently. Woolman used the typing ploy to keep agents in their place, typing some trivial memo while they waited, sending a clear message about hierarchy of command. Woolman's hands flew over the keys, a sure sign that he had been desk-bound for years. Jett was still a hunt-and-peck typist; something he was proud of.

While he waited, Jett studied the back of Woolman's head. Woolman was virtually bald, a gray fringe just above his ears being his only hair. He kept the fringe neat, making frequent visits to a stylist. Jett supposed it was the scarcity that made Woolman's fringe so precious to him. Shortly, Woolman paused, turning, leaning back in his chair, one hand massaging each arm rest. Woolman's face was soft and round, with deep horizontal creases across his forehead. He was pudgy now, though once he had been an effective field agent of some note—but that was then and this was now.

"Well?" Woolman said.

"We lost one; one badly injured."

"What was his ability?"

"Fire. Not as powerful as the one in seventy-eight."

"Fire?" Woolman said, with distaste.

Woolman had been on the nineteen-seventy-eight team that had faced the most powerful Special ever tracked. Four agents had died then, literally burned to a crisp. Another four were injured, Woolman one of them. Woolman's legs still bore the scars of the skin grafts. Ever since, his weakness had been fire.

"You said he wasn't powerful," Woolman said. "Yet, he killed one?"

"Powerful enough, but he wasn't smart. He should have hit us when we were all in the car."

"What about containment?"

"It was the middle of the night; only a few witnesses. A garage was burned; some other minor damage. We're arranging for restitution and got the bodies out before anyone was sure of what happened. The neighbors think we captured a federal fugitive."

"Who's the casualty?" Woolman asked finally.

"Knox. Steele will survive but he has third-degree facial burns. He won't be a field man anymore."

Making notes on a yellow pad, Woolman looked thoughtful, his gray eyes blank as if staring at some inner screen. Jett knew he was thinking about replacements, not sympathizing with the families of the dead and injured. Jett often wondered if Woolman's M and A scores were lower than his.

"Did you backtrack him?" Woolman asked.

"Not far. It was snowing pretty hard."

"He only had about four hours. How far could he walk?"

"From the look of his shoes he had walked some miles across country. That part of Minnesota is pretty rural, lots of wooded areas," Jett said.

"And ten thousand frozen lakes."

"Exactly."

"Any idea where he was going?"

"He was trying to make a phone call," Jett said, placing the quarter in front of Woolman.

Woolman picked up the coin, looking at the date.

"Did he complete the call?"

"No."

Woolman paused now, his fingers drumming a tuneless rhythm.

"I've been talking to the technicians at Rainbow about a permanent solution to the problem of the Specials," Woolman said.

Jett had heard rumors about problems at Rainbow, the facility that contained the Specials, and he knew that breakouts had become more frequent, a sign they were losing containment. The CIA had long wanted the Office of Special Projects shut down, but a permanent solution hadn't been considered feasible. The visit by the CIA chief told him that the situation was changing. Jett also knew that any permanent solution would be more dangerous than the worst Special the Office had ever dealt with—far more dangerous than the fire thrower Woolman had fought in nineteen-seventy-eight. The thought of what a permanent solution would entail aroused Jett like no other mission had.

"If we decide to go with the permanent solution, you would be my choice as team leader. Of course, it's not set yet; there are technical details to work out."

"Whenever," Jett said.

Jett stood to leave.

"I suppose I'll have to visit Steele," Woolman said.

"I'll do it," Jett said, knowing Woolman couldn't stand the thought of walking into a burn ward. Jett would have visited Steele anyway, not out of compassion, but out of loyalty to a team member.

"Damn fire throwers," Woolman said, fingers drumming nervously.

Jett nodded, then left, smiling to himself. The fight with the fire thrower had provided the most excitement he'd had in three years, even giving him a small adrenaline rush. Jett wondered how Woolman would have reacted? Would he have collapsed at the first fireball, pants soaked with urine? It gave Jett a feeling of strength to know another man's weakness.

SCHIZOPHRENIC

August
University of Oregon Campus, Eugene, Oregon

With his clothes rumpled, shirt cross-buttoned, and hair unkempt, Ronald Simpson looked like a transient, but until a year ago he had been a successful stockbroker on the fast track with his brokerage. Now diagnosed schizophrenic, he sat on a cot to be fitted with the helmet containing the leads that connected him to a cryogenic computer. The cot was placed in the middle of a semicircle made up of three work stations, each packed with equipment. Elizabeth Foxworth worked with Ronald while her friend, Monica Kim, stood behind Dr. Wes Martin at one of the stations. Monica was quiet, since quiet visitors were the only ones Wes tolerated.

Ronald's nervous habits made fitting him with the helmet—called an EET—difficult for Elizabeth. Normally, he habitually rubbed his face with his hands and then finger-combed his greasy hair over and over. The helmet disrupted his sensorimotor routine, however, and not running his fingers through his hair disturbed him. Still, he wanted to cooperate and kept catching his hands on the way to his head, forcing them back down. He tried sitting on his hands, but, as if they had a mind of their own, they pulled free and went for his scalp, where they were frustrated by the cap covering his head.

Elizabeth reassured him, and he responded with his litany.

"Yeah, gonna be okay, everything's gonna be okay."

Finished, Elizabeth nodded to Shamita Patel at the center station, who signalled that she was receiving Ron's brain waves. As senior engineer, Shamita had developed the micro electroencephalograph built into Ron's helmet and the cryogenic central processor that was the heart of their supercooled supercomputer. Only five cryogenic supercomputers existed in the world—the CIA had three—but theirs was the only one used to intercept brain waves. Shamita was nearing fifty; her once jet black hair was graying, the patches of gray standing out like dandelions in a spring lawn. A sober person, she compensated by wearing colorful clothes. Today over black slacks, she wore a loose shirt covered with bright flowers.

Elizabeth now looked to Len Chaikin, who would monitor Ronald's physiological responses using receptors mounted in the temples of the helmet and others taped to his chest. During the development phase of the engineering, Len had acted as Shamita's hands, doing the physical construction of the circuit boards from Shamita's designs, as well as designing and installing the liquid-hydrogen cooling system. Good looking, with regular features, blue eyes, and brown hair, Len was the kind of man you wanted to call pretty instead of handsome. Len had an irreverent and irrepressible sense of humor, and to Wes's annoyance, used it indiscriminately. Now he signalled to Elizabeth that he was receiving Ronald's blood pressure, heart rate, respiration, and galvanic skin response.

Ready for the next step, Elizabeth asked Ron to move his limbs one at a time, while Shamita studied her monitor, noting the neural activity associated with each movement.

"Yeah, gonna be okay, everything's gonna be okay," Ron said, moving his arms and legs as directed.

They repeated the movement sequence three times until Shamita confirmed the neurological map. Next, Ron was asked to touch his toes, clap his hands, and pass a ball from hand to hand.

"Yeah, gonna be okay, everything's gonna be okay," he said to each request as he complied.

In a few seconds Shamita had confirmed that Ronald's brain was organized like most people's, with the motor and sensory regions on opposite sides of the central fissure, running horizontally across the brain. Motor control was upside-down and backwards, with the right side controlled by the left side of the brain, and the left side controlled by the right side of the brain. Control of the toes was located near the top of the cortex and control of the tongue low on the side. The computer quickly recognized Ronald's psychomotor organization as standard, and the mapping proceeded.

"I've got motor cortex," Shamita said finally.

"Relax him," Wes said.

Elizabeth asked Ron to lie down, which he did with difficulty, his head bobbing up and down.

"Yeah, gonna be okay, everything's gonna be okay."

Suddenly his body went limp, his eyes closing.

"What did you do?" Monica asked.

"His brain waves are monitored by sensors in the EET helmet, and once we localized motor functions we used antagonistic signals to interrupt certain neural pathways and relax some of the larger muscles," Wes said. "At the same time we blocked part of the activity in the reticular activating system."

Wes gave a perfunctory explanation, having given it many times to visitors who never really understood what it meant. If Monica Kim followed the pattern, Wes expected her to accuse him next of paralyzing Ronald.

"You put him to sleep," Monica said.

Wes was pleasantly surprised by Monica's understanding. Most visitors were from the Kellum Foundation, which funded Wes's research and couldn't be refused access. The others were fellow neuropsychologists, or social workers like Elizabeth, who didn't have enough knowledge of his work to even approach an intelligent question. Monica Kim had already demonstrated more depth than any of Elizabeth's previous friends. At five foot five she was five inches shorter than Elizabeth and opposite her in almost every way. Elizabeth was a striking woman with red hair and green eyes, and while she dressed conservatively, she drew the attention of men wherever she went. Monica wasn't beautiful, but she was pretty, with black hair and almond shaped eyes.

"You might find this interesting, Monica," Len said, motioning for her to come to his station.

"Aren't you just monitoring his physiological signs?" she asked.

"Well, yes, but there's more to it—"

"Thanks anyway, Len, I'll stay here," Monica said, standing behind Shamita, watching her map Ronald's cerebral cortex.

The equipment and software were designed for multiple subjects, but today the scientists were intercepting only one subject's cerebral activity. By sending competing signals to certain regions of the subject's brain, they could temporarily shut down selected brain activity. With two or more subjects they could shut down a portion of one brain's activity and substitute the activity from another brain, combining two or more minds into one. Today's experiment wasn't designed to blend minds; instead they would try to create order in the very confused mind of a schizophrenic. Shamita would select out brain functions, Len would receive physiological signs, and Wes would monitor both from his station.

"How do you decode the brain's signals?" Monica asked.

"We don't," Wes said. "Brain waves are multiplexed signals . . . It's complex."

"You're not assuming a hierarchical feature matrix?" Monica asked.

Impressed, Wes warmed to Monica.

"Originally we did work with the hierarchical feature detector model and there is good evidence this is how people make sense of their environment. For example, if you show a person a horizontal line tilted at an angle, a single neuron will respond. Tilt it a little more and a different cell responds. Another cell will respond to the width of the line, another to its length. These individual cells then send their signals to other cells called complex cells, which then respond only to certain combinations of width, length, and angle. The signals from the complex cells are sent to hypercomplex cells, which again only respond to certain combinations from the complex cells, and so on through a network of billions of cells with trillions of combinations. However, our work at this level didn't take us where we wanted to go."

"You disproved the hierarchical model?" Monica asked.

"No, we decided it was irrelevant," Wes said.

Elizabeth interrupted, asking if they were ready to map the auditory cortex. Shamita nodded, and Elizabeth turned on a CD player which played a variety of sounds, Shamita watching her monitor for Ronald's neural responses.

"We were able to isolate hierarchical cell structures that fit the model in both the visual and auditory cortexes, but interactions between cells increase exponentially with each new level," Wes continued. "It's difficult enough to track cell activity among a dozen cells, let alone millions. It finally dawned on us that we needed to be working at a macro level, not the micro level. It was like trying to appreciate the *Mona Lisa* by looking through a microscope at the molecules of paint.

"When we treated brain waves as complex wholes and stopped trying to disassemble them, we made rapid progress. Now we look at the brain waves as functioning much like FM-radio broadcasts. In order to broadcast stereo, frequency-modulated radio combines several waves into a compound wave that can carry more information than the individual waves—it's called multiplexing. The signal is split again at the receiver back into the original waves. The cortex functions in much the same way, by compounding signals and then compounding the compounds—that's multiplexing. With our equipment we intercept the multiplexed signals and re-route them through fiber optic lines and then back to the cortex."

"Or to another cortex," Monica said.

"We don't do that anymore," Wes said, remembering the disaster that had resulted from his first experiments with integrating minds. Using autistic savants, he and his team had integrated the fragments of genius from four savants, creating a single mind with amazing abilities. Unfortunately, his team had been infiltrated by someone with psychokinetic abilities whose power had been magnified by linking with the savants. People had died—Len had nearly been killed. In a perverse way the experiment had been an overwhelming success, but the cost had been too great. The fact that Monica didn't ask why they stopped integrating minds made Wes suspect that Elizabeth hadn't kept any secrets from her.

"I'm surprised your computer can keep up with the brain," Monica said.

"Actually, neural activity is relatively slow. It's based on chemical diffusion across a semipermeable membrane. Single neurons are microscopic, so the process is sufficiently rapid for mental activity, but remember we're working at a macro level involving millions of neurons."

"Isn't your computer supercooled?"

"It's a cryogenic computer. We use the liquid nitrogen to supercool our CPU. The superconducting chip processes the information faster than the brain itself, which allows us to keep up with the multiplexed brain waves. The light-wave transmission through the fiber optic lines is much faster than that of the neurons—the speed of light, actually. As long as we keep the length of the transmission lines short enough, and we work at a multiplexed level, it works."

Elizabeth finished the audio sequence and began tactile stimulation. Using Wes's software, the computer displayed a model of Ron's brain from three perspectives on Wes's screen. Elizabeth and Shamita worked together, mapping Ronald's sensorimotor functions; the results were displayed on Wes's monitor.

"See the schizophrenic bleed, Wes?" Shamita said.

"Yes, especially visual to auditory." Then, explaining for Monica, Wes added, "Schizophrenics tend to confuse sensory information—hear colors, feel sounds, that sort of thing."

"I've had some experience with schizophrenics," Monica said.

Monica said it as if it was important, and Wes briefly caught Elizabeth's eye. She was up to something.

"This is auditory function here," Wes said, pointing to the temporal lobe of the brain, about halfway down the side. "There are auditory regions on both sides of the brain." Then, pointing to the back of the brain, he said, "This is where visual information is received. Notice the sharp increase in electrical activity in both auditory regions as Elizabeth plays the tape, and notice this activity connecting the two regions."

"We can also get infrared images," Wes said, typing on the keyboard and calling up a new view of Ron's cortex. "The EET helmet Ron's wearing also detects temperature differences. As neural activity increases, temperature increases. The red and orange colors indicate the highest levels of activity."

Wes pointed to the color image on the screen. It showed green and yellow in most regions, but orange with red centers in the visual and auditory regions. Then, tracing with his finger, he said, "Notice this activity connecting the different regions. This kind of flow between regions is unusual, even for schizophrenics."

"I've never seen anything like it," Monica said, studying the screen intensely. "The flow seems . . . forced."

"Exactly," Wes said. "Ron is very unusual. It's like he's picking up sensations his brain doesn't know how to process—they're not visual or auditory. That's why we're interested in him."

"We're interested in helping him, too," Elizabeth said suddenly.

"Of course, I didn't mean . . ." Wes sputtered, embarrassed by his tendency to get absorbed by technical problems and forget the person involved.

Wes typed on the keyboard again, and the electrical activity of Ron's brain reappeared on the screen.

"Here's where we can do some good," Wes said. Then to Shamita he said, "Patch auditory, visual, olfactory, and haptic regions."

The wave pattern changed only slightly, but Wes's trained eye could see a decrease in the flow between regions, and the brain waves approximate a normal pattern.

"His respiration is slowing, Wes, heart rate too," Len said. "Galvanic skin resistance is increasing." Then, looking at Monica, Len said, "This is pretty interesting, Monica, you might want to come look at this."

"It means he's relaxing, Len," Monica said. Then to Wes she said, "Why the reduction in anxiety?"

"The world makes more sense to him now. It's not as cluttered and confusing."

"I thought he was asleep."

"It's more like a hypnotic trance than sleep. He's both conscious and unconscious. We can communicate with him, at least if he's coherent. Let's begin, Elizabeth. Shamita, give him full audition and restore speech function."

"I'm getting some pretty interesting readings here, Monica," Len said.

"No, Len," Monica said.

"I'll let you push some of the buttons," Len said.

Monica laughed, shaking her head.

"Ignore him," Elizabeth advised. "Just like you would a family dog."

"Until it starts humping your leg," Len said, then hummed to himself.

Shamita laughed, but didn't look up from her monitor.

"Elizabeth, talk to Ron," Wes told her.

"Ron, can you hear me?" Elizabeth said.

"Yes."

"How do you feel, Ron?"

"I feel . . . I feel tired."

"Too tired to talk to me?" Elizabeth asked.

"I feel good."

"Do you know where you are?"

"The university."

"That's right. Do you know who I am?"

"Elizabeth."

"That's right—"

"You have beautiful red hair."

"Thank you, Ron, now do you—"

"Green eyes. You have green talking eyes."

"Talking eyes, Ron?" Elizabeth prodded.

"Yes."

"What do you mean when you say my eyes talk?"

"They say things I don't understand."

"What kind of things?"

"I don't understand them. I can't explain."

"Try."

"Redaudable circlingology compounded by the violet voice of green smell."

Everyone in the room exchanged glances, Len shrugging and saying, "His vitals are picking up."

"Relax, Ron, you're safe here. We're your friends," Elizabeth said, waiting for him to repeat his mantra—he didn't.

Monica leaned close to Wes's ear. "Is his response what you were look-ing for?"

"Yes. Many schizophrenics try to verbalize concepts that can't be grasped. We're trying to help him make sense of them."

Actually, the work with Ron was just the first step in an ambitious proj-ect, and Wes suspected Elizabeth had shared the details with Monica.

"Ron, I want you to open your eyes," Elizabeth said. "Now look at my eyes, Ron. Are my eyes speaking now?"

"No. They are pretty eyes."

"Thank you."

With a hand-slice across her throat, Elizabeth signalled Shamita to cut off Ron's hearing.

"Wes, let's gradually reinstitute the sensory bleed. He's high-functioning; if we can keep him from being overwhelmed he might be able to make sense out of his perceptions."

Wes agreed, and Shamita slowly widened the parameters, allowing lim-ited sensory overflow.

"Tell me when my eyes begin to talk, Ron."

"Can I blink? My eyes are dry."

"Blink whenever you need to, Ron," Elizabeth said.

"They're talking."

"What are my eyes saying, Ron?"

"It's something I can't understand. Something like violet . . . maybe blue, shifting, around and around until the color green smells triangular. Circles within circles feeling brown until they fly apart smelling like cinna-mon."

There was more, all recorded digitally, none of it making any sense. When Ron became agitated they relaxed him, then brought him out slowly. As soon as the helmet was off he sat up, rubbing his face, finger-combing his greasy hair, saying over and over, "Yeah, gonna be okay, every-thing's gonna be okay."

"Thank you for helping us, Ron," Elizabeth said.

"Yeah, gonna be okay, everything's gonna be okay."

Elizabeth helped him from the room to where his wife was waiting out-side. He was rubbing his face and hair as he walked out the door. A few minutes later Elizabeth was back.

"The change was remarkable," Monica said. "A portable version of this machine could change his life."

"That's an interesting idea," Len said, coming to stand by Monica. "We could talk about it over coffee?"

"You can't let someone walk around with a liquid nitrogen backpack," Wes said. "Besides, the program isn't self-monitoring."

"We thought at first schizophrenics like Ron would benefit from repeated sessions," Elizabeth added, "but they always revert. It's as if their systems can't be trained to process in any other way."

"Or something external is forcing that pattern on them," Monica said.

"You told her, didn't you?" Wes glared at Elizabeth.

"You can trust Monica," Elizabeth assured him, smiling.

"If I understand it," Monica said, "you've identified a small group of schizophrenics who are anomalous. They don't respond to drug therapy or psychotherapy and they are characterized by peculiar perceptions. You're pursuing the hypothesis that they are receiving psychic transmissions from somewhere—maybe another solar system."

"I know it sounds crazy," Wes apologized.

"Not at all," Monica said.

"It sounds nuts to me," Len said, "and I'm part of the project."

"It's creative," Monica said. "Elizabeth said you were open to new ideas."

Now Elizabeth and Monica exchanged looks, and Wes steeled himself for what was coming.

"Do you know much about dreaming, Wes?" Monica asked.

"He never dreamed someone as good-looking as Elizabeth would ever go out with him," Len said.

"I understand the neurology of dreaming," Wes said quickly, to stop the chuckling.

"What about dream interpretation?" asked Monica.

"It's nonsense," Wes said, not caring if he offended Monica. Something was coming and he didn't care if he discouraged her. "I've read Freud's *Interpretation of Dreams*, and I don't accept the idea of manifest and latent content of dreams. If you dream of walking upstairs you're not dreaming about sex, you're dreaming about walking upstairs. An umbrella is an umbrella, not a penis."

"You said penis," Len said, then snorted and laughed.

"Most dreams reflect day-to-day worries and are made up of people you know and everyday events," Wes continued. "Nothing mysterious about them."

"Do you dream, Wes?" Monica asked.

"Of course."

"Ever dream the same dream more than once?"

"Yes."

"How often?"

"Several times, I suppose."

"What would you think about someone who dreams the same dream every night?"

Now Wes paused, looking for the trap.

"I don't know if that's unusual—"

"It's very unusual," Monica said. "I've analyzed dreams as part of my practice for years and I've never met anyone who dreams the same dream night after night without variation."

"There must be some stressful event in the person's life that is causing the dream," Wes said.

"Not that I can find," Monica said.

"You think there's a neurological cause?" Wes asked.

"I think the source of the dream is external, just like Ron's confused perceptions."

"Someone dreaming the same dream over and over is interesting, but—"

"It's not just one person," Monica said. "It's seven."

"Then it's not as unique as you led me to believe," Wes said, feeling the mystery slip away.

"You don't understand. I have identified seven people who dream the same dream every night."

Shamita and Len were staring in wonder, and Wes knew he had missed the significance.

"So they dream the same thing over and over. What leads you to believe the source is external?"

"You're not getting it, Wes," Elizabeth said. "All seven people dream exactly the same dream every night. It's one dream they all share."

"Well, there are many common dreams," Wes said. "Most people have dreamed of forgetting they have a test at school or a presentation at work or of showing up somewhere naked. Is it that kind of dream?"

"No," Monica said. "When people dream they are naked, they are in a variety of places—where they work, in a park, at a concert. It's a common theme but the details vary. That's not the case with this dream. The details are identical for each dreamer. People in this group dream they are on a ship in the middle of a desert and there's no way off."

"I dreamed I was on the Love Boat once," Len said. "Fifteen hundred passengers and I was the only one that didn't get laid."

Shamita elbowed Len and Wes glared at him, Len faking embarrassment.

"All of them dream it every night?" Wes said, drawn by the strangeness. "How long has this been going on?"

"Years. For one of the dreamers, more than fifty years."

"What?" Wes was surprised.

"It's killing them, Wes," Monica said. "That dream is killing the dreamers and I need your help to save them."

MYSTERY

Elizabeth and Wes met for dinner two or three nights a week, adding fuel to the campus gossip that they were lovers. In reality they were somewhere between friends and lovers, taking their relationship seriously, but letting it develop at its own pace. They were both married to their work, Wes to his research and Elizabeth to counselling her clients, so making room for each other came slowly. Meals together, and occasional intimate moments, sufficed for now, but like an addict getting hooked on a narcotic, the more time Wes spent with Elizabeth, the more he needed to be with her.

The University of Oregon was surrounded by mature neighborhoods on three sides, many of the stately old houses now sororities and fraternities. A moderate climate and ample rain made the lawns and campus verdant spaces grow a deep Oregon green. The original business district bordered the other edge of the campus, and beyond that the strip malls that housed the retail chains. Restaurants were sprinkled around the campus, most serving fast food and catering to the eat-cheap needs of the students, but mixed in were gourmet restaurants favored by the faculty and Eugene residents. Elizabeth had picked one of these, an old house remodelled into an intimate restaurant which served primarily vegetarian dishes with a few chicken entrees for the unconverted.

Elizabeth was seated when Wes arrived, having come directly from her seven o'clock counselling appointment. She had ordered an Oregon wine, bottled in the Chehalem valley, and poured him a glass as he sat down.

"Have you thought about the dreamers?" Elizabeth said, before he could get his glass to his lips.

"There's nothing I can do, Elizabeth. I don't know what you told Monica, but she seems to expect more than she should."

"I told her you have experience dealing with the paranormal."

"There's no such thing," Wes started to argue, the waitress interrupting as he did.

Elizabeth was a regular customer who was systematically working through the menu, sampling every salad they offered. Tonight Elizabeth chose a dinner-sized salad combining avocados and broccoli. Wes asked for the chicken and mushroom dish he always ordered, knowing the mushrooms would outnumber the chicken pieces two to one. As a scientist, Wes was attentive to details, and was sure there had been a lower mushroom-to-chicken ratio the first time he and Elizabeth had visited the restaurant. Slightly paranoid, he suspected that his diet was being monitored in the kitchen, the vegetarian staff gradually reducing the chicken in his food, slowly weaning him from his meat addiction.

"Elizabeth, there is no such thing as the paranormal," Wes continued when the waitress was gone. "That's just a term used by the ignorant for events not yet understood."

Wes didn't deny the existence of phenomena that operated outside the normal laws of physics; he had experience with them, but he saw those phenomena as indications that the laws needed to be revised, not as something supernatural. To Wes, everything was explainable, and once explained, controllable.

"Exactly, Wes, there has to be an explanation for why all these people are sharing one dream. All we're asking is that you help us understand it. It's something you're good at."

Wes wasn't flattered; he felt manipulated. Elizabeth was a creative problem solver, connecting seemingly random events. Wes was a plodder, systematically hypothesizing and data gathering, eliminating one possibility at a time. While very different from Elizabeth, Wes had often benefitted from Elizabeth's chaotic approach to problem solving.

The waitress brought their order, setting two small plates of food and a basket of warm bread on the table. Wes's chicken and mushrooms were covered with a cream sauce, a few peas mixed in. Wes spread out the concoction, selecting a random sample and counting the mushrooms and chicken pieces. The mushroom-to-chicken ratio was now three to one.

"What can I do?" Wes said, starting with the mushrooms, saving the chicken as if it was dessert.

"Meet with some of the dreamers. Listen to their stories. Give us a fresh perspective on the problem. Maybe you'll see something Monica and I missed."

"Just talk with them?" Wes asked.

"And brainstorm with us," Elizabeth said, smiling.

In the soft light of the restaurant Elizabeth's green eyes and long red hair made her nearly irresistible. When she smiled, Wes's caution evaporated and he heard himself agreeing to meet some of the dreamers. Once again Elizabeth had overcome his natural caution, and Wes marvelled at the power she had over him. Always a fiercely independent researcher, Wes's unconventional theories had led him to be shunned by mainstream science. Yet he had the strength to resist the pressure to return to the mainstream. So it surprised him how easily Elizabeth could manipulate him. Even more surprising was the fact that he didn't mind giving up his independence for her.

THE ONE DREAM

Sun City, Arizona

Wanda Johnson smoked her first cigarette when she was sixteen years old, and had smoked every day since for sixty years. Now, whenever a coughing fit took her, she talked of quitting.

"My friend Ellie went to a hypnotist to quit smoking. It cost her two hundred dollars. He hypnotized her and told her she would lose her taste for tobacco. Know what? She still smokes. Didn't do a damn bit of good. I might try it, though. They say some people are better subjects than others."

They were sitting in Wanda's mobile home, having come directly from the airport to Wanda's trailer park. Most of the trailers in the Shady View Court had screened rooms built off of one side where the elderly residents would sit in the evenings, enjoying the pure, Arizona air. Wanda's trailer had one of these extra rooms, but Wes, Elizabeth, and Monica sat inside with the door closed, letting the air conditioner knock the temperature down thirty degrees.

Wanda's plump body shook with another cough. Her hair was gray and cut short, giving her a boyish look. She wore dangling orange earrings that looked like fishing lures, and sat in a rocker with doilies covering holes where cotton batting poked through. Everything smelled of cigarettes; the air was thick and hazy from Wanda's incessant smoking.

As professional listeners, Elizabeth and Monica sat patiently, letting Wanda direct the conversation. Wes fidgeted through the small talk, when they discussed everything from airline food to Wanda's cactus garden. While Wes acted interested, inside he worried about diverting grant funds for the flight to Arizona. The Kellum Foundation had long supported him and he wanted to keep their trust. Twice he tried to break into the conversation, to get Wanda to the point, but Elizabeth stopped him both times with a hand on his leg.

"What's the point of quitting now?" Monica asked. "You're seventy-six years old. The stress of quitting would do more harm than smoking."

"Have you seen the price of cigarettes?" Wanda said. "I could go to Las Vegas twice a year if I didn't smoke." Then, after a deep drag on her cigarette, "Would you like more tea?"

"No thanks, Wanda," Monica said. "We really came to hear about your dream."

"My friends are sick to death of hearing about my dream, so I'm glad to have someone new to tell it to." Wanda sipped her tea. "It's always the same. I'm on a ship, but the ship isn't on an ocean. It's in the middle of a desert, hardly anything growing anywhere you look. There's no sky. When you look up there's nothing to see—just nothing. There's no one else on the ship. I walk all over the deck and through the cabins—never see anyone. The ship isn't quite right, though. You can go through the same door twice and not come out in the same place."

Wanda looked thoughtful, then said, "Dreams are queer like that, aren't they? It's been so long since I've dreamed anything else I can't remember what other dreams are like."

Wanda's eyes glazed, her mind drifting back to before the dream began.

"I remember dreaming I went to school in my pajamas," Wanda said after a long thought. "I must have been seven or eight. Or maybe I didn't dream it? Maybe I really did go to school in my pajamas?"

"Many children dream of wearing their pajamas to school," Elizabeth said.

"You don't say. It would be fun to dream that again."

"Wanda, is there more to your ship dream?" Elizabeth asked.

"Just the feeling. I'm afraid—in danger—I want to get off the ship, but I can't. The more I wander, the more I want to get off. By the time the dream ends I'm desperate to get home."

"What kind of ship is it?" Wes asked.

"Looking for symbolism?" Wanda said. "My dream's been analyzed over and over and no two experts gave me the same answer."

"Just curious," Wes said.

"It's not a cruise ship, I've been on one of those. It's a Navy ship. It's got the big guns mounted in turrets, a single smoke stack, and there's a crane on one end. There's guns all over the ship. It's got to be a Navy ship."

"Is there a name? Any identifying marks?" Elizabeth asked.

"Not that I've ever seen, and I've seen every bit of that ship."

"Did you ever try to get off of the ship?" Wes asked.

"Every night, honey. That's what I do all night long."

"I mean jump over the side," Wes said. "Have you ever jumped off?"

"It's a hell of a long way down. I'd be hurt."

"But it's just a dream," Wes said.

"It's so real," Wanda said, eyes blank as if she was seeing the images from her dream. "I really feel like I'm there. I'd be afraid to jump. You know what they say, don't you? When people die in their dreams they really die."

"How could you know that?" Wes asked.

"I read it somewhere," Wanda said.

"But if someone died in their dream and never woke up, how would you know they dreamed that they died? If they were dead they couldn't tell you what they had dreamed the night before."

"A seance, I suppose," Wanda said. "There's scientific ways to know," she added seriously.

Wes opened his mouth to argue, but Elizabeth's hand pressed his leg again.

"You've been dreaming this dream for a long time, haven't you, Wanda?" Monica said.

"I'll say," she said, reaching for a package of Lucky Strikes. They waited while she lit up another cigarette and took a deep drag, blowing the smoke out through her nose. "Since World War II," Wanda went on, traces of smoke still flowing from her nose. "I was only married to my first husband a few weeks before he shipped out. I never really got to know Johnny, but he was oh so handsome in his uniform. Swept me off my feet, he did. A honeymoon and then he was gone. Slam-bam-thank-you-ma'am," she said, and then chuckled. "A few months later a telegram came telling me my Johnny was dead. The dream started after that."

"A Navy ship lost in the desert with no way to get home! The dream is about her husband," Wes whispered to Elizabeth.

"I heard that," Wanda said. "My eyes are bad, not my hearing. I don't blame you for thinking that, I thought the same thing myself at first. When the dream wouldn't go away I went to see a psychiatrist."

"Who was that?" Monica asked.

"Dr. Goldman. He was Jewish, don't you know? They say they're the best, and that's why I picked him. Freud was Jewish, you know?"

"I'd heard that," Elizabeth said politely.

"That was back when I lived in Trenton. I suspect he's long dead. He wasn't a young man even then. I liked him but he didn't help a bit. Finally, I told him the dream went away just to make him feel good, paid my last bill, and never went back. I tried three or four other psychiatrists—some Jewish, some not—but they didn't help either."

"Don't you ever dream anything else, Wanda?" Monica said. "Maybe early in the morning when the dream is over."

"Not that I remember, but I suppose it's possible. They say you can't remember all of your dreams."

Using small talk, Monica and Elizabeth wound the meeting down, making sure they left Wanda with a positive feeling. Stepping from Wanda's air-conditioned trailer into the Arizona summer was like running into a wall. They hurried to their car and turned the air conditioner up full.

"I'm beginning to think this was a wild goose chase," Wes said from the backseat. "Her first husband was a sailor lost at sea and the dream is about a Navy ship. Isn't the connection clear?"

"No," Elizabeth said, as she drove them out of Wanda's trailer park.

"You're forgetting about the other dreamers," Monica said. "They don't all have relatives who died in the Navy."

"Have you asked?" Wes said.

"I don't have to," Monica said.

"Isn't it an obvious connection?" asked Wes.

Monica and Elizabeth were in the front seat and exchanged a look that made him feel foolish.

"Besides, the dream isn't that unusual," Wes said.

"Don't forget the others dreaming the same dream."

"There's two hundred and fifty million people in this country dreaming every night. If you searched you could find a hundred people dreaming about ships in the desert. I don't see why we need to visit any more of these people."

"A hundred people dreaming exactly the same dream every night?" Monica said sarcastically.

"Wes is worried about losing his grant money over this," Elizabeth said. "I'll make a deal with you, Wes. If you're not convinced after the trip to Tulsa, I'll cover the cost."

Elizabeth had cut to the heart of it, making Wes feel cheap. Sulking in the backseat, he listened to Monica and Elizabeth chat all the way to the airport.

TEAM

Tulsa, Oklahoma

Karla Compton was five foot seven, brown hair, brown eyes. She was attractive, but not beautiful—just what a good agent should be. With makeup she could be pretty, without makeup she was plain. With a little work she could be ugly. She dressed in khaki pants and a print blouse, purchased at a J. C. Penney's. She had two closets in her apartment, one with clothes she wore when working, the other with outfits from upscale stores that she wore on personal time. On a given morning she could draw on a wardrobe ranging from Kmart jeans to designer dresses. Having been to Oklahoma before, she was dressed middle class and carried her gun in her purse. Nathan Jett wore Dockers and a white, square-cut polo shirt which covered the holster on his belt. They were checked into a Holiday Inn, waiting for the call that would tell them when and where to respond to a pending breakout. Two other agents, Pierce and Sloan, sat on the end of the bed watching preseason football. Compton was standing on the balcony, looking out toward the airport, the hotel pool just below. Jett studied her body, not out of lust, but wondering how long she would last against him. She looked fit, but couldn't weigh more than one hundred and thirty pounds, giving him nearly a seventy-pound advantage. He joined her on the balcony, leaning over, watching the kids splashing in the pool.

"You still studying karate?" Jett asked.

"Tae Kwon Do," she replied.

"Ever use it in the field?"

"Some."

She was as laconic as he—no wasted energy or words.

"What's the biggest guy you ever took down without help?"

Now she turned to him, face expressionless.

"Is there a point to this?"

"Yeah. If I work with someone I want to know I can count on them," Jett said.

"If you need help, just ask."

"I never need help."

"Then you can count on that, too."

She had an attitude, and Jett liked that, but he still had doubts about her in a fight. Sloan shouted excitedly at the television, Pierce complaining. Jett and Compton both turned, thinking the same thing. Anyone excited about a preseason football game had no future in the agency.

The phone rang and the others waited for Jett to pick it up.

"We've got a breakout," Oscar Woolman said. "You're close and it happened less than thirty minutes ago."

Jett listened carefully to the directions; he never wrote anything down. When he hung up he nodded to the others. Visibly excited, Pierce and Sloan checked the load in their weapons. Jett noticed Compton simply pick up her purse, as sure of her weapon as he was of his. They checked the bedroom, bathroom, drawers, and garbage cans, making sure nothing of theirs remained. They would never return to the hotel, and some would not return from the mission at all.

MARGI

Tulsa, Oklahoma

Wes sat on a vinyl kitchen chair, sweat trickling down his neck, his wet shirt sticking to the back of the chair. Margi Winston put a glass of lemonade in front of him, hand shaking as she did. His glass had Kermit the Frog on the front, Monica and Elizabeth had plastic cups with a Dairy Queen logo, and Margi drank from a beer mug. She was trying hard to be a good hostess, and if she had owned a set of matching glasses she would have used them. Her house was small—two bedrooms, kitchen, and living room. The neighborhood was run down, the street had no curbs, the asphalt was broken and crumbling along its edges.

"The air-conditioning's broken," Margi said, swirling the ice cubes in her glass. "I haven't had time to get it fixed yet."

Monica had briefed them about Margi's situation on the trip to Tulsa. She was an outpatient now, but had been hospitalized for months, losing her job and then her health insurance. When her mother died she inherited the house she lived in but was behind in the taxes and would lose it soon. The air-conditioning wasn't fixed because she couldn't afford the repairs.

Now Margi sipped her lemonade, holding her mug with two hands, unable to completely stop the shaking.

"This is Dr. Martin and this is Elizabeth Foxworth," Monica said. "Elizabeth is a social worker like me and Wes is a psychologist."

"Can they help me?" Margi said immediately.

"I don't know," Monica answered truthfully. "Wes—Dr. Martin—has been doing experiments that could give us a new approach to your problem."

Wes squirmed, having made no commitments and being loaded with doubt.

"I'll try anything," Margi said, trembling in her chair, eyes tearing. "I need something."

"Tell them about your dream," Monica said.

"It's always the same. There's a ship in the desert and I'm on it but I don't want to be. I want to get off so I go looking for a way but I can't find one. I walk all over the ship but there's no way to get off. Night after night I walk the ship but I can't get off."

Margi paused, sipping her drink, staring at the table, sweat beading on her forehead, her hands tight around the beer mug holding her lemonade.

"The ship is so confusing. I've tried to memorize the passages, to learn my way around, but I can't. Sometimes you climb down a ladder and you're in the engine room, and the next time you climb the same ladder you come out on the deck. Go through a door once and you're in the kitchen, go through again and you're in the radio room."

Margi's short blonde hair was unkempt, her skin was pale, her blue eyes were set in dark hollows. With a slight figure normally, now she was beyond thin, bordering on emaciated. She was thirty years old but looked forty, prematurely aged by stress. Another month or two and she would resemble a concentration camp survivor—if she lived that long.

"What kind of ship is it?" Monica asked.

"It's a Navy ship."

"Destroyer? Battleship? Aircraft carrier?" Wes prodded.

"It's not an aircraft carrier, because it doesn't have runways—you know, the big flat area for the planes to take off. It does have airplanes, though—two of them. They're on the back of the ship. I don't know the difference between a destroyer and a battleship, but this ship has great big guns."

"How many funnels does it have?" Wes asked.

"Funnel?" Margi said, hands so tight on the beer mug her knuckles were white.

"Smoke stacks," Wes said.

"One, I think," she said. "Is that important?"

Margi looked stricken, as if she had missed the one important part of her dream that was the key to saving herself.

"No, it's not important. I was just curious," Wes said.

"What do you see when you look over the side of the ship?" Elizabeth asked.

"Desert."

"And when you look above?" Elizabeth went on.

"Nothing."

"Have you ever tried jumping over the side of the ship?" Elizabeth asked. "You might get off that way."

"It's too far," Margi said. "It would break my legs."

"Does the ship have a name?" Elizabeth asked.

"I don't know."

"Are there letters or a name painted on a wall anywhere?" Elizabeth said.

"No. But I'm not sure I've seen all of the ship. Sometimes I still find a room I haven't been in."

"Have you ever seen anyone else on the ship?" Wes asked.

"Never."

"Is there a mirror? Can you see yourself?" he asked.

"I don't remember any mirrors."

"How long have you had this dream?" Monica asked.

"Seven years last July," Margi said, eyes tearing, hand shaking so hard now she had to put her glass down.

"Margi, I can't promise anything, but if there's any way we can help, we will," Elizabeth said.

When they left, Margi was sitting in her kitchen weeping, hands trembling in her lap.

Once back in the car Wes turned the air conditioner on full and then said, "That was odd about the airplanes. What she described wasn't an aircraft carrier but she said it had airplanes. That's the kind of confabulation you get in dreams—mixing details."

"It was odd," Elizabeth agreed.

"Wanda didn't mention the airplanes," Wes pointed out. "Maybe these aren't exactly the same dreams."

Wes was driving, with Elizabeth next to him and Monica in the rear seat, and now both women glared at him.

"Just because Wanda didn't mention the airplanes, it doesn't mean they weren't in her dream," Elizabeth said.

Wes didn't point out that the opposite was true also; instead, he quickly changed the subject.

"Quite a different reaction than Wanda," Wes said.

"Interesting, isn't it," Elizabeth agreed. "Wanda treats the dream like an old friend and Margi is disturbed by it."

"Not just disturbed," Monica said. "The dream is killing her."

"Lack of REM sleep?" Wes asked.

"Yes."

REM stood for rapid eye movement and was associated with dreaming. Sleep studies had shown that rapid movement of the eyes under the eyelids was a reliable indicator of dreaming. As a graduate research assistant, Wes had worked on a dream deprivation study. College students recruited for the study slept in the lab and then Wes or another graduate student would monitor their eyelids through the night, waking them every time REM sleep appeared. The idea was to deprive them of dreaming and see the effects. Those college students they kept from dreaming quickly became irritable and anxious. Physiologically they showed signs of severe stress, and none of the students could stand more than a week of dream deprivation.

"Margi sleeps, but she can't dream normally so she doesn't get the physical benefit," Monica said. "No matter how long she sleeps, she never feels rested. She needs to dream about her life and her problems, so her mind can edit out the day's worries just like an overworked muscle needs rest to cleanse itself of the lactic acid that builds up during exercise."

"Wanda has had the dream for fifty years—why is she thriving?" Elizabeth asked.

"Wanda is one of those rare individuals who need very little sleep," Monica said. "When she was young she averaged only five hours a night. Now she sleeps only three and a half."

"I had a professor like that," Wes said. "He slept four hours a night and thought his graduate students were lazy if they slept any more. He didn't seem to understand the concept of individual differences."

"Wanda's mind handles wastes differently than most people's," Monica continued. "She would be a good subject for future research, Wes. At the other end of the spectrum are those that need ten or eleven hours of sleep a night. Margi is one of those. Her mind processes waste inefficiently so she needs more sleep—more dream sleep."

"Margi has lasted seven years with the dream," Elizabeth said thoughtfully. "I wonder if there aren't others who didn't last that long?"

"I know of two people who committed suicide that had complained of a persistent dream," Monica said.

"About a ship?" Wes asked.

"About a ship," Monica confirmed.

They rode a few minutes in silence, Wes behind the wheel. Wes wasn't convinced they weren't dealing with coincidental dreaming, but he was intrigued with the difference in physiological response between the two women. There had to be a neurological basis for the difference, and his mind went to work on the problem.

"Wes, are you listening to me?" Elizabeth said.

"Sorry, I was thinking of something."

"Why did you ask if there was a mirror on the ship?" Elizabeth repeated.

"I got to thinking about the similarity of the dreams—not that I'm convinced they're the same dream, but if the dream is being forced on them from the outside, then they're not the ones who are wandering the ship. It makes you wonder who they would see if they looked in a mirror."

"We should have asked Wanda if she had seen a mirror," Monica said.

"If she'd seen someone else in a mirror she would have mentioned it," Elizabeth noted.

"But she wouldn't mention airplanes if she had seen those?" Wes said, pointing out the inconsistency in Elizabeth's logic.

Wes checked the rearview mirror. Elizabeth was glaring at him. Soon her green eyes were animated again, her cheeks flushed. She was a beautiful woman with high cheekbones and fine facial features, but all Wes could see was the look that told him she had plunged into the puzzle of the dream and wanted him to jump in with her.

"If we routed Margi's dream through your computer, Wes, could you insert a mirror with your program?" Elizabeth asked.

"It doesn't work that way," Wes said. "We can intercept and transfer the brain's signals at a multiplexed level, but we can't generate our own."

Elizabeth and Monica looked disappointed, and they rode in silence, Wes still thinking about Elizabeth's suggestion. He couldn't program a mirror and insert it into a dream, since he couldn't decode the multiplexed brain waves—only another brain could do that. Then he thought of another way to see into the mirror.

"Wes, you just missed the exit," Monica complained.

He put his idea on the back burner while he looked for the next exit, but when he looked over at Elizabeth he could see she was reading his mind again.

"By the way," Monica said, "who is paying for this trip?"

"I guess I will," Wes said.

"Convinced?" Elizabeth said.

"Intrigued," he replied. "Where to next?"

"Home," Monica said. "Our next dreamer lives three blocks from the campus."

MELEE

A CIA Keyhole satellite detected magnetic field build-up, the early indicator of a pending breakout. After an escape the satellite could track the magnetically charged Special until the charge dissipated. At that point helicopter and ground units triangulated on residual energy clinging to to the escapee. The residual dissipated rapidly, so it was important to locate the Special within twenty-four hours. Linked by secure satellite phones, Jett and his team were directed to the Special. The Special was in an industrial area.

Compton drove the car; Jett, with a computer in his lap, gave directions. The industrial park housed light industry and was a mix of large warehouses, manufacturing plants, and the few remaining houses of a once proud neighborhood. The homes were in disrepair, the paint scoured away by the one-two punch of the hot Oklahoma summers and the deep freeze of winter. Few of the homes were still occupied; an old washing machine lay in the yard of one, an old woman smoked on the front porch of another. Most were boarded up, ready to make room for the expanding industrial park.

Jett studied the map on his screen, then contacted the tracking teams, confirming that the Special wasn't moving. Once they had found two Specials dead, neck and legs broken as if they had fallen from a great height. He had mixed feelings about that possibility here. It meant containment would be easy, but it also eliminated the risk—he craved risk.

"He hasn't moved," Jett said.

Compton stopped for a light.

"That's too bad," Pierce said.

Jett could hear the relief in Pierce's voice. Then Jett's computer beeped and the computer map scrolled. The Special was on the move.

Compton's foot pressed the accelerator as soon as the light changed. Pierce and Sloan checked their weapons. The Special was moving slowly, clearly on foot; Compton expertly guided the car as Jett gave directions. They closed fast, quickly passing within the margin of error of the tracking system, which could only get them within a few blocks—then it was a matter of leg work. They began cruising, the other teams patrolling the perimeter to make sure the Special did not get past Jett's team.

"We're looking for a sailor outfit, right?" Sloan asked.

"He'll look like one of the village people," Pierce said.

"They're not all sailors," Jett reminded them, "and they're not all men."

Compton sighed, disgusted that Pierce and Sloan needed to be reminded of basic details. Pierce and Sloan were whispering now, but Compton and Jett ignored them, eyes drawn to a clump of people in a parking lot. Compton slowed in front of a plant called "Midwestern Wire." Through the legs of the bystanders Jett could see a man dressed in white, sitting on the pavement, a sailor's cap next to him.

"That's him," Jett said, Compton accelerating without being told, stopping down the block.

Jett called the other teams, assigning positions at nearby intersections. He and his team kept their eyes on the crowd, waiting for the others to get in position.

"He looks injured," Compton said.

Jett could see a patch of red on the sailor's forehead, and the man was rocking slightly, holding one arm.

"They might have called an ambulance," Compton said.

Jett understood immediately and said, "Go find out."

Compton left, and Jett ordered Pierce into the driver's seat. Compton walked to the edge of the crowd and talked to one of the men. Then she turned and nodded at Jett, staying with the crowd. Jett got back on the phone, giving orders to his perimeter teams. A minute later Compton strolled back to the car.

"He's talking," Compton said. "The crowd thinks he's out of his head."

Sirens sounded, coming closer, then stopped.

"We've got to shut him up," Pierce said. "Let's go."

"Sit down," Jett ordered as Pierce pulled on his door handle.

Pierce hesitated, flushing from anger, but then sank back into his seat.

Jett's phone buzzed and he held it to his ear. Then he ordered Pierce to drive. Pierce started to protest, but Jett slapped the back of his head. They left the crowd and drove two blocks away to where one of their teams was holding the ambulance. The attendants had been taken away, uniforms left behind.

"One was female," Jett said, tossing a uniform to Compton.

They changed in the ambulance, Compton wiping off her makeup and tying her hair back, effectively changing her looks so that those in the crowd wouldn't recognize her from her first trip. When they were ready, Jett turned on the siren and drove to the wire factory, Pierce and Sloan following. Grabbing a medikit from the back of the van, Jett and Compton pushed through the crowd to the man who was still sitting on the ground, injured. He was wearing sailor dress whites, the pants bell-bottomed. The uniform was torn in places, but was in remarkably good condition for clothing as old as Jett knew it had to be. The man in the uniform was young, maybe twenty years old, with black hair and dark brown eyes. He wore dog tags, and there was a wedding band strung from his neck chain. The sailor had a head wound and held his left arm. Jett took charge, examining the wound, talking to the man.

"Do you have any other wounds besides your head?"

"My arm."

Compton touched the arm, feeling the length of it.

"It hurts. I think it's broken."

Compton felt the sailor's legs and his other arm, then announced, "Nothing else is broken."

"Sir, can you stand?" Jett said. "We need to get you into the ambulance."

"I think so."

Jett and Compton helped him to his feet.

"Shouldn't you use a stretcher?" a woman said from the crowd.

Now the Special looked at the woman and then at Jett.

"You should have checked his blood pressure and heart rate," the woman said, coming through the crowd. She was middle-aged, and studied them suspiciously.

Now the Special looked frightened.

"I'm okay," he said. "Let me go!"

Jett tightened his grip, Compton speaking to calm the Special.

"It's going to be all right," Compton said. "We're going to treat you in the ambulance."

"He could have internal injuries," the woman said.

"Let me go," the Special said.

They were only a few steps from the ambulance when the Special began to struggle.

"I'm not getting in there," he said, pushing on Jett with his good arm.

Jett held on, Compton tightening her grip on the other side, hurting the broken arm. Pushing with his legs, the Special slowed them, and now they were pulling him toward the ambulance. Then Pierce stepped around the ambulance, reaching into his coat and pulling his weapon. The Special reacted instantly, stiffening in Jett's grasp. Suddenly, as if hit in the stomach by an invisible boulder, Pierce buckled in the middle, breath exploding from his body. As the Special turned toward Jett, Jett head-butted him, then shoved him toward Compton, the three of them falling in a tangle. It was a wrestling match now, the Special's broken arm giving them the advantage; but as they struggled he seemed to feel his injury less. Just as they had him pinned face down, the crowd circled them, men in work clothes pulling on Jett and Compton.

"Get off of him," someone said.

"You're hurting him," another said.

"We're federal agents," Jett shouted, but still the men held him, pulling him away. The men were reluctant to handle Compton as roughly, and she made them pay, kicking one full in the groin. He collapsed, hands in his crotch. With an elbow she broke the nose of the man behind her, then turned and drove a fist into the solar plexus of another.

The men holding Jett were distracted by Compton's assault. Twisting, Jett broke the grip of one man, then shoved him back, getting space for his free arm. Swiftly he turned and smashed the nose of another—no fancy karate moves, just a rock-hard fist to the face. The man collapsed to his knees, hands to his face, the blood already flowing. Jett caught another man on the jaw, knocking him to the ground; the others backed away. A gunshot into the air ended the melee, Sloan advancing, ordering the crowd away. They had no time to leave before the Special struck again.

A soundless hurricane blew through the crowd, bodies tumbling away from the Special. Pressed against the ambulance, Sloan tried in vain to aim his gun. Jett lay flat, his bulk giving him some resistance. The Special was moving again, slowly, still clutching his arm. The hurricane ended, leaving a confused mob scattering in all directions. Jett got up to follow the Special, not looking for Compton, knowing she would be right behind.

The Special crossed the road to a parked car, leaning against it and then turning back toward Jett. Jett dove behind the ambulance, Compton following him. An invisible blow from the escapee rocked the ambulance up onto two wheels; it briefly threatened to fall over on them before crashing back down. Jett counted to three, then popped himself up, risking a quick look. The Special was running; he was already halfway across the parking lot on the other side of the street. Jett trotted after him, Compton veering right so that they wouldn't be a single target. Sloan came thumping up behind, running next to Jett, who shouted for him to spread out.

When the Special rounded the corner of the next building, Jett sprinted to follow, Sloan pounding along behind. As he paused at the corner, a blast of air roared past, sending two men rolling out from behind the building. The workmen wore stained blue overalls; one lay still, the other grabbed his leg where a piece of steel protruded. Staring at the injured man, Jett shook his head.

Containment's going to be a bitch, he thought.

Peeking around the corner he could see along the length of the warehouse to a storage yard behind. The Special was nowhere in sight. Cautiously, he jogged along the side of the building, trying to balance speed with caution. The Special was running, but once exhausted he would put his back to a wall and fight.

Jett paused at the end of the building, Sloan still following. The storage yard was filled with stacks of pallets, fencing made of cement, and mounds of sand and gravel. A scoop loader was working the gravel pile, hauling it inside the building. No sign of the Special. An eight-foot chain link fence cut off escape to the left and ran the length of the property—no way out.

"He's gone," Sloan said. "Just disappeared."

"Shut up," Jett said.

Jett studied the pallets and stacked fencing, looking for hiding places. There were nooks and crannies, but nothing that would immediately draw someone to it as a place to hide. Then he looked closely at the sand pile, seeing foot-sized depressions running to the top. Without a word he ran to the sand, following the trail to the top where the fence was only three feet high. Jett jumped the fence, Sloan landing right behind. Police sirens sounded in the distance—they would have to terminate the Special soon.

There was an old house on the other side. Jett squatted next to the fence, studying it. Sloan started forward, but Jett pulled him down.

"Wait," Jett said.

Then he saw Compton appear at the corner of the house, pointing at the back window. Boards covered most of the windows, but this window had missing boards and the glass underneath was broken. Sloan followed Jett to the house, where they joined Compton.

Nodding, Jett pulled out his phone.

"What's the situation?" Jett asked the man who answered.

"We're holding the cops for now, but they won't cooperate long. Worse, the media's here. A TV crew picked up the police call."

"Ask what happened to Pierce?" Sloan whispered.

Jett would have ignored Sloan, but he worried that Pierce might be delirious and need to be shut up.

"What about Pierce?" Jett asked.

"Dead. His spine was broken."

"Send a unit to back us up. We've got the Special contained and we're moving in."

"Well?" Sloan whispered.

"He's dead."

Sloan's face went red, his lips tightening. Jett had seen the signs before; it was rage—something Jett had never felt.

"I'm going to kill that bastard," Sloan said, starting to stand.

Jett held him down while Compton watched dispassionately.

"We'll go in, but we coordinate entry," Jett said.

"Okay, but I kill him," Sloan insisted.

"If you get there first," Compton said, smiling slightly.

"Just stay out of my way!"

"We'll enter the same way he did," Jett said.

"I'm first," Sloan said.

Jett watched Sloan creep toward the window, then looked at Compton. She was still smiling. They followed Sloan, taking up positions on either side of the window, then signalled Sloan that they were ready. Having had a minute to calm down, Sloan was less reckless and peeked into the room first. Satisfied, he placed both hands on the sill and leaned inside, pulling one knee up. Suddenly the window exploded—the frame, boards, and remaining glass were blown away, Sloan with them. Jett lay on the ground picking splinters out of his face and hands. Compton was doing the same. Sloan lay twenty feet away on his stomach, his head twisted at an impossible angle.

"I was afraid of that," Compton said matter-of-factly. "Now what?"

"I could order you inside," Jett said.

"Don't waste your breath."

A black van pulled up, three of their men spilling out, taking cover and waiting for directions.

"Make him come to us," Compton said.

Jett thought for a second, then told Compton to hold her position, and ran to the van.

"Find some containers, siphon out some gas," he ordered. "We're going to burn him out."

Ten minutes later they had three glass jugs of gas, rags sticking out the top. Jett directed his men to surround the building. With everyone in position he handed Compton one of the jugs.

"We'll only have a few minutes once the fire starts," he said. "The police are only a couple of blocks away and antsy."

Lighting the rag, Compton threw it through the window, the jug shattering and spreading the gas. Flames lit the interior. The other jugs were thrown through windows in the front. The old wood-frame building caught fire quickly. A minute passed, and another; nothing happened. Smoke poured from the building, a tell-tale plume streaming into the sky. Shouts of "Fire!" came from down the street, and workers came out of a plant across the road. Jett called for another team to keep the crowd back, but his men were spread thin. The standoff had to end soon.

Suddenly, wood splintered in the front of the house, sounding as if a wrecking ball had broken through the wall. Then came another blast of wood and glass. Jett held his ground, looking at Compton.

"It's a diversion," he said.

Compton nodded, smiling slightly. He lifted his gun, supporting it with his left hand. Then the back door blew out, broken into dozens of pieces. Smoke billowed from the door, and through the smoke came the Special. Jett and Compton put six bullets into him before he made two steps, and continued to fire as he fell. They replaced their clips before advancing to make sure the Special was dead.

As they were checking the body the police arrived, with a fire engine right behind. A few seconds later a television van roared up. As soon as the van stopped, the satellite dish on the top rotated, finding its uplink. A reporter and cameraman piled out of the van, the woman reporter arguing that they should set up the shot by the body, the cameraman arguing that the burning house was "more visual." A crowd was gathering, too, and Jett reeled with the task ahead. He had to deal with injured civilians, two dead agents, the body of a Special riddled with bullets, a burning house, and a television crew filming the aftermath. As if reading his thoughts, Compton said, "Hoover Dam couldn't contain this."

BULLETIN

Monica and Elizabeth shared social work stories, boring Wes. They were in the airport bar, drinking overpriced coffee, waiting for their flight. There was golf on a TV hanging from the ceiling, and Wes watched it despite knowing little about the game.

Wes used to spend his spare time working on his computer programs or in the lab—his time off was barely distinguishable from his work. Since meeting Elizabeth he had changed. He took walks with her now, and three times a week they worked out together at the campus facilities. Walking the stair-stepper and lifting the weights was repetitive, but afterward he found his mind clearer, better at problem solving. He now kept the gym schedule even when Elizabeth couldn't make it.

The golf match was interrupted, the logo for a local channel coming on with the voice of an announcer saying, "We interrupt this program for a special news bulletin." The logo was replaced with a woman reporter standing in front of a burning house, with firefighters, police, and clumps of people in the background. The reporter's curly blond hair was wilting in the Oklahoma summer heat, and her white blouse clung to her body. Beads of perspiration dotted her face.

"We're at the scene of a fire, Roger, which you can see behind us, but there is more to the story than just a fire. We have reports that two, maybe three men were killed and several others injured. The incident began a couple of blocks from here at the Midwestern Wire factory. Workers called for an ambulance when they found an injured man in the parking lot, but when the ambulance arrived a fight broke out and one man was killed."

"Barbara, how was the man injured?" Roger broke in.

"I have an eyewitness who can tell us what happened."

Barbara stepped sideways, the camera following her. A man waited nervously, but with a look of self-importance. He wore blue work clothes, was balding, and had a dark moustache. The reporter held the microphone to his face and said, "What is your name, sir, and where do you work?"

"I'm Avery Singer and I work at Midwestern Wire."

"What did you see today, sir?"

"Well, this sailor was lying in our parking lot and my friend Willie sees him and calls me over. He's hurt bad so we yells and tells them to get an ambulance."

"Was the man conscious?" Barbara asked.

"Sort of, but he wasn't making any sense. He was like out of his head or something."

"What happened next, sir?"

"Well the ambulance comes but the ambulance guys don't seem to know what they're doing. I mean they just picked the guy up and dragged him to the ambulance. He started yelling for help and then some guy came around the ambulance with a gun and wham, the guy with the gun got hit in the stomach so hard it killed him!"

"Who struck him?" Barbara asked.

"I'm not sure. No one was close. Maybe the sailor kicked him. Anyway, we tried to help the hurt man and all hell broke loose. It was a big fight and then all of a sudden another guy with a gun shows up and then it was like being in a tornado except there wasn't any wind. Everyone was knocked down except the hurt guy—he was a sailor, did I mention that?"

Wes nudged Elizabeth hard enough to break into her conversation, then pointed at the television. "Listen to this report."

Elizabeth rolled her eyes for Monica, but both women listened as the reporter continued the interview.

"A tornado with no wind?" the reporter probed.

"That's what it felt like," Singer said.

"Tell us what happened to the ambulance," the reporter continued.

"I was getting to that. Something hit it and tipped it almost all the way over."

"An explosion," the reporter suggested.

"Nah. I didn't hear anything like that. It just tipped."

"Another windless tornado?" the reporter said.

"Maybe," Singer said, irritated. "I'm not crazy. Ask Willie about it. He'll tell you the same."

"Thank you, Mr. Singer," the reporter said, stepping away. "I have another witness who can describe the events here by the burning house." She stepped next to another man, Hispanic, dark hair, shorter than the reporter. "What is your name, sir?"

"Hector Ramirez."

"What did you see, Mr. Ramirez?"

"I saw a sailor run into that house, the one that's burning. These ambulance people were chasing him, and another guy. That guy got killed."

"What happened, sir?"

"He tried to climb in the window and it blew up. Spit him right back out."

"There was an explosion?"

"Must have been. What else could do that?"

"Go on, Mr. Ramirez."

"Some other guys came, and pretty soon they threw something in the house—I think it was gasoline. Anyway, the house caught on fire. Then wham, wham, the whole front of the house blew out and then the side of the house blew and the sailor came running out. The ambulance guys shot the sailor a couple dozen times."

Elizabeth and Wes exchanged glances, Monica watching curiously.

"Sound familiar?" Wes said, thinking of his previous experience with a psychokinetic killer. With just the power of his mind the man had crushed Len's chest and then knocked Wes down a flight of stairs. By the time the police finally cornered the psychokinetic in a 7-Eleven, the man had literally destroyed the building, collapsing the roof using only his psi power.

Elizabeth knew what Wes was remembering.

"It could be any number of things," Elizabeth said. "Anyway, this has nothing to do with your experiments."

"Sure," Wes said.

"We don't know what happened, Wes. It doesn't mean psi abilities are involved."

Monica was listening intently, and Wes knew they had said too much. The report ended, the golf match returned. Wes pretended to watch it while he wondered about the strange events described in the news bulletin, hoping that Elizabeth was right and that what had happened had nothing to do with his experiments.

SOLUTION

The Office of Special Projects had a small conference room in a corner which was used mostly for staff reviews and agent debriefings. The conference room door was glass, and through it Jett could see that the space was filled to overflowing with a mixture of civilians, CIA, and Navy brass. He sat waiting outside Woolman's office, watching the lips of those in conference with Woolman, wishing he were a lip-reader. The brass were agitated, and the normally sedate CIA chief was red-faced and sweating. Something big had happened, and the fact they had gathered at OSP told Jett that it involved the Specials.

Shortly, the meeting broke up, those in the conference room departing one at a time to keep the gathering secret. The CIA chief let the others leave first, staying with Woolman. When he did leave, he was grim-faced and oblivious to the others in the office. Now only one person remained in the conference room with Woolman, gathering papers into a briefcase. Woolman left him, walking directly to his office and ignoring Jett, but leaving his office door open. Jett waited a few minutes to let Woolman compose himself, then stepped in, closing the door behind him.

Woolman was tense; beads of sweat formed on his bald head. As his fingers drummed the tabletop, he seemed unaware of the snare-drum rhythm filling the room. Jett was better at monitoring his body language than Woolman, never letting toe-tapping, tongue-wagging, or finger-drumming reveal his inner state. He saw fidgeting as a weakness, since it could be a window into a person's mind. Woolman's finger-drumming told Jett that he was anxious; his anxiety was expected—taking out the Special had been messy. But the unusual gathering in the conference room told Jett that something more important was going on.

Woolman had a family—a wife and two daughters. There were no pictures of them, of course; families were a liability in their line of work, and those with dependents didn't like to advertise the fact. Few field agents were married, and he knew of none who had children. Since families made you vulnerable, when agents married they were either reassigned to the office or transferred to the Secret Service. Jett wondered if this is how Woolman ended up with a desk job. He also wondered what kind of woman would marry Woolman. The man never smiled, never joked, and never showed even the slightest interest in female staff or agents. It was likely Mrs. Woolman had her own pathologies that made her need a fidgety man with a cold exterior.

"Your mission was a disaster. It was all over the news."

Woolman was debriefing Jett, but clearly was distracted by his previous meeting.

"It couldn't be helped. There were a dozen people around when we found him."

"The ambulance ruse was good," Woolman said.

"One of the women in the crowd was a nurse and queered the whole thing. She could tell we didn't know what we were doing and turned the crowd against us."

"Bad luck," Woolman said.

The rhythm of Woolman's fingers was rapid now, individual beats nearly indistinguishable.

"Containment in the information age is damn near impossible—cellular phones, Internet, satellite broadcasts, and every Joe Blow with a video camera."

"It is a challenge," Jett said.

"It used to be only the intelligence services had access to these technologies. Now I see women in grocery stores talking on cell phones, and they could be connected to anyone on the planet."

Jett also had trouble picturing Woolman in a grocery store pushing a cart, selecting heads of lettuce and squeezing bread to find the freshest loaf. If there was a domestic side to Woolman, it was as well hidden as his warm side.

"There's another problem," Woolman said abruptly. "As you must have realized we're getting more breakouts."

Jett knew the frequency of his tracking assignments had increased, adding to his job satisfaction.

"We thought the Specials were testing a way to punch through Pot of Gold's containment field. Now we suspect they had something else in mind."

Pot of Gold was the code name for the place where the Specials came from.

Touching the intercom button on his phone, Woolman said, "Send Dr. Lee in."

Dr. Lee was the project director at Rainbow, the facility that monitored Pot of Gold. As he entered, Jett recognized him as the last man left in the conference room. Dr. Lee was Chinese-American, short, oval-faced, and wore a gray suit with a red-and-blue striped tie. The suit was expensive, the tie tasteful. Jett could see that behind his wire-rimmed glasses there were layers of creases around his eyes, although the rest of his face was smooth, making his age hard to judge. Jett guessed that Dr. Lee was older than Woolman.

"Dr. Lee, meet Nathan Jett."

Shaking hands, Dr. Lee said, "I've heard you do good work."

"I've heard the same about you," Jett lied politely. He knew little about what Dr. Lee or any of the technicians at Rainbow did.

"Dr. Lee, Mr. Jett has been cleared for your briefing."

Dr. Lee smiled in response, then said, "Two days ago the aircraft carrier USS Nimitz was cruising off the Pennsylvania coastline when it disappeared. No other ships in the flotilla were significantly affected."

Jett's blood pressure rose slightly. On the face of it, Dr. Lee's story was impossible to believe, but Woolman didn't tolerate nonsense and had no sense of humor. That, combined with the strange meeting in the conference room and the rumors of problems at Rainbow, gave the disappearing-carrier story credibility.

"Nothing the size of the Nimitz simply vanishes," Jett said.

Dr. Lee smiled, then looked to Woolman, who drummed his fingers a few times and nodded.

"There was more to it," Dr. Lee said. "The ship was enveloped in a green light, and when the light faded, the Nimitz was gone. It encountered the green light twice before, and the John F. Kennedy reported a similar phenomenon at approximately the same latitude and longitude. I became involved when it was discovered that the electromagnetic waves recorded by ships in the flotilla are similar to those generated by Pot of Gold."

Again Dr. Lee smiled, using his smile to release tension just as Woolman used his finger drumming.

"We see three possibilities," Woolman cut in. "It may be that another nation has discovered the technology that created Pot of Gold and used it to capture the Nimitz. It's the usual list of suspects: Japan, Russia, China, North Korea. However, our intelligence tells us they have no credible research program in resonant magnetic fields. They continue to be nuclear focussed. The second possibility is that a private agency has developed this technology. There are a few corporations and foundations with the resources and the will, but again there is no evidence of a sustained effort."

"Not even the Kellum Foundation," Dr. Lee added.

Woolman shot Dr. Lee a glance that said he had revealed too much, and Jett took note of it. Jett knew of the Kellum Foundation and its reputation for funding unconventional research. The foundation had been an early supporter of cold fusion research, pouring millions into that dead end.

"The third possibility is that the Specials have learned to manipulate the containment field and somehow managed to pull the Nimitz into Pot of Gold," Woolman continued, finishing with a finger drum roll and a nod to Dr. Lee.

"Beginning about two years ago, we began to notice changes in the shape of Pot of Gold's field. Asymmetrical bulges appeared which we had difficulty containing. Our field loses integrity without symmetry. The asymmetry also increased field porosity, leading to the increase in the number of escapes. That's why you have been so busy," Dr. Lee said, finishing with another nervous smile.

"Until the Nimitz disappeared, all indications were that the Specials were probing the containment field, preparing for a mass escape," Woolman said.

"How many Specials?" Jett asked, feeling the beginning of the slightest adrenaline rush.

"An army of them," Woolman said. "Based on interviews with survivors there could be as many as three hundred."

Jett's heart stepped up its rhythm at the thought of facing three hundred Specials with psi abilities.

"Dealing with that many would be a challenge," he said.

"Yes," Woolman agreed, "not to mention keeping it quiet. There's another problem," he added, deferring to Dr. Lee.

"We've done some work with Specials that were picked up," Dr. Lee said, again ending with a smile.

Jett knew that very few Specials were captured alive, and most of those were female.

"It seems that once their psi abilities are activated, that trait can be passed on to their offspring."

He smiled broadly this time, revealing how nervous he was. Jett understood his discomfort; Dr. Lee had just hinted that he and Woolman had been involved in human breeding experiments where it was unlikely that any of the "offspring" were allowed to live past the testing period.

"We've been unable to isolate the gene responsible for their psi abilities and cannot suppress either their power or their ability to pass that trait on—short of sterilization," Dr. Lee said with another nervous smile.

Jett knew the CIA and military had long been interested in psi powers, but only as a weapon they could control. Neither the CIA nor the military would tolerate psi powers spreading uncontrolled through the population, and in truth Jett didn't relish the idea either. No one without psi abilities would enjoy discovering that there were people one rung above them on the evolutionary ladder.

"We were preparing to handle the threat of a mass escape, but the Nimitz incident makes that problematic," Woolman said.

"Because of the nuclear weapons," Jett said.

"Yes, those and more. If the Specials have control of the Nimitz, and ride her back to the world, they will have an arsenal greater than the arsenals of most nations of the world. If the nuclear safeties have been compromised, then we would be dealing with a nuclear power."

"They could force a stalemate," Jett said.

"There won't be a stalemate," Woolman answered. "We can't have them getting into the general population."

"The loss of the Nimitz has been contained for now by keeping its battle group at sea and blacking out most communications, but we can't keep this secret much longer," Woolman said.

Jett guessed that there would be five or six thousand crew on the Nimitz, and a couple thousand more in its carrier battle group that knew of the disappearance. They would all have family and friends who they wrote to and called regularly, and it wouldn't be long before those family members began to worry about their loved ones. He estimated that they might keep the loss of the Nimitz secret for two or three weeks before the communications dam broke; leaks would begin immediately.

"It has been decided that the first course of action is to determine if the Nimitz is in Pot of Gold."

Jett felt his heart speed up slightly, the tiny adrenaline rush building, and he relished the feeling. Whoever was sent into Pot of Gold would be facing Specials on their own turf.

"Dr. Lee believes he can successfully insert a team into Pot of Gold and retrieve the team members," Woolman said.

Jett knew there had been attempts to enter Pot of Gold before, with disastrous results. The only survivor had suffered third degree burns over much of his body and lived just long enough to tell of the horrors that had befallen the rest of his team.

"I believe that's been tried," Jett said.

Woolman frowned at the breach of security, but was hardly surprised. The agents were a breed apart, and loyal to each other. That loyalty was a prerequisite for survival. Deception was the norm in their work, but they kept few secrets from each other. What one agent knew, others would know.

"There were two incursions, actually," Dr. Lee said. "Three agents went in the first time and we never heard from them again. The second attempt was seven years ago. One man made it back but was severely burned. He is the only eyewitness to the conditions inside Pot of Gold. He confirmed that Pot of Gold is full of Specials and they're insane."

"You haven't had any success in either shutting down Pot of Gold or getting agents back," Jett said. "What makes you think you can do it now?"

"We created an aperture to let the teams inside," Dr. Lee said, "and then opened an exit at the same spot at a predetermined time. Except for the burned agent, no one else made it to the exit point at the predetermined time. This time we have portable hip units that will allow you to pass safely through the field at any time and point you choose. Once you've accomplished your mission you can exit Pot of Gold immediately and not have to fight your way back to the exit point."

The hip units were a significant advantage that the earlier teams didn't have. Still, there were other concerns.

"Once inside, you're dealing with Specials on their own turf," Jett said. "The advantage is all theirs—they know the terrain, they have the built-in weapons."

Now Dr. Lee flashed a nervous smile and waited for Woolman to explain the rest of the plan.

"We sent our own Special in on the last attempt," Woolman said.

This was new, and Jett's heart picked up its pace ever so slightly.

"As we expected, his abilities were magnified inside Pot of Gold, but there were too many Specials for him to deal with. They pounded him senseless and then turned him into a human candle and threw him out when we opened a door."

"The one who made it out was your Special?" Jett said.

"He's not dead," Woolman said. "They burned him as a warning to us."

Jett's heart thumped a little faster—he was beginning to feel the way he did when he faced a Special.

"He's willing to go back," Woolman said.

"After what they did to him?"

"He's insane, of course," Woolman said.

In Jett's line of work, insanity didn't necessarily disqualify you.

"If he couldn't handle them before, what will be different this time?" Jett asked.

"Two things," Woolman said. "Dr. Lee, tell him about the weapons."

Dr. Lee took off his glasses and cleaned them with a tissue while he spoke, still smiling. "We learned from the agent who survived that the team's weapons didn't work inside Pot of Gold. We know that time is slowed inside and we now believe that certain chemical reactions are impossible. Specifically, rapid reactions."

"Like the explosive kind necessary for a gun to fire," Jett said.

"Exactly," Dr. Lee said. "For a bomb, too. That's why we have to send a team in. Don't worry, we have a solution."

Jett never worried, but he was wondering.

"We've developed a weapon powered by compressed gas."

"Pellet guns?" Jett asked skeptically.

"Not a toy, Mr. Jett." Dr. Lee said.

He finished with his glasses and put them back on.

"The gas charge doesn't have the power of gun powder, but we've compensated by using prefragmented Teflon-coated bullets. The reduction in propellant power is compensated for by improved penetration. You don't have quite the range and power of a nine millimeter, but in the confined spaces of Pot of Gold the weapons should be sufficient."

"You said there were two things different about this insertion into Pot of Gold."

"We have a contact in the Kellum Foundation," Dr. Lee said, "which specializes in funding nontraditional research—research the National Science Foundation wouldn't touch. Some of the research has dealt with the paranormal. They recently funded a project that turned up the most powerful Special we've ever run across this side of Pot of Gold. He killed several people—psychokinetic, unheard of ability, at least the equal of those in Pot of Gold. Unfortunately, he was killed."

Dr. Lee's smile broadened, and Woolman's fingers began drumming again, telling Jett that the important part of the story was still to come.

"There are several peculiarities surrounding that incident," Dr. Lee said. "For one, there was a report of a man who was immune to the abilities of the Special. We have eyewitnesses who claim that while others were bowled over like tenpins from the Special's psychokinetic powers, this man walked right up to the Special and was able to hold him."

"Immunity to psi forces?" Jett asked.

"The Special's psychokinetic powers worked on everyone but this one man. Think of it as another kind of talent," Dr. Lee said.

"He could be useful," Jett said. "Does he have the necessary skills? Weapons training? Hand-to-hand combat?"

Dr. Lee kept his smile, but looked uncomfortable and deferred to Woolman.

"He has no training," Woolman said, fingers drumming.

"That's a limitation," Jett said.

"It's worse than that," Woolman said. "He's retarded."

ANITA

Anita was seven and Pollyanaish. Polite, outgoing, cheerful, she was a child even Wes was comfortable with. She wore her brown hair in pigtails and was missing two front teeth, giving her the classic seven-year-old smile. Still, her eyes were dark hollows, telling of her severe sleep disturbance. She sat on the edge of her sofa wearing shorts and a pink tee-shirt with two white rabbits on the front, hands in her lap. Her mother, Shirley Andrews, sat next to Anita. She was a larger version of the daughter, sharing her clear skin, fine facial features, and long, thin arms and legs. Anita's mother watched Wes, feeling that his coming represented new hope. He felt as if he was raising her hopes under false pretenses.

"Do you like rabbits?" Elizabeth asked.

Nodding her head yes, Anita said, "Bunnies are the softest animal in the whole world and when I get better I'm gonna get one." Then the little girl looked to her mother, who confirmed the promised rabbit with a nod. "I've got bunny hair things, too," she said, turning her head so they could see her pigtails held with bands that wrapped around pink bunnies. "I've got bunny earrings, too, but I can't get my ears pierced until I'm twelve."

"Very sensible," Elizabeth said.

"I can only get one hole in each ear, too," Anita said.

"I see," Elizabeth said.

"My friend Keri has her ears pierced."

"Does she have bunny earrings?" Elizabeth asked.

"No. Just little gold balls."

"I'm wearing hoops," Elizabeth said, leaning forward and showing Anita her earrings.

"I think I'm wearing roses," Monica said. "I can't remember, though. What are they?" she asked, leaning forward so Anita could see.

"Ooh, little flowers. I like those," Anita said, "but I like bunnies better."

Wes sat quietly through the small talk, waiting for Elizabeth and Monica to establish a relationship with the little girl. He knew it was the right approach, but disliked the inefficiency. If he had come alone he would have asked about the dream immediately, and probably frightened the little girl into silence. He had always been all business—efficient and machinelike, generating publications and pulling in grants, always on the cutting edge of neuroscience. Totally left brain, logic and rationality, his interpersonal skills were woefully undeveloped; that made him and Elizabeth an odd couple. The feelings of others were of utmost importance to her, and if a person was comforted or a friend made, it didn't matter to her if a technical problem went unsolved. In this case, however, helping Anita meant solving a technical problem, and Wes and Elizabeth needed each other. Finally Wes heard them bringing the earring conversation to a close.

"Tell us about the dream," Monica said.

"I'm on a boat and I can't get off. I just walk up and down, down and up, up and down. Then I wake up."

"When you're on the deck of the ship—you know, outside—what do you see when you look up?" Monica asked.

"Great big cannons," Anita said.

"Above those, way up in the sky?" Monica said.

Anita turned her head up and closed her eyes.

"Nothing. I don't see nothing."

"What do you see when you look over the side of the ship?" Monica asked.

"Nothing," Anita said. "Just sand."

"Is there anyone else on the ship?" Monica asked.

"No. Just me."

"Are there airplanes on this ship?" Elizabeth asked, glancing at Wes.

"Yes, two of them. It's the kind that has two wings. I forget the name."

"Biplanes?" Elizabeth suggested, flashing Wes a triumphant smile.

The fact that Anita had seen the airplanes solidified Monica and Elizabeth's claim that Margi, Wanda, and Anita were dreaming the same dream; but the peculiarity of finding airplanes on a battleship was yet to be explained, and the fact that they were biplanes was yet another oddity.

"I guess so," Anita said.

"Is there a mirror on the ship?" Elizabeth asked.

Anita paused, looking at her hands in her lap. Then she reached for a pigtail and put the end in her mouth, sucking on it.

"I dunno. Maybe in the bathroom."

Wes leaned forward. None of the others had mentioned finding a bathroom.

"There was a mirror in the bathroom?" Elizabeth asked.

"I dunno," Anita said. "Maybe. I can't see that high."

"Okay, Anita. You said there was no way off the ship. Have you ever thought of jumping over the side?" Monica asked.

Anita's mother reached over and took the pigtail out of the little girl's mouth. Unconsciously, Anita's right hand put her other pigtail in.

"It's pretty far," Anita said.

"It's only a dream," Monica said. "You wouldn't get hurt."

"If I jump will the dream go away?" Anita wanted to know.

Monica looked to Wes and Elizabeth, then said, "No, but it might help us figure out a way to stop the dream."

Anita put her head down and said, "I'd be too scared."

Elizabeth walked over and sat next to her on the sofa. With her arm around Anita's shoulders, she said, "Would you be too scared if I went with you?"

Anita looked up, hopeful but confused.

"Jump off the ship with me?" Anita said. "You'll be in my dream?"

"Yes, I'll jump with you," Elizabeth said, looking at Wes.

"I don't know," Wes started, remembering the disaster that had resulted the last time he integrated multiple minds. Then he saw Anita and her mother staring at him, the mother's eyes pleading, the little girl's hopeful look coming from eyes that hadn't had a normal night's rest in months.

"All right, we'll try," he said.

Elizabeth smiled triumphantly.

With her mother's permission, Anita spent the night in the university's sleep lab, wearing a nightgown covered with pink bunnies and one of Wes's scalp caps while her brain waves were broadcast through fiber optic cables to the computer with the supercooled processor. At the corner of her eyes were tiny sensors that would pick up muscle contractions indicating eye movement. Len, Wes, and Shamita were at their terminals, Monica looking over Wes's shoulder. Elizabeth sat on the edge of her cot, scalp cap in place, waiting her turn.

It wasn't a full mind meld since they needed only to let Anita's brain dream for both of them, but Wes was nervous, having pushed the envelope of neuroscience before and paid the price for it.

"That's one tired little girl," Len said. "Her alpha waves are desynchronizing and we have six cps."

"Cps?" Monica questioned.

"Cycles per second," Wes explained. "Alpha waves characterize relaxation. When they slow and desynchronize, you are in light sleep. If Anita follows a normal sleep pattern her brain waves will continue to slow, and then we'll get sleep spindles—bursts of electrical activity."

"There we go," Len said a few minutes later, "our first spindle—fourteen cps."

Monica left Wes to stand behind Len, who was monitoring Anita while Shamita mapped Elizabeth's brain.

"I knew I'd interest you eventually," Len said to Monica.

"Your monitor interests me," Monica said.

"Yeah. My monitor is bigger than Wes's."

"Quiet, you'll wake Anita," Shamita scolded.

"I don't think a bomb would wake that little girl," Len said, whispering now. "I've got fifty percent delta waves at two cps and it looks like she's cycling back up to light sleep. We should get rapid eye movement any second now." Then a minute later he said, "I've got REM sleep—she's dreaming."

Elizabeth lay down, while Wes called up her brain wave pattern, waiting while she settled into a comfortable position. In a minute Len indicated that he had clear physiological readings on both subjects. As usual Shamita took longer, processing more slowly, making fewer errors but using more time.

"Frontal, temporal, parietal, occipital, all clear and nominal," Shamita said finally.

"Elizabeth, we're going to put you under now," Wes told her.

"Ready," Elizabeth said.

Wes nodded to Shamita, and she began to intercept Elizabeth's brain waves, filtering out sensory information, convincing the brain that it was falling asleep. Elizabeth was semiconscious, however, able to communicate with those controlling her brain. When Elizabeth was in a state similar to a hypnotic trance, Wes took control, letting Anita's brain waves flow into Elizabeth's brain.

"It will take a minute for your brain to adjust, Elizabeth," Wes said.

It took five minutes of adjusting parameters, but then Elizabeth's brain wave pattern was a near-perfect duplicate of Anita's. They were dreaming the same dream.

THE DREAM

Elizabeth found herself walking down a narrow corridor, Anita in front of her wearing a pink dress and patent leather shoes. The girl's long hair was combed and curled. She was stepping through an oval doorway, all metal—it was a ship's hatch, and she had to step up and over a metal flange to pass through.

"Anita, I'm here," Elizabeth said.

Anita started, turning with wide eyes, mouth open. Elizabeth saw that the pink dress had an embroidered bunny on it, and that Anita had both of her front teeth.

"You scared me," Anita said, close to crying.

"I'm sorry. I told you I would be with you."

"Can you come every night? I don't like it here alone."

"I'd like to make it so you never have to come here again."

"Do it, please?"

"I'll do what I can," Elizabeth said, taking the little girl's hand. "That's a very pretty dress."

"My grandmother gave it to me."

Now Elizabeth looked around, noticing the detail of the ship.

"This doesn't feel like a dream," Elizabeth said. She slapped a wall, feeling the impact, but not hearing the "smack" sound. Then she ran her hand along it, feeling the cool of the metal.

"Wes, can you hear me?" Elizabeth said.

"We're here, Elizabeth," Wes said. *"Are you sharing the dream?"*

"Yes. It's amazing. I'm actually in her dream."

"Who are you talking to?" Anita asked.

Squeezing her hand, Elizabeth said, "I'm talking to Wes. Wes and Len and Shamita and Monica can hear me when I talk."

"How come I can't hear them?"

"Wes, why can't Anita hear you? She's asking."

"Audition is virtually shut down during dreaming. If we feed it to her it could disrupt the dream."

Elizabeth paused, knowing that Wes's explanation was too complicated for a seven-year-old.

"Wes says your job is to dream and mine is to listen and talk. I'll tell you everything they say. Except Len's stupid jokes."

Anita smiled at that, saying, "I like Len, he's funny."

"Okay, if Len tells me any jokes I'll tell them to you."

"Tell us what you're seeing, Elizabeth," Wes said.

"They want to know what I see," Elizabeth said to Anita. "I'm in a corridor—a ship's corridor. We're standing in front of a hatch—oval shaped. There are two hatches in one direction along this corridor and a sealed hatch at the other end. There are two more in the other direction ending in another closed hatch. The detail is amazing. Textured walls, bolts, rivets, the lights in the ceiling are in wire cages. There's a bell on the wall—like an alarm."

"What color?" Wes asked.

"Red," Elizabeth said.

"Unusual," Wes said.

"Is it the wrong color for a ship's alarm?" Elizabeth asked.

"There shouldn't be any color at all," Wes said. *"Most people think they dream in color but actually it's rare."*

Elizabeth thought about her own dreams, unsure if they were in color. Certainly there were no bright, high-contrast colors.

"It looks different with you here," Anita said, pulling on her hand.

"In what way?"

"I can see things better."

"What do you mean?"

Shrugging her shoulders, Anita said, "I dunno, it just looks different."

"Tell me if you see anything different that you can point at."

Anita nodded.

"Can you show me where the bathroom is?"

"Maybe," Anita said, then turned left.

Elizabeth followed her, noticing that there was no sound, and when they pushed open the next hatch there was no hinge groan. The corridor continued on the other side, and they stepped through the hatch. They were in a long corridor, pipes running above them. At the end of the corridor was a steep ladder. Elizabeth followed Anita up and then along another corridor, pausing at a closed hatch. It had a name plate but there was nothing written on it.

"It's one of these doors, I think."

They had seen no one on the ship, but Elizabeth had a growing sense of dread, as if something unexpected could happen at any second. Opening the door, she found two bunks and a small desk. There were blankets on the bed, but they had no edges. Elizabeth looked closely, then ran her hand over one blanket. It had the right feel, but conformed seamlessly to the thin mattress. Now sensitized, she noticed other missing details. Screws were missing slots, the desk had no drawers, and there was nothing on top of it. There were pipes running along the ceiling but no joints or couplings. The lack of detail should have made it feel more dreamlike, but it didn't.

"Anita, have you been in this room before?"

"I dunno. Maybe."

"You thought this was the bathroom?"

"Sometimes it is."

"Have you ever seen a room like this one?"

Anita looked around then said, "Yeah, but it didn't have a bed before."

Elizabeth urged her to look for the bathroom again. Anita skipped the remaining hatches in the corridor, taking Elizabeth back the way they had come and down the stairs they had climbed. Then the girl turned, leading Elizabeth back in the direction they had come to seemingly the same door, but when she opened it this time there was nothing on the other side but darkness.

"Isn't this the same room?" Elizabeth asked.

"I dunno. It changes."

Anita started forward and Elizabeth stopped her.

"What's in there?" Elizabeth asked.

"The bathroom, maybe." Anita walked into the room and faded from view.

"Wes, are you still there?" Elizabeth said.

"*Of course,*" Wes replied.

"Are Anita's vital signs normal?"

"Len says everything's nominal for Anita," Wes said. *"What's going on?"*

"We're looking for the bathroom," Elizabeth said.

Elizabeth stepped through the doorway into the room and suddenly found herself standing on the deck of the ship. Anita was a few steps away, looking over the side.

"There," Anita said, pointing. "That doesn't look the same."

Elizabeth leaned over the side and saw a patch of ground sparsely spotted with sagebrush. It was a small area; a hundred yards away in all directions there was nothing—a wall of nothing. Above her, there was nothing to see but haze. If it hadn't been gray, she would have called it a whiteout.

"How is it different, Anita?"

"There's lots more green stuff."

Looking over the edge, Elizabeth understood why none of the dreamers had ever jumped off. It was a three-story drop to solid ground.

"Are we going to jump, Elizabeth? Are we?"

"Let's find the bathroom first," Elizabeth said, not sure now that she could leap.

Turning, Elizabeth got her first full look at the ship, and it was overpowering, like no dream she had ever had. They were midship, looking up at the superstructure. There was a single large funnel with masts fore and aft. A variety of antennae were attached to the masts, as were other structures. There were crow's nests on both masts. Forward of the funnel was the largest visible structure, at least five stories tall. The bridge would be there, Elizabeth knew. Mounted forward of the bridge were two huge gun emplacements with a smaller gun and turret between the bridge and the first big gun. Smaller gun turrets were to her right and left, and toward the stern was another medium-sized gun and more of the smaller gun turrets. Mounted on the stern were two more of the big guns, and right on the stern Elizabeth could see a biplane mounted on a rail. Over the top of the big gun she could see another biplane on the far side. Never had she seen such a spectacle in her own dreams, yet as she looked closely she could see the lack of detail—the guns closest to her had barrels, but they blended into the steel of the turret where there should have been a joint. There was a life raft mounted to each of the turrets, but no ropes or fasteners holding them on.

"Let's go, Elizabeth," Anita said, pulling her hand.

Anita pulled her back through the hatch they had just left and into a corridor which looked exactly like the one Elizabeth had first found herself in. They walked the length of it to another corridor and up another set of stairs—identical to the ones they had climbed before. A few steps later Anita stood before the same door as before—at least, Elizabeth thought it was the same door.

"It's usually the bathroom after it's outside," Anita said.

It was the bathroom—the head—this time, with a double row of sinks down the middle, toilets along one side, and a steel trough that served as a urinal along the other side. Looking closer, Elizabeth could see that there were no faucet handles, only spouts. The urinal had no drains and the toilets no flush mechanism. Over each sink hung a small frameless mirror.

"It's different in here too, Elizabeth," Anita said. "Before there wasn't no place for the water to come out," she said, pointing at the sinks.

Elizabeth hesitated, nervous about what she would see in a mirror. Holding Anita's hand she stepped in and turned to face the closest mirror—she saw nothing.

"*Elizabeth?*" Wes cut in. "*What's going on? Your heart rate and blood pressure are up.*"

"We found the bathroom, Wes. There are mirrors but they don't reflect."

"Hold me up," Anita said. "I want to see too."

When Elizabeth bent down, she saw something out of the corner of her eye—something in the mirror. Standing again she saw nothing but the glass. Eyes on the mirror, she bent again—she saw nothing. Assuming it was her imagination, she picked Anita up. Anita made faces in the mirror, and Elizabeth smiled. Then Elizabeth saw it again—a flickering face. Abruptly dropping Anita, she quickly looked behind her, but saw only wall.

"What's the matter, Elizabeth?" Anita said.

Looking back, she stared deep into the glass, but saw nothing. Then she looked just left of the mirror, letting her peripheral vision do the seeing—there was movement. Glancing back, she caught sight of a face—no faces. Were there flickering faces in the mirror? It was a subliminal perception, just below the point at which her conscious mind could be sure.

"Aren't you going to hold me up?" Anita said.

Elizabeth lifted the little girl again.

"*Your heart rate just took another big jump, Elizabeth,*" Wes said.

"I'm just a little nervous. We're going to go outside now."

"And jump, Elizabeth?" Anita said. "Are we really gonna jump?"

Elizabeth said yes, but wasn't sure she would. Anita led them back along the their path and through the same hatch to the outside. They walked to the rail and looked over the edge.

"I'm scared," Anita said.

"Me too. You don't have to jump if you don't want to," Elizabeth said.

"Hold my hand?" Anita asked.

"I will."

"Elizabeth, both of your heart rates are up now," Wes said.

"We're getting ready to jump," Elizabeth said.

"You don't have to do this."

"I know. We want to." Then, to Anita, Elizabeth said, "Are you ready?"

The little girl nodded, looking as if she was about to take her first roller coaster ride. Elizabeth sat on the rail and swung her legs over. Then she helped Anita up next to her, the little girl tucking her pink dress under her legs.

"On three?" Elizabeth said.

"Let's just go," Anita said, wiggling forward.

Elizabeth wasn't ready, but Anita was about to slide off, so she gripped her hand tight and jumped, pulling the little girl with her.

When she was ten, Elizabeth had moved to a two-story house, and every night when she first started dreaming she would find herself standing at the top of the stairs, knowing she had to jump, but too afraid to. Finally, she would get the courage and leap off the top step, floating slowly toward the bottom, always drifting to other dreams as the bottom rose up to meet her. This was like that. She and Anita were falling, but very slowly and in fits and starts. They weren't picking up speed, and occasionally they paused in midair as if gravity had taken a rest. A fall that should have taken a few seconds took minutes, but about ten feet from the bottom they suddenly lurched and fell in a normal fashion, landing with a very real and jarring thud.

"Are you all right, Anita?" Elizabeth said.

"Yes. I think so."

Elizabeth looked back up the side. It was a bizarre sight—the ship's hull buried in the sand, but not deep enough to keep the great bulk from tipping. The brush around them was mostly sage. Looking closely she saw that the plant lacked detail and looked artificial. There was no smell.

"What's going on, Elizabeth?" Wes said.

"We're off the ship. The landing was pretty hard but we're not hurt." Then Elizabeth remembered that she was actually lying on a cot in Wes's lab. "Were we hurt?"

"Len says you and Anita are fine. Your heart rate is coming down, too."

"It's just like they described it, Wes. The ship is in a desert. There's sagebrush for about a hundred yards but nothing else."

"See if you can find a name or number on the ship," Wes said.

"Wes wants us to see if we can find a name on the ship," Elizabeth told Anita.

She took Anita's hand, and they walked along the ship toward the bow. There were no markings of any kind, nothing but flat gray paint everywhere they looked. Finally, they reached the point where the anchor hung— except the anchor was attached to the hull instead of hanging from a chain.

"There are no markings, Wes," Elizabeth said. "I'm going to see how far I can get from the ship."

Still holding Anita's hand, she walked across the desert, which ended about a hundred yards away. She stood there looking at nothing.

"It's just like the sky," Anita said.

Elizabeth's eyes registered a foggy gray, but as she tried to focus on the nothingness her eyes began to hurt, then her head.

"Wes, I'm going to try and walk out of the desert," Elizabeth said.

"Careful, Elizabeth," Wes said.

"It's just a dream, right?" Elizabeth said. "Wait here, Anita."

Letting go of Anita's hand, Elizabeth stepped forward until her toes were right on the edge of the desert. Then she reached forward until her fingertips touched the nothingness. Suddenly her body felt as though it was on fire, and with a deafening buzz and crackle Elizabeth was knocked onto her back.

"Elizabeth, are you hurt?" Anita screamed. Kneeling next to Elizabeth, she took her hand. "Wake up, Elizabeth, wake up."

Unresponsive to Anita's pleas, Elizabeth lay unconscious. Then, to the little girl's horror, Elizabeth became transparent.

"No! Don't go!" Anita said. "Don't leave me!"

Elizabeth's hand melted away, and Anita's fingers passed through what had been skin. Now all Anita could see was an outline of where Elizabeth had been.

"Don't leave me alone, Elizabeth! Please don't leave me!" Anita pleaded.

Then Elizabeth was gone.

RALPH

Worthington, Ohio

Slurpee in hand, Ralph strode up High Street, headed for home. Ralph had a muscular upper body and long legs, and walked with oversized strides, arms swinging in a simian way. At the sight of his large protruding lips, overhanging brow, and serious look, passersby stepped aside, staring from the corners of their eyes. Ralph wore a Hawaiian shirt with baggy shorts and blue thongs. In his shirt was a pocket protector packed with pens. Ralph had no use for the pens, since he could barely write, but they were *his* pens, given to him by the owners of the shops along High Street.

Ralph turned into the auto parts store, heading directly to the counter in the back.

"Hi Roger, hi Meg," Ralph said loudly, which was his only way of speaking. "How's business?"

"Business is fine, Ralph," Roger said.

"What kind of Slurpee do you have there, Ralph?" Meg asked.

The two customers at the counter looked at the peculiar man, then turned away, pretending not to notice his oddities.

"Lemonade. It's pretty good. Want I should get you one?"

"It's too early for me, Ralph," Meg said.

"Not now, Ralph," Roger said. "If you come by later, I might."

"Well okee-dokee then," Ralph said. "See ya."

Then Ralph was out the door, loping up the street, long legs pumping effortlessly. The hardware store was next, and Ralph popped in, stopping by the checkout stands.

"Hi Shirley," Ralph said to the middle-aged woman at the cash register. "How's business?"

"Slow, Ralph. It will pick up after lunch."

"Want I should bring you a Slurpee?"

"No thanks, but maybe Gaylord wants one." Shouting to the rear of the store Shirley said, "Hey Gay, Ralph's here. You want a Slurpee?"

"Naw!" came Gaylord's reply. "Maybe an Eskimo Pie when it gets hotter."

"Well okee-dokee then," Ralph said, and left.

The routine was repeated all along Ralph's route; at the barber shop, the paint store, the Chinese restaurant, the beauty salon, and the real estate office. Meeting and greeting was a routine Ralph had used since he was a child and still living with his parents.

Born to older parents who thought they were long past childbearing age, Ralph had been their pride and joy. An easy, cheerful baby, he was the center of their lives, and they loved him all the more knowing they would have precious little time with him. His mother was nearly fifty when he was born, and his father even older. They were traditional parents; Ralph's mother stayed home with her son, enjoying every minute of parenthood. She found playing with her son, pushing him in the stroller, and later walking hand in hand with him more satisfying than her thirty years as a legal secretary. His father also loved parenting; he played catch with Ralph, took him fishing, and used his carpenter's skills to build him the best playhouse a boy could imagine. It was a pirate ship–shaped jungle gym, with a sand box and rope net for climbing.

Ralph had been popular with the neighborhood kids, not just because of his special toys or the bottomless cookie jar in his kitchen, but because of his genial personality. Ralph went along to get along, and never held a grudge. A friend who threw sand in his face one day was welcomed back the next. Ralph and his parents couldn't have been happier, until Ralph started school.

By the end of first grade Ralph was behind his grade level. With a social promotion they pushed him into second grade, where he continued to fall behind. Because he was easy to work with, he was promoted again to the third grade, but it was clear by the end of that year that he could not keep up with his peers. It was painful for his parents when the school retained him to repeat the third grade, but Ralph took it in stride, climbing onto the bus each morning with a smile on his face and a Daffy Duck lunch box tucked into his backpack. Each day that year he waved goodbye to his mother from the bus window. It was Ralph's last year in a regular class.

The next year Ralph was assigned to special education and driven to school by his mother. Cheerful to a fault, he accepted his new situation though he was briefly saddened because he missed riding the bus with the other children. Quickly adapting, he was popular with the staff and his classmates, and was often a positive influence on emotionally unstable children.

As early as age five Ralph began walking up and down his block, talking to anyone and everyone. By the time he was ten he was ranging several blocks from home and knew by name most of the residents in his neighborhood. By age twelve he was known far and wide; passersby called to him by name as he came down the street, and business owners greeting him warmly as he visited, often asking Ralph to run errands for them. When he was thirteen his father died, and over the next few years the pirate ship fell into disrepair. The paint peeled from the ship, the rope climbing net frayed and finally broke under Ralph's weight. Three years later his mother died. With no relatives to take him in, Ralph was made a ward of the state and began moving from foster home to foster home, the only constants his wandering ways, his need to meet and greet people, and his always genial personality.

Ralph was finishing his greeting routine now, checking with Nigel, who was sitting in the booth at the Chevron station taking money from the self-serve customers. Satisfied that Nigel didn't need anything, he turned on Selby Street, headed for Dr. Birnbaum's house, which was where he lived.

Ralph walked into an old neighborhood which had been rejuvenated when the third-generation families put money into remodelling. Many of the original single-story homes now were two-story, others had room additions, still others had garages converted into family rooms. Mature trees lined the streets, and in the yards grew closely cropped grass outlined with large shrubs. In new neighborhoods gardening meant planting, seeding, and fencing. Here, gardening was pruning, clipping, and raking.

Ralph greeted everyone he passed on Selby Street with a hearty "hihowyadoin," stopping to shake hands with people he hadn't met before—there were few of those. Ralph knew everyone and everyone knew him.

He spotted the strange car in front of his house a block away, and his legs picked up their rhythm. His "hihowyadoins" were clipped now, and he finished with a quick "I gots to get home. I think we gots company." Ralph was up his walk and in the door in six strides, pleased to see that they did indeed have visitors.

A man and a woman sat on the couch opposite Dr. Birnbaum, who was in his motorized wheelchair. Severely injured in a traffic accident, Dr. Birnbaum had barely survived, and the accident had exacted a heavy toll on his body. His empty left pant leg was neatly folded and pinned, as was his left sleeve. His face was heavily scarred on the left and the eye on that side hung low, eyelid open over a blind eye. The right eye, however, was animated and bright with intelligence. Ralph walked directly to the visitors, extending his hand.

"Hihowyadoin," he said. "My name's Ralph, what's yours?"

"Nathan Rand," the man said, standing to take Ralph's hand.

Ralph pumped the man's hand vigorously, grinning from ear to ear. Visitors were a treat to Ralph, exciting him more than Christmas mornings.

After a score of hand pumps, Ralph turned to the woman, who took his hand in a limp grip.

"I'm Karla Simon," she said.

"It's okay to squeeze tight," Ralph said. "You won't hurt me or nothing." Ralph felt Karla's grip tighten, and he pumped her arm.

"Glad to meet ya," Ralph said. "Want to stay for lunch?"

"Well . . ." the woman began.

"We can't," the man said. "Thanks for the kind offer, though."

Ralph was still pumping the woman's hand, and now she tried to pull away. Still grinning and pumping, Ralph finally released her hand, then sat next to her, his hip against hers. She scooted away.

"These are FBI agents, Ralph," Dr. Birnbaum said. "They were about to tell me what they came to see me about."

"Well okee-dokee then," Ralph said.

"Well, we really wanted to talk about Ralph," the man said, hesitating.

"You can talk in front of him," Dr. Birnbaum said. "If it's something he can't hear, then I don't want to hear it either."

Dr. Birnbaum watched the two agents look at each other, and then without a word the decision was made.

"We've heard that Ralph has a special ability," Agent Rand said.

"Where did you hear that?" Dr. Birnbaum asked.

"I don't know the name of the person, but they work for the Kellum Foundation. I understand they're funding some of your work."

"Ralph is special in many ways," Birnbaum said cautiously. "He's as gentle as a lamb, as strong as a gorilla, and you'll never meet anyone with a sweeter temperament."

Ralph listened with a big smile on his face, the corners of his generous mouth curling up toward his ears, his thick lips thinning.

"Most remarkable of all is his sense of position. Ralph never gets lost. He's a human homing pigeon. We've dropped him off in random parts of the city and he's found his way home every time. We've tried it in Cincinnati, Cleveland, Akron, and Circleville, and every time he turned toward home or any other place we designated. Isn't that right, Ralph?"

"Yep. I didn't like that cave, though. It was scary. There were too many dark places."

"That's right, he even found his way out of Mammoth Caves. We took him deep into the caves to screen out electromagnetic radiation. We thought he might be using it to orient. It didn't matter. Ralph picked his way through the cave system to the tourist trails, then followed them out."

"I got a banana split at the Dairy Queen that time," Ralph said.

"I can't imagine why the FBI would be interested in his homing ability," Dr. Birnbaum said.

Dr. Birnbaum studied their faces, but their steady eyes and neutral smiles revealed nothing.

"Actually, it's his other ability we're interested in," Agent Rand said.

"I don't know what you're talking about," Dr. Birnbaum lied.

"His resistance to PK," Rand said. "It's in Doctor Martin's reports as well as yours and Ms. Foxworth's."

Dr. Birnbaum frowned, then turned to Ralph.

"There's gum in my dresser, Ralph, why don't you get yourself some and then watch TV?"

"It's in your sock drawer. I already found it, but I didn't take some."

Ralph stood and turned to the agents.

"You want I should bring you some?"

"No thank you, Ralph," they said.

"Well okee-dokee then," he said and loped out of the room.

"No one was to have access to those files," Dr. Birnbaum said as soon as Ralph was gone.

"We're the FBI," Agent Simon said.

"We had permission," Agent Rand added. "As we understand it, Ralph was immune to the psychokinetic power of a man calling himself Gil Masters."

"I knew him as Carl," Dr. Birnbaum said, surprised at how much they knew. "We never knew who he really was or where he came from."

"This man could knock holes through walls using nothing but his mind?" Agent Rand continued.

"Yes. He did horrible things. Many people died."

"Yet Ralph could walk right up to him and Gil couldn't touch him," Agent Rand said.

"Yes."

"Could Ralph be resistant to other psychokinetic powers?" Agent Simon asked.

"What power are you thinking of?" Dr. Birnbaum asked.

"Nothing in particular," Agent Rand said.

"In your report you suggest that Ralph might be the evolutionary answer to a mutant like this psychic," Agent Rand said.

"I hypothesized that if psychokinetic power could evolve, then resistance to it could coevolve. Nature always provides a balance. If the tyrannosaur has a fearsome set of jaws, then the herbivores must have armor plate and defensive horns like the triceratops. In response to the lion's claws and teeth, the gazelle has speed. To control the rabbit population, the fox and the hawk evolved. To control insects there are birds. If the next step in evolution is psychokinesis, then there must be compensating abilities."

"Seems reasonable," Agent Rand said. "However, immunity to psychokinesis is a passive defense, like the white fur of the snowshoe rabbit. It's only effective until the hawk spots the rabbit."

"I won't let you take him," Dr. Birnbaum said suddenly.

Agent Simon raised her eyebrows in surprise. Agent Rand looked bewildered.

"Excuse me?" Agent Rand said.

"The only reason you would need someone with Ralph's resistance to PK is to stop another psychokinetic like Gil Masters."

Dr. Birnbaum studied the agents. Agent Simon's face was pink, but Agent Rand remained emotionally opaque.

"Nothing of the kind," Agent Rand said "We're just gathering data for a new training program. The computer is supposed to simulate every conceivable scenario and solution. Using someone with Ralph's abilities will become a part of one of those scenarios."

"There is another psychokinetic," Dr. Birnbaum insisted.

"We're just doing research," Agent Rand said, standing. "Say goodbye to Ralph for us."

Dr. Birnbaum followed the agents to the door, making sure that they got into their car and left. Even after they drove up the block and out of sight, he sat watching. He knew they were lying, and that worried him, because if they needed the help of a retarded man, the situation must be dire indeed.

PICKUP

Six blocks from Dr. Birnbaum's house, Jett and Compton transferred to a van and then drove back and parked down the street. Sitting in the back of the van they watched the house through mirrored windows, waiting for Ralph. They had watched the house before visiting, and knew his routine. Dr. Birnbaum couldn't keep him penned up for long.

Two hours later Ralph came out, turning toward the business district.

"More Slurpees," Compton said. "He's insatiable."

Jett studied Ralph as he passed the van. Most people noticed Ralph's loose lips, overhanging brow, and peculiar posture, but Jett saw his broad shoulders, narrow hips, and muscular legs. There was good raw material in that body, but it was undeveloped. Ralph had the power but not the skills. Jett was sure he could make short work of Ralph if it came to a fight.

"How do you want to do this?" Compton asked.

"The easy way," Jett said, reaching into his coat and pulling out a large pack of gum.

They caught Ralph a block before he reached High Street. Jett stepped out of the passenger side of the van, reaching out with his hand.

"Ralph, I'm glad we found you. Dr. Birnbaum said you might be going this way."

"Hihowyadoin" flowed out of Ralph. Walking down the sidewalk, Ralph had looked serious, like a man on a quest. Now, his face reshaped into a big, sloppy grin, and he pumped Jett's hand.

"Hi Nathan," Ralph said through a wet smile.

"Ralph, I wonder if you would mind helping us with something."

Jett opened the sliding door, motioning to Ralph to get in.

"I'm not supposed to go places with strangers," Ralph said, concerned.

"We're not strangers," Jett said. "Doctor Birnbaum introduced us, remember?"

"Yeah, sure," Ralph said, smiling again.

"Besides, Doctor Birnbaum said it would be all right if you came with us."

"I don't know, Nathan," Ralph said.

"You can call me Nate," Jett said.

"I don't know, Nate," Ralph said. "I was gonna get me a Slurpee and I'm kinda thirsty."

"Karla and I were just about to go to the A & W for root beer floats. Would that be okay?"

"Well okee-dokee, then," Ralph said.

Ralph climbed into the back of the van.

"Got any gum?" he said.

Jett was handing it over the seat before Ralph finished asking.

HOSPITAL

Elizabeth spent the night in the hospital, sensors taped to her chest, leads connecting to a heart monitor by her bed and to another at the nurses' station. A nurse was always on duty at the station, watching the bank of monitors, each of which was labelled with the room number where the signal originated. It was an impressive technological array, but impersonal. The only humanizing touches were pieces of tape stuck next to each display with the handwritten names of the patients. The designers of the state-of-the-art cardiac wing hadn't thought to leave spaces for the names of the patients, and that disturbed Wes. It was the kind of mistake he would make.

Wes stopped at the nurses' station and studied Elizabeth's cardiac rhythm. He had read hundreds of physiographs as part of his research. The monitor under the tape labeled "Elizabeth Foxworth" showed a normal rhythm. Wes was relieved, although he noticed that the monitor next to Elizabeth's, labeled "Norman Greene," showed a man in serious trouble.

Elizabeth was sitting up in bed, wearing a hospital gown, leaning over the tray table in front of her and drawing. Discarded sketches littered her bed. Even in hospital garb, she was beautiful. Wes wanted to say something clever, but all he could muster was a weak "Hi." She looked up and smiled.

Wes returned her smile, embarrassed by the size of his grin. Wes wasn't comfortable with anything he couldn't control, and his emotions had always been bigger than he was.

"How are you feeling?" Wes asked.

"I'm wasting a hospital bed," Elizabeth said. "They're releasing me after lunch."

"The arhythmia didn't return?"

"They monitored me through the night and I'm back to a normal rhythm."

"I never should have put you in Anita's dream. We'd never tested the technique."

"Who would you have tested it on?" Elizabeth asked.

"A volunteer."

"I volunteered," she reminded him. "You did the right thing, and we learned a lot from Anita's dream."

"It almost killed you, Elizabeth."

"You're exaggerating," Elizabeth said, reaching out to take Wes's hand.

"It wasn't a simple dream," Wes said. "Your heart was stopped! You had all the signs of severe electric shock except the burns."

"Maybe Wanda Johnson was right. Maybe if you die in your dreams, you really do die."

"I can't believe that," Wes said.

"I agree. What Anita and the others are experiencing isn't a dream. It's something real. We need to find out more about it."

"It's too dangerous. I won't risk you again. Not anyone."

"If we don't do something, Anita and Margi will die. They have to dream normally again, Wes. No medicine or psychotherapy has helped them. You are their only hope."

Wes sat on Elizabeth's bed, thinking of little Anita wasting away like Margi, being drained little by little, night after night. Instead of sleeping snugly, dreaming kid dreams, she was being dragged away in the dark, forced into an endless walk down the corridors of a ghost ship. Uncomfortable, Wes shifted his weight, crumpling one of Elizabeth's sketches. It was a crude floor plan.

"I was trying to remember the layout of the ship," Elizabeth said. "I thought if I had a map I could get around better the next time, but Anita and the others are right. The corridors don't connect in a consistent or logical way."

"I won't put you back in that dream," Wes said.

Elizabeth rubbed his back, then leaned her head on his shoulder.

"I won't jump off the ship this time."

"There could be other dangers."

"If we integrate all the dreamers, the ship might make more sense. It's probably fragmented the way it is because each of them are only getting bits and pieces. Together we might get clarity, and I might be able to see those faces in the mirror."

Wes was weakening, but before he could give in his cell phone rang. It was Dr. Birnbaum.

"They've taken Ralph," Dr. Birnbaum blurted.

Wes knew Ralph from his first experiments with mind integration. Ralph had been a friend of one of the autistic savants that Wes had used for the integration, and had turned out to be a thorn in Wes's side. A large man with a powerful physique, Ralph was educable but mentally retarded, as gentle as one of Anita's bunnies, and the most annoying person Wes had ever met. With an unquenchable thirst for Slurpees and a lumberjack's appetite for ice cream, he had mooched money from Wes constantly, at a time when Wes needed to be concentrating on the experiment. Wes had gradually grown to tolerate him. On the other hand, Elizabeth cared deeply for Ralph.

"Who has taken Ralph?" Wes said. "What are you talking about?"

"There were two of them posing as FBI agents."

"What's going on?" Elizabeth asked, tugging at Wes's sleeve.

"It's Dr. Birnbaum. He says someone has kidnapped Ralph."

Surprised, Elizabeth let Wes talk.

"How do you know these people took him?" Wes asked.

"He went for a walk and never came back. You know Ralph always comes back. I called the FBI and found out they never sent agents to my house."

Ralph had a propensity for wandering, walking for miles in all directions and introducing himself to everyone he met. He had a preternatural sense of direction, and never seemed to get lost. Still, Wes couldn't forget that the man was retarded, so it was easier to believe that Ralph had finally wandered too far than to believe that he had been kidnapped by phony FBI agents.

"Did you check the hospitals?"

"Of course. I'm telling you he was kidnapped."

"Why would anyone want to kidnap Ralph?" Wes said.

"They knew about your work with the savants and about Ralph's resistance to psi powers."

Wes's mind-integrating experiment had created a powerful psychokinetic who had seemed unstoppable until they discovered that Ralph was immune to his power. While others were being blown around like paper in the wind, Ralph had walked up to the psychokinetic and tackled him.

"How could they know?" Wes said.

The catastrophe that had resulted from Wes's first experiments could never be covered up, but the details of what had happened, and the special psychokinetic abilities involved, had been closely guarded.

"They said they had copies of the reports from the Kellum Foundation, but I checked and no one at the foundation has released the reports, nor has anyone requested them."

Wes was silent, thinking through the implications. Besides a select few inside the Kellum Foundation, the only others who knew about Ralph's resistance to psychokinesis were his team members and Dr. Birnbaum. He trusted his team, and Dr. Birnbaum was a foster father to Ralph. If there had been a leak it had to have come from within the foundation.

"There can only be one reason why they want Ralph," Dr. Birnbaum said.

"I know," Wes agreed.

If Ralph had been kidnapped for his ability, then somewhere there was a dangerous psychokinetic.

"We're coming out to Columbus," Wes said, feeling that he had to do something.

He said goodbye and then turned to explain to Elizabeth, but she was already pulling the sensors off her chest. She knew Ralph was in trouble from the half of the conversation she had heard. As she pulled the leads from her gown, the monitor signalled a cardiac emergency. The nurses would arrive soon, but Wes and Elizabeth ignored the monitor, both worrying about a large retarded man with a penchant for Slurpees and long walks.

KIDNAPPED

Jett had dressed Ralph in a pair of his sweat pants and one of his tee-shirts. To Jett's chagrin the tee-shirt was tight across Ralph's chest. It was late evening, and they were weight lifting in the hotel fitness center. Ralph had cleaned and jerked one hundred and fifty pounds with little effort, but his form was so poor that Jett couldn't risk trying him on anything heavier. Woolman would park Jett behind a desk if Ralph injured himself.

Instead of trying him on free weights, Jett took Ralph to the universal gym, where there was less risk of injury. Jett disliked machine lifting. Machines restricted movement, limiting the number of muscle groups worked. Switch from the machine to a free lift and you could feel the difference right away; you worked muscles used for balance—muscles that the machine couldn't touch.

Jett watched Ralph climb onto a padded bench, and try to figure out where to put his feet for leg lifts. Ralph's awkward moves, his clumsiness, and his homely face reminded him of his brother. Jett's twin brother, Jason, was the opposite of Jett in almost every way. Where Jett had been a handsome boy, athletic, and good in school, Jason was unattractive, with mud-brown hair that refused to stay combed, and a long thin face that was permanently etched with the lines and creases of sadness. A poor student,

Jason was always behind in class. At recess it was even worse. Clumsy and frail, Jason was seldom asked to play and frequently teased. Nature had played a cruel joke on Jason, creating a boy whose deficiencies made him a target for his peers, yet giving him a thin emotional skin. Where Nathan Jett felt little physical or emotional pain, Jason suffered doubly from every insult, joke, and whisper as though he was meant to feel for both of them.

Born to an alcoholic couple, Jason and Nathan Jett had received minimal care from their mother, who was frequently drunk and abusive. Their father took over as abuser when he was home. Jett's earliest memory was of a beating. He was three, sitting at the kitchen table, a half-finished glass of milk in front of him. His father was shouting at him for not finishing his milk, but when Nathan reached for the glass his father slapped it out of his hand, the glass shattering against a cabinet and spraying milk. Blaming Nathan for the broken glass, his father slipped his belt from his belt loops while Nathan Jett hunkered down, ready for the beating. He took that pain stoically—he could always take pain—but his brother couldn't, and Jason suffered cruelly from his father's belt.

When they weren't abusing Jett and his brother, Jett's mother and father abused each other. One night when the boys were six, a screaming match erupted downstairs, and Jason came to hide in Jett's bed, shivering from fear. Their mother usually took a beating when their parents fought, and would later take it out on the boys. Violently loud, the fight suddenly ended with a crash and a thud. Later they heard their father's truck leave.

Jett fixed his brother breakfast the next morning: Wheaties and slightly sour milk. His father stormed in as they ate, ignoring the boys and washing his muddy hands in the sink. When he was finished, he wiped his hands on a dish towel, studying the boys. Jett stared back defiantly while Jason kept his eyes on his cereal bowl.

"Your mother's run off," his father said finally. "She run away because of you rotten kids."

That was all his father ever said about where their mother had gone. Over the next few years Jason asked occasionally about her, but Jett's only answer was, "She's someplace better than this."

Nathan Jett became mother to Jason then, making sure he was ready for school, which was easy since school was the one refuge from their father. Because they were poor they received free lunch tickets, the source of one good meal a day. They survived after school as best they could, doing their chores first and then homework in their room, never daring to ask their father for help. Jett was quick, finding the school work easy. Jason struggled to learn to read, even with his brother's help, and found even simple addition nearly incomprehensible.

By third grade Jett was doing his brother's homework, but the teachers soon found out, since Jason's homework was nearly perfect, while in class he couldn't pass a test on the same material. Jett expected his father to beat him after the teacher called, but instead his father whipped Jason for being "so damn stupid," as if the heavy blows would improve his IQ.

Like Ralph, Jason was clumsy, but he didn't have Ralph's intimidating size to protect him. Kids in their grade feared Nathan Jett and never teased his brother, but older kids saw Jason as an easy target, calling him names and teasing him mercilessly. Jett fought boys two and three years older than himself over his brother, winning as many times as he lost and getting a reputation for ferocity and ruthlessness that finally protected his brother from all but the worst bullies.

Rejected by his peers early in childhood, Jason was a misfit and outcast who was ill equipped emotionally to be marginalized. In Ralph, Jett saw many of the same deficiencies that his brother had suffered from, yet Ralph was cheerful and outgoing and had survived to adulthood.

"Hey look, Nate, I'm doing it," Ralph said.

Jett watched Ralph's leg lifts, fondly remembering times like these with his brother.

"Try this one," Jett said, motioning Ralph over to the bench press. "You lie down here and then push the bar up."

Jett demonstrated, pressing two hundred pounds, sharply expelling his breath as he did.

"Now you try it."

Ralph was beaming, his fleshy lips stretched in a huge sloppy grin.

"Is that heavy, Nate? It looks heavy. I bet it's heavier than ten Slurpees. Maybe even a million."

Compton came into the fitness center, clearly disapproving. She was dressed in her JC Penney clothes; tan slacks and yellow short-sleeve polo shirt. They were staying at a Holiday Inn and she had dressed to fit in.

"It's a lot heavier than Slurpees, Ralph."

"Least you can't spill this," Ralph said. "Course I never spill. Leastwise not too much."

Ralph slid under the bar, copying Jett's position.

"Now I just push up, right, Nate?"

"Right, Ralph."

Ralph pushed, extending his arms to full length.

"Do I gots to hold it up long?"

"That's fine, Ralph. Put it down carefully."

Ralph showed little strain with the lift, so Jett moved the locking key up another fifty pounds.

"Try lifting again, Ralph."

"Is it heavier, Nate? Is that what you did back there?"

"Yeah, it's heavier."

Compton came closer, still disapproving, but interested.

"Hi, Karla. Nate and me are lifting weights."

"I can see that. When you get done here, you need to go back to the room. Yogi Bear is on the cartoon channel."

"Boo Boo too?"

"Of course."

"I like Boo Boo better'n Yogi. I think he's smarter than the average bear too, don't you?"

"Yes," Compton said.

"Try the lift," Jett said.

Ralph pressed, moving the bar slightly, but then dropping it back.

"It's kind of heavy, Nate."

"Too heavy for you?" Jett asked.

"Lemme see," Ralph said.

Ralph pushed, extending his arms until his elbows locked. Then, without being told, he dropped the weight.

"I did it," Ralph said, beaming.

Jett reached for the locking key, intending to take it up another fifty pounds. Compton stopped him.

"It's your turn, Nate," she said.

Agents customarily used only last names. Compton was using "Nate" to mock him.

Jett took over Ralph's position under the bar. He pressed the weight confidently, knowing his limits. Compton nodded in appreciation, then set the weight at three hundred pounds.

"Try it now," Compton said.

With another sharp exhale, he pressed until his arms were fully extended; they wobbled slightly with the effort.

"My turn, Nate. This is fun. Did you know your face gets red when you do that?"

Ralph matched Jett's lift, then waited while Compton reset the weight.

"It's at three-twenty-five, that's as high as it goes," Compton said.

Jett's personal best was four hundred and ten pounds, but he didn't routinely lift at that level.

Ralph pressed the weight, expelling his breath like Jett, his face turning red. There was no wobble in his arms.

"Can you do it more than once, Ralph?" Compton asked.

"Sure I can," Ralph said, then pressed the weight five times in quick succession.

"That's lots heavier, Nate," Ralph said as he got up to make room for Jett.

"Yeah, lots," Compton said, smiling.

"If you need help just let me know," Ralph said.

"I won't need help," Jett said, irritated by Compton's smile. "If you want in on this, just say so," he told her.

"I might bulk up and need new clothes. The agency is already on me about my clothing allowance," Compton said.

Jett positioned himself, then went through his breathing routine, ending with a deep breath and a sharp exhale. Just as he started his press Ralph spoke.

"Yuck, he blew spit out his mouth."

Compton snorted, and Jett lost his focus. The bar remained exactly where it had started.

"Is it too heavy, Nate?" Ralph asked.

"Don't talk while I'm trying to lift."

"Okay, Nate. I won't say a word. My lips are sealed." Ralph took an imaginary key out of an imaginary shirt pocket, pretended to lock his lips, then put the key back.

Jett looked at Compton, who smiled and made a zipping motion across her lips.

Jett went through his breathing routine again and then pressed with all his might, blowing loud and long as he did. He pressed the bar until his elbows locked, then lowered it to his chest. Knowing what Compton expected, he lifted again, and a third time. When he got to his fourth lift he barely made it; he collapsed on his fifth try.

Ralph went through the routine of unlocking his lips with the imaginary key.

"I did it one more than you, Nate. You want to try it again? I could help you?"

Compton unzipped her lips with an exaggerated motion.

"You want I should help you, too?" Compton said.

"Funny," Jett said to Compton. "Go watch cartoons, Ralph."

"Well okee-dokee, then. I hope Yogi's still on. I want to see Boo Boo."

"Say hi to Boo Boo for me," Compton said.

Jett towelled his face and neck, waiting for Ralph to leave. He knew Compton had something to say.

"What the hell are you doing, Jett?" she asked. "You know he shouldn't leave the room."

"He's like a wild animal," Jett said. "He's got too much energy to sit around all day. I brought him down to work some of it out."

"If you feed him Slurpees and ice cream, he'll sit in front of a TV twenty-four hours a day."

Jett ignored her, settling into the seat for leg lifts.

"You brought him down here to test him, to see how he matched up against you. Well, now you know—he's stronger than you."

"Strength isn't everything," Jett said.

"That's my line," Compton retorted.

"I'm saying he doesn't have the intelligence to use his strength to full advantage."

"If you're saying intelligence beats strength, then I agree."

Jett paused between lifts, shaking his head. "I'm not saying that. A gorilla will kill a computer nerd every time," he said. "There's an optimum combination of intelligence and strength."

"And you have that combination?"

Jett smiled, then began his leg lifts again.

"You know, Jett, a computer nerd with a gun is more than a match for a gorilla."

She was quick, another ability Jett admired. Unfortunately, she used her mental agility against him.

Compton's cell phone rang. After a clipped "Yes," she listened for a moment, then hung up.

"They're ready to open the door to Pot of Gold."

It was time. Jett felt his pulse quicken ever so slightly, and it pleased him.

FOUNDATION

They spent a day with Dr. Birnbaum talking to police, neighbors, and two psychics whom Birnbaum had tested in the years before his accident, but turned up no clues to Ralph's whereabouts. The Columbus Police Department was investigating but had no leads. The local news carried pictures of Ralph, generating many calls of concern from the seemingly hundreds of people Ralph had introduced himself to, but no concrete leads. It was clear that the authorities in Columbus were doing everything possible to find Ralph, so the next day Wes and Elizabeth flew to Chicago to meet with a trustee of the Kellum Foundation, promising Dr. Birnbaum that they would stay in touch.

Robert Daly was sixty, but looked fifty—the fifty of someone who could afford a personal trainer and cosmetic surgery. He was fit, handsome, tan, and looked prosperous in his tailored suit. Assured of his own financial future and that of his children, Daly now spent his days determining which supplicants would get handouts from the deep pockets of the Kellum Foundation. Wes had expected to meet with a staff member, not one of the trustees, and now found he was nervous. If money was power, and to a researcher it was, then this man had the power to make or break Wes.

"Dr. Martin, Ms. Foxworth, it's wonderful to finally meet you both face to face," Daly said, smiling. His teeth were white, even, and probably caps.

They shook hands and exchanged greetings, then Daly led them into his office.

Wes sat on a leather couch, with Elizabeth next to him. Daly sat in a matching chair, his legs crossed, looking like a CEO. One side of his office was arranged like a living room with a couch and armchairs, end tables, lamps, and a coffee table. A large desk and office furniture occupied the other half of the office. Most of the office was leather and mahogany, but the desk was a simple glass surface held up by four large, strangely twisted, ornate brass legs. It was the ugliest desk Wes had ever seen, but he had no intention of mentioning it.

Elizabeth got right to the point of their visit.

"Have you been told why we're here?"

"Yes. Is there any news about Ralph?"

"No," Elizabeth said. "No one saw anything, no one heard anything. The police have no leads to follow."

"That's why we're here," Wes said.

"How can we help you?"

Wes thought Daly's reactions appeared genuine; his tone expressed concern. But Wes could tell by Elizabeth's crossed legs, folded arms, and furrowed brow that she didn't find Daly convincing.

"The couple claiming to be FBI agents knew about my previous work," Wes said, "and they claimed to have heard about Ralph from someone in the foundation."

"But you've published your results, and there was quite a bit in the news—with the deaths and injuries. Surely, that's where they got their information."

"They had details that could only have come from my reports to the foundation."

Daly looked disturbed, uncrossing his legs, then recrossing them. Finally, he said, "Perhaps one of your assistants spoke of your research."

"I trust my people one hundred percent," Wes said.

"And I have equal confidence in my people," Daly said.

They were at an impasse.

"Wes works only with a handful of people, Mr. Daly. The foundation must employ a hundred."

"Two hundred and twenty-seven, actually," Daly said in crisp syllables.

"The chance of a leak goes up exponentially with the number who know," Elizabeth suggested.

"Only a fraction have access to the records," Daly said. "We're security conscious here. As you know, we fund cutting-edge science and maintain close relationships with our researchers. Leaking results would harm that special relationship and open them, and us, to exploitation."

The foundation funded "fringe science," or what mainstream scientists called "pseudoscience." Wes suspected that much of the research ended with null results. Wes's success had made him the wonder boy of the foundation.

"I know my assurances won't satisfy you," Daly said, then waved his hand in dismissal when Wes started to protest. "I wouldn't be satisfied if I were you. I've never met Ralph, but I read your reports and he sounds like a very special man. Here's what I will do. First, I will have our security office begin an investigation to see if we can find a leak. Second, I'm prepared to commit the foundation to helping get Ralph back. Would a reward help?"

"Yes, I suppose it would," Wes said.

"Let's start with fifty thousand dollars," Daly said. "If that doesn't turn up a lead in a week or so, we'll double it."

"Thank you," Wes said.

Daly looked at his watch.

"I'm afraid I have another appointment," he said.

He walked them to the door, shaking their hands and ushering them out.

"Don't worry, if it's humanly possible, we will find Ralph," Daly assured them.

Then they were out the door and walking to the elevator.

"I don't trust him," Elizabeth said.

"He promised to investigate," Wes told her.

"The foundation is going to investigate itself," Elizabeth said. "That's like having the police investigate the police."

"If he's trying to cover up something, then why offer the reward?" Wes asked.

The elevator doors opened, and they stepped in. There was one other man inside who got out at the next floor. When the doors closed again, Elizabeth picked up where she had left off.

"Fifty thousand dollars is nothing to the Kellum people. Especially if you know you'll never have to pay it."

"What do you mean?" Wes asked.

"Maybe he knows where Ralph is, and maybe he knows Ralph is never coming back."

The doors opened and they were in the lobby, passing through security and then out into the hot Chicago sun. They walked to the parking lot in silence, Wes worrying about where Ralph was and what was happening to him.

DALY

Robert Daly dropped two ice cubes into a tumbler, then added lemonade-flavored Snapple. Taking the drink to his chair, he turned to face the window behind his desk and looked out at the Chicago skyline. He sipped the lemonade, then swirled the ice cubes in the tumbler as he used to do when his drink was bourbon. He missed drinking, especially at times like these. Booze relieved stress—at least temporarily.

He hadn't been completely truthful with Dr. Martin and Elizabeth Foxworth. He didn't know anything about what had happened to Ralph, or how the kidnappers had found out details about Dr. Martin's research, but there might be a leak at Kellum. There had been other incidents, and the trustees suspected that an intelligence agency had penetrated the foundation. In turn, they had their own moles in the intelligence community, thus maintaining a balance of power. Daly was convinced that they gained more than they had lost in the spy game.

The Kellum Foundation was named after its founder, Dr. Walter Kellum, who had earned his fortune as a pioneer in radio and television technology. When Dr. Kellum was declared dead after World War II, his fortune was sufficient for a small foundation; the revenue stream had increased exponentially in lockstep with the television industry. Now the Kellum

Foundation was ranked as the fifth largest foundation in the United States, but in fact its pockets were the deepest of any private foundation in the world. With resources hidden in a dozen nations, the foundation operated much like the intelligence community, with a public budget open to scrutiny and a black bag budget used to fund projects the trustees euphemistically labelled "controversial." Daly knew that most of the black bag projects wouldn't pass the scrutiny of university ethics committees, and certainly would be lightning rods for the media and social activists. Some were clearly illegal. However, the black bag projects were often the most promising, and Daly and the other trustees wouldn't let archaic laws and outdated sensibilities keep them from their goal.

Like its budget, the foundation's charter had both a public and a private component. The public charter reflected Dr. Walter Kellum's lifelong commitment to modernism—the belief that through science and the scientific method, the human condition could be steadily improved. Consistent with that public mission, the foundation funded basic research, primarily in the natural sciences, but occasionally in soft-science psychology projects like Dr. Martin's mind-linking experiments. Daly had seen the early potential in Dr. Martin's work, and the success of his project had been beyond the foundation's expectations.

Dr. Kellum had written the foundation's charter during the Second World War, and because he knew of the horrors of the Nazi extermination camps, he had also written a shadow charter, not to be seen by the public. According to the secret charter, the trustees were to find ways to protect mankind from itself before its nihilistic tendencies led it to self-destruct. A Darwinian evolutionist, Dr. Kellum had set aside his fortune to be used to stave off human extinction and promote human evolution in the hope that an improved human being would emerge. To Dr. Kellum, humanity was like a child, needing the protection of a parent. The foundation existed to fill that paternal role.

While the mission to promote human evolution would be seen by most as benign, there were passages in the shadow charter that could be misinterpreted. These passages argued that the general social good might occasionally require the sacrifice of society's members. Some would argue that Dr. Kellum's paternalistic views were much like those of the architects of the Holocaust, but Daly believed that there was a critical difference between them and that the difference justified the foundation's actions.

With an original board of trustees named in Dr. Kellum's will, and careful selection of subsequent trustees, the foundation had stayed true to its mission through the Korean conflict, the Cold War, the Cuban Missile Crisis, the Vietnam War, the social revolution of the sixties, the economic crises of the seventies, and the collapse of the communist world in the eighties and nineties. Each crisis served to validate the mission of the Kellum Foundation and reinforce the trustees' support of covert activities that prevented any of the crises from developing into worldwide conflict.

Through the years it became clear to the trustees that fulfilling their goal meant more than simply funding research, since development and application of technology required stable social structures and a receptive culture. Shortly after its founding, the Kellum Foundation had begun funding political campaigns, as well as subversive political movements that the trustees judged likely to produce the kind of social stability they desired. Donations, bribes, and loans usually accomplished their goals, but on occasion assassination had been necessary. Committed to promoting the general welfare, the foundation had not balked.

Swirling the ice in his drink, Daly considered the implications of Ralph's kidnapping. The fact someone had penetrated deep enough into the foundation to access Dr. Martin's work was worrisome, particularly so because of the timing. Daly had just initiated a project that was dependent on Dr. Martin and his mind-melding technology, and Dr. Martin had been making good progress with the dreamers. While Daly could see no immediate connection between the project and Ralph's kidnapping, the coincidence was troubling, and he wasn't a man to leave anything to chance. After another sip of lemonade, Daly picked up his phone and punched a single number, then asked his secretary to find the Chief of Security.

PLEA

When they returned to Eugene, Elizabeth had a dozen messages, three from Anita's mother. Elizabeth called her first.

"She's worse, Elizabeth. I'm afraid . . . she's confused a lot, and she's hallucinating. She hardly eats enough to stay alive and she's stick thin. I took her back to the doctor, but he just prescribed vitamins and more sedatives. They don't stop her from dreaming."

"The same dream?" Elizabeth asked.

"Yes," Anita's mother said.

Then she was silent, sniffling. Elizabeth pictured tears streaming down her face.

"Can you help her? Can Doctor Martin do something?"

"We'll try."

Now Anita's mother cried openly, sobbing thank-yous into the phone. Elizabeth let her pour her emotions into her gratitude before promising that she would call as soon as possible. Elizabeth was still worried about Ralph, and worrying about Anita again, too, only added to her emotional burdens.

She found Wes in his lab, scrolling through program code. She stood in the doorway watching him. The lines of code flew past, and she wondered if he was actually reading them or just mesmerized by the pattern, his mind somewhere else. Abruptly he stopped the scroll, used the mouse to highlight a line, then typed in changes—he was reading the code, even at that speed. Did his focus mean he wasn't worried about Ralph? She knew him well enough to know that he was good at burying his emotions. He turned at her knock and asked about Ralph immediately.

"I've heard nothing," Elizabeth said.

Wes looked disappointed, despite his claims not to like Ralph.

"Anita's declining, Wes. She's disoriented and hallucinating. She has to have a normal night's sleep and dream again."

"Maybe after they find Ralph."

"There's nothing we can do to help find Ralph," Elizabeth said. "But we might save Anita."

Wes frowned, again staring at his screen. The lines of code were stationary now. When he spoke he didn't look up from the screen.

"I've been thinking about what you said about each of the dreamers getting bits and pieces of the same dream. When we integrated you with Anita, she said that the dream had more detail. Maybe Anita is a receiver picking up a transmission from somewhere."

"Like our theory that some schizophrenics are actually picking up thought transmissions."

"Exactly. When you were added, we improved Anita as a receiver. Since you don't dream the ship dream, we can assume you are a poor receiver, but even your presence improved Anita's reception. It stands to reason that if we brought together the other ship dreamers and integrated them to make one receiver, we might dramatically improve reception."

"Put me in the dream again, Wes."

Wes winced at the thought of risking her life again. Elizabeth felt his hesitation and hurried to reassure him.

"Anita needs me to be with her, and I want to look in that mirror again."

Wes nodded, reluctantly agreeing.

Thinking of the faint reflections she had seen, Elizabeth wondered what she might see this time. They had been calling the nightly walk on the ship a dream, but she wondered if it wasn't really a nightmare they were about to bring into focus.

RAINBOW

New Mexico in August was a hellish place. The land was barren, the animal life invisible, all creatures hiding in deep burrows to avoid the heat by avoiding daylight. Vegetation was sparse—deep green and gray over red earth baked hard by a relentless sun. The mountains in the distance were rugged, jutting into pure sky. They had an Indian name, but Jett couldn't remember what it was. Everything here had an Indian name. Thunderheads were building by the mountains, but from the dusty smell of the air Jett knew it hadn't rained in weeks, and wouldn't. There was a stark beauty to this land, but aesthetic appreciation was something akin to emotion, and Jett couldn't experience it. What he did appreciate was the challenge of living here.

There were snakes out there, coiled under rocks, and rabbits and mice in burrows. He thought there might be bobcats too, and certainly hawks, but he had no hope of seeing them. Not in this heat. It wasn't even noon, and already the day was over a hundred degrees. The animals who survived here were tough, disciplined, and well adapted to the rigors of the climate. He respected the humans who met the challenge of life here, too—not those who brought air-conditioning and swimming pools, but those who had come first and lived without modern conveniences. There was a Navajo reservation nearby, he knew. He respected those people and the white men who had followed, displacing them, fighting for the land. The reservations here were huge, testifying to how worthless the land was. Crossing the fought-for land in an air-conditioned van, he felt pampered, and had an urge to turn off the air-conditioning and roll down the windows.

"Want some gum, Nate?" Ralph asked.

Compton was driving, wearing white shorts and a white tank top with a blue Nike swoosh over her left breast. Jett was in the passenger seat of the van, and Ralph rode behind them, his head between the seats, loudly smacking his gum.

"What kind, Ralph?" Nate asked.

"Spearmint. I chewed all the Juicy Fruit. I think I gots one piece of that pink stuff if you want it."

"Not that pink stuff—that stinks. Pee-yew!" Jett said, holding his nose.

Ralph gave a little snort that passed for a laugh and broke into a huge grin. Ralph and Jett had been repeating that routine since they had first played it out on the airplane. Compton glared. She hated the routine, Jett knew, so he kept playing his role with Ralph just to needle her.

"Are we there yet?" Ralph said, head still between the seats, gum smacking loudly.

"Yes, Ralph, we're almost there," Compton said tersely.

Jett was amused by her irritation. Until they had picked up Ralph, she hadn't shown any more emotional depth than Jett had, but in Ralph's presence she was a different person; an emotional person.

"I was just asking cause I'm gonna have to go again," Ralph said.

"You couldn't possibly have to go again already," Compton said.

"I didn't say I had to go," Ralph said. "I said I was gonna have to go."

"We all have to go sometime," Jett said.

"When you gotta go, you gotta go," Ralph said.

Then together they said, "And we really gots to go!" Ralph snorted again, and smiled so wide that you could see his wisdom teeth. It was another of their routines, and Compton shook her head in disgust.

Jett found that he enjoyed Ralph's company. Ralph reminded him of his brother, Jason.

Jett's relationship with his brother ended after eighth grade. Jett's father had taken the call from the principal, having ignored repeated requests to visit the school. When his father's work boots pounded up the stairs, Jason cowered on his bed while Jett took position between his brother and the door. Storming in, belt in hand, his father paused, seeing the look on Jett's face. Jett wasn't the physical equal of his father yet, but his father was perpetually drunk, and if it came to a fight the outcome wasn't assured. Realizing this, his father held the belt in his hand, making no move to use it on Jason.

"That was your principal," his father shouted. "Your idiot brother ain't going to high school. They're sending him to a school for retards. He's damn stupid, and ain't good for nothing, and he won't learn nothing at that school except to wipe his ass and tie his shoes! That's all retards can learn."

Feeling the belt in his hand, he looked past Jett again, longing to use it, but stopped by the steel in Jett's eyes.

"Just like his mother. Damn stupid," his father said, then stomped out.

Jett held his brother through that night, listening to him cry off and on. Jett didn't cry, but for one of the few times in his life he worried—worried what would happen to his brother without him.

Jett went to high school, excelling in class and standing out as an athlete. His father came to games occasionally, where he watched Jett score touchdowns and hit home runs. He bragged about his son, too, although he had never played ball with his boys or coached them in any way. Jett and his brother's first baseball gloves were bought with money Jett had earned mowing neighbor's lawns.

Jason didn't fare well at his new school. He became morose and withdrawn, not coming out after school to play street ball, hiding from the shame he felt about being different. One day Jason wasn't on the city bus that he took to and from his special school. Jett went looking for him, riding his bike along the bus route. When Jett saw the flashing lights of the police cars and ambulance, he knew immediately it was for his brother. The emergency vehicles were at the railroad crossing; a train was stopped on the tracks. Jett pushed through the crowd and past the police to see the pieces of his brother's body being zipped into a yellow rubber bag. For the one and only time in his life, Jett shed a tear.

The police called it an accident when they took Jett home and told his father. "He wasn't good for nothing anyway," his father said, and Jett snapped, jumping him. Jett beat him senseless before the police managed to pull him off and cart him off to jail. The football coach took him in after that, and he went to Boston College on a football scholarship. He never saw his father again. Now he seldom thought of his long-dead brother, but being with Ralph brought back those memories.

They were following a poorly maintained two-lane road. The blacktop was crumbled along its edges, and potholes were frequent hazards. Now Compton slowed, turning onto a dirt road that headed into the desert. It was nothing but two ruts, and they were bounced around inside the van.

Compton's recklessness amused Jett; he suspected that she was in a hurry to get somewhere where she could get some space between her and Ralph. Despite the rough ride, Ralph's head still bobbed between their shoulders.

"It's bumpy," Ralph said. "I think it's bumpy, don't you, Nate? Do you think it's bumpy, Karla, do you?"

"I can't talk, Ralph, I have to concentrate on driving."

"Okee-dokee then," Ralph said, smacking his gum. Then he said, "Want some gum, Nate?"

Compton cursed under her breath as they started the routine again.

"What kind, Ralph?" Nate said.

"Spearmint. I chewed all the Juicy Fruit. I think I gots one piece of that pink stuff if you want it?"

"Not that pink stuff—that stinks! Pee-yew!" Jett said, holding his nose.

This time when Ralph snorted, something flew out of his nose, landing on Compton's white shirt. It was yellow and wet. Jett smiled, feeling an urge to laugh. Compton's face turned pink. Jett worried she might lose control and break Ralph's nose with one of her fancy Tae Kwon Do moves. Fortunately, they reached the fence and she stopped, waiting while Jett got out to open the gate.

Jett used a shiny new key in the rusty lock. The lock mechanism responded to a twist of the key, and he removed the chain. Compton drove through, then Jett locked the gate behind.

He had been to Rainbow only once before and remembered the road as two ruts angling into the desert. When Rainbow was constructed there had been a paved road, well maintained chainlink fencing, and guard posts. Once the facility was finished, the paving had been removed to make the facility appear unimportant. There had even been a budget to keep the road looking unused and poorly maintained, like some forgotten path to an abandoned government base. With technological advances Rainbow had been automated and the budget cut, since fewer technicians were needed to monitor the facility, and soon the road really was under-used. Now, however, Jett could see the ruts cutting deeper into the desert, fresh red soil churned up along the sides, mixed with crushed sage. The trouble at Rainbow had dramatically increased the traffic to the facility.

After thirty minutes of rough road they saw the complex, a two-story rectangular structure covered with rusty sheet-metal siding. A door and window were set in the end they approached. In front was a gravel parking lot. There were no cars in the lot, and everything was coated with a thick layer of red dust. Jett noticed many criss-crossing tire tracks. Along the side of the building to the left were large sliding doors. Compton headed for these, and they slid open as she approached, letting them into Rainbow's dark interior.

A dozen cars were parked inside; now armed guards appeared, four of them surrounding the van.

"Are those policemen?" Ralph asked. "They don't look like policemen."

The guards wore street clothes and carried automatic rifles. Jett recognized half of them as OSP agents he had worked with in the past. He recognized two of the others as CIA, and suspected the rest were CIA or NSA. There were no uniforms in sight, telling him that the army was mustering somewhere else. An agent Jett knew as McIntyre came to the car, asking for identification. While Compton handed their ID cards out the window, Jett sized up the guards; only McIntyre was a good match. He was six feet tall and probably weighed one hundred and eighty pounds. He had a ruddy complexion and blonde hair with a reddish tinge. McIntyre looked them over, too, quickly dismissing Compton and focussing on Jett. He nodded slightly, acknowledging Jett from previous missions. Compton made her own assessment. She was less obvious than he and McIntyre, but Jett knew that she had measured each guard herself, noted their readiness or lack thereof, and was ready to act if necessary. Looking at the gearshift, he noticed with approval that it was in reverse and the engine was idling.

Agent McIntyre studied their ID cards, then stared long and hard at Ralph. Ralph rolled down his window and leaned out.

"Hihowyadoin?" he said. "I'm Ralph and this here's Nate and this here's Karla. What's your name?"

The agent stared back, slightly amused.

"Call me Mac," he said.

"You gots a 7-Eleven around here? I'm pretty thirsty."

"No," McIntyre said, handing back the ID cards. "Please get out of the van."

The air was hot outside the van. Even so, Jett guessed that it was twenty degrees warmer outside the building. Ralph stepped close to the guard.

"Got any gum?" he asked.

"No," McIntyre said.

Jett pulled Ralph along, holding his arm to keep him from introducing himself to everyone they passed. There were three lower levels to the complex at this end, and they used the stairs going down. At the bottom they passed through another security station. Most of the lower levels of the complex were devoted to the nuclear reactor which had been installed in the early seventies, eliminating the heavy power drain from the local supplier. The reactor took only a fraction of the space; the rest was devoted to cooling grids and heavy water storage facilities for the spent fuel rods. The floor they had entered on was divided in half. The end they were passing through was filled with the banks of electronics necessary to monitor Pot of Gold and to keep the Specials inside. At the far end of the facility the space was a full three stories high, and in the middle of this space were three huge black rings sitting parallel to each other. Stairs led up to the middle of the first ring and a platform ran through the middle of all three.

"Looky there," Ralph said. "They look like giant chocolate-covered donuts." Then, after a slow thought, "I'm hungry. Got a candy bar or something?"

Jett pulled a Hershey bar out of his pocket and handed it to Ralph.

There were offices and a ready room along the back wall, and they found Woolman waiting in one. He studied Ralph, who had chocolate on his face and hands, then called out to a young woman seated outside his door. Her hair was black, eyes brown, and she moved gracefully. Jett noticed that her sweater bulged along her hip, suggesting a holstered weapon.

"Take Ralph down for a can of pop," Woolman said.

The young woman looked at the large retarded man doubtfully.

"Pop?" Ralph said excitedly. "Do you gots orange? I like orange the best but grape's pretty good, too. I don't like that Dr. Piper stuff."

"Dr Pepper," the woman said.

Ralph snorted and then smiled, the chocolate smear cracking open to reveal his teeth. Then his arm shot out and he hit himself on the side of the head with a loud thump.

"How could I be so stupid?" Ralph said. "I said Dr. Piper." Grinning like a fool, Ralph said to the secretary, "Hihowyadoin?" Ralph's hand shot out, and the woman reached for it reflexively, letting Ralph pump her arm. When he finally released it, her hand was sticky with chocolate.

"Let's stop at the rest room on the way and wash our hands," she said, wondering what she had done to deserve this assignment.

"Good," Ralph said. "Cause I gots to go. And when you gotta go, you gotta go!"

Then Ralph turned to look at Jett, and together they said, "And I really gots to go."

Ralph snorted and grinned, and followed the woman out of the room.

Jett realized that Woolman was staring at him.

"You two seem to be getting along," Woolman commented.

Instantly, Jett's smile was gone.

"I'm just kidding him along," Jett said.

"It wouldn't pay to get attached to him," Woolman said. "You know what he's here for."

"I don't get attached," Jett responded firmly.

Woolman studied Jett's face as if he was seeing him for the first time. Jett knew his behavior was disconcerting to Woolman, and his position as team leader was in jeopardy. Finally, Woolman turned to Compton.

"What about you? How do you feel about Ralph?"

"He's irritating," Compton said. "If I'd had to ride another mile in the car with him I would have sedated him."

Satisfied with Compton's hostility, Woolman sat down behind the desk. Unconsciously, his hand came up and began to drum on the table. There were chairs in the office, but Jett and Compton weren't invited to sit.

"Dr. Lee reports that the field around Pot of Gold has been stable since the disappearance of the Nimitz, although it's assumed a new shape," Woolman said, fingers drumming a background beat.

Jett took that as evidence that the Nimitz was inside.

"Your primary objective is to determine if the Nimitz is inside. If it is, then signal us and we'll send in the marines."

Jett knew Woolman meant that literally, and that they would attempt to retake the Nimitz and clean out Pot of Gold one Special at a time.

"If the Nimitz is not in Pot of Gold, destroy the generators before exiting. Rainbow will then collapse Pot of Gold. Under no circumstances destroy the generators in Pot of Gold with the Nimitz inside."

"I understand," Jett said.

Dr. Lee had explained that they were uncertain of what would happen when Pot of Gold collapsed; the most likely scenario was that anything inside would be crushed, including the two nuclear reactors in the belly of the Nimitz and the carrier's complement of nuclear warheads. While crushing was unlikely to detonate the warheads, it would release weapons-grade plutonium, which was the most toxic substance known. Even then, the release of the radioactive material wouldn't concern them if it remained inside Pot of Gold, but no one was sure what would happen to the contents of Pot of Gold once that little side pocket of the universe was eliminated.

"We insert you in one hour," Woolman said. "The rest of the team is here and ready."

Woolman dismissed them by nodding to the door, but Jett held his ground. Compton took a step, then stopped when Jett didn't follow.

"We should leave Ralph here," Jett said. "He won't be any help."

Woolman's gray eyes came up to stare at him again, his fingers pausing mid-cadence.

"How do you figure that?" Woolman asked.

"He's got the intelligence of a ten-year-old. At the first sign of trouble he'll panic."

Woolman held Jett's gaze for a few seconds, then shuffled through the papers on his desk, picking out a sheaf stapled at the corner. Turning several pages, he paused as if reading before saying, "Dr. Martin's report says Ralph remained cool even when under attack. He saw his friends hurt in front of him yet remained calm and walked right up to the Special that was attacking them. It doesn't sound to me like he panics."

Jett noticed that Woolman referred to the psychokinetic that had attacked Dr. Martin's group as a Special. Had there been an escape from Pot of Gold in which the Special had not been found? Or did Woolman refer to everyone with psi power as a Special?

"Do you think he'll panic, Compton?" Woolman said. His eyes were still on Jett, even as he spoke to Compton.

"He's too stupid to panic."

Jett knew Compton meant that Ralph wasn't smart enough to know he should be afraid, but Jett doubted that was true. Intelligence overrode instinct; the lower the IQ, the more instinctual the person. Ralph's willingness to risk his own life to protect his friends might be the most intelligent thing about him.

"If he gets in your way, kill him," Woolman said.

"Yes, sir," Compton said.

Jett said nothing and followed Compton out the door. Ralph was coming down the corridor, a can of orange pop in each hand.

"I gots you one, Nate. I didn't get you one, Karla, cause I didn't know what you liked. They got grape and they got Mountain Dew. You don't have to put money in the machine or nothing. I already drank three cans."

Ralph burped long and loud. Jett smiled briefly, then remembered where they were going with Ralph. He held the smile on the outside, but inside he was remembering Agent Steele. His face had been blackened by the flames and the roasted skin pulled away from the meat underneath. Even when Steele writhed on the ground, screaming, Jett hadn't felt a thing for him. Now he hoped that Ralph wouldn't end up like Steele.

LINKED

The dreamers were gathered in Wes's lab, ready for the integration. The team had integrated five minds in the original experiment, but when that experiment ended tragically, Wes had dismantled the equipment. Fortunately, most of the equipment was still functional, and since they would only integrate four minds this time, they could piece together the necessary components. Fiber optic cabling, electroencephalographic transducer helmets, couplings to join the fiber optics to the supercooled computer, and miscellaneous pieces of cooling and power equipment were put together by Len, who did the engineering using Shamita's designs.

Cots were placed in the center of the room, heads toward the computer that would intercept their brain waves, with the fiber optic lines kept as short as possible. Three computer stations were set up in a half circle outside the cots. Len monitored physiological functions from sensors taped to the dreamers' chests, wrists, and the corners of their eyes, and sensors built into the EET helmets. Shamita controlled the intercept of brain waves, correlating brain function with brain region, and then intercepting selected functions and, on command, inhibiting others. From his station Wes monitored the integration using the software he had developed, directing Shamita in the creation of a synthesized consciousness. This time their goal was to bring the minds of Anita, Margi, Wanda, and Elizabeth together to share a dream. With his program up and running, Wes watched the final preparations of the dreamers. Len worked with Wanda; he was bothered by her smoking.

"You can't smoke in here," Len said, fanning Wanda's smoke from his face.

"Says you," Wanda replied, sucking long and hard on her cigarette, then blowing the smoke from her nose.

Len was fitting her with an EET helmet, making sure the cap fit tight so the sensors could pick up the minute electrical activity of her brain waves. She blew more smoke in his face.

"You see those gas tanks over there?" Len said. "We use liquid gas to cool the computers. You can't smoke around that stuff. You could blow this whole place up."

"What kind of gas?" Wanda asked, flicking ash on the floor.

"Liquid nitrogen," Len said.

"Who you trying to fool? Air is mostly nitrogen," Wanda said, her cigarette hanging from the side of her mouth. The tip moved up and down as she spoke, dislodging small amounts of ash with each syllable. "This whole damn room is filled with nitrogen and you don't see any flames do you? I'm not stupid, young man, and I would take it kindly if you wouldn't treat me like a doddering old fool. If you're bothered by my smoking, then just come out and tell me the truth. Don't make up lies about setting the place on fire."

"You're right, I should have been honest," Len said. "I don't like your cigarette smoke. Would you mind not smoking in here?"

"Hell yes, I mind," Wanda said. "They knew I was a smoker when they asked me here, and if you don't like it then it's just too damn bad."

Wanda stubbed out her cigarette and then shook another one from the Lucky Strike package, lighting it with a Bic lighter. Len finished fitting her with the helmet but lingered, watching her defiant smoking.

"Wanda, you remind me of my mother."

"Is that so?" Wanda said.

"She died last year, and when the funeral director asked how I wanted her body handled, I said 'Embalm, cremate, and bury her. Take no chances.' "

Wanda guffawed, then went into a fit that was half coughing and half laughing. When she recovered she looked at Len with a smile.

"You're all right, Lenny," Wanda said.

"Does that mean you'll stop smoking?" Len asked.

"No."

Monica was with Margi. Margi wore a flowered shirt over blue shorts, and her legs were so thin the shorts gaped around her thighs. She twitched occasionally, and her eyes were in constant motion, flicking from side to side at even slight movements. They were mapping Margi's motor cortex; she moved her legs and arms as Monica directed, while Shamita recorded from her station.

Margi had deteriorated noticeably since they had visited her in Tulsa. Her eyes were set in even deeper hollows, and her cheeks had become concave. Her lips were cracked as if she were dehydrated, and her short blonde hair was oily and tangled. Emaciated, tense, and often confused, she was dying in a balanced fashion; psychological death and physical death perfectly synchronized.

Elizabeth entered with Anita, her mother letting go of her hand only when they reached the door to the laboratory. Anita had deteriorated, too, Wes realized; she looked tired and had dark circles under her eyes. Her hair was again fixed in two pigtails, and she wore jeans and a sweatshirt with Bugs Bunny on the front. She still needed new front teeth, but most noticeable was her lack of energy—a little more life had been drained from her. She shuffled her feet, hung her head morosely, and didn't speak until spoken to. Elizabeth fussed over her like a mother, carefully fitting her EET helmet, talking to her constantly, reminding her of when she had worn it before. After placing the sensors at the corners of Anita's eyes, Elizabeth took the cot next to hers, putting on her own helmet and adjusting it until Shamita signalled that she had good contact. Margi's and Wanda's cortexes were already mapped, and since they had used Elizabeth and Anita before, Wes called up their stored cognitive maps. They were ready.

"It's time to relax," Wes said. "I know it will be difficult in a strange situation, but try to go to sleep."

The lights were dimmed and they lay in silence. Anita, Margi, and Elizabeth closed their eyes and began breathing deeply, following Wes's instructions. Wanda still held a cigarette between her lips; she lay with her eyes open, blowing smoke rings into the air which Len systematically destroyed with waves of his hand. Wanda chuckled the first time he did that, enjoying Len's irritation. Wes worried that she would keep the others awake, but Anita relaxed almost immediately, first showing Alpha waves on Len's monitor and then the sharp bursts of electrical activity called sleep spindles.

"Anita's passing through stage four sleep," Len whispered. "We've gone from two cps to four cps with spindles of fourteen to sixteen cps." Then a few seconds later he said, "Here comes REM."

"We won't wait for the others to sleep," Wes said, knowing it wasn't necessary. "Put them under."

One by one, Shamita intercepted their brain waves, then sent interference signals that shut down parts of their motor cortex.

Margi lost her nervous shakes and lay still, eyes slowly closing. Wanda was still smoking when she was relaxed; Len snatched the cigarette from her lips before it fell, crushing it out violently. Elizabeth went under last. Wes watched on his monitor as their minds ceased to function independently, slowly coming to match brain wave activity. They were becoming one mind, and sharing one dream.

INSERTION

Six agents would enter Pot of Gold to scout for the Nimitz. Jett had declined Woolman's offer of more. If it came to a fight, and it could, they would be fighting in narrow corridors, and under those conditions even six might be too many.

Jett's team was preparing in a series of cubicles along one wall, where each team member dressed and was fitted with equipment. Each agent was given a hip unit to be used for returning, and a weapon specially designed to operate in Pot of Gold. They had trained with the weapons before picking up Ralph, and been briefed on the layout of the ship.

Jim Peters was in the first cubicle. He was nearly as tall as Jett, but leaner, with a lanky figure and white-blonde hair. His eyebrows were so light, they were nearly invisible, giving his face an open, expressionless look. He might have been skinny in high school, but now he had enough bulk to make him useful. A technician tightened the straps to his unit, and Peters looked up and winked. Jett nodded a greeting in response. Jett disliked people who communicated with various facial expressions. Peters was a reliable agent, however, and Jett had worked with him before.

Billy Thompson was suiting next to Peters. Thompson was a black man, and Jett had strong feelings about people of color. Minorities were either a plus or a minus in his line of work, and rarely a wash. Black men like Thompson stood out in white communities, drawing unwanted attention; in mixed-race communities they gave you an advantage. This was one of those times when it wouldn't matter what color Thompson was.

Thompson had played professional football for two years, never getting into a regular season game. He was cut the third year and not picked up by another team. He had the size of a lineman, and near NFL speed. Those who had seen him in action said he would be a good match for Jett. Now Thompson was suited up, checking his weapon. He nodded to Jett as he passed.

Compton was in the next cubicle, stepping into the fire-resistant coveralls Dr. Lee had provided. She wore snug-fitting underwear, designed by the same person who had created the fire suits they would wear. Thompson or Peters might have appreciated Compton's figure, but Jett noticed only the lack of muscle mass. She wouldn't last long against him despite her fancy Asian fighting skills. Compton saw him looking and turned, pulling her coverall on and zipping the front.

The survivor of the second entry into Pot of Gold was in the next cubicle. He was dressed, but his burn scars grew out of his coveralls and onto his face like some hideous ivy climbing the wall of a building. The scars were thick ropes along his neck, spreading into overlapping plates of scar tissue that covered most of his face. His eyes peered through hollows bored in the scar tissue, and Jett thought it a miracle that he had kept his sight. The flames had licked up to his eyebrows before being extinguished. There was hair on the right side of his head, but on the left side were merely patches of hair among the scars.

When Jett had first met Robin Evans, he had not been impressed. Evans was retired from active duty and living on a disability pension, and Jett thought he would be soft, his skills atrophied. Instead, he found him in excellent physical condition; also, his fighting skills had honed quickly. He wasn't in Jett's league, but he was an acceptable team member. Evans was a survivor who had spent years undergoing skin grafts and reconstructive surgery. He was tough physically—all scar tissue—and had a will to live that had kept him alive through an experience most people begged not to survive. Evans lived for the chance to get revenge on those who had roasted him alive. Jett knew he might be reckless, but recklessness can be managed, and it can be used.

Ralph was in the final cubicle, waiting for Jett. He was wearing one of the silvery coveralls and admiring himself. When Jett came in, he was staring at his arm while a technician finished putting on his hip unit, and holding a can of orange pop in his hand.

"Hi, Nate," Ralph said. "This thing is so shiny I can see myself. Can I keep it? Can I? I want to show it to Doctor Binbam."

"We'll see, Ralph," Jett said.

Jett undressed, slipping on the same undergarments he had seen Compton wearing, and then stepped into the coverall. Ralph watched—to Jett it felt like having a dog watch you undress. It's not embarrassing, only disconcerting. The technician switched his attention to Jett, helping him into the harness holding the power pack, and the hip unit, which wrapped around his waist and literally sat on his hip. Dr. Lee had explained that the unit circling his waist was a coil designed to generate an intense magnetic field. They wouldn't use it to enter Pot of Gold, but once inside they could use it to exit.

The technician checked Jett's hip unit and then switched it to standby, a yellow light glowing on the belt in front of Jett. Finally he handed Jett his weapon, an oversized black pistol with an armored hose that attached to cylinders of gas in the lower part of his pack. The tank was pressurized, and the gun fired a .222 caliber Teflon bullet. The bullets were fed down the pressurized armored hose so there was never a need to reload.

"Is that a gun, Nate? It looks like a gun sort of," Ralph said. "Guns are bad, Nate. You shouldn't play with them."

"I'm allowed to, Ralph. I have a license to carry a gun."

Ralph folded his arms across his chest and leaned back, hips pushed out, lips puckered.

"I don't know, Nate, I don't like guns much. You could hurt somebody with a gun."

"It's not a real gun, Ralph," Jett said. "It's an air gun."

"A Daisy? It's a BB gun?"

"Yeah, sort of a BB gun."

Now Ralph's face reformed into a smile. "Well okee-dokee then."

Next, the technician placed the special bomb in the top half of Jett's pack. Chemical explosives wouldn't work inside Pot of Gold; nor would nuclear devices, Jett had been assured. So Dr. Lee had designed a different kind of bomb suited for Pot of Gold. Evans carried an identical bomb, and Peters and Thompson each carried a signalling device to be used to contact Rainbow.

Now Jett looked Ralph over from head to foot, making sure his suit was sealed tight, his harness secured, his hip unit functional. As he was finishing, the others gathered outside the cubicle. When Ralph saw Evans, his face reshaped into concern.

"Did something happen to you?" Ralph asked.

Evans stared back, mute. Jett knew Ralph wouldn't give up until he had his questions answered.

"He was burned," Jett said.

"I bet it hurt. I burned my arm on a stove one time. I gots a scar too. You want to see it?"

"No!" Evans said, then rested his hand on his gun. "Shut him up, Jett, or I will."

Evans's threat brought back a memory from Jett's childhood. He was playing basketball in the school yard when a neighbor girl came to tell him that Jason was in trouble. Jett found his brother in an alley, three older boys on top of him, pulling his clothes off. Nose bloody, dirty face streaked with tears, he was clinging desperately to his underpants while the older boys laughed. Barely slowing, Jett scooped up a hand-sized rock. He broke the nose of the first boy with his weighted fist, knocking him out of the fight. When the other boys stood to face him, Jett threw the rock at the head of the biggest one, and when the boy's hands came up to protect his face, Jett kicked him in the groin, then pounded his head when he bent over from the pain. The third boy ran while Jett beat the second boy into a fetal position.

Jett had been mother, father, and guardian angel to Jason, but after his brother stepped in front of the train, Jett had repressed those protective instincts. Now he found himself facing off with another bully, that buried protective feeling digging its way out of its grave. Silently cursing himself for caring, Jett stepped in front of Evans, his face inches from the mat of scars.

"No one touches Ralph," Jett said.

Evans stared long and hard before looking away. Jett turned to each of the others in turn. Thompson was checking his straps, disinterested. Peters winked at Jett, which Jett took as acquiescence. Compton merely looked at him quizzically. Then Jett introduced the others before Ralph asked. Ralph shook hands with Peters and Thompson, but Evans turned away. As usual, Ralph took the rebuff good-naturedly.

"Let's get to the portal," Jett said.

"I gots to go to the bathroom," Ralph said. "And when you gotta go, you gotta go. And I really gots to go."

Ralph smiled, but Jett didn't join in their routine.

"For real, Ralph?" Jett said.

"For reals!" Ralph said.

The others groaned as Jett began helping Ralph out of his harness and coverall.

After the bathroom trip, Jett hurried Ralph into his equipment. He had to get the mission underway before Ralph could irritate them any more. All agents were government killers, and while they wouldn't kill Ralph at Rainbow, he wanted to be sure that Ralph left Pot of Gold alive.

Jett herded Ralph toward the back of the facility and up the stairs to the platform leading to the three large black rings. The rest of the team waited on the platform. Jett checked Ralph's hip unit again, and then his own. They were both glowing yellow. When the others had their weapons ready, Jett shouted down to Dr. Lee.

"We're ready!"

Dr. Lee was leaning over a technician's shoulder, his glasses balanced precariously on the end of his nose.

"Yes, yes. The door will open soon."

"I don't see a door, Nate," Ralph said. "Do you see a door?"

"Shut him up," Evans said.

Evans was tense, and needed silence to prepare for what was ahead.

"Here we go," Dr. Lee shouted.

It started with a low hum, just above threshold. The hum built quickly, getting proportionally louder and higher in frequency. Jett's skin prickled and his hair felt as if it were alive.

"You look funny," Ralph said. "Your hair's sticking up, Nate."

"It's static electricity," Jett said.

"Neat," Ralph said, then reached out with his finger toward the railing. A blue spark an inch long arced between his finger and the rail. "Ouch," Ralph yelled, shaking his hand.

"I forgot to tell you," Dr. Lee yelled. "There is danger of shock! Don't touch anything metal."

"Don't touch the rail," Ralph said. "It hurts."

Now the air was crackling, and Jett felt as if his body was carrying a charge that could stun an elephant.

"Don't touch each other," Jett said.

They all moved apart, except for Ralph, who was holding his hand out in front of him, palm up. His hand was glowing. Jett's were glowing too.

"This is it," Dr. Lee said. "Go as soon as you see the opening."

The buzz was all around them; then suddenly the air sizzled. Jett looked down the platform through the archways created by the half doughnuts and saw a shimmery wave. Quickly it became a green oval.

"That's it, let's move," Jett ordered.

He hurried forward, Ralph and the others following. Slowing just before he reached the oval, Jett put a leg in first. It disappeared, but he felt nothing. With Ralph and his team right behind him, Jett stepped all the way into the green light and vanished.

INTO THE DREAM

Elizabeth was back in the ship, in the same corridor as before, except this time it didn't feel anything like a dream. The detail was rich, and there were smells; oily, thick smells of diesel and grease.

"Hello, Elizabeth," Anita said.

Anita was with her, wearing her hair down and her pink dress with the bunny on the front, and it confused Elizabeth. Wanda was supposed to have been with Elizabeth in the dream. She had the most experience exploring the ship, and was the least affected.

"Wes, are you there?" Elizabeth asked.

"Yes, Elizabeth."

"Anita is here with me, not Wanda,"

"She must be the strongest receiver," Wes said after a long pause. *"As the dominant one, she's controlling the dream. We can try adjusting the parameters and try to bring out Wanda."*

Elizabeth thought it over, but decided against it. The link was working, and as long as they didn't jump off the ship and touch the edge of the world, there should be no danger.

"Anita and I will explore the ship, Wes. Is that okay with you, Anita?"

"You won't leave me?" Anita said.

"I won't leave you."

Elizabeth hugged Anita and stroked her hair. When they separated, she realized that Anita looked worse than she had in the last dream. There were hints of bags under her eyes and her hair was mussed. Elizabeth understood that this time she wasn't just seeing Anita's image of herself. Now she was seeing an image shaped by her memory of Anita combined with the memories of Wanda and Margi.

"It's much more detailed now, and I can hear sounds," Elizabeth said.

"You're talking to Wes again, aren't you, Elizabeth?"

"That's right."

"Wes, this doesn't feel like a dream," Elizabeth said. "I feel like I'm really on a ship."

"Maybe you should come out?"

"No. We'll find the bathroom and look in the mirror again."

"Be careful, Elizabeth," Wes said.

"This way, Elizabeth."

Anita started down the ship's corridor. This time Elizabeth could hear Anita's feet on the metal floor. There were more visual details, smells, and sounds. Integrating Wanda, Margi, and Anita had improved the quality of the dream—if it was a dream.

Elizabeth followed Anita to the next hatch, and this time when they pushed it open the hinge groaned. Anita started through the hatch, but then gasped and turned back, wrapping her arms around Elizabeth and burying her face.

"What's wrong?" Elizabeth said.

"Len says Anita's heart rate just jumped—respiration and BP are all up," Wes said.

Anita didn't respond, so Elizabeth gently pulled her arms loose, saying, "Let me look. I'll be right back."

Elizabeth pushed the hatch open further and found herself staring at a man's contorted face. Startled, she jumped back just as the little girl had.

"Elizabeth—" Wes began.

"I know, my pulse and respiration are all up," Elizabeth said, cutting Wes off. "Give me a second, Wes."

Looking back, Elizabeth saw that the face was just as before. She pushed the hatch wider. The man wasn't whole. It was the body of a sailor protruding from the corridor wall. Most of the head was visible, as well as one leg, an arm, and half of his chest. The rest of the sailor ended at the wall. Watching the wide-open eyes, Elizabeth touched the sailor's chest—the eyes remained frozen. Elizabeth felt along the sailor's chest where it met the wall, but could find no gap. It was as if the sailor was part of the wall.

"Wes, I'm looking at a man who seems to be part of the wall."

"Is he alive?" Wes said.

"No. At least he isn't moving and shows no response to touch."

There was silence as Wes discussed the sailor with Shamita and Len.

"Elizabeth, we don't know what to make of the man in the wall. It's your call. Do you want to continue?"

Elizabeth went back to Anita and held her close.

"It's just a man, Anita. He's sticking out of the wall, but he's just like a statue. He can't move and he can't hurt you. I know it's scary—it scared me too."

"I never saw anything like that before," Anita said.

"There might be other new things, Anita, because this isn't just your dream, it's Margi's and Wanda's too. Do you want to go on? Help me find the mirror again?"

"I guess so," Anita said.

"It's important if we're going to stop the dream, Anita."

Nodding, Anita separated from Elizabeth and took her hand, stepping toward the hatch.

"We're going on, Wes," Elizabeth said.

As they passed the man in the wall, Anita stared wide-eyed, studying him from all angles. Then they were past him and down the corridor to a staircase. Elizabeth followed Anita up to the deck above and found herself outside, looking down on the big guns mounted on the bow.

"This is where they steer," Anita said, pulling Elizabeth along.

They entered a hatch and were in the pilot house; the ship's wheel, compass, and communications tubes were here. The detail was perfect, and the ship looked ready to sail. From the pilot house they passed through the chart room and then into another compartment filled with old-fashioned electronic gear. Elizabeth recognized only a radar scope. Then they passed outside, climbed down, and back in though another hatch, finding themselves in a compartment with radio equipment. After that they emerged behind one of the big guns and climbed down a ladder and entered another corridor where Anita stopped again, reaching back for Elizabeth's hand. There were two sailors in the corridor ahead. One was sticking up through the deck, only his shoulders and head showing, his mouth and eyes open, frozen in an expression of surprise. The other sailor stood at the far end, all of his body visible, his face turned away.

"There are two more men, Wes," Elizabeth said. "One is in the deck, the other is standing in the corridor at the far end." Then, to Anita, she said, "Let me go first."

Taking Anita's hand she led her toward the body in the deck, her eyes locked on the man, watching for movement. They passed the man, Anita staring in amazed horror, and then came to the standing man. This sailor was dressed in navy denims and stood perfectly still like a department store mannequin. Elizabeth scooted around him, her back to the wall, her eyes watching his face. His eyes were open, his face turned toward the corridor ahead. There was no fear in his eyes, nor any expression except a little weariness as if he was just up from a nap. He was a young man, maybe eighteen or nineteen.

"Let's hurry," Anita said.

Anita opened the next hatch and stepped in, disappearing. Elizabeth followed, finding herself outside on the deck of the ship near the bow, under one of the big guns.

"See, it changes," Anita said, expecting to be in the bathroom. "We have to try again."

"Wait," Elizabeth said, and walked to the rail. She looked out at the nothingness that had knocked her out. Before, it had no detail; and adding Margi and Wanda to the integration hadn't changed that. Then Elizabeth leaned over the side and looked toward the bow. The anchor was still there, but this time it was hanging from a chain. Then she saw the number.

"Wes, are you still there?"

"*Of course,*" Wes said.

"I'm looking at the bow of the ship. There's a number painted there."

"*You didn't jump off, did you?*"

"I'm leaning over the rail. The number is CA137."

"*I've got it,*" Wes said. "*That's enough. I'm going to bring you out.*"

"Not until I look in that mirror."

"Let's keep going, Elizabeth," Anita said. "I'm scared."

"All right. Wes, we're moving on to find the mirror."

Anita led Elizabeth to a hatch. Just before she followed Anita through, Elizabeth looked down the deck toward the stern and saw a shimmering green light. Wanting to investigate, she hesitated, but knew she had to keep up with Anita since the same hatches didn't always lead to the same places. Then she stepped through the hatch.

POT OF GOLD

Jett stepped onto the deck of the USS Norfolk, walking forward to give the others room. Toward the bow he saw a man stepping through a hatch. Freezing, he held up his hand to warn the others of the danger.

"Why is your hand up, Nate?" Ralph asked. "Do you have to go to the bathroom? When you gotta go, you gotta go."

"Shut up," Evans hissed.

Jett shot Ralph a stern look, making a zipping motion across his mouth.

"Gotcha," Ralph whispered at a volume greater than most people speak.

Ralph pretended to take a key from his pocket and lock his lips, then with an exaggerated gesture he dropped the key back into his pocket.

With a hand motion, Jett sent his team to take cover under the eight-inch gun turret mounted near the stern. Jett could see off the starboard side of the ship clear to the opaque edge of the world of Pot of Gold—there was no supercarrier.

"Peters, Thompson, circle around the stern," Jett ordered. "Check the port side for the Nimitz."

Peters and Thompson ducked under the catapults that held the biplanes, and using a see-saw maneuver, moved out of sight. Then Jett stepped close to Evans, whispering into his reconstructed ear.

"Let's see what you've got."

Evans pulled a wooden block from his pocket and set it on the rail of the ship, then backed away and stared at the block. The block rocked, spun, and then shot off the rail into the desert.

"I'm not at full strength yet," Evans said.

Jett nodded, then surveyed the ship. They were near the stern under a gun turret, the gun barrel pointed aft. There was a wide expanse of deck between the gun and a crane mounted on the stern, and on either side were the biplanes fitted with pontoons and mounted on the catapults. Forward of their position, the superstructure towered over the turret; the radio and radar masts were the highest points. Gun emplacements were mounted all along the superstructure, with a five-inch gun mounted just forward of the eight-inch and three forty-millimeter antiaircraft guns mounted behind those. A large funnel blocked his view forward. No one was in sight.

Peters and Thompson returned, moving stealthily. Thompson shook his head as they arrived.

"There's nothing on the port side except more desert," Thompson said. "The Nimitz isn't here."

Jett's orders were clear. If they did not find the Nimitz they were to report immediately. Jett had Peters turn and squat so he could remove the signal laser from his pack. The device was a tube laser attached to a large capacitor capable of powering a short series of bursts. There were only two settings on the device, one signalling presence of the Nimitz, the other its absence. Jett twisted the end of the laser to the negative setting, put it down so it was aimed vertically, and turned it on. The device hummed, emitting an invisible beam.

"Let's find the generators," Evans said.

Reading emotion through Evans's scars was difficult, but the tone of his voice hinted that he was happy. Without the Nimitz, killing the Specials was now top priority.

Jett led the way, the team spreading out behind him as best they could on the narrow deck. Peters hung back, covering the rear. Jett led them to the hatch through which the man had entered and opened it a crack, checking the corridor on the other side. It was clear, but as he opened the hatch wider and stepped in, he came face to face with a sailor. Instantly his gun was on the man's forehead—the sailor didn't move.

"He's frozen," Evans said from behind. "There's another one."

Jett looked down the corridor to see a sailor's body sticking up through the deck—nothing but a head and shoulders. The sight would horrify most people, but Jett felt only a slight adrenaline surge.

"Hihowyadoin?" Ralph said, hand outstretched to the first frozen man.

"Shut up," Evans hissed again.

"What's the matter with him?" Ralph said, puzzled.

"It's a statue," Jett said. "Like a mannequin in a store window."

"Oh," Ralph said, but stared at the man, not quite able to accept Jett's explanation.

With a sign from Jett, his team checked the compartments on either side of the corridor, working toward stairs where he heard movement. When his team signalled all clear he started down the stairs. At the bottom he signalled Evans forward.

"Everything look the same to you?"

"Yes. Of course, the last time I saw it there was a lot of smoke in my eyes."

Jett knew that the smoke had come from his own burning flesh.

"If you see anything that looks different, you tell me," Jett said.

"The only thing that's going to be different this time is a whole lot of bodies."

Jett ignored the threat, knowing that Evans was right. One way or another the Specials were going to be cleaned out of Pot of Gold and the easiest way was to find the power source; that's where he was headed. If the Specials tried to stop them, he would take them out one at a time.

Weapons ready, Jett's team headed into the bowels of the ship, Ralph trudging along dutifully, lips locked in a fleshy pucker.

Moving cautiously, they checked open hatches, someone always covering their rear. As well-trained professionals, they were light on their feet and moved with military crispness, covering every hatch, every intersection—except for Ralph, whose artless plodding gave away their position every step of the way. Peters, Thompson, Compton, and even Jett hushed him, urging him to walk softly, but he was incapable. Evans, however, glared malevolently with merciless eyes. Jett knew it wouldn't take much more to set Evans off. What sanity he'd once had, had been baked out of him.

They passed through the pilot house, the chart room, the radio room, and the fire control center, following the sounds ahead. Three more times they came to sailors who were frozen—two embedded in bulkheads, the third frozen midstep on a ladder. Ralph stared at each one long and hard, not able to accept that these men were mere mannequins.

Then Jett turned a corner and saw movement ahead. The man they had seen on the deck was there, turning into a compartment. A short distance behind him were three sailors and a woman. They were following the first man, unaware of Jett and his team. Jett signalled the others to stop, but Evans didn't. He had seen the Specials, and there was murder in his eyes.

FACES

Elizabeth and Anita stepped into the bathroom—"head," is what it would be called on a ship, Elizabeth realized—and it was much as she remembered it. The facilities were designed for men. A long trough was mounted against one bulkhead, serving as a urinal. Toilets were set along the other side, separated by low partitions. Down the middle was a double row of metal sinks. Each sink had a mirror mounted over it. There was more detail than before, with faucets and handles, spouts and drains. Elizabeth went directly to the same mirror as before.

"Wes, are you there?"

"What is it, Elizabeth?" Wes said.

"We're in the bathroom—the head—and I'm looking in a mirror."

"Lift me up, Elizabeth? I want to see too," Anita said.

"I'm looking in the mirror, but I don't see myself. I see a man."

"Standing behind you?" Wes asked.

"No, I'm looking at myself, but I'm a man." Elizabeth said. "He's young, maybe twenty-five, with short brown hair. It's oiled and combed to the side. He's got a blue shirt on and the sleeves have been cut off."

The hatch creaked and Elizabeth and Anita turned, startled to see four people step into the compartment. Three were dressed in the blue dungarees and work shirts of sailors. The fourth was a black woman wearing green bell-bottom pants and a yellow shirt covered with big orange flowers. Most striking was her hair, which looked like a perfectly shaped ball. Elizabeth remembered the style from the sixties and recognized it as an afro.

"Have you got someone, Dawson?" the sailor in front asked.

The group approached, crowding in. Elizabeth backed up, making room. There was a hatch on the other side, and she backed toward it instinctively, ready to run.

"Elizabeth," Wes said. "What is going on? Your vital signs—"

"There are people here," Elizabeth said.

"Who are you talking to, Roger?" the sailor said. "You made contact, didn't you?"

"I'm scared," Anita said.

Then another man stepped into the room. His presence was nightmarish, making what had felt real seem like a dream again. His facial features were barely distinguishable behind thick scar tissue. Anita gasped and clutched Elizabeth's leg. The others turned to face the newcomer, as shocked as Elizabeth by his sudden appearance.

"We're dissolving the integration!" Wes said.

The disfigured man wore a silvery suit with a wide belt, and straps that held a backpack. In his hand was a gun, but he didn't fire. Instead, he stared at the group in front of Elizabeth, and suddenly they were knocked aside, tumbling like tenpins, slamming into the bulkheads. Elizabeth had seen it before—the man was using psychokinetic power. When he turned on Elizabeth, she pulled Anita close. Before he could strike, another man in a similar suit stepped into the room, a gun in his hand. One step behind, walking with his long stride, his fleshy face shaped into a concerned look, was Ralph. Before she could speak she was hit in the chest with an invisible fist, which knocked her into the back bulkhead. Anita was pulled with her. Gasping for breath, Elizabeth collapsed, Anita kneeling with her, face buried in Elizabeth's lap.

"Ralph," she said hoarsely as she felt the integration begin to dissolve. Details disappeared as the dream was deconstructed—seams, rivets, bolts, faucets and pipes vanished. She tried again to get enough breath to call Ralph's name, but it was useless, she was losing the dream. As her vision faded to black, she saw Ralph reaching for the scarred man.

SKIRMISH

Evans killed the first two men with head shots. The Teflon slugs punctured their skulls but didn't have the energy to blow out the other side; instead, the prefragmented bullets came apart, rattling around in their skulls, destroying soft neural tissue, pithing them like you would a frog in biology class.

The third man threw himself in front of the woman, saving his own life. Evans's shot passed just over his crew cut. Evans had another shot lined up when Ralph reached him, wrapping him in his meaty arms, pinning him. Jett covered the man and the woman Evans had targeted and ordered Compton to cover the remaining man. Peters and Thompson crowded in, fingers twitching on their triggers, wondering why there were still three Specials alive.

"Let go of me!" Evans screamed.

"You gots to calm down," Ralph said, his voice even.

"You're dead, Ralph! You're dead!"

Jett turned from the Specials, pointing his gun at Evans.

"Stop struggling!" Jett ordered.

Evans's face was impossible to read through the thick scar tissue, but he relaxed, ignoring the gun in his face.

"No one touches Ralph," Jett said.

"I won't kill him," Evans said finally.

Jett couldn't trust Evans. Like Jett, his psychological profile made lying as easy as killing. Jett stepped aside, keeping his gun on Evans's head.

"Let him go, Ralph."

"I dunno, Nate, he did something real bad to those men."

"Let him go!" Jett repeated.

"Okay, sure, Nate. If you say so."

Ralph released his grip, stepping back, staring at the two dead men with his face contorted into concern. Evans flexed his arms to restore circulation, then checked his weapon. Jett relaxed, turning to the man who they had first seen on the deck. He was slumped against the far bulkhead, just coming to. Glassy-eyed, he felt the back of his head, his fingertips coming away damp with blood. Suddenly Evans's arm snapped toward the couple cowering on the floor, his gun firing twice. Both died instantly. Ralph immediately wrapped his arms around Evans again.

Evans struggled briefly, then relaxed. Now Evans looked at Jett, smiling with the lips of a corpse.

"I only promised not to kill Ralph."

"Thompson, take his weapon," Jett ordered.

It wasn't as simple as taking the gun from his hand, since they had to disconnect the pressure hose from the gas canisters in his pack. Thompson disconnected the gun, storing the weapon in Compton's pack. Then Jett ordered Ralph to release him again. Strangely, Evans didn't protest. Jett knew it was because in Pot of Gold Evans was a Special and was never without a weapon.

"It's better that you don't have a gun, Robin, even if it is just a BB gun," Ralph said.

Evans glared at Ralph, his eyes glistening with hate.

With the other Specials dead, they turned to the lone survivor. Compton moved aside to let Jett get closer in the cramped head. The Special Evans had knocked against the back wall was fully conscious now.

"Please don't kill me," he begged. His eyes were riveted on Evans, either horrified by the man's appearance, or aware that it was Evans who had done the killing.

"How many more of you are there?" Jett asked.

"You came to kill us," the man responded.

"We only want to get to the generators," Jett said. "We came to shut them down."

"We're never going home," the man said.

Jett knew that much was certain. There was a way out for his team, but none for the Specials. The Specials were powerful and uncontrollable, and a threat to those on the outside.

"We'll find the generators with or without you," Jett said. "If you help us we won't kill you."

"We don't need him," Peters said with a wink, then squatted next to the man. "But I think I can get him to talk."

Peters put his gun on the sailor's knee.

"Whatcha doin?" Ralph said, trying to push through.

Thompson gripped Ralph's arm, holding him back.

"Don't hurt me," the sailor said.

Jett held up his hand, and Peters held his fire, giving Jett another wink.

"This is your last chance," Jett said. "Make yourself useful."

"They won't let anyone get near those generators," the man said, looking down at the gun still pressed against his knee.

"Who won't let us near them?" Jett asked.

As if in answer, footsteps sounded in the corridor. Peters dragged the captive to his feet, using him as a shield. The others turned to face the door, taking cover behind sinks and toilet stalls—there was precious little cover. With all guns trained on the door, Jett dragged Ralph to the side, reminding him with a hand motion that his lips were locked, then pushed him behind. Just ahead of Jett, Compton whispered, "Shouldn't Ralph be in front?"

She was right. This was why they had brought Ralph. Then the footsteps stopped just outside the door. The tension grew as they waited for something to happen.

"He's reading us," the sailor said. "I can feel him."

Jett took that to mean that someone outside was using a psi power.

"We've got to get out of here!" the sailor said.

Jett motioned Peters to keep the sailor quiet.

The hatch slammed shut. With the ringing still in their ears, the hatch opened and slammed again and again. The sound was deafening. Ralph put his hands over his ears as the door continued to pound. Suddenly it stopped; the hatch was open. Outside, the corridor began to glow, quickly growing brighter than day. Soon it was too bright for their eyes.

"Jerry Rust is out there," the sailor said, clearly terrified. "We have to go now!"

The glow spread into the room, and Jett looked down, trying to keep his pupils from constricting. Finally, the light was so bright that he feared being blinded and closed his eyes. Jett used his ears now, listening for the attack.

The light grew even brighter until his eyelids glowed, so he covered them with his left hand. His skin grew warm while they waited, and he wondered if this was the attack. Then he heard a step; when he opened his eyes someone was in the doorway. As Jett raised his gun he was hit by an invisible wall.

He was knocked back, Ralph catching him, holding him up. Compton was driven back too, slamming her head on the pipe under the sink. She bounced off, lying flat. Jett was off balance, being held up by Ralph, but he fired over Compton's head, knowing she had the sense to stay down. He was still functionally blind, unable to aim with any accuracy. Thompson fired too, and then Compton. The figures in the doorway were nothing but blurs, but Jett could see that they held some sort of weapons and were taking aim. Suddenly, the attackers were knocked back through the doorway—Evans had used his power. A bullet fragment bounced off the wall next to Jett. The room was filling with their own riccochets.

"Hold your fire!" Jett shouted.

"Yeah," Ralph said. "One of those BBs hit me in the leg and it hurts."

"Cover me," Peters said.

Peters dragged the frightened sailor to the far end of the head, opening the far hatch, peeking through a crack first, then opening it wider.

"You go first," Peters said to the sailor. "If you run I'll kill you."

The sailor nodded, then let Peters push him through the door into the corridor to the other side. Near panic, the sailor checked the corridor in both directions. Peters went next and then signalled the others. Jett motioned Compton to the back hatch as the attack resumed. This time Jett's team was ready, backs against the wall, tensed for the psychic blow. It felt like a punch in the face. Jett's nose stung, blood trickling from his left nostril. His team opened fire, aiming carefully now, the bullets angling into the corridor. When the room began to glow again, Jett ordered retreat.

Evans went through first and then Compton, who fired a burst through the open door as she retreated backward. Jett pushed Ralph toward the door, noticing that his leg was bleeding.

"It hurts, Nate," Ralph said. "Those BB guns hurt people. I'm never gonna play with one."

Jett reached the door and then crouched to cover Thompson, who backed toward him. The glow in the doorway was painfully bright. Now the room was getting hot. Jett's skin was warm to the touch when Thompson passed him, stepping into the corridor. Jett stepped through, pulling the hatch closed behind him, dogging it.

Jett checked Ralph. His wound was minor, little more than a gash.

"We better move, Jett!" Compton said. "This hatch is getting hot."

Jett touched the hatch, feeling the heat. Then he had a thought.

"Ralph, come here, touch this door."

"Okee-dokee, Nate," Ralph said.

Ralph put his hand on the door, his face expressionless.

"What do you feel, Ralph?"

"It's smooth, Nate."

"Is that all you feel, Ralph?"

"I suppose," Ralph said, looking puzzled.

"So he is immune," Compton said. "He wasn't knocked over with the rest of us and he doesn't feel the heat. I wonder if the light affected him?"

Jett and Compton exchanged puzzled looks.

"But I felt the heat and that light was as bright as looking at the sun," Compton said.

"Induced hallucinations?" Jett suggested.

"We've got to get away," their captive said, backing down the corridor.

"The heat isn't real," Jett said.

Then Jett remembered the blood coming from his nose. He touched his upper lip, his finger coming away sticky with blood.

"Nate, can I take my hand off now?" Ralph asked. "It's getting awfully hot."

Compton and Jett exchanged quick looks.

"Run!" Jett yelled.

They made only a few steps before the hatch blew, heat and smoke boiling down the corridor. Jett had Ralph by the arm, dragging him along when they were knocked to the ground, the heat and smoke washing over them. Jett held his breath and rolled over, firing toward the head. The smoke dissipated, and he could see the hatch again—there was no one. Then they were hit from behind.

Peters and the sailor were thrown back into the others, rolling over Jett and Ralph. Thompson and Compton came up firing, Compton yelling to the others to run. Evans stared down the hall using his special ability. The smoke swirled, but there were no thumps from falling bodies and no satisfying screams.

Peters and the sailor were up and running, Evans following. Jett pulled Ralph to his feet and got him into a fast walk. Ralph's sensorimotor system wasn't wired for running; a fast, loping walk all he could manage. Reaching a junction, they took cover around the corner where Peters waited with the sailor and Evans. Thompson and Compton came next, retreating down the corridor, firing into the gloom. Before Compton and Thompson could reach the junction, they were sent flying, they landed flat and skidded along the deck.

Jett straffed the smoke blindly, then reached out and dragged Compton around the corner to safety. Thompson crawled to the far side. It was a mistake. Now he had to cross the intersection to get to the others. Thompson signalled Jett that he would cross to their side on the count of three. He held up three fingers and then dropped them one by one. With the last finger Jett and Compton opened fire. Thompson waited only a second before making his move.

Thompson's football career had ended because he was a step too slow for the pros, and now his life ended for the same reason. A fireball came out of the gloom, catching Thompson midstride. Enveloped by the fireball, he was knocked to the deck. His body was partially protected by the fire-resistant silver coverall, but his head was exposed and the flames concentrated there, his hair bursting into flame. Screaming in agony, Thompson started to rise—running was always the first impulse. Then he dropped and rolled, beating the flames on his face and head to no avail. Peters' gun sputtered, Teflon bullets piercing Thompson's skull. Now he lay still, his body still burning, but the agony over. Jett turned on Peters.

"He could have made it," Jett said. "Evans did."

"I wish to God I hadn't," Evans whispered through rebuilt lips.

Peters winked at Jett, then was off with the captive sailor.

"They'll be coming," Compton said, grabbing Ralph and pulling him after Peters.

Jett and Evans locked eyes, Jett wondering how much sanity was left beneath those scars. Evans broke the stare and followed the others. Gun in his hand, Jett thought of shooting Evans. It would be the safest move to make, but for the first time in his life he didn't think of it as killing, he thought of it as murder.

EXPERIMENT

Shamita finished dissolving the integration while the others looked after the dreamers. Wes was at Elizabeth's side, worry etched into his face. Monica stood between Margi and Anita, alternating her attention between the two. Len attended to Wanda, who was the first to wake.

"Where's my cigarettes?" Wanda said, reaching for the pocket in her sweater.

In a flash, she had a Lucky Strike in her mouth and the Bic lighter in her hand. When she struck the lighter Len blew out the flame.

"Smartass," she said, then struck the lighter.

Len blew out the flame again. Staring him straight in the eye, Wanda thumbed the little wheel that adjusted the flame size. Then, with another spark, a three-inch flame shot from the top of the lighter. Wanda held it still, daring Len to blow it out.

"Ha! Smartass!"

She lit the cigarette and blew the smoke in Len's face.

"You know this means war, don't you, Wanda?" Len said.

"Don't pick a fight you can't win," Wanda replied.

"Never underestimate your enemy."

"I wouldn't think it would be possible to underestimate you," Wanda said, then finished with another "Ha!" and a laugh that ended in a wracking cough.

Anita woke at the same time as Elizabeth, the two of them sitting up and reaching out for each other. Then Elizabeth remembered the dream.

"I saw Ralph," Elizabeth said. "He was on the ship."

Confused, Wes looked from Elizabeth to Shamita, who shrugged her shoulders.

"You must have added him to the dream, Elizabeth," Wes said.

"Not with their cortex parameters," Shamita said. "Elizabeth was receiving only, not transmitting."

"There was a monster," Anita said.

"It wasn't a monster, Anita. It was a man who had scars on his face. I'm sure you've seen people like that before."

Anita shook her head.

"Not like him. The dream's worse, not better."

"I know it seems that way, Anita, but we learned something. We have a number for the ship."

"Will that help?" Anita asked.

"It might," Elizabeth told her.

"Wes, you better take a look at Margi," Monica interrupted.

Margi was sitting up, but she was dazed, her eyes unfocused, her head lolling from side to side. Wes checked her pupillary response with a flashlight. It was sluggish. Len returned to his monitor and reported depressed vital signs, but nothing critical. Wes signalled Elizabeth to get Anita out of the room.

"Let's go see your mother," Elizabeth suggested, lifting her off the cot.

"Let me walk her out," Wanda said, glaring at Wes. "I gotta find myself a place where I can smoke in peace anyway."

When they were gone, the team gathered around Margi. She was still groggy, but responsive. Suddenly her eyes teared.

"I dreamed I was doing the dishes."

"On the ship?" Wes said.

Margi was crying for joy.

"No, at home with my mother. I was drying while she washed. It didn't last long, but it felt so good."

"It's possible," Len said. "When we began to dissolve the integration there was a brief period of individual sleep. The others slipped into delta wave sleep, but Margi was showing alpha. She might have dreamed normally for a few minutes."

"Can you do it again?" Margi asked. "Make me dream of my mother?"

Wes was about to explain that they didn't know how it happened, when Elizabeth rescued him.

"We won't give up, Margi. We'll all keep trying."

"Thank you. You don't know how much that meant to me," Margi said, her face and voice animated. "My mother and I did the dishes every night when I was little. I hated it then, because I wanted to go out and play with my friends. Now I know how special that time was. We talked like two grown-ups. I would tell her about school, and she would tell me about her day. Sometimes we would argue, sometimes we would laugh over silly things."

Margi's smile suddenly faded, and her speech took on the raspy sound of exhaustion.

"And I was there with her . . . in my dream."

Elizabeth helped Margi to her feet, then walked her to the door, making sure of her balance before letting her go.

"She's exhausted," Wes said when she was gone. "We can't use her again."

"That little bit of normal dreaming did more harm than good," Shamita said. "She had forgotten what she was missing until we reminded her."

"What was that about Ralph?" Wes asked.

"He was on the ship, and there were others," Elizabeth told them. "We were in the head when four people came in. There were three men and a woman. She was a black woman and her clothes and hair were right out of the sixties."

The others looked at each other, wondering about the oddness of the black woman on a Navy ship.

"They called me Roger, and asked me if I 'had someone?' Then the man whom Anita called a monster came in. He had terrible scars and wore silver coveralls. He had a gun but didn't use it. He didn't need to. He had psychokinetic power. There was another man dressed the same way, and then Ralph. I'm sure it was him. Then the scarred man knocked me down and everything went black."

"You must have contaminated the dream," Wes said. "None of the other dreamers know who Ralph is, and the psychokinetic man—well, that comes from your past experience."

Shamita shook her head. "Unless we're getting faulty readings, Elizabeth wasn't sending."

"There's nothing wrong with that hardware," Len said defensively.

"But then how do you explain it?" Wes asked.

Elizabeth's face was blank, her eyes seeing something far away.

"I know one of the men. He's the one in Dr. Birnbaum's sketch. He's the man that kidnapped Ralph. Wes, this isn't a dream. It's a place, and it's a real place where they've taken Ralph."

"I don't know, Elizabeth, it's too coincidental. Ralph is kidnapped and a few days later he shows up in your dream with the man you saw a sketch of."

"What about the black woman?" Elizabeth asked. "I'd never seen her before."

"You said she was wearing clothes from the sixties?" Wes asked.

"Bell-bottoms, and she had her hair in an afro."

"Isn't that just the kind of odd detail a dream would have? Think about it Elizabeth—why would someone kidnap Ralph and take him to a ship where there are sailors and a woman dressed like one of Charlie's Angels?"

"It is strange, but we need to follow up on what we have. The ship's number is CA137. We can check naval records."

Wes was skeptical, but knew from experience that Elizabeth's hunches were often right. He also knew that her hunches could get a person killed.

LEADS

Elizabeth was on the ship again, walking quickly, feeling as though she were being rushed, pushed along by an irresistible force. The ship's compartments connected endlessly—big compartments with giant boilers that powered the steam turbines, smaller compartments with diesel motors attached to sixty-kilowatt generators serving as backup power for the ship's guns and water pumps. She had never been on such a ship, but she knew what the machinery was for. That knowledge was part of her dream. The largest open space was in the stern where the hangar was located. There were no airplanes stowed there now, but two were mounted on their catapults, ready for action. In the hangar she felt more fear than anywhere else on the ship.

She had memories too, flashbacks of fires on a ship—not this one—caused by enemy shelling, and of sailors with hoses, fighting the fires. She was one of those men, she knew, holding a nozzle, feeling the heat from fires that refused to go out. Then the ship suddenly rocked from another hit—a fourteen-inch round, she knew somehow. Then the memory was gone and she was trudging through the ship again.

The compartments went on and on, all painted navy gray, all connected in an incomprehensible, endless loop. A few compartments were empty, some had hammocks slung from the walls, most were filled with machinery. The monotony should have bored Elizabeth, put her to sleep, but there was no sleep in this dream and no rest either. She walked the ship all night, helplessly dreaming someone else's dream.

Elizabeth woke as tired as when she lay down. She checked her clock radio to make sure it was morning. She vaguely remembered hitting the snooze bar, and noticing the clock showed six-thirty. She had risen at this hour six days a week for the last four years, but today she felt hung over. Her head felt pressurized, as if the pressure inside was now slightly greater than outside. She felt generally uncomfortable and fuzzy.

Elizabeth thought of Margi and Anita, and the way they were suffering—sleeping, but never resting. Now she understood their longing to sleep, and especially to dream normally again. She had a powerful need to dream herself, and this was only her first day with the dream.

The phone rang and she reached out, taking two tries before she grasped the receiver. Her lips were thick and her voice sluggish when she spoke.

"Did I wake you?" Monica asked.

"No, I was up," Elizabeth said.

"I had an idea last night about how we might find out what ship the CA137 is."

There was a few seconds' lag as Elizabeth's mind cut through the fog and remembered that they had seen the number when she was in the dream.

"Yes, the CA137. I remember. How . . . where . . . what is your idea?"

"Why not call Doctor Birnbaum? He knows all kinds of odd things."

"I suppose I could," Elizabeth said, not sure how she felt about calling him. "He will want to know about Ralph anyway."

"It's just an idea," Monica said.

"It's a good one. Thanks for calling."

Elizabeth hung up and lay back on her pillow. It would be nine-thirty in Columbus, so she could call anytime. It took her fifteen minutes to shake off her lethargy and pick up the phone again. Dr. Birnbaum answered on the second ring.

"It's Elizabeth, Dr. Birnbaum."

"Do you have news about Ralph?" he asked, clearly concerned.

"Not exactly," Elizabeth said, then explained about the mind integration and what she had seen during the dream.

"Ralph was there with the man who kidnapped him?" Birnbaum said.

"Yes. I'm sure it was them."

"That's odd," he said.

"There's something else. We have a number for the ship. It's the CA137, but according to the records we checked, the ship was planned but never built. You don't happen to know the ship, do you?"

"It does sound familiar, but I can't place it."

"Wes is going to call the Navy today."

"Let me work on it. I'll call you back in a couple of hours."

"Call me at the university," Elizabeth said, then hung up and lay back, eyes closing. She couldn't sleep. After twenty minutes she forced herself out of bed and dressed.

DIRECTION

Robert Daly sat at his desk in the Kellum Foundation headquarters. A grant application was spread out in front of him. His glass-topped desk had no drawer to store pencils, pens, erasers, and paper clips, no place to hold files or stickies, no hiding place for his scissors, calculator, or stapler. All of those were tucked away in the credenza behind him. Just last week he had owned a real desk with drawers; a great mahogany desk with the surface area of a small aircraft carrier. Even with his computer, pencil holder, phone, desk calendar, Rolodex, and stacks of folders, there was still room to work. Now that desk was gone, broken into pieces to get it through his door. He was sad to see his old friend go, and dismayed when he saw his new desk.

The replacement desk was more than just a desk; it was a work of art designed and built by his son the artist. It was the only commission his son had received last year, given to him by his mother. Smiling graciously, Daly had accepted the gift and tolerated the parade of potential customers his wife had ushered through his office. There were no new commissions. Daly was in a position of power and was used to obsequious supplicants fawning over him, but no one was so desperate for Daly's favor as to buy one of his son's ugly, nonfunctional desks. Knowing that family harmony depended on his response, he praised the desk. To his horror, his wife believed him and soon commissioned matching office furniture.

The grant application on his desk was typical of what the Kellum Foundation funded. The applicant had been working at a major university on grant money, but his grant had not been renewed. The researcher had been experimenting with a new approach to producing nuclear fusion. To produce fusion, two hydrogen atoms need to be combined, creating one helium atom and releasing the excess energy. Instead of using particle accelerators to reach the energy level necessary for the fusion to occur, the researcher had been experimenting with polarized electric fields to compress matter to the densities necessary for fusion. He had never achieved fusion, but had stumbled across an anomaly he thought more interesting. He found that electrons fired near the compressed mass arrived before they had been released. Professional colleagues called the result spurious, but he was convinced that the electrons were travelling back in time.

With his grant running out, the researcher was desperately seeking alternative funding. Daly would send the application to the staff for scientific evaluation, but it was likely to be funded. It fit with the foundation's overall goal—in fact, almost everything did.

Daly's phone buzzed and he reflexively reached across his desk. There was no phone there. Anything on the desk "detracted from what the piece was trying to say," his son had insisted. Turning to the phone behind him, he punched his secretary's line.

"Mr. Daly, we're getting Internet hits on the web sites you were interested in."

"From Doctor Birnbaum?"

"Yes."

"Thank you," Daly said, hanging up. Shifting to his computer he accessed the Internet and opened his search engine. He had the sites marked and found Dr. Birnbaum's inquiry on the second bulletin board he checked. He had spent an hour carefully wording his reply, knowing that Dr. Birnbaum would pass it on to Dr. Martin. He decided not to mention the disappearance of the Nimitz. Dr. Martin and his people didn't need to know about the Nimitz, since they weren't ready yet to make the connection with the ship dream.

After reading Dr. Birnbaum's message, Daly found that his preworded reply needed only slight modifications. Then Daly clicked on "send" and sat back. Dr. Martin and Ms. Foxworth were close to where he wanted them to be, and the information he had just sent should get them even closer.

NORFOLK

Elizabeth sipped her third cup of coffee. Normally a single cup of coffee woke her up in the morning, but not today. Wes came in, looking at her with concern.

"You don't look well," Wes said.

"Good morning to you too," she said.

"I didn't mean—"

"It's okay, Wes. I didn't sleep well," Elizabeth said.

Wes waited for her to explain.

"I had the dream last night," she went on. "I was on the ship again."

Wes collapsed onto the one chair in her small, neat office.

"Somehow I made you receptive to the dream," Wes said. "I never should have put you in the dream again."

"I insisted, Wes. No one knew this would happen."

"I shouldn't have taken the chance."

"Wes, look at this the other way. If linking with the dreamers made me a receiver, then maybe we could link each of the dreamers with nonreceivers and stop them from dreaming of the ship."

"We can try that," Wes said.

Wes accepted the idea too quickly, and she knew there was little chance it would work. An uncomfortable silence followed. Elizabeth realized that like Margi and Anita, she would only stop dreaming of the ship when she stopped dreaming forever.

The phone rang. Elizabeth answered, then punched the speaker phone.

"It's Doctor Birnbaum. He knows something about the ship. Can you hear us, Dr. Birnbaum?"

"Yes. Is that Wes with you? Good, he needs to hear this too. I tracked down your ship, the CA 137. It's a World War II vintage Baltimore class, heavy cruiser. It was to be named the Norfolk but according to the Navy the ship was never built."

"So there is no such ship," Wes said.

"Not officially," Birnbaum said. "Other sources say it was indeed built at the Philadelphia Naval Yard and launched for sea trials in 1943."

"So why would the Navy lie about it?" Elizabeth asked.

"Have you ever heard of the Philadelphia Experiment?" Dr. Birnbaum said.

"No," said Wes.

"Yes," said Elizabeth.

"It's a World War II secret government project that has achieved nearly the same level of notoriety as the UFO crash at Roswell."

"Urban myth?" Wes said.

"There is a nugget of truth at the core of most myths, Wes," Dr. Birnbaum said. "The Philadelphia Experiment began with the DE 173, the USS Eldridge. The Navy was experimenting with electronic camouflage, trying to find a way to make its ships invisible. The Eldridge was fitted with specially modified naval-type degaussers—basically a magnetic field generator. The generators were rigged to pulse, rather than generate a constant field. They found they could increase the strength of the magnetic field exponentially if they pulsed the generators at resonant frequencies. They believed the intense magnetic field would bend light, making the ship invisible."

"Is that possible?" Elizabeth asked.

"I don't see how," Wes said. "Only matter as dense as a black hole can warp light."

"I would have agreed with you yesterday," Dr. Birnbaum said, "but then I learned the experiment was conducted by the Navy Office of Scientific Research in August 1943 and that Albert Einstein was a consultant to that office between May 1943 and June 1944. He primarily worked for the

Bureau of Ordnance but some believe he had a hand in the Philadelphia Experiment."

"If the experiment had been successful, the Navy would have invisible ships today," Wes said.

"Something happened, but not what they expected," Dr. Birnbaum said. "The Eldridge disappeared all right, but there are rumors the ship was actually transported to Norfolk, Virginia and back again."

"Impossible," Wes said.

"The Navy publicly denied it," Dr. Birnbaum said, "but the Navy was so pleased with the initial experiment they funded the creation of larger generators and a second experiment. My source tells me they used the newly launched CA 137, the USS Norfolk for the second one. They took her out to sea with a skeleton crew and powered up the generators. The ship disappeared just as the Eldridge had, but this time the Norfolk never reappeared. The observation ship carried witnesses who swear the ship just vanished and never returned."

"And now it shows up in dreams," Elizabeth said.

"There's more to the myth," Dr. Birnbaum said. "It gets even stranger. There are reports that a few months after the experiment with the Eldridge, some of her crew—this is going to be hard to believe—became semi-transparent and could move through walls. Some got stuck and became part of the wall."

Wes and Elizabeth looked at each other, incredulous.

"In the dream there were sailors like that, some in the deck," Elizabeth said.

"Just like on the Eldridge," Dr. Birnbaum said. "It seems less and less like myth."

There was silence now as Elizabeth and Wes tried to make sense of it all.

"Dr. Birnbaum, the ship in the dream had airplanes on it, but you say it is a cruiser, not an aircraft carrier," Wes said.

"Airplanes? You say there were airplanes on the ship in the dream?" Dr. Birnbaum said.

"I saw two airplanes," Elizabeth said.

"Were they F-14s?" Dr. Birnbaum asked.

"No, they were antiques—biplanes—and they were mounted on the back of the ship," Elizabeth said.

"Those would be scout planes," Dr. Birnbaum said. "World War II–era cruisers carried as many as four planes and launched them with catapults. They were used mostly for reconnaissance and artillery control. Sometimes they landed at sea and were recovered, sometimes they just let the planes crash because it wasn't safe to pick them up."

"Why did you think they might be F-14s?" Wes said.

"When I was searching the Internet I came across a chat room where they were talking about the USS Nimitz. There are rumors that the ship has been sunk or blown up, or that it simply disappeared. The only fact that everyone agreed on was that communication with the Nimitz has been cut off."

"Could they have revived the Philadelphia Experiment?" Elizabeth asked.

"They most certainly wouldn't try it with a supercarrier," Dr. Birnbaum said.

The rumors about the Nimitz were an odd coincidence, but the ship Elizabeth and the others had reported from the dream was nothing like an aircraft carrier.

"The Philadelphia Experiment was fifty years ago," Wes said.

"But we're dreaming about it today," Elizabeth said, "and we see Ralph on the ship."

"It's too fantastic," Wes said. "People passing through walls?"

"Interdimensional shifting?" Dr. Birnbaum suggested. "Perhaps the resonant fields pushed the Eldridge through a dimensional hole and out the other side to Norfolk, and then back. The sailors were somehow changed in the process, perhaps slowly, and months later the full effects were seen?"

"How does this help us find Ralph?" Elizabeth asked.

"We need to find the ship," Dr. Birnbaum said.

"There might be another way," Wes said. "I don't know how to find our way to the ship, but I bet Ralph knows how to find his way home."

"What are you suggesting?" Dr. Birnbaum said.

"I think we should ask Ralph to come home."

JOURNEY

Jett and his team followed the captured sailor through the Norfolk, guns ready, alert for attack. Ralph plodded along behind Jett, distracted by open hatches, connecting corridors, and especially frozen men. Their guide's course wove them from port to starboard, fore and aft, in and out of the ship, around gun turrets, and through the pilot house and chart rooms. From the deck he led them deep into the bowels of the Norfolk, through crew berths slung with hammocks and to boiler rooms. Huge diesel-fired boilers connected to steam pipes dominated one room; the pipes were designed to carry the steam to the turbines in the engine room. The second identical boiler room was through connecting water-tight doors; it connected to an engine room with its great turbines. On the far side there was another boiler room, but the boilers here were missing. From there they moved to a fourth boiler room and another engine room. Jett knew from studying the design of the Norfolk that the redundancy was by design and not the result of the twisting of space that the field created. However, sometimes compartments did not connect as they should, and instead of the empty boiler room leading to the fourth boiler room, it led to the deck. This kind of space distortion made forming a mental map of their route nearly impossible.

Twice they emerged in the airplane hangar, a great, empty space designed to store seaplanes like those mounted on the deck above. Once, they passed through the chart room to emerge in a magazine, half filled with shells for the five- and eight-inch guns. Along the twisting, turning route, they encountered men frozen in place or protruding from bulkheads. A set of hands decorated the outside of a forty-millimeter gun turret on one pass, a leg protruded from a boiler on another. Most bizarre of all was a ladder they climbed, which was as much human as it was metal.

Jett's briefing on the conditions inside Pot of Gold hadn't prepared him for something so foreign to human experience. Ralph studied all the frozen men, finding it hard to pass anything so lifelike without introducing himself.

After hours of following the sailor, Jett called a halt as they emerged from the superstructure. They took cover under a twenty-millimeter gun emplacement at midships. Jett eyed the machine gun, longing to climb into the gun emplacement and feel the steel of the weapon. Guns were the tools of his trade.

The deck was empty, no frozen men or bodies protruding from bulkheads. They hadn't seen or heard anyone in pursuit since Thompson was torched. Jett ordered Peters to guard the hatch they had just come through, and told Evans to move down the deck to secure an avenue of escape.

"Are we getting close to the generators?" Jett said.

"Closer," the sailor answered, squatting.

The sailor was a young man, maybe twenty-five, but he carried himself like someone much older. His generation had fought and won a world war, coming home war-weary and older than their years. Jett understood men like this sailor, since he, too, had taken on adult responsibility in his teens.

"What's your name?" Jett asked, squatting next to him.

Suddenly Ralph's arm went out and he thumped himself on the side of his head.

"How could I be so stupid?" Ralph said. "I didn't get to meet ya!" He thrust out his hand. "I'm Ralph, and this here's Nate, and this here's Karla, and this here's Jim, and that's Robin over there."

"I'm Roger Dawson," the sailor said, taking Ralph's hand.

"Hihowyadoin?" Ralph said. "Got any gum?"

"I can't remember the last time I saw a piece of gum."

Standing, Jett pulled a pack of Juicy Fruit from a pocket in his silver coveralls and handed it to Ralph.

"Share it," Jett said.

"Juicy Fruit," Dawson and Ralph said at the same time.

"How close are we to the generators?" Jett asked again as Dawson unwrapped the stick of gum.

Getting to his feet, Dawson said, "Did we ever get to Mars? Someone said we flew a rocketship to the moon and that next we were going to go to Mars."

"The generators?" Compton said, pushing her gun into Dawson's side.

"Men did walk on the moon, but we haven't gotten to Mars yet," Jett said.

"Imagine that," Dawson said. "Someone actually touched the moon."

"The generators?" Compton said, poking Dawson hard enough with her gun barrel to make him wince.

At five foot seven, Compton was three inches shorter than Dawson and fifty pounds lighter, but she was well conditioned and knew every nerve nexus in the human body. Dawson saw her through his 1940s eyes; women weren't trained to kill back then. Dressed in her silver suit she looked cute and harmless to him.

"Stop poking me with that gun, honey, or I'll take it away from you," Dawson said.

Suddenly Compton's left arm whipped out, striking Dawson across his chest, the edge of her hand impacting his solar plexus. Dawson's lungs deflated explosively, and he buckled in half, arms wrapped around his waist.

"Don't call me honey," Compton said. Then she jammed the gun into Dawson's ear, causing him to wince again. "When you can breathe again, the first words our of your mouth better be about the generators or they'll be your last."

"You didn't have to hit him," Ralph said. "It's not nice to hit people, Karla."

Ignoring Ralph, Compton kept the gun pressed against Dawson's ear. It took a minute for him to get control of his breathing, and then he waited another minute, either collecting his thoughts or defying Compton—either of which was foolhardy.

"I'm taking you to where you need to go," Dawson finally gasped. "There are thirty-two known levels on the Norfolk. We started on level twelve and we're now on level twenty."

"What do you mean 'levels?' " Jett said.

"It's what we call them. I don't really understand it myself. You need to talk to the Professor."

"We don't need to understand it," Compton said. "We just need to know how much farther it is."

Scared, Dawson avoided eye contact, Compton's gun still nestled in his ear.

"What level are the generators on?" Compton asked. "Level twenty-two? Level thirty? I'm running out of patience."

"Level one," Dawson said.

Compton cursed, her finger tightening on the trigger. Dawson's lips moved as in prayer.

"Wait!" Jett ordered Compton. Then he asked Dawson, "Why are you taking us the wrong way?"

"I'm taking you to the Professor. He can explain it all."

"Take us to the generators," Jett said.

"We can't get to them. They have them. They won't let you anywhere near."

"Who?" Jett said. "The people who attacked us?"

Evans came down the deck, listening to the exchange.

"Yeah. It was them that killed your friend. They protect the generators. They're all crazy. That's what we call them, Crazies. They think that machine gives them eternal life—eternal hell if you ask me."

The OSP agents knew that the Specials they hunted wore 1940s' vintage Navy uniforms, but Jett knew that few of them had ever wondered why. Jett however, had put it together long before Woolman had cleared him for a full briefing. What he hadn't known about before the briefing was the social structure that had evolved in Pot of Gold. Based on interrogations of the few surviving escapees, Dr. Lee had sketched a picture of the evolution of society in Pot of Gold.

After Pot of Gold was sealed, the officers and scientists had lost control. As special powers emerged in some crew members, those with the strongest powers became restless, seeing their rightful place as being at the top of the chain of command. As it turned out, the greatest power wasn't telekinesis or the ability to generate fire or electricity; it was the power to manipulate others. A chief petty officer, Layton McNab, developed the ability to manipulate other people's minds, reshaping their beliefs, desires, and loyalties. Dogmatically religious, McNab gave what had happened to the Norfolk a theological twist and, by preaching and using telepathic manipulation, he converted more than half the men to his cause. Renaming himself Prophet, he led his cult in a Jihad—a holy revolution. Most of the officers were killed in the first battle, the rest in the skirmishes that followed. Those who followed McNab were called Crazies by the ones who remained loyal, and the loyalists were labelled heretics by the rebels. Eventually the two factions established territories and, while still hostile, now coexisted with a minimum of conflict. Dawson was one of the loyalists.

"What about you, Dawson?" Jett asked. "Don't you like being young forever?"

"It's hell. You don't eat, you don't drink, you don't even piss. Even this gum doesn't taste good."

"He's right. It doesn't taste that good," Ralph said. "Maybe we got bad pieces. Want another?"

Dawson declined, then continued as Ralph unwrapped another piece.

"The Professor says the normal laws of physics don't operate here. Time and space are all messed up. That's why this ship is the way it is."

"We're wasting time," Compton said.

Evans stepped close to Dawson. Jett tensed, ready to save the sailor's life.

"Take us to this Professor," Evans said.

Even inches from the hideously scarred face, Dawson showed no revulsion.

"Follow me," Dawson said. "You can relax. The Crazies aren't anywhere near. I can sense them when they come."

"And you'll warn us?" Evans said.

"They'll fry my ass as quick as yours," Dawson replied.

Dawson led off again, back into the ship and up another flight of stairs. Jett noted that his team stayed vigilant even after Dawson's assurances. At the next level Peters called a halt and walked up to Jett, tapping on his hip unit.

"It's dead," Peters said. "The ready light's dead. There's a ding in the side over here."

"Maybe the light's out," Jett said, trying to head off what was coming.

"It might be the light," Peters said with a wink. "Or it might not. I better trade units with Ralph just to be sure."

This time Peters didn't wink; he was waiting for Jett's answer. Compton and Evans were waiting too, their confidence in him eroding with every second he took to respond.

"You wanna switch, Jim?" Ralph said. "I don't mind if the little light's out. I dropped my flashlight once and broked the bulb. I still liked it anyway cause my daddy gave it to me. I still gots it somewhere."

"Yeah, let's switch," Peters said. "When we get back I'll buy you an ice cream cone."

"Maybe a dip cone?" Ralph said, a big grin on his face.

"Sure, a dip cone."

"Well okee-dokee then," Ralph said, fumbling to get his unit off.

"Let's get moving again," Jett said, trying to salvage his authority. "Let's go see the Professor."

MOTEL

Wes didn't want to use Elizabeth, but was reluctant to use Margi since she had been slow to recover from the last integration. He had little choice, however, since it could take weeks to track down another person tuned in to the ship dream. He decided to evaluate Margi, hoping that her brief normal dream had made her stronger. Wes had booked a motel room near the campus for Margi, but when he called to ask her to come to his office there was no answer. After calling repeatedly for the next two hours he and Elizabeth went to the motel.

Wes knocked several times, but Margi didn't answer. The motel had interior halls, and there was no window they could peek through.

"She could be out somewhere," Elizabeth suggested.

"She's too exhausted to go anywhere," Wes said.

"I don't think she would have gone home without telling us. Your experiment was her only hope," Elizabeth said.

"I'll get the manager," Wes said.

The manager wasn't on duty, and the assistant was reluctant to let Wes into a rented room. Wes explained their concern for Margi's well-being, but even then Wes had to show every piece of ID in his wallet before Mr. Waltham would agree to check.

Mr. Waltham knocked repeatedly before using his pass key. Opening the door slowly, he shouted into the room.

"Ms. Winston? Are you here, Ms. Winston? It's the assistant manager, Mr. Waltham."

Finally, Mr. Waltham pushed the door open wide enough for Elizabeth and Wes to squeeze past. The bathroom was to the right as they entered; Elizabeth paused at the closed door, knocking. Wes continued into the room. There were two queen-size beds. Both beds were made, although one was rumpled as if someone had lain on top of it. Personal items were scattered around the room, and Margi's suitcase was in the closet, clothes hanging from the rod above.

"Mr. Waltham, we need to open the bathroom door," Elizabeth said.

Wes joined Mr. Waltham and Elizabeth at the bathroom door. Mr. Waltham again knocked several times, calling to "Ms. Winston" before he used a small hook on his key ring to spring the bathroom lock. With a click, the catch released, and again he began the calling routine. He stopped abruptly when he smelled the foul odor. With an assertive shove, Elizabeth moved ahead of the assistant manager, pushing the door open. Taking two steps in she turned to the bathtub and gasped. Wes stepped in next to her, and Mr. Waltham followed. Margi was floating in the bathtub, face up, eyes closed, head submerged. Her bowels had released when she died and the water was fouled with her waste. She floated lifeless in the brown soup, her nude body already beginning to bloat.

Mr. Waltham gasped, then hurried out to the phone to call for paramedics. Wes estimated that it was at least twelve hours too late for help.

He turned away, sickened by the sight and saddened by his inability to help Margi. He stepped back into the hall; before Elizabeth followed, she took a towel and covered Margi's body.

"Was it suicide?" Mr. Waltham asked.

Wes shook his head. "They'll have to do an autopsy, but I don't think so. She had a sleep disorder. I suspect she slipped into a coma and drowned."

Mr. Waltham was not listening, either dwelling on the horror of what he had seen or contemplating the impact of the death on his occupancy rates.

Elizabeth pulled Wes aside.

"You'll have to use me in the integration now," Elizabeth said.

"It's too dangerous."

"Do you want Anita to end up like Margi? Or me?"

"You're too sensitive to . . . to whatever it is. That last session affected you more strongly than the others. Margi dreamed of the ship for seven years before it killed her. That last integration equalled two years' worth of

Margi's dreams. I'll find a solution to this, Elizabeth, without risking you. I'll enter the integration with Anita and Wanda. Shamita can control the meld."

"There's no reason to believe you'll respond any differently than I did," Elizabeth said. "You could end up receiving the dream. If we're going to solve this we can't both have our sleep disrupted."

Wes searched for other options, but none came to him. They hadn't seen anyone in the dream when Elizabeth was in Anita's dream by herself. It was only after they integrated the three dreamers with Elizabeth that the details had emerged. Wes doubted that Wanda and Anita alone would be sensitive enough. The reception increased exponentially with the addition of each dreamer.

"All right, Elizabeth, we'll integrate with you, but as soon as you find Ralph you get out. No exploring."

"Agreed," she said.

The elevator opened at the end of the hall and the paramedics emerged, Mr. Waltham following behind, wringing his hands. There was nothing the paramedics could do, but Wes respected the fact that they wouldn't take Mr. Waltham's word that Margi was dead. There was hope until they decided there was no hope. That was the way he thought about Elizabeth and the dream. Wes estimated that Elizabeth had no more than a few weeks before she, too, slipped into a coma and drowned in her bathtub. Remembering Margi's bloated body, he vowed not to let it happen.

PROFESSOR

Dawson brought them in off the ship's deck and down into its interior, past crew berths and aft toward where the hangar should be. Then he stopped just before a staircase and waited until they all caught up.

"We're almost there," Dawson said. "It's one deck down."

Peters and Compton checked their weapons.

"Don't kill them," Dawson said. "They won't hurt you."

Evans grabbed Dawson by the front of his shirt, pulling him to within inches of his scarred face.

"Don't tell me they don't like to hurt people."

"It wasn't my people. It was the Crazies that hurt you."

"I won't let them hurt you, Robin," Ralph said.

Still holding Dawson's shirt, Evans turned to Ralph, splitting his hatred between the two men.

"Let him go, Evans," Jett said.

Evans ignored him until Jett rested his hand on his gun.

"What's happened to you, Jett?" Evans said. "You're nothing like your reputation."

"I get the job done, that's why I'm in charge," Jett told him.

Peters and Compton listened to the exchange with interest.

"When we get to the bottom, we'll have to put our hands up," Dawson said.

"Like this?" Ralph said, sticking his arms up and banging his knuckles on overhead pipes. "Ow!"

Jett's team waited for his response. He could only push them so far before they rebelled.

"We're going down those stairs ready, not with our hands in the air," Jett said.

"They'll kill you," Dawson said. "They know you're coming. They're ready for you."

"How could they know we're coming?" Evans asked.

"They won't hurt you," Dawson said quickly.

"How?" Compton said, jamming her gun in Dawson's ear again.

"I told them. Margolin—he's one of us—he can hear what I'm thinking. I told them about you so they would get out of the way. I didn't want you to kill anymore."

"Back the way we came," Jett ordered.

"It's too late," Dawson said. "They're behind us too."

"It's a trap," Compton said.

Without being told, his team spread out, guns covering both directions of the corridor and up and down the stairs.

"Pick a direction," Evans said, "and I'll punch a hole through them."

"You can't win," Dawson said. "There are too many of them. We have a fire thrower, and kinetics like you."

Jett knew his team would never go down those stairs with their hands in the air, and he also knew Dawson was underestimating his team's chances of getting through the Specials. With Evans's psychokinetic power and their weapons, he guessed two, maybe three of them would make it, but Ralph wouldn't.

"I'll go down," Jett said. "The rest of you can stay here until I'm sure it's safe."

"Dawson stays," Peters said.

"Ralph goes," Evans said.

"Can I, Nate, can I?" Ralph said.

"Sure, Ralph," Jett said, knowing it was the best way to keep him alive.

"Can I hold the sides going down?" Ralph said. "It's kind of steep and I don't know if I can do it with my hands in the air."

"Sure, Ralph," Dawson said. "Be careful when you put your hands up at the bottom so you don't bang your knuckles again."

Ralph thumped himself on the side of the head, saying, "How could I be so stupid?" Then he started down the stairs, Jett following.

At the bottom Ralph turned left as if he knew where he was going. As soon as Jett's head cleared the bulkhead, Jett he could see that Ralph was walking toward someone. A black woman stood at the end of the corridor. She was plump and wore a green apron with white pockets over a blue dress with tiny white polka dots.

"Hihowyadoin?" Ralph said, hand extended.

Just as Ralph reached her the woman disappeared.

"Where did she go?" Ralph asked. "Did you see that, Nate? She's a magic person or something."

Ralph reached the junction and then looked left and right.

"Oh, there she is, Nate. This is the way."

"Put your hands up," Jett reminded him.

"Oh yeah," Ralph said, then lifted his arms, banging his knuckles again.

Jett raised his hands, managing to spare his knuckles, and followed, turning the corner to see the woman in the green apron halfway down the corridor. She disappeared again when Ralph reached her.

"That's neat," Ralph said. "How does she do that?"

There was an open hatch to Ralph's right, and he looked in.

"There you are," Ralph said, then stepped in.

When Jett got to the hatch, Ralph was shaking hands with a group of people. Jett leaned in cautiously, catching sight of men standing to the right and left of the hatch. Making sure they could see his hands, he stepped through. Men on either side poked him in the sides with crude spears made from pipe. Others aimed crossbows at his chest. The men were mostly sailors, but there were civilians too, wearing a mix of every kind of clothing including farmer's overalls, a polyester suit, and a tuxedo. They were a wild-looking bunch, some with facial tattoos, others wearing necklaces made of copper shell casings, nails, or in one case forks. More wild still were their eyes, which were bright and distant, making Jett wonder if he hadn't fallen into the hands of the Crazies.

"Take his gun," someone commanded.

They pulled his gun from his holster, but the cable kept it attached to the backpack.

"He's got it wired on," one of the sailors said.

"Get a pair of dikes," another said.

"I can take off the harness," Jett said. "If you let me put my hands down."

"Slowly," one of the sailors ordered, pressing the spear into his side.

Jett released the latches on the harness, letting them slide the backpack off. He kept the hip unit, hoping they wouldn't think it was a weapon. They looked it over, but left it when they couldn't see any danger.

"Go on in," one of the sailors said. "But move slowly."

More men with crude weapons parted in front of him, letting him and Ralph enter. The room was a machine shop with lathes and drill presses. There were bits and pieces of other machinery around the room which looked as if they had been cannibalized, and there were piles of pipe and buckets filed with wedges of galvanized pipe. Thirty people filled the room, mostly bizarre and crudely armed sailors in denim work uniforms, but behind them were a dozen women in a bewildering variety of clothes. The middle-aged black woman in the green apron was there, and next to her a woman wearing a skirt with a hemline just below her knees and the kind of nylons with a seam up the back of the leg. The woman next to her was young, maybe twenty, and wore a pink mini-skirt and matching sweater with white boots that came to her knees. Behind the women Jett saw children peeking out around their legs. One boy was about ten, two girls maybe five and two. Knowing that he planned to destroy Pot of Gold, the presence of the women and children made him uncomfortable.

They watched him with a mixture of emotions: anger, hatred, fear mostly; but some expressed hope. The crowd parted, clearing a path to a metal table. An object sat on the table, shaped like a ship, but filled with multicolored wires. Behind the table was a man wearing thick glasses with wire rims. He wore a short-sleeved white shirt and gray slacks. He looked fifty, and was thick around the waist. Balding, his little remaining hair was combed across the bald spot in thin lines, making his scalp resemble a musical score awaiting notes. Ralph had finished working the crowd, shaking every hand, and now reached the bald man as Jett approached.

"Hi, I'm Ralph, what's your name?"

"Nice to meet you, Ralph. I'm Walter Kellum."

Hearing Kellum's name, Jett flashed back to the meeting in Woolman's office. He remembered them talking about corporations and foundations that might have the resources to develop the technology to create a Pot of Gold. Dr. Lee had said that "not even the Kellum Foundation" was supporting that kind of research. Now Jett found a Kellum inside Pot of Gold, although he didn't know what it meant.

"This here's Nate," Ralph said.

"Nice to meet you," Kellum said. "I'll bet you've come for your missing aircraft carrier."

DOORWAYS

Jett shook Walter Kellum's hand. He had to lean across the table to do so; the man made no move to come around to his side, and sailors with machetes guarded both ends of the table. Sailors and civilians with a variety of homemade weapons were crowded in behind him and Ralph. They guarded Kellum like a king.

"Welcome, Mr. Jett. So, you've come to kill us."

"I'm here to locate the Nimitz, nothing more," Jett lied. "You say it's here, but we've been on deck many times and not seen it."

"Just what were you planning to do once you find the Nimitz?" Kellum asked, carefully keeping information from Jett.

"We're a scouting party. We are to locate and report."

As he spoke, Jett realized that their second signal laser had been destroyed when Thompson was burned. Now the only way to inform Rainbow about the Nimitz was to return through the barrier.

"And when you make your report, what will the government do? Send in troops to retake their aircraft carrier? And if they can recapture the Nimitz, then how will they get it back to the world?"

Using marines was exactly what Jett expected, but somehow they needed to find a way to get the Nimitz home. Kellum might be the key to making that happen.

"If you help get the Nimitz back, I'm sure you and the others here would be welcomed back, too," Jett said, trying to sound sincere. "It would be a show of good faith."

"You can all come to my house if you want," Ralph offered.

"Either you're lying or you've been duped," Kellum said. "They've kept us trapped in here for more than fifty years, and now you expect us to believe they would welcome us home?"

"Times have changed," Jett said.

Kellum circled the model ship with his hand.

"There are two resonant magnetic fields surrounding the Norfolk. The inner field flows from the synchronized magnetic pulse generators I created. We call the inner field the amniotic field since it contains us just like the amniotic membrane contains a fetus in its mother's womb. The outer field—the chorionic field—is generated by an outside source. I assume you know by whom, since they got you inside. They could drop that field any time they wanted."

"The outer field is purely defensive," Jett said. "Those that have gotten out have harmed innocent people."

"My people were killed because they were different, not dangerous. Besides, not all of us have developed unusual abilities."

Jett knew that those who escaped were all considered to have psi abilities and were killed as soon and as efficiently as possible. The policy was based on experience. The first Specials who emerged from Pot of Gold had killed many. Impressed, the military had tried to control them, to use them as weapons, but the Specials proved uncontrollable. The early escapees were insane, and Jett knew a powerful telekinetic had killed most of the scientists assigned to the early project. It was that early experience, and fear of living in a world where a select few have psi powers, that had sealed the fate of the men on the ship and brought the Office of Special Projects into existence.

"The Specials who got out were dangerous," Jett said, regretting using the word "Special."

"Then why would we be welcome on the outside now?" Kellum said.

The men and women packed into the machine shop murmured, then quickly grew still, waiting to hear Jett's reply.

"For one thing, you seem to have found the key to extending the life-span. You haven't aged a bit," Jett said.

Dr. Kellum paused, knowing that Jett was stalling, but then straightened his glasses, pushed the wisps of hair higher on his forehead, and said, "The words 'day,' 'night,' 'week,' or 'year' have no meaning here. If outsiders didn't occasionally stumble across an opening to the Norfolk, we wouldn't have any sense that time has passed at all."

"People get in?" Jett probed.

"That's where the women and children came from, and some of the men too. Their stories are all the same; out walking or playing and the next thing they know they're on the Norfolk." Motioning to the woman in the waitress uniform, Dr. Kellum said, "Tell him how you got here, Peggy."

Peggy was a teenager, pimples dotting the chin of her pretty face. As a child her hair must have been blonde, but it was darker now, with blonde highlights; slivers of her childhood.

"My boyfriend picked me up from work," Peggy said with a deep Texas accent.

Jett saw that she still wore a Denny's name tag that said, "My name is Peggy."

"We were fighting—he didn't like the way I was with the customers. He thought I was coming on to them, but I only did it for the tips. Blondes get bigger tips, and if you're friendly you can make a lot. He started yelling, and I yelled back, and he yelled some more. Then I just told him to stop that truck of his and let me out."

Now Peggy looked far away as if it was happening to her again.

"I started walking down the road, and he followed me, hollering at me to get back in the truck. He wouldn't leave me alone, so I crossed the highway and started cutting across a field. It wasn't nothing special, just sage. He got out and came after me and grabbed my arm. I got loose and started off again. He kept coming after me, cutting me off, herding me this way and that like I was some yearling calf. Finally, I had enough and took off running. He chased me, and I started zig-zagging to get away, and then suddenly I was here."

"Tell him when it happened," Dr. Kellum said.

"It was June 6, 1984," Peggy said. "I guess Zach is a married man now with kids as old as me," she added sadly.

Jett didn't say it, but he thought it possible that Zach was doing time for the murder of his girlfriend. They had left a restaurant together fighting, and she had disappeared without a trace. A jealous boyfriend would be a prime suspect, and Texans liked their crimes solved.

"See Bobby back there, hiding behind Wilma?" Dr. Kellum said, indicating the oldest boy standing behind the woman with the seamed nylons.

"He was chasing a butterfly around his backyard and ended up in the engine room on level thirty-two. He was there a long time before we found that level. A man named Kennedy was president when Bobby showed up, and he says he remembers seeing a debate between President Kennedy and a man named Nixon on television. I worked on the development of television and I knew then it would become a great civics tool."

Then Dr. Kellum smiled in a sad way.

"I'd love to see television. Peggy said it's in color now."

He acted as if he wanted Jett to describe the state of modern broadcasting, but Jett had no desire to regale him with the marvels of high-definition reception or digital satellite broadcasting. He had a mission to complete, and needed to find a way to get on with it.

"The amniotic field convoluted time and space, which created the different levels of time on the ship," Dr. Kellum continued. "The field is porous, however, and there are holes. Your chorionic field seals most of those holes, but there are routes in and out. Peggy, Marge, Sarah, Bobby, and the others all stumbled across an entrance."

Jett knew that the technicians at Rainbow actively worked at keeping the Specials inside Pot of Gold. Impending escapes were preceded by power fluctuations that slowly built, indicating the general geographic area where the escape would take place—all within a few thousand miles of Philadelphia. Jett hadn't known about people finding their way into Pot of Gold, but of course that wouldn't concern Woolman.

"Occasionally, some of our people disappear," Dr. Kellum said. "We know they found a way out, but they never come back. But there is order to the universe, so the twists and turns of time and space inside the Norfolk can be understood. There must be a pattern!" he insisted, indicating the ship model in front of him. "That's what this is for."

"That's neat, Walter," Ralph said with a mouth full of gum. "Did you make it yourself?"

Dr. Kellum's thick glasses magnified his eyes, giving him an owlish appearance.

"We built it, Ralph," Dr. Kellum said, sweeping his hand to include the men and women gathered in the room. "We've all worked on it. You see, it isn't really a model; it's actually a three-dimensional map."

Ralph's eyes glazed over as he looked at the ship. Even his jaws stopped in mid chew.

Jett looked at the multicolored wiring that made up the guts of the ship and traced a yellow wire that went up and down and all around through the ship. If it was a map he would never be able to follow it.

Dr. Kellum pointed at a silver disk soldered to the end of a red wire on the deck near the stern.

"That's level twelve, where you entered," Dr. Kellum said, "but we can't get out that way because your people have it sealed, and even if we did get out we would be killed."

"So we must be here," Jett said, pointing at a white wire that wound deep into the ship.

Dr. Kellum ignored him, his owl eyes focussed on the ship. "We know of two other unsealed exits," he said, pointing to other disks soldered to the ends of wire, "but they don't go anywhere, or go somewhere we don't want to go. There are other exits out there, I'm sure of it."

"Why are you telling me this?" Jett asked.

"Why? Because you're one of us now. There's no way out for you or Ralph, or any of the others. They sent you on a suicide mission, Nathan Jett."

Dr. Kellum waited for Jett to respond, but he didn't. Jett did have a way out, but he wouldn't share it. Instead, he played along to gain Kellum's confidence.

"Did they tell you how we got here?" Dr. Kellum asked.

"I know some of the story," Jett said.

"I'm not sure anyone on the outside knows the whole story. I'm not sure I fully understand it, and I created this place."

Dr. Kellum waved his hand over his head as he talked. He was an animated man, using his hands as well as his voice to communicate.

"We didn't understand what we were creating when we began. We hoped that by creating an intense magnetic field we could bend light around a ship, making it invisible—a decided military advantage. Our first experiment was with a destroyer escort, the USS Eldridge. We fit her with Navy degaussers specially designed to pulse. Pulsing the degaussers in tandem created resonance, exponentially increasing the power of the combined magnetic field. The first experiment took place in Philadelphia, and I watched from the dock as the ship was slowly surrounded by a green glow. As the generators came up to power, the light got brighter and our hair stood on end. Then the Eldridge shimmered and disappeared right before our eyes. A few seconds later it was back.

"Later we heard reports that the ship was sighted off the coast of Virginia at the same time it had disappeared in Philadelphia, but we laughed them off. We shouldn't have. Given that first success, the Office of Naval Research made our project high priority, just below the Manhattan Project. We received funding for a full-scale test and were given another ship.

The cruiser Norfolk was turned over to us for a few weeks of experimentation. She was fresh out of the Philadelphia Shipyard and ready for sea trials. Dr. Einstein and I had worked out the original pulse rates and frequencies, and now we refined these to increase the intensity of the field.

"The second-generation magnetic field generators had ten times the power of those used on the Eldridge. We took the Norfolk thirty miles offshore and then slowly brought the generators up to full power. It happened just like with the Eldridge—the green glow, the slow build-up of static electricity—but this time I was on the ship and felt the full force of the charge. The static build-up was so intense, I almost stopped the experiment, but suddenly the static was gone. Then it happened. The ship shuddered, and then the outside world faded away and was replaced by the opaque field you see all around the ship. We found ourselves in a desert—here—and a hundred yards in all directions there was nothing. Only then did we begin to understand what we had created.

"You see, the magnetic field we created was modified by the steel of the ship—thirteen thousand tons of it. If only we hadn't used a ship," Dr. Kellum said, shaking his head. "The field was distorted, flowing up and down the corridors, twisting time and space. There are two poles now—one astern, the other forward of the bow. This distortion created the different levels of time you have experienced. You see, as you travel through the ship you are really travelling through different moments in time. That's why you seem to have multiple ships. Think of it this way: right now you exist in this second, and then this one, and then this one. If you could travel back a second, you would see yourself as you were a second ago."

"Time travel," Jett said.

"Of a limited sort," Dr. Kellum said. "Different moments in time are fixed for the ship and exist in parallel rather than in series, which is how we normally experience time. Since these moments are parallel, we can move between them. Right now we are in this machine shop at this moment. Walk through the ship until you are on another time level, and it's a different moment in the same machine shop. It's the same all over the ship, with different moments of time frozen and parallel. The only exception is the boiler room where we installed the generators. Those generators are the nexus for the field and they exist at only one moment in time."

"What about the men that are part of the ship and standing in the corridors?" Jett asked.

"The field affects each of us differently," Dr. Kellum said sadly. "Unfortunately, for some of the men there was a lag as the field took hold of them.

When it finally did, they occupied space the ship had moved to and they merged with the ship, the men and the structure of the ship occupying the same space but at two different moments. Those men and the ones in the corridors have simply stopped moving with time at all."

"You must have tried to turn off the generators," Jett said.

"Not immediately. You see, we took the Norfolk out with a third of her normal complement—five hundred men. Some of those disappeared as the field reached full strength, and a hundred more merged with the ship. We didn't want to turn off the field until we understood what had happened. By the time we lost hope of saving them, the paranormal abilities had emerged, and Chief McNab began to prophesize and preach. By the time we discovered his ability to control the minds of others it was too late. Many of the crew were already fanatic followers. The judgement of God, he said. Maybe it was. More and more men went over to his side. I knew we were losing control, so I ordered the power lines to the generators cut—it made no difference; the generators continued to run. Everything continued to run. You see the lights burning all over the ship? The power lines were cut long ago, yet they still burn. Wherever this place is," Dr. Kellum said, gesturing with his arms again, "provides its own power. It also sustains us. We don't eat or drink, yet our bodies are replenished."

"How do you explain that?" Jett asked.

"Do you know the second law of thermodynamics?" Dr. Kellum said.

"It's entropy; the tendency for systems to move from order to disorder."

"It's more than a tendency, it's written into the fabric of the universe—it's a law. But given that law, then how did order come to exist in the universe in the first place? Why do galaxies and planetary systems form, or for that matter, why did our own atoms organize into molecules, the molecules into cells, and the cells into complex biological systems? And given the fact of entropy, why doesn't a system move from order to disorder instantly? Why does it take time at all, and why do some systems exist for eons with little decay?"

"A force that counters entropy?" Jett suggested.

"Very good," Dr. Kellum said. "Think of that force as anti-entropy. With our experiment we intended to bend light, and we succeeded beyond expectations, but I believe we did more. We pushed ourselves into the substrate of the universe—slipped between the layers, so to speak—into a region where the anti-entropy force is strong and entropy is weak. This ship and the people on it are maintained by this force, a force as fundamental as gravity."

Jett wasn't a theoretician, but he connected Dr. Kellum's theory to what had happened to time itself. With no entropy—no deteriorization—there was little or no passage of time. It stood to reason that if another little pocket like Pot of Gold could be created in a layer of the universe where entropy dominates, decay would be virtually instantaneous, and time would literally fly by.

"With McNab proselytizing among the men and turning them against the officers, we had only one course left to us. We decided to cut through one of the steel casings and destroy the generator coils, but McNab mutinied when he found out. He was too powerful by then, and we couldn't stop him. Most of the others died, and he drove us out of level one. He has controlled the generators ever since."

"So it was McNab that pulled the Nimitz inside?" Jett said, probing for information again.

"McNab is a very ordinary man with an extraordinary ability to manipulate those around him. He can't begin to fathom the complexities of magnetic resonance and its relation to gravitational fields."

"If he didn't pull the Nimitz inside, then who did? Or is it here at all?"

Again Dr. Kellum avoided discussing the Nimitz, holding back information. Jett was sure that Dr. Kellum was hiding something important.

Now pointing at the ship with the wires inside, Dr. Kellum said, "There is a pattern, and when I have discovered it, we will all go home."

Dr. Kellum's followers erupted in cheers, bringing Ralph out of his trance.

"Your toy ship map isn't right, Walter," Ralph said. "You want I should fix it for you?"

Dr. Kellum smiled at Ralph, the happy wrinkles around his eyes magnified by his thick glasses.

"Thanks, Ralph, but we've been working on it a long time. A very long time."

"Sure, sure. I understand. You think I might break it or something, but I won't. I could fix it for you in a jiff. See where that yellow striped one goes down in there? Well it should go up one before it goes down. And where you got that little cap thing on the orange wire—that means dead end, right?—it doesn't end there."

Ralph started to reach into the model, but Dr. Kellum grabbed his hand.

"Please don't touch it," Dr. Kellum said.

"I could fix it," Ralph said.

"No," Dr. Kellum said sternly. Then, more kindly, "What are you wearing around your waist?"

"It's how we're gonna get home again," Ralph said. "The light on mine's busted, but I don't mind. I like it anyways."

Dr. Kellum came around the table, looking first at Ralph's hip unit, and then at Jett's.

"How is it supposed to work?" he asked.

Jett hesitated, and was prodded with a spear. His underresponsive nervous system registered no pain. He felt no fear, just the the tension of readiness. He knew he could kill the man behind him, and three or four others before they got him. It wasn't the time, though.

"It generates a magnetic field that allows us to get back out," Jett said.

"It's too small," Dr. Kellum said. "It won't work."

"Miniaturization has paralleled every technological advance since you've been in here," Jett said.

"You can't miniaturize the laws of physics," Dr. Kellum said.

Dr. Kellum removed his glasses and wiped them with a handkerchief from his pocket, then he put them on and said, "Let's go find out. We'll go to the barrier and you can test it."

Jett realized that if they took him to the field surrounding Pot of Gold, he could escape and notify Woolman about the Nimitz—still, he hadn't seen the Nimitz with his own eyes yet, and he couldn't trust Dr. Kellum's word. The Professor was saner than the men and women surrounding him, but Jett was sure he was holding something back.

"I don't need to try it," Jett said. "I know it works."

"You mean you won't try it until your business here is finished. Until we're all dead?"

Jett didn't protest. Dr. Kellum couldn't be reasoned with, and his followers were as fanatic as the Crazies.

"I want you to turn on your little device and put your hand into the barrier. You have to know they sent you in here with no way out."

Jett saw no point in arguing. They had his gun, and the rest of his team was surrounded. He would go with Dr. Kellum and watch for his opportunity. The Norfolk's crew had little of their military training left, and somewhere, sometime, they would get careless.

"I came down here with my hands up as a sign of good faith," Jett said. "I gave up my gun to show you could trust me. Now show me that I can trust you. Give me my gun back."

"If I did, I would be dead in the next instant," Dr. Kellum said.

"I don't need a gun to kill," Jett said.

Dr. Kellum's eyebrows rose in alarm, and the guards with machetes stepped closer. If Jett had trained them, they would have taken those positions when Dr. Kellum had first come around the table.

"I'll make this deal with you, Mr. Jett. Come with me to the barrier, and if your device works, I will give you your gun and you and your friends are free to go."

"And if it doesn't work?"

"Then I'll give you your gun and you and your friends are in the same boat we are—no pun intended," Dr. Kellum said, smiling at his own joke.

Jett nodded agreement, and Dr. Kellum shouted orders, sending a small party of armed men on ahead. He led Jett to the door. Jett paused when Ralph didn't follow. Ralph was again mesmerized by the model.

"I could fix their toy ship, Nate. Really I could."

Jett handed him another pack of gum to shut him up, then pulled him away from the miniature ship. A small group of guards fell in behind. Two of these men had their heads shaved and their scalps tattooed—one with an American flag and the other with a battleship. They both carried spears, and Jett felt as if he was on safari, being accompanied into hostile territory by friendly natives. Except he wasn't sure these natives were sane.

INTEGRATION

The dreamers returned to the lab at ten P.M. While Wes could simulate sleep by reducing cerebral activity, he thought that natural dreaming would maximize dream sharing, and without Margi they needed the extra sensitivity. Elizabeth and Anita arrived first, both so sleepy that they could hardly keep their eyes open. Sadly, even when they were allowed to sleep, the ship dream would deny them rest. They would wake tomorrow a little worse off than today.

Wanda came last, a cigarette in her mouth. Familiar with the routine, Wanda walked straight to her cot, sat on the side and waited for her helmet. When she sat, Len left the lab. Wanda waited on her cot for Len. When he didn't return immediately, Monica took his place, fitting her with her helmet. Then Len was back, a string of garlic around his neck, another in his hand. As he entered he took a bite, chewing noisily.

Len walked directly to where Monica was working with Wanda. A Lucky Strike hung from Wanda's lips, the smoke curling around her head pushed into swirls by the air-conditioning currents. Stopping face to face, Len leaned forward, and with a lot of breath, said, "How are you today, Wanda?"

"Is that garlic?" Monica asked.

"Yes it is," Len said with more breath than necessary, his face still inches from Wanda's.

"Expecting vampires?" Shamita said from her console.

"I'm teaching Wanda a lesson," Len said, again breathing into Wanda's face. He took another bite of garlic. Wanda remained impassive, a bit of ash falling from the end of her cigarette.

"Len, it stinks," Monica said. "Take that putrid necklace off and stop chewing that stuff."

Len ignored Monica and leaned even closer to Wanda's face, until their noses almost touched.

"I'll make a deal, Wanda. If you stop smoking in here, I'll get rid of the garlic."

Now Wanda sucked in a lung full of smoke and blew it into Len's face.

"Ha!" Wanda said. "My mother's maiden name was Petrocelli. I was weaned on garlic."

Then she took the clove from his hand and took a bite, chewing it.

"You think cigarettes smell bad—just wait till you smell it mixed with garlic. Ha!"

Len's face fell and he looked ill. Without a word he turned and stomped from the room, returning a minute later without his garlic. Glum, he sat at his console, checking to see that all the leads to the dreamers were functional.

"You won the battle, Wanda, but the war isn't over," Len said as he worked.

"Do your worst, Lenny," Wanda said. "There ain't nothing you can do to make me stop."

"I love a challenge," Len said.

"Everything's a challenge to you," Wanda said, blowing smoke out through her nose.

Monica waved her hand through the smoke, then went to stand at Wes's console, waiting for the integration.

Wes held Elizabeth's hand as she settled down on the cot, and pulled a sheet over her. There were bags under her eyes and wrinkles he'd never noticed around her mouth. Something had happened to her at the end of the first integration—something physical and not at all dreamlike. She was a receiver now, and it had cost her dearly.

"You'll have to let go of my hand if you want me to go to sleep," Elizabeth said. "I'm not used to having someone hold me at night."

"I'd like to change that," Wes said.

She smiled, then closed her eyes, nestling her head into the pillow. They turned down the lights and waited. Wanda went under first, making snorting noises and jerking as she fell asleep. The snorting and myoclonia were both normal for her sleep routine. A few minutes later Len whispered that Anita was showing sleep spindles and was well on her way to dreamland.

"They're all asleep," Len said finally, "but they're at three different stages. Wanda will get to the dream first."

"Let Anita set the pattern; she dominates anyway," Wes said. "Set the parameters for Elizabeth like Margi's—that should approximate the quality of reception we had before."

"How conscious do you want Elizabeth?" Shamita asked.

"Just supraliminal. The more dreamlike, the less it will drain her."

Minutes passed as the brain wave patterns of the dreamers were coordinated and then slowly synchronized, Anita's brain setting the master pattern. Then, with a microimpulse here and a blocking impulse there, the electrical activities of the other brains were coordinated into synchronous patterns.

"We're almost there," Shamita said.

Wes watched the perfectly synchronized brain waves on his screen and knew that in a few seconds Elizabeth and Anita would once again find themselves on the ship.

SOURCE

Elizabeth found herself sitting with her back to a bulkhead on the dream ship. The detail was rich and clear again. There were people wearing silver suits like the one Ralph had worn, but no Ralph. One was a woman who leaned against another bulkhead. She had short brown hair and her face was hard, determined. With a start, Elizabeth recognized her from Dr. Birnbaum's sketch—the woman who had helped kidnap Ralph. Another man squatted a short distance down a corridor. He was tall and thin, with nearly white-blond hair. She looked the other way and saw the scarred man squatting near the top of a steep staircase. They were at a corridor junction, with stairs leading to the decks above and below. Everything around them was steel, painted navy gray. Then she remembered Anita. The little girl was next to her, holding her knees to her chest. She was staring at the scarred man, terrified.

"Don't be afraid, Anita," Elizabeth said.

"I can't help it. He's a monster."

"What did you say, Dawson?" the woman asked.

Elizabeth realized that the people in silver suits could hear her, but not Anita.

"Where's Ralph?" Elizabeth said.

The woman stared at her, puzzled.

"You know where he is, Dawson."

The blond man and the scarred man turned to listen. The woman had called her "Dawson." Elizabeth held out her arms and looked at them. She was wearing the blue shirt with the cut-off sleeves. Her arms were the muscular ones of the man she had seen in the mirror. He was channeling her, letting her see through his eyes.

"Why are they calling you Dawson?" Anita asked.

"They don't see me the way you do," Elizabeth replied.

The people in silver suits stared as she appeared to talk to herself.

"I'm not who you think I am," Elizabeth said.

The others exchanged looks, the woman stepping closer, pointing one of their strange pistols.

"What's the game, Dawson?"

"It's not a game. My name is Elizabeth Foxworth and I'm a social worker. Right now I'm lying on a cot at the University of Oregon."

"Elizabeth, this is Wes," a voice broke in. *"Your vitals are elevating— Anita's too."*

"Don't pull me out, Wes. Give me some time."

The woman aimed the gun between Dawson's eyes.

"Who are you talking to now? Who's Wes?"

"He's schizophrenic," the scarred man said.

Elizabeth spoke quickly. "Dr. Wes Martin is here with me in the laboratory. He's the one that created the machine that allows us to link minds together. We found people who have been dreaming of this ship and we think someone on the ship is telepathically transmitting from here. Probably this man," Elizabeth said, pointing at herself. "Using Doctor Martin's equipment, we linked the minds of people dreaming of this ship in order to make them a better receiver. When we did, we linked with this man's body, and now I'm seeing through his eyes."

"He's talking nonsense," the scarred man said.

The blond man watched the exchange from his position, but his only contribution was a wink whenever Elizabeth caught his eye. The woman stared, her jaw set, her finger tensed on the trigger.

"I say we kill him and break out of here," the scarred man said. "We don't need him to get the job done."

"We wait for Jett," the woman said.

"Jett's lost his nerve," the scarred man said. "Look at the way he protects that moron."

"Is she going to shoot you, Elizabeth?" Anita said.

"No. It's only a dream, Anita."

"Who's Anita?" the woman asked.

Elizabeth started to explain, but was cut off.

"Just shut up and sit there, Dawson, or Elizabeth, or whoever you want to be."

Then the woman in the silver suit turned away.

"Elizabeth, what's going on?" Wes asked.

"I can't speak for a while, Wes. You'll have to trust me."

The woman whipped around, the gun back in Elizabeth's face.

"Not another word," she hissed.

The gun frightened Elizabeth even though her left brain told her it was "just a dream." Her right brain wasn't as easily convinced, and insisted on imagining the horrible consequences of a bullet in her face. Then, in her mind, she saw the black woman with the afro haircut shot dead, and the others peppered with bullet holes, blood trickling from their wounds. There was an image of a burning man, too—a black man, his flesh turned crisp and peeling away from the meat underneath; then the flames repeated the process and burned away another layer.

All these thoughts ran through her mind, and yet they were alien to her. Real yes, but not memories of events she'd seen. These were Dawson's memories, like the dream of fighting a fire on a ship, shells exploding all around. She was sharing the mind of the man wearing the blue shirt with the cut-off sleeves, and she was feeling his fears.

She tried to displace the gory images that made her recoil from the gun, tried to regain control, but her own emotions were elusive, too insubstantial to be grasped. Then the strongest emotion yet poured in, pushing out everything else. She didn't understand what it meant, but she knew something—or someone—was coming, and it terrified the man whose body she shared. A warning bubbled up from the inaccessible depths of their shared mind, and she couldn't help but speak.

"They're coming," she said out loud, voice trembling.

"Who?" the woman, Anita, and Wes asked at the same time.

Elizabeth dug deep into her mind, finding no clear image. Then she relaxed, letting the Dawson mind direct the flow. Out of the depths came more images of death and burned flesh, of bright lights and bloody mayhem. Then an answer formed, but it was meaningless to her.

"The Crazies," she said through the man's lips. "The Crazies are coming."

The thick tissue that was most of the scarred man's face was capable of only slight emotional expression, but his eyes clearly showed a mix of hate and fear.

The silver suits came alert now, the blond man peeking around the corner and down the corridor. Then there was the sound of thumping above them, and the sound of a hatch being slammed closed.

"Give me my gun," the scarred man said to Compton.

"No, Evans," the woman said.

Elizabeth began putting names to the faces of the people in the silver suits. Evans was the scarred man with the angry eyes. Then Elizabeth heard running feet in the corridor above, followed by the screech of metal on metal. Someone screamed above them, and the corridor at the scarred man's end lit up as if a strobe light had flashed. Elizabeth and the Dawson part of their unified consciousness both cringed, tensing their shared body, getting ready for fight or flight.

"Give me my gun!" Evans ordered again.

The sound of running came closer, and then a half dozen men and one woman ran down the corridor in front of the blond man. Most wore sailor uniforms, but a few of the men and the woman were dressed in street clothes, adding to the surreal feeling of the ship.

"Compton, the Crazies will be here any second and you're going to need me," Evans said.

"Use your power," the woman said.

Elizabeth noted the woman's name, and also her reference to the scarred man's "power."

"We'll need both when they get here, and you know it takes time to hook the gun up," said Evans.

Compton waffled only a second.

"Get his gun," Compton said, backing up toward the blond man.

The blond man dug in Compton's pack, then tossed the gun to Evans, who set about reattaching the weapon to the pressure hose. Elizabeth noticed that Compton kept her gun trained on Evans while he attached the hose to his gun.

Now there was more thumping and banging, closer than before. It was coming from Evans's side, and Compton moved forward to reinforce his position. The blond man kept his position, protecting them from a rear attack. Evans had his gun reattached now, and was checking the pressure gauges and his load. Elizabeth kept down on the floor, arm around Anita, whispering comforting words to her.

"What's going on, Dawson?" Compton asked.

"I know it's hard to understand, but I'm not Dawson right now, I'm

Elizabeth. At least some of me is. A little girl named Anita is here with me, too."

Compton stared icily, her gun swinging toward Elizabeth. She acted as if she thought Elizabeth was lying, but it was Dawson's body Compton saw and Dawson's voice she heard. The idea that Dawson was channeling for a social worker in Oregon would be hard for any rational person to accept.

"I need to get a message to Ralph," Elizabeth said through Dawson's body.

"I need to know what is happening," Compton repeated, her words cold steel.

Elizabeth knew that Compton was desperate. They expected an attack at any moment, and Dawson had been some sort of guide for them. When Elizabeth took control of Dawson's mind, she turned Dawson from an asset to a liability. They had no reason to keep him alive now, and Elizabeth expected a bullet at any second. She feared being in Dawson's body when it died, not knowing what that would do to her own mind and that of the other dreamers, but she also feared for the Dawson part of her. It wasn't his fault that they had taken control of his body, and she feared for him as she would for a friend. Then, from that deeper part of her mind where Dawson's consciousness dwelled, a new thought came to her.

"The Crazies know the outsiders are here," Elizabeth said suddenly. "They're coming to kill them."

As the words came out of her mouth, Elizabeth realized that she was with the outsiders.

"You're scaring me, Elizabeth," Anita said.

"Don't worry, Anita, I won't let anyone harm you," Elizabeth said. "It's just a dream, remember."

"Elizabeth, can you talk yet? Your vital signs are roller-coasting up and down," Wes said.

"I'll explain when I can, Wes," Elizabeth said, knowing that Compton and the others were preparing for attack and ignoring her.

They heard more running, and then men with spears and crossbows crossed in front of Evans, hurrying somewhere. Suddenly, the men were knocked down like bowling pins, tumbling back down the corridor and out of sight. Evans turned and put up one finger, the others tensing, getting ready. Suddenly a fireball streaked past, and they all turned their heads reflexively to protect their vision. Anita whimpered, and Elizabeth hugged her close, comforting her as best she could, her own voice trembling. Then there was an earsplitting "whump" from down the corridor, followed by a loud sizzling.

"Time to move," Compton whispered to Evans. "I'll take Dawson down the stairs first, then Peters, then you."

Evans stared back defiantly, and Elizabeth feared he would refuse. Evans wanted to fight.

The corridor was quiet now. Then Elizabeth heard footsteps on the metal deck. Compton pulled Elizabeth to her feet, signalling with quick motions to Peters, who nodded, then turned back to cover his end of the corridor. Now Compton leaned close to Elizabeth's ear, whispering.

"If you want to live, keep your mouth shut and come with me."

Compton brought her gun up to Elizabeth's eye level, and Elizabeth nodded. Then Compton pushed her toward the stairs.

"Go down, and if any of your people start shooting, you'll be the first to die," Compton whispered.

Elizabeth started down, trying to climb softly, but the metal stairs rang with every step. The deck below looked like the one above, nothing but intersecting corridors. There were hatches down the corridor, but none were open. Far down the corridor she saw a leg and arm protruding from the wall, but thankfully no head. She found that Anita was with her when she reached the bottom, and she comforted her as best she could, the little girl staring down the corridor at the body parts sticking through the wall.

Compton came down right behind her, gun pointed at Elizabeth, her eyes sweeping right and left. As soon as Compton was down she snapped her fingers and Peters followed. With a hand motion she sent Peters forward to check out the next corridor junction. He approached cautiously, finding nothing and signalling Compton. Compton snapped her fingers again, the signal for Evans to climb down. When Evans didn't appear, she snapped her fingers again, but there was no Evans. Then she pointed her gun at Elizabeth.

"If you move I'll kill you," Compton whispered.

Anita was invisible to everyone but Elizabeth, so only Elizabeth saw her recoil at the threat. As Compton climbed back up to the deck above, Elizabeth knelt and whispered to Anita.

"It's just a dream, Anita. She won't really hurt me."

"She's so mean," Anita said.

"She's scared, just like you and me. As soon as we find Ralph we'll go home, I promise."

"I don't know how much longer I can stand this, Elizabeth," Wes said.

"Wes is watching over us," Elizabeth said to Anita. "He just talked to me."

Anita nodded, and Elizabeth stood again, watching Compton, who had reached the top and was whispering to Evans. Elizabeth couldn't hear what she said, but suddenly all hell broke loose.

The first thing Elizabeth heard was a sputtering sound, then screams and shouting. Suddenly the opening at the top of the stairs lit up and Compton ducked, sliding recklessly down the stairs. A fireball flashed across the opening, followed by a loud thump and sizzling sounds. Now there was the clang of metal on metal, a hundred tiny metal sounds as if it was hailing nails.

"Where's Evans?" Peters shouted loud enough to be heard over the din above.

Suddenly sounds of the metal hail could be heard directly above them, moving toward the stairs.

"Get back," Compton shouted, and shoved Elizabeth against a bulkhead, holding her there with an arm across her chest.

Then the hail reached the staircase and a dozen small objects shot through the opening, ricocheting off the stairs and walls. One hit the wall next to Elizabeth with a metallic thunk, dropping to her feet. It was a jagged piece of metal.

"Let's go," Compton shouted, pulling Elizabeth from the wall and shoving her toward Peters, who still guarded the corridor.

"Evans?" Peters said when they reached the junction.

"He's decided to do a Custer on us," Compton said.

Peters shrugged, and said, "Then it's just you and me and the Dawson-Elizabeth-Anita thing."

"And Jett," Compton said.

"If you say so," Peters said with a wink.

The deck above them, where Evans fought, now glowed as if the noonday sun was shining through. Heat was flowing down through the opening, the temperature quickly rising ten degrees.

"Let's go," Compton said.

Peters took Elizabeth now, pushing her into the corridor.

"Which way?" Peters asked.

"I don't know," Elizabeth said.

There was a loud thump, and then clanging from above. Now Compton pointed her gun at Elizabeth's face.

"We don't have time for this, Dawson. Which way?"

"I'm not Dawson," Elizabeth said. "I'm Elizabeth. I tried to explain."

"Fine, Elizabeth," Compton said. "Take us to wherever Jett is, or you're no use to us."

"Let's just go, Elizabeth," Anita said. "I don't like it here."

Elizabeth closed her eyes, trying to let the Dawson part of her take more control. A vague sense of direction came to her.

"I think they went to the right," Elizabeth said.

"That's better," Peters said, shoving her down the corridor.

Compton followed, watching their backs to make sure they weren't pursued. It was unlikely. The battle in the corridor above continued to rage.

BARRIER

Dr. Kellum led them through engine rooms, boiler rooms, the hangar deck, and then up through crew berths, a mess, and the fire control room; then he repeated the trek with a slight variation. Jett understood that he was leading them through a pattern that was the equivalent of twisting a combination lock in the right order. The corridors were rarely wide enough to walk two abreast, and most of the trek was spent going single file. Sailors carrying crossbows and spears led, followed by Kellum, Jett, and Ralph, and then more guards behind. Without being obvious, Jett studied the weapons of Kellum's soldiers. Most were cutting or stabbing weapons: short knives, machetes, and spears. The long-range weapons were crossbows. They were all homemade, of course; the Navy didn't issue medieval weapons.

Crossbows had changed little in design since their invention, the only modern improvements being in materials. The type of weapon carried by Kellum's men was basically a carved wooden stock shaped like a rifle stock and designed to fit against the shoulder. The crosspiece was a bar of metal like one leaf of a car spring, and it varied in length and thickness. Jett estimated that the thickest might draw eighty pounds. The crossbows had metal stirrups mounted at the ends of the stocks. To draw the crossbow, the archer would have to step in the stirrup, then use both arms to pull the bowstring back and set it in the notch. There was a simple trigger mechanism, with a small leaf spring that kept the notch up until the trigger was pulled, the notch dropping down into the stock and releasing the bowstring. The bolt the weapon fired rested in a groove carved into the top of the stock and projected through a hole in the metal crosspiece. Kellum's men carried their crossbows cocked, a quiver of bolts on their belts. The bolts were fifteen inches long with fletching only on two sides. The bolts were tipped with broadhead arrow points, designed to penetrate flesh and do as much damage as possible—even more as the arrow was removed. Based on what Jett could see of the weapons, he judged that they would be effective for only forty or fifty yards, which was more than enough in the confines of the Norfolk. He knew there were more powerful versions of crossbows, called "arbalests," that required pulley systems to cock them. These were slow and cumbersome, but had a range of two hundred yards or more. The absence of arbalests, and the quick-fire long bow, was probably due to the narrow confines of the corridors and compartments of the Norfolk. Long-range weapons weren't needed.

After ten minutes of walking up and down in the ship, Jett turned to Ralph, who trudged along with his own peculiar posture, seemingly fascinated by every hatch they passed.

"This is very confusing, Ralph," Jett said. "I don't know if I could find my way back."

"That's okay, Nate, I could show you," Ralph said.

"Are you sure, Ralph?"

"Sure, sure, Nate. It's easy. You just go down there and turn right, and then down there and then through all those big machine rooms, and then up there and through that room with the swinging beds and then the one with the kitchen in it, and then back down to the machinery room. Course, I think it would be shorter if you went that way, and up them stairs and through the room with the big wheel that steers the ship, and then down to the rooms with the big machinery, and then—"

"Fine, Ralph, as long as you know," Jett tried to interrupt, but Ralph continued.

"—and then left again, but don't go right."

"Why not right?" Jett said before Ralph could get started again.

"It goes outside," Ralph said.

"You mean on deck?"

"I dunno. It's not on Doctor Kellum's map, but it's just like the other doors. He should have a blue striped wire there and a cap thing, but he doesn't. I could fix it, Nate. Really I could, and I wouldn't break it or nothing."

Jett had seen Ralph's special resistance to psychokinetic force in action with Evans. Now he was was coming to see that Ralph's sense of direction was just as special. He suspected that Ralph really did know of an exit off the ship yet to be discovered, and more importantly, yet to be used by a Special and therefore not blocked by Dr. Lee at Rainbow. Jett checked behind him, making sure the guards were a few steps behind.

"Let's not tell anyone about that door, Ralph," Jett said.

"How come, Nate?" Ralph said too loudly. Ralph seldom tried to whisper, and when he did it came out louder than most people's normal voices.

"We don't want them getting their hopes up. Not until we're sure there's a door there."

"Okee-dokee, I guess, Nate. I won't tell no one if you don't want me to."

"Thanks, Ralph. It's for the best. Need some more gum?"

Ralph did, of course, and Nate fished a pack of spearmint gum out of his silver suit.

Dr. Kellum led them through what should have been an interior hatch, but when they stepped through the dark opening they found themselves outside on the deck of the ship between two of the gun turrets. It was another level of time, as Kellum had explained it, but in this moment there was a cargo net slung over the side. Dr. Kellum climbed over the side, the flab around his waist drooping as he awkwardly stepped over the rail onto the net. Two sailors climbed over on either side of him, arms hovering, ready to catch the ungainly professor.

Ralph followed Jett's example, and straddled the rail, carefully selecting a foothold before swinging over and starting down. Jett watched Ralph closely.

"You don't have to worry about me, Nate," Ralph said. "I had a jungle gym in my backyard when I was little. My daddy built it for me. It looked like a pirate ship and there was rope just like this."

"Don't talk, Ralph. Watch what you're doing."

"I can talk and climb," Ralph said. "I can talk and do anything."

"I know you can, Ralph, but I can't," Jett lied.

"Well okee-dokee then, Nate. I'll zip it closed."

Ralph stopped his climb, looped an arm through the ropes, and went through the motions of locking his lips with a key and then dropping the key in a pocket. After that they climbed in silence, Jett watching Ralph's awkward moves, ready to help. Dr. Kellum waited at the bottom with his bodyguards. Four more sailors stepped off the net behind them, and more of Kellum's clan waited on the deck. Kellum led them across the desert to where it ended in an opaque wall, then turned to Jett.

"There is no way out for us, and if I'm right, no way out for you either."

Kellum motioned for Jett to step to the barrier and try his escape device. Jett hesitated, not sure he wanted to know.

"It might only work once," Jett said. "It has a limited power source."

"You don't have to pass through the whole barrier. Just put your hand through. That should leave you plenty of energy in reserve."

Jett slid the switch to the "on" position and saw the ready light flash, just as Dr. Lee had explained would happen. He waited a minute as he had been instructed, letting the unit charge and generate a neutralizing field. Just as Dr. Lee had described, the light became steady, telling him that the field had reached sufficient strength. Dr. Kellum stood opposite him, and Ralph next to him, peeling the foil off another piece of gum. The sailors were standing around him in a semicircle, watching hopefully. He realized that they wanted the hip unit to work, since it would mean another way out of Pot of Gold.

Jett reached out slowly with his hand until it was inches from the nothingness that was the barrier.

"Do you know what you're about to touch?" Kellum said.

Jett paused, hand outstretched.

"Think of it as a sheet of pure electricity."

Jett hesitated. He wasn't afraid, but he was tense, like when he was tracking an escaped Special.

Jett extended one finger and brought it slowly toward what Kellum called the amniotic field. The surface didn't reflect, and he couldn't focus on it to judge depth; he found that he had misjudged the distance and his reach was short. Now he leaned forward, misjudging it again, this time touching it with his finger before he expected. As soon as he did, his body became a conductor, and the electricity flowed through him. It scrambled his efferent nervous system and disrupted the messages that controlled his muscles, creating spasms. He jerked and writhed uncontrollably. Then the disruption reached the hypercomplex neural net that was his brain, overriding every neural impulse, firing every neuron. Awareness of the world went first, and then his sense of self. He had no complex thoughts now, only sensorimotor concepts of spasms and pain. Then he had no consciousness at all.

CONCERN

How are her signs, Len?" Wes said.

"Elevated. Whatever she's dreaming is a real horror show."

"What about Anita and Wanda?"

"Anita is as bad as Elizabeth. Wanda barely registers a pulse. Either she has the nerves of a lion tamer or she's not in the dream."

Wes could only imagine what was going on in the minds of the three people stretched out on the cots in his lab, their faces passive. The unified brain wave pattern on his screen looked like so many others he had seen; they were uninterpretable except by Elizabeth, Wanda, and Anita, whose common experiences gave meaning to the electrical storms going on in their brains.

Wes was at his station, watching his monitor, while Len and Shamita studied theirs. Monica was there too, walking from station to station, looking at the displays, occasionally walking past the cots to study the faces of the dreamers.

Typing a few commands, Wes called up the physiological readings from Len's computer. As Len had said, Anita and Elizabeth showed signs of extreme stress, while Wanda appeared to be sleeping normally. Shamita had Len's displays on her monitor too, and chewed her lip anxiously.

Shamita always dressed in bright colors—today she was wearing a bright pink-and-yellow top that looked like something left over from the tie-dyed days of the sixties. Despite her cheery clothes, Shamita was a serious person with a dry sense of humor. She was all business in the lab, unlike Len, who found humor in anything and everything.

"Let's bring them out," Shamita said. "It's too risky."

Having been reluctant to perform another integration in the first place, Wes was ready to pull the plug on the experiment.

"Let's not be too hasty," Monica said.

Monica had been standing by the dreamers, listening to the exchange, watching intently.

"It's not hasty," Shamita argued. "Look at the pulse and blood pressure readings."

"I'm concerned about them, too," Monica said, forehead furrowed with worry wrinkles. "But what's best for them in this case is to let them finish what we sent them to do. Unless we can find the source of this dream and stop it, we can't save Anita or Elizabeth. Give them a chance to tell Ralph to come home. It may be their only hope."

Wes waffled, torn in two directions. Elizabeth was more than a part of his life; she was the person who infused him with life. And he loved her. There was Anita to consider, too. Wes was uncomfortable with children, but he liked Anita, and the hope he saw in her mother's eyes each time they met pained him. Anita's mother was desperate because time was running out for her daughter.

Wes still used "dream" to describe what Elizabeth and Anita were experiencing, but it was much more than a dream and more dangerous than a nightmare. Elizabeth's cardiac distress had proved that. Somehow they were connected with something real in another place. Knowing that it was more than just a dream made him responsible for what happened to his dreamers. Still, in the final analysis, he had to choose between watching them die slowly or risking shortening their lives to save them. Then he pictured Margi's bloated body floating in her own waste. He didn't want the woman he loved to end that way.

Wes walked to Elizabeth and sat so that his lips were near her ear.

"Can you talk now?"

"Quickly," Elizabeth said.

"Elizabeth, I can't let this go on much longer."

"Don't bring me out," Elizabeth said.

"What is happening?"

"I'm with the people in silver suits."

"Like the one Ralph was wearing?"

"Yes."

"Are they listening to you?"

"Yes."

"I understand. I'll give you a few more minutes, but you and Anita are weak. If you don't find Ralph soon, we'll have to find another way."

"I understand," Elizabeth said.

Wes returned to his console and said to the others, "We'll maintain the integration for now."

Shamita shook her head in disagreement. Monica put her hand on Wes's shoulder and gave him a slight squeeze.

"You're doing the right thing," she said.

He wished he was as confident as she. He was filled with doubt, and a part of him sensed something new about Monica—he didn't trust her. She had been too quick to insist that they keep the integration going. Anita's well-being should have been her first concern, and it wasn't clear that continuing the integration was the best thing to do. Why was Monica so certain?

Taking Elizabeth's hand, he watched her eyelids, seeing the movement beneath them that indicated dreaming. He wished he could be there with her.

BATTLE

Jett opened his eyes to see Ralph's face, his jaws chewing away at a fat wad of gum, his wet fleshy lips slightly parted. His breath smelled of spearmint.

"He's not twitching anymore. That's good, isn't it, Walter? It's not good to twitch like that, is it?"

Jett was on his back looking straight up. He could see the opaque field that was Pot of Gold's sky. There were heads leaning over him, Ralph's the closest, but also Dr. Kellum's and some of his men, including the bald man with the battleship tattoo. Jett's heart was pounding in his chest and his body tingled from head to toe. His arms responded sluggishly, as if he was pushing through water.

"Look Doctor Kellum, he's moving his arms, too!" Ralph said. "That's good, isn't it?"

Then Ralph pushed his face closer so that his nose nearly touched Jett's. "Do you feel like talking, Nate?"

"Get out of my face," Jett said in slow, crisp speech.

"I think he's getting better," Ralph said.

Hands gripped his shoulders and he was helped into a sitting position. Dr. Kellum was cleaning his glasses again. He smiled smugly.

"I told you it wouldn't work. They sent you on a suicide mission. You were expendable, just like us."

Jett struggled to his feet with the help of Ralph and a sailor. He unbuckled his belt and dropped the useless hip unit on the ground.

"You might as well take yours off too, Ralph," Jett said.

"Is it okay if I keep mine, Nate? I think it's neat and I don't mind if the little light doesn't work."

"You can have mine if you want it, Ralph. My light works."

Like a kid on Christmas morning, Ralph lit up, his lips spreading wide in a huge grin.

"Thanks, Nate. Thanks a lot."

While Ralph busied himself switching hip units, Jett faced his new situation. He wasn't suicidal and he never accepted a mission where he didn't have a plan to extricate himself and his team. Lee and Woolman had lied to him about an escape route so that he would take the mission. Now he had few options. He had signalled Rainbow that the Nimitz wasn't in Pot of Gold, but now realized that the Nimitz might actually be inside. Woolman had been clear that retrieving the Nimitz was top priority, so if he could find the ship, he and his team might be able to return with it—if he could tell Woolman it was inside. Except the other signal laser had been destroyed when Thompson was burned. His only other hope was Ralph, who stood like a bipedal cow, chewing his wad of gum.

"Still want to destroy the field generators?" Dr. Kellum asked.

"I've got something else on my mind right now," Jett said honestly.

Survival was on his mind; survival, and finding a way out so he could return to Rainbow and kill Lee and Woolman.

"If you destroy the generators, we'll all die," Kellum said.

"Not as long as you have the Nimitz," Jett said. "You got it inside, didn't you? Why not just get on board and ride it back out again?"

"I only wish it was that easy," Kellum said. "First of all, I don't have the Nimitz—McNab and his Crazies have it. Second, riding it out, as you put it, would be a sure way to die. Your aircraft carrier came here in a very different way than the Norfolk. With the Norfolk, we had the magnetic pulse generators installed in one of the boiler rooms. When we began the experiment we first synchronized the pulses to create resonance, and then brought the power up slowly. The field gradually formed around the hull of the Nimitz and created two poles—positive at the bow, negative at the stern. As I told you before, the electric charge that was generated was so great, I nearly terminated the experiment, but the field expanded out around the ship before it reached full strength. None of us on the Norfolk ever felt the field's full power."

"Like I did when I touched it?" Jett said.

"It hurt, didn't it, Wes," Ralph said. "I bet it hurt lots."

Kellum smiled at Ralph, warming up to him like everyone did.

"You just got a taste of it," Kellum said. "I estimate we were in here two decades before I came up with a way to get out. I knew people occasionally found their way in and out. That's why we were mapping the ship, trying to understand the pattern to the twists in time and space. Finally the significance of those holes in the field hit me. You see, the field that surrounds us is really electromagnetic radiation, which propagates in waves. The waves interweave to create the field that you touched. I reasoned that if you stretched the field, the holes in the fabric of the field would get larger—so large, in fact, we could all escape. Here's how I explained it to my people."

Pulling up one of his pant legs, Kellum put his fingers inside his argyle sock and stretched it until his fingers could be seen through the fabric.

"See, the holes get big enough that you can see through them."

"That's neat," Ralph said.

"Do you create the holes in the amniotic field by changing the settings on the generators you built?" Jett wanted to know.

"No, they don't respond to the controls. Once the field was created and we found ourselves here, the generators began drawing their power from the fabric of this universe. My idea was to build a second set of generators to make the field asymmetrical and to stretch the field, making more and bigger holes."

"McNab let you do this?" Jett asked, remembering what Dawson had said about the Crazies protecting the generators.

"Not right away, not for a decade in your time. McNab's cult is based on the belief that we are in purgatory, awaiting service to God. I met with McNab a dozen times before I convinced him to agree to let me build the new generators. One day he claimed he got a revelation from God and gave me permission.

"We had to strip the copper wiring out of the Norfolk on four time levels to get enough for the new generators, and even then they're half the size of the originals. I wanted something we could control, something like what we had on the Eldridge. Construction of the generators took years in our time. Then it took a long series of trials before I got the frequency right so the generator pulses would resonate. But I did it, and it worked, and we would be out of here now except for one mistake.

"We built the new generators in the desert just off the stern of the Norfolk. When we turned them on we found we could slowly bring them up to

power and reshape the existing field. We started by creating a second negative pole that pushed against the existing pole at the stern of the Norfolk.
This compressed the existing field, creating a bulge. Then I decided to
reverse polarity and try stretching the field. When I did, the fields were
now in series—positive pole to negative pole—and the combined fields
elongated the field. When it stretched, the field lost some of its opacity and
we could see a ship. It was an aircraft carrier, and the biggest ship I had ever
seen. It was passing through the same latitude where we had conducted
our original experiment. Then we discovered the ship was being pulled
into the field just like a magnet attracts a nail. But either the field was too
weak, or the ship did not pass close enough."

Jett realized that the ship must have been the John F. Kennedy, the first
carrier to encounter the effect.

"It was after that experiment that McNab reneged on our agreement. Two
of my assistants had been corrupted by McNab, and they took control of the
new generators. Next thing we heard, McNab was fishing for a warship to pull
in. He wanted one with uranium bombs—what do you call them?"

"Thermonuclear weapons, hydrogen bombs, fusion bombs, they have
many names," Jett said.

"That's what McNab was after, and now he has them."

"Then he intends to escape using the Nimitz? Can it be sent back the
way it came?"

"It can go back. The only thing holding it here are the new generators.
But no one can go back with it. As I said, the Nimitz was pulled in through
the field. Most of the crew of the Nimitz were either killed when it entered
or frozen in time when the ship shifted out of normal time/space. We've
heard that some of the crew below decks survived, insulated from the
intense shock of the field. By now McNab will have converted them or
killed them, but no one would survive a trip the other way."

"Even if they insulated themselves?" Jett asked.

"It won't matter. The field will ignite the explosives, oil, and aviation
fuel on the carrier, and any other combustible. Coming this way it doesn't
matter, since the field dampens rapid chemical reactions, but going back to
the world, the ship would become an inferno."

"So what is McNab planning?" Jett said.

"I don't know," Kellum replied.

"I've been outside many times, and I didn't see the Nimitz," Jett said.

"The generators exist only on level one, and the Nimitz is on that level.
I told you, the field is generated around Norfolk, not the Nimitz. The carrier just serves as a pole to elongate the field."

Even though he had been betrayed by Woolman, Jett found that he couldn't abandon his mission. His high *A*-scores—for authoritarianism—meant that he followed the chain of command, even if that chain had decided he was expendable. Besides, McNab was the craziest of the Crazies, and now he had access to nuclear weapons. If he could get back to the world, he would be ruthless.

Shouting came from the deck of the ship, and one of the sailors called over the rail.

"Margolin's sensed the Crazies! They're after the newcomers."

"Hurry to the ship," Dr. Kellum said, starting to jog. "We can't get caught down here."

He didn't have to explain. If the Crazies took control of the deck, they would be caught on the open ground of the desert, their back to a sheet of electricity—a perfect killing field.

Ralph loped along in his peculiar fashion, oversized strides keeping him close to Dr. Kellum. Ralph's face showed concern, his jaws continuing to work the gum. They were nearly to the cargo net when the deck above was strafed. It wasn't gunfire—none was possible—but Jett knew the sound of metal hitting metal. There was a scream from above, and shouting. A fireball rocketed over their heads into the desert, setting a small patch of brush on fire—it burned, but with a dull flame and much smoke, quickly dying to a smolder.

Jett reached the net ahead of the others, waiting for Ralph and Dr. Kellum.

"My gun?" Jett said.

Dr. Kellum hesitated a second, then there was more strafing above, another scream, and the thud of a body hitting the ground. Dr. Kellum motioned to a sailor, who handed over Jett's gun, helping him on with his pack. Two sailors started up the net while Jett made sure the weapon was pressurized. When Dr. Kellum was on the net, Jett took Ralph's arm to help him up.

"I can do it, Nate. I had one in my backyard, remember?"

Jett ignored him and helped him up. A half dozen fireballs shot randomly off the deck, hitting the amniotic field and dissipating.

They were halfway up the net when a sailor shouted from above.

"We can't hold them much longer. Hurry!"

Before the sailor could pull back over the rail, there was the rat-a-tat-tat of metal on metal, and something tore into the sailor's face. He fell back with a scream, hands covering the bleeding wound.

Suddenly there was the crackle of static electricity, and the deck above was lit up. A half dozen men screamed.

Jett had never felt this vulnerable before. Hanging from the net, he was completely exposed, only the curve of the ship's hull giving him and the others some protection. More fireballs flew from left to right—from the attackers toward the defenders. Two impacted above them on the left side of the net, setting it on fire. The fire died, but the blackened net continued to smolder.

"Climb right," Jett ordered.

The sailors did as they were told, but Dr. Kellum looked first to see why. The first of the sailors reached the top, risking a quick look onto the deck and then ducking back down, nodding encouragement to the others, waiting for them to climb up close. When they were all near the top, the sailors looked to Dr. Kellum, expecting orders. When Dr. Kellum hesitated, Jett took charge. Pointing to the sailors in front, he lifted two fingers and then pointed over the rail with one. Military-trained, the sailors accepted Jett's commands, confident in his natural leadership abilities. Jett then indicated that Dr. Kellum would go next, followed by Ralph and then himself. The other sailors were to follow.

At Jett's signal, the first sailor went up and over, sprinting across the corridor to shelter behind a forty-millimeter gun turret. Just as the second sailor climbed over the top, the left side of the cargo net snapped. The net dropped a foot, and then another foot as the second rope in the net broke. Instinctively, Jett reached out to grab Ralph's arm.

"I told you, Nate, I had one of these in my backyard," Ralph said, hanging on tight. "Course, it never gots on fire."

Jett shushed Ralph, who had forgotten that his lips were locked. The flames were gone, but the net was still smoldering, and the next rope would break soon. Dr. Kellum was due to go over next, but Jett held his leg, then climbed up next to him, peeking over the top. There was a body directly below the rail, and two more to the right—both burned and smoking. To the left there was another body lying on its back. This one wore a tee-shirt that said "University of Maryland." The tee-shirt was soaked in blood. There was movement to the left, eyes peeking out of corridors and hatches. The battle was either at a stalemate or it was a trap. Jett assumed a trap.

Another rope snapped and half the fibers of the next gave way. Jett checked Ralph again, but he was still hanging on just below Dr. Kellum. One of the sailors below Ralph had his hand on Ralph's back, steadying him. Jett looked back over the railing, checking to see if it was still clear, then climbed over, squatting, gun covering the corridor. He felt for the pulse of the man on the deck, not because he cared, but because Dr. Kellum's followers would see. There was no pulse. Jett was relieved. He had no intention of dragging a wounded man through a battle.

Movement down the corridor alerted him, and he dropped flat behind the body just as a cloud of metal shards rocketed by. Two impacted the man he hid behind; the rest ricocheted all around him. From behind him, one of Dr. Kellum's Specials conjured up a fireball and it whistled past, Jett feeling the heat. On impact the fireball burst into a thousand candle flames and sprayed in all directions. A sailor ran from his hiding place, his hair on fire.

Now Jett could see why weapons development hadn't proceeded much beyond simple crossbows. It wasn't just that the close quarters limited the need; it was also that the the abilities of the Specials were more effective weapons.

Jett popped up, then reached over the rail, pulling Dr. Kellum over. Keeping his body between Kellum and the Crazies, he helped Ralph onto the deck.

"I told you I could do it," Ralph said proudly.

Jett motioned Dr. Kellum and Ralph to move to the right, away from the Crazies. Before they could, another cloud of metal whistled down the corridor. Jett tackled Ralph and Dr. Kellum. Neither man had the reflexes to survive on a battlefield. One of Dr. Kellum's sailors was caught with one leg over the rail. Jagged bits of metal ripped into his neck and chest, spraying bloody flesh and bone fragments. The impact carried him back over the rail, and he fell silently to the desert below, landing with a bone-breaking thud.

When the barrage stopped, Jett lifted his head to see a man standing in the corridor. He had wild, black eyes, and his black hair was long and matted. He was dressed in black biker boots, jeans, and a denim jacket. His hand was extended, and his face was nearly purple with exertion. There were sparks between his fingers, growing in length and intensity, and now they shot off his finger tips like tiny lightning bolts.

"It's Cobb," Dr. Kellum said.

Jett raised his gun to fire, but was struck, electricity arcing from his hands to his extended gun arm. Out of control, his arm tingled and twitched. The shock spread up his arm to his torso, his nervous system shorting out, neurons firing randomly, muscle groups working against each other. Then the electric charge increased in intensity and he felt as if his whole body had been plugged into a light socket. Ralph and Dr. Kellum convulsed behind him. The intensity was building, and for the second time that day he was being electrocuted.

Suddenly, there was a whistling rush of wind as something flew over Jett. It was a steel hatch pulled from its hinges and launched by one of Dr. Kellum's Specials. As the hatch passed them, the current was attracted to the steel door. Arcing light spread around its perimeter, looking like a grotesque fourth of July sparkler. Jett got relief from the shock as the door flew over, but still he couldn't use his muscles. Then there was the deep sound of heavy impact as the hatch hit steel, and clanging and crashing as it came to rest on the deck.

Now a steady stream of metal fragments came from Dr. Kellum's Specials. Even if Jett had had muscle control, he wouldn't have been able to rise for fear of having the top of his head taken off. He knew the cover fire couldn't last much longer, but he had the strength of a four-year-old, the coordination of a baby. Then there were hands on him, pulling him along the deck under the strafing fire. He saw Ralph and Dr. Kellum being dragged, too.

Pushing with his feet, Jett tried to help, but his legs were still weak and his efforts only made the rescuers' job harder. One of the life rafts lashed to a gun turret had burned and was smoldering. Through the smoke he saw movement and the long black hair of Cobb. The stream of metal fragments was sporadic and then stopped. The sailors pulling them dropped into a crouch, trying to hurry and knowing that they had lost their cover. Jett felt doubly exposed. He was physically weak, and his body was between the enemy and the sailors trying to rescue him. Then a Crazy leaned out of a hatch and held up a gloved fist full of bits of metal—they were about to get strafed. Warning shouts came from Kellum's people, but there was no cover here, and the sailors were dragging them as fast as they could. Jett knew that if the situation were reversed, he would drop his man and sprint to safety; he was thankful the men trying to save him had higher M-scores than he did.

They were moving too slowly to make it to cover, so Jett raised his numb arm until he could see his gun. Concentrating on his index finger, he told it to squeeze. His whole arm shook as his short-circuited efferent network carried the signal from his brain to his hand and then to his finger. The first of the metal fragments whistled past his head just as his finger twitched and pulled the trigger—the gun fired with a "sput" sound.

His shot was wild, striking ten feet past the Special holding the metal fragments, but still he ducked. Jett's second shot was five feet closer, but low, coming off the deck with a whine, the bullet coming apart in tiny fragments. Muscle control was returning rapidly now, and Jett fired a round into the smoke from the burning life raft, trying to keep Cobb out of the fight.

"Here comes Rust," one of Kellum's people shouted.

Jett knew what Rust could do—he was a fire thrower. Rust was farther down the deck, dressed in a brown polyester leisure suit. With a neatly trimmed Elizabethan beard and rows of new hair plugs, he looked like a man obsessed with his own appearance. He was staring at Jett.

Jett willed his sluggish muscles to realign. Then, as if it had been conjured from hell, a fireball streaked toward them. Warnings were shouted; the sailors dropped Jett and lay down flat on the deck. Jett felt the heat as the fireball passed overhead. He had enough control to sit up now, and he came up firing, Rust ducking for cover. Then the hands were on him again and he was being pulled as he fired wildly. A few steps later many hands pulled him to safety, dropping him next to Ralph and Dr. Kellum.

"I don't feel so good," Ralph said.

"Yeah," Jett said.

Sailors helped Dr. Kellum to his feet. Hands took hold of Jett once again, helping him to stand up. Ralph was walking with only a hand on his shoulder to steady him.

Dr. Kellum's people were pulling out in waves. Two Specials hung back, providing cover with fireballs and metal fragments. Now they raced through compartments and between decks, working the combinations to new moments of time. The hangar, boiler rooms, chart room, and crew berths flew by in a blur; then they were on the deck and climbing to the conning tower and through the pilot house into the bowels of the ship again. On a pass through the chart room, Jett tripped, catching himself on a chart table. As he got up he saw that he had tripped over the shoulder of an ensign, most of whose body was buried in the deck and the base of the chart table. Ralph helped Jett to his feet.

"Do you still gots that tingly feeling, Nate?"

"Leave me alone," Jett snapped.

"You're crabby, aren't you, Nate? I can tell, but I don't mind."

Jett kept quiet so that he wouldn't trigger more verbal dribble from Ralph. Now there were more shouts from behind.

"Those people are mad at us, aren't they, Nate?"

"Yes. Keep moving."

A short distance later they joined another group of Dr. Kellum's people.

The old black woman was in this group, and spoke to Dr. Kellum, who then turned to Jett.

"The Crazies attacked your friends," Dr. Kellum said. "My people had to pull out."

Jett's mind went to work on scenarios for completing his mission without them, and for escape. He was relieved that he hadn't left Ralph behind.

"My people saved the map," Dr. Kellum said as they started moving again. "We can use it to get us to levels McNab doesn't know about."

Suddenly those in front stopped, crouching, and like railroad cars backing up behind a braking engine, those behind stopped abruptly. Ralph stood dumbly until Jett pulled him down. When all of them were still, they could hear sounds of battle behind, but also sounds coming from in front. They were trapped.

Jett waited for Dr. Kellum to issue orders, but none came. Kellum was a benevolent dictator to his people, a brilliant man, an inventor, and Solomon-like in his judgment of disputes. But he was not a general. Precious seconds passed. Taking charge, Jett ordered those in front and behind to get into the compartments on either side of the corridor. They were crew berths, slung with hammocks. Jett remembered from the schematics he had studied that most of the crew berths were located toward the stern of the ship. The hatches of the berths were closed; Jett left his cracked so he could see down the corridor.

A minute passed. Then he heard the sound of approaching footsteps. Jett preferred to let the Crazies pass, but some of Kellum's Specials could feel the minds around them. If there was one of those who could feel minds among the approaching Crazies, Jett would spring the ambush.

A man came into view, dressed in Navy denims. It was Dawson. Right behind him in their silver suits were Compton and Peters. Suddenly Jett had an emotional surge—he was happy to see his team. When he pulled the door open, Compton reacted, her gun coming up and sputtering three times, but missing Jett's head by inches.

"Hold your fire!" Jett shouted, waving his silver-coated arm out the door.

Compton was smiling when he stepped out.

"Hi Karla, hi Jim," Ralph said, coming out behind Jett.

"Ralph!" Dawson suddenly shouted, trying to push through to Ralph.

The corridor was filling with Kellum's people, a strange mix of sailors and civilians from different eras.

"Ralph, it's me, Elizabeth!" Dawson shouted.

Ralph just smiled and waved. Compton pushed through the crowd, coming to stand by Jett and Dawson.

"He started doing this after you left," Compton said. "He says his name is Elizabeth."

"It may be," Kellum said.

Dr. Kellum studied Dawson through his thick glasses.

"Some of my people are telepathic. Dawson is the most powerful, and sometimes he links with people on the outside."

Jett had seen so many bizarre abilities in his years with the OSP, he considered anything possible.

"Who are you?" Jett asked Dawson.

Dawson looked past him toward Ralph.

"Ralph, I need to talk with you," Dawson shouted.

Jett reached out and grabbed Dawson's shirt in both fists, slamming him against the bulkhead, getting his attention.

"I said, who are you?"

"I'm Elizabeth Foxworth, and I'm a social worker."

Ralph was coming now in response to Dawson's call, but he stopped to talk with another man, and then a woman, shaking their hands and going through his introduction routine.

"A social worker?" Jett probed.

Jett sifted through his memory, searching what he knew about Ralph. The reports about Ralph's special ability spoke of an Elizabeth Foxworth who had been assigned to Dr. Martin's mind melding experiments. If Dr. Martin had found a way to communicate through Dawson, Dawson was a link to the outside world.

"Elizabeth Foxworth?" Jett said.

"Yes," Dawson said, surprised. "I need to talk with Ralph."

Ralph started forward again at the sound of his name. Jett kept Dawson pressed against the bulkhead, wondering how to use the connection to the outside.

"Why do you want to speak to Ralph?" Jett asked.

Dawson ignored him and tilted his head to talk to Ralph, who was close now.

"Ralph, I have a message from Elizabeth and Wes," Dawson said. "You need to go home, now."

"I thought you were Elizabeth," Jett said.

"I'm both. Ralph won't understand if I tell him the truth."

"Understand what?" Ralph said.

Jett released Dawson, letting him speak to Ralph.

"You've been gone too long and everyone's worried. Dr. Birnbaum doesn't know where you are."

Ralph looked concerned and leaned back, arms folded on his chest, lips puckered and protruding. Then, after a long think, he turned to Jett.

"Nate, I gots to go home now. I don't like to make people worry."

Jett knew that if Ralph could find an exit, he could use it to extract his team. Even though a part of him wanted to face off with McNab and deal with the threat from the Nimitz's nuclear weapons, he couldn't pass up this chance.

"I understand, Ralph," Jett said. "When you gotta go . . ."

Ralph joined him and they said together ". . . you gotta go."

Ralph grinned from ear to ear, but his mouth quickly returned to a concerned pucker when there were more shouts from the end of the corridor. The bulkhead at the end of the corridor began to glow; Jett could feel the heat from thirty feet away. Those closest backed away. Men with crossbows moved closer, fitting bolts to their weapons, aiming them as you would a rifle. The bulkhead melted, rivulets of liquid metal running onto the deck, sizzling and smoking. Soon there was a hole which spewed crossbow bolts. The two men in front spun from the impact of the shafts, looking like human pincushions. They fell dead where they lay, and the panic was on.

"Compton, you take the point. Peters, cover the rear," Jett ordered.

Peters pushed through the surging crowd like a salmon swimming upstream. As Compton turned, Jett realized that Evans was missing.

"Where's Evans?" he shouted above the growing din.

"Either dead or killing Specials," Compton said.

Jett had never trusted Evans, but they could have used his ability and his weapon. Reaching for Ralph, Jett pushed him forward.

"Lead us to the door, Ralph. The door you told me about, remember?"

"Sure, Nate, I know."

"Good. Take us there."

Jett noticed that Dawson had Ralph's arm and was pulling him along too.

"Remember you promised to go home, Ralph," Dawson shouted.

"Sure, sure, I remember," Ralph said, leading the party past the last crew berth and past the magazines for the stern eight-inch battery.

"Remember to go home," Dawson said again.

Then Dawson released Ralph's arm, letting him move ahead at his own speed. Jett heard Dawson say, "Wes, bring us out."

Suddenly they were sprayed with metal pieces, one burying in Dawson's leg. Dawson fell, and the panicked crowd behind pressed past. Jett helped Dawson to one side, letting Kellum's people pass.

"We've got to keep moving," Jett said to Dawson.

"The integration is dissolving," Dawson said, eyes glassy.

Peters and the rear guard backed toward them. One of Kellum's psychokinetics sprayed a handful of metal shards. Jett noticed that the man's nose was bleeding.

The Crazies were at the other end of the corridor, dashing from one crew-berth hatch to another, working forward. They were even wilder looking than Kellum's people, being two rungs lower on the civilization scale. Most had facial tattoos, and many had crosses dangling from their necks or painted on their clothes. Their ears were pierced and they wore dangling copper earrings, many of them crosses hammered out of copper shell casings. They were a ragged bunch, and more reckless than Kellum's people.

When one of the Crazies sprinted for a hatchway, Jett picked him off, realizing as the man fell that he wasn't tattooed and he wore a purple jersey. Jett knew the Nimitz flight deck crew wore colored jerseys so that they could be easily distinguished from flight control in the ship's tower. Crew in purple jerseys were called "Grapes," and were responsible for fueling the planes. Jett spotted another man in a green jersey—he would have been on the catapult or arresting wire crews. This was the first concrete evidence Jett had that the Nimitz was indeed in Pot of Gold.

"We're going home now, Anita," Dawson said, looking to the side as if he was seeing someone.

Jett pulled Dawson to his feet. The man was confused, his face blank.

"Let's go," Jett ordered.

"What's going on?" Dawson said suddenly.

"Are you Elizabeth, or Dawson?" Jett asked.

"Dawson."

Supporting Dawson with one arm, Jett fired with the other as they backed down the corridor, fighting with the rear guard. The connection with Elizabeth Foxworth had been broken; Jett's link with the outside world was gone. If Ralph didn't find a way out, Jett would need Dawson to connect again. Dawson was limping, blood spreading down his leg. Jett let him move ahead, then dropped back, helping Peters pick off Crazies.

EVANS

Evans was hiding in a powder magazine. The heavily armored room was packed with shells for the six- and eight-inch guns, and ammunition for the forty-millimeter and twenty-millimeter guns. Evans had fought the Crazies using his gun and his power. There had been too many for him, and he had been forced back, retreating slowly, leaving dead bodies and wounded men behind. He knew Compton thought he was suicidal, but he wasn't. A man can't die twice, and he had died years ago when the Specials had burned away any chance he had of a normal life. Only fantasies of revenge had kept him alive.

The red-hot fragment that pierced his suit had cauterized the wound, stopping the bleeding. It would scar, and Evans laughed at the thought. It must have been a ricochet—otherwise the fragment would have penetrated all the way to his lung. Instead, he dug the fragment from his chest. There was a wound on his neck, too, but the thick scar tissue absorbed the fragment. They had taken their best shot at him and he had survived, taking out four or five Specials. He could kill them a few at a time, but eventually they would get him. If Jett and Compton had stayed on task, he would have had allies, and the decks of the ship would be running with the blood of the Specials.

Something was wrong with Jett. He had a reputation as a ruthless agent, but the Jett he had seen on this mission would never have been retained by the agency. Evans couldn't count on Jett—he had a thing for the moron, Ralph. He had gone off with Ralph and was likely dead. If the Specials were going to die, he was going to have to do the killing, and the best way to do that was to destroy the generators.

Standing, Evans noticed that his chest ached, but less than when he first hid in the magazine. He was healing at abnormal speed, since the efficiency of his body's repair mechanisms was facilitated in Pot of Gold. Evans had no sense of which way to go, knowing only that the generators had been installed in one of Norfolk's boiler rooms. He trudged up and down corridors, working his way to the lowest decks, checking the boiler rooms and finding them empty, then working higher into the ship, trying to find his way to what the captured sailor called "level one." On his fifth trip through the ship he heard sounds.

Cautious, Evans waited, listening, trying to identify the sound. After a minute his mind matched it with his past experience. It was a hacksaw cutting through metal. Evans advanced slowly along the corridor. The sound came from a compartment near where he had battled the Crazies. He paused by the hatch, his back to the bulkhead, and listened.

The "stroop, stroop, stroop" sound of the saw stopped and there was the dull clink of a small piece of metal. He waited until the saw began again, then peeked into the compartment. There were two men inside. One wore the overalls of a farmer, his shoes still caked with dirt from the patch of ground he had worked. The other was a seaman dressed in work denims, white sailor cap on his head. The farmer was sawing through a pipe locked in a pipe vise. The sailor stood next to him, holding the pipe unnecessarily. There was a bucket below, and after a dozen strokes a piece of the pipe fell into it. Evans waited until the farmer started another cut before he stepped into the room.

Evans didn't know if they were Crazies, and he didn't care. It was more important to know if they were Specials. He doubted it. If they had significant talent they wouldn't be given menial jobs.

"Don't move," Evans said, menacing them with the gun.

The farmer turned to face him, his chin covered with a day's growth of beard. His face had the weathered look of a man who spent sixteen hours a day outside. He stared with dull eyes—no spark, no anger, no fear. The sailor's eyes were bright with intelligence.

"You got no business here," the farmer said, taking a step toward Evans.

Evans aimed for the farmer's foot, but the shot caught him in the ankle and he went down with a yelp, both hands reaching for his wound. The sailor's eyes never left Evans, who now wondered if he'd shot the wrong man. The sailor had nerve; he kept his head the way an agent would.

The farmer was moaning, but both Evans and the sailor ignored him, eyes locked.

"You're going to lead me to the generators," Evans said.

The sailor shook his head no.

"Turn around," Evans ordered.

Slowly the sailor turned, facing the workbench. There were tools and pieces of pipe on the bench, so Evans ordered the sailor to put his hands behind his head, fingers laced. Then he went to the pipe vise next to the moaning farmer. The pipe was held by a chain that looped it. The chain could be tightened with a ratchet until the pipe was held tight. Evans released the catch and loosened the chain, sliding the pipe out. It was a length about three feet long, one end cut at an angle where they had been working. The bucket was a quarter full of one-inch slivers of pipe.

"Put your arm in!" Evans ordered the farmer, pointing at the loop of chain.

The farmer didn't look up, so Evans poked him with the sharp end of the pipe. He flinched, eyes still dull, but now moist.

"Put your arm in or I'll kill you," Evans said.

The farmer got to his knees slowly, wincing from the pain in his ankle. Half crawling, dragging his limp and bleeding leg behind, he inched toward the pipe vise and put his left arm through the loop. Evans wrapped the chain just below the farmer's elbow, then tightened it, the farmer yelping with the pain and then sobbing as the chain cut through his flesh and the blood started to flow.

"Turn around," Evans told the sailor.

When the sailor saw the farmer, his eyes widened at the sight of the man bleeding from his ankle, his arm locked in the vise. It was the sign of weakness Evans had hoped for. The farmer could stand it no longer and reached for the release on the ratchet. Keeping his gun on the sailor, Evans brought the pipe down on the farmer's wounded ankle. The farmer yelped, his free arm reaching for his ankle.

"Don't touch the vise," Evans ordered.

The sailor was wide-eyed now, shocked by Evans's cruelty.

"You're going to lead me to the generators," Evans repeated.

"You can't go there," the sailor said. "It's not our territory."

Evans took two sideways steps toward the vise and swung the pipe around in a big arc, putting all his strength into the blow. He hit the farmer's arm halfway between the wrist and the elbow, snapping the arm in half. The farmer screamed and clawed ineffectively at the vise, too wracked with pain to work the release. Broken in the middle, the arm hung limp, connected only by muscle and skin. To Evans's satisfaction the sailor stared open-mouthed. Then he turned, bent over, and threw up—nothing came out.

"I'll take you to the generators. Just don't hurt him anymore."

Evans ordered the sailor to the corridor.

"Let me help him first," the sailor pleaded.

"No."

"Let me get him out of the vise, at least."

"He can let himself out," Evans said.

The sailor left reluctantly, looking back at the farmer. Evans let the farmer live because he wanted the sailor to have hope. He would kill the sailor eventually, but hostages with hope were easier to manipulate. The moans of the farmer followed them down the corridor.

DISSOLVED

Should I call for an ambulance, Wes?" Shamita said.

They were all gathered around Elizabeth's cot in the lab where she lay unconscious. Wanda sat on the edge of her cot, cigarette in hand, blowing smoke rings toward Len. Len periodically waved his hand to clear the rings, but otherwise ignored Wanda. Anita, in her Bugs Bunny tee-shirt, kneeled on her cot, one pigtail in her mouth, chewing anxiously and straining to see over the adults who stood around Elizabeth. The room was silent except for the whir of disk drives, the drone of computer cooling fans, and the soft pumping sounds of the liquid-nitrogen cooling system.

"Maybe you better get an ambulance," Monica said.

Monica's belated concern irritated Wes. She had pushed him to continue the experiment.

"Do it, Shamita. Call an ambulance," Wes said.

Shamita was moving before Wes finished speaking.

"Len, keep your eye on her vital signs," Wes said.

Len returned to his station, glaring at Wanda as he passed.

Wes held Elizabeth's hand, talking to her, saying her name over and over, coaxing her back to the world. The others had woken immediately when the link was dissolved—even Anita, who was the strongest receiver.

Elizabeth still wasn't conscious six minutes after dissolution, and her body was reacting as if it was still in the dream.

"Her heart rate is coming down, Wes," Len said. "Coming down fast. Blood pressure is dropping."

Elizabeth's eyelids fluttered, and everyone took an expectant breath. After a half dozen blinks the faces around her came into focus.

"Elizabeth, can you hear me?" Wes asked.

"I talked to Ralph," Elizabeth said. "I told him to come home."

"BP is still dropping. Heart rate is down to fifty-five," Len said.

"Don't talk," Wes told her.

"What about Anita?" Elizabeth said suddenly, trying to sit up.

Wes held her down with a hand on her chest.

"Anita is fine," Monica said.

"And Wanda?" Elizabeth wanted to know.

"There's nothing wrong with me," Wanda said loudly from behind. "I'm as tough as a cockroach. You couldn't kill me with a rock if you tried."

"Much as we'd like to," Len said.

"Ha!" said Wanda, blowing a stream of smoke at Len's head.

Elizabeth smiled weakly at the continuing war between Len and Wanda, then her eyes lost focus and her eyelids drooped.

"Heart rate is forty-nine beats per minute," Len said. "Her blood pressure is continuing to drop."

"Stay awake, Elizabeth," Wes said. "Tell me what you saw, what you did."

Elizabeth's eyes opened again.

"I saw Ralph," Elizabeth said weakly.

"Yes, tell me about Ralph."

"If he comes home . . ."

"Yes, Elizabeth, if Ralph comes home, what?" Wes said.

"If Ralph gets home, don't let him go back to the ship."

Wes hesitated. To save Elizabeth, he had to find the source of the dream and stop the dream transmission. He didn't know how to get there without Ralph.

Weak as she was, Elizabeth sensed his hesitation.

"Don't go to the ship," Elizabeth said. "Promise me you won't go to the ship?"

Wes couldn't promise. He would do whatever he had to, to save Elizabeth.

"I can't promise, Elizabeth . . ." Wes began, but never finished. Elizabeth was unconscious.

EXIT

They fought a running battle with McNab's Crazies, racing through the ship, following Ralph from one level to another. Casualties were light, and the wounded healed quickly, benefitting from the same force that had kept them from aging for fifty years. As they moved through the ship they picked up more of Kellum's people, pockets of men, women, and children who joined the flight. The increasing numbers slowed them, increasing their vulnerability.

"They're coming again," Dawson said suddenly.

The crowd immediately reshuffled positions, those with weapons hurrying to help those in the back, unarmed women and children moving forward.

"How far is the door, Ralph?" Jett asked.

"I'm not so good at guessing, Nate."

"How many turns and stairs?"

"Three turns, two stairs—up and down the same one two times—and three turns."

"We're in a hurry, Ralph. If you get us there quick I'll give you a pack of gum."

Ralph grinned and picked up his pace until he was moving at his full speed, somewhere between a walk and a run. They made the turns and climbed between decks, Jett losing track of the combination. Finally they came out on deck behind the funnel, then climbed down into the ship again. Soon Jett found that they were in a corridor with a mess hall on one side; a kitchen was separated from the tables by a serving counter. There was a hatch opposite the mess, and Ralph stopped.

"That's like one of those thumbtack things Walter has stuck on the ends of the wires," Ralph said.

"A door to the outside?" Jett said.

"Guess so," Ralph said.

Jett undogged the hatch and pulled it open, revealing a green mist.

"He found one!" Dr. Kellum said in amazement.

Murmurs of surprise rippled through the crowd. Jett reached toward the mist, but Dr. Kellum stopped him.

"Bring a spear up here," Dr. Kellum shouted.

"Nate, aren't you forgetting something?" Ralph said.

Jett handed over one of his last two packs of spearmint gum, and Ralph tore into it, feeding stick after stick into his mouth.

A spear was handed to Dr. Kellum, who slowly poked it into the green mist until only the part he held was visible. Then he pulled it back, looking at the tip.

"What's that all about?" Jett said.

"Not all these doors go somewhere safe," Dr. Kellum told him. "This ship is a maze of time-and-space loops all twisted around and turned back in on itself. This door might lead home, or it might not."

Dr. Kellum handed Margolin the spear and called for the "sampler." The sampler was a pole with a bellows attached to one end. A rope ran from the bellows to the end of the handle through a series of eyehooks. A spring had been fitted between the handle attached to the pole and the loose bellows handle. The rope ran to a latch that was holding the spring. The bellows was collapsed and latched. Dr. Kellum pushed the bellows end of the pole into the green mist, until he held only the handle. Then he pulled on the rope to release the catch at the other end. He gave the bellows a couple of seconds to expand, and then pulled the pole back out.

"Volunteer?" Dr. Kellum yelled.

Two or three people shouted in response, and Dr. Kellum pointed to a chubby sailor who pushed through to the front. Dr. Kellum held the bellows close to his face and then squeezed the handles, expelling the air caught inside. A yellow cloud puffed from the bellows, and the chubby sailor breathed some of it in. Instantly he was wracked with a fit of coughing and wheezing. He bent in half, held by those on either side. He retched three times in succession, all three dry spasms. When he had control of himself and was breathing normally again, Dr. Kellum thanked him for volunteering.

"We can't use this door," Dr. Kellum said.

"Ralph, take us to another door."

"They're close," Dawson warned from somewhere back in the crowd.

Ralph was already moving down the corridor.

"Stop!" Dawson shouted. "There's something wrong. They're ahead of us now."

"What? That's not possible," Dr. Kellum said. "These are new levels. They've never been to this part of our territory. How could they find a way past us?"

"I can feel it too," another of Kellum's people said, also sensing the minds of the Crazies. "There's some ahead of us for sure."

"That's cause we're not too far from the beginning," Ralph said, while he unwrapped another stick of gum.

"Bring the map," Jett ordered.

A middle-aged man wearing blue polyester slacks and a white dress shirt brought the ship model through the crowd. Kellum took the model and held it out to Ralph.

"Where's the beginning?" Jett said.

Ralph pointed to a black wire that wound through the ship.

"We're about to join up with the black level?" Dr. Kellum asked.

Ralph shook his head up and down.

Kellum's face lit up as if he had just had a revelation.

"It makes sense," Kellum said. "Einstein believed space and time curved, and that if you travelled far enough you would ultimately come to the beginning. We're trapped in a microcosm of a universe that curves back in on itself."

"But with exits," Jett said.

Jett stepped to the mess and spotted a hatch on the other side—most of the ship's compartments had at least two exits. He shouted to Peters and Compton in the rear.

"Get everyone through here. We don't want to get surrounded."

Then Jett took Ralph's arm.

"Are there other doors, Ralph?"

"Sure, but it's lots farther if we go this way," Ralph said.

"We can use the map," Kellum said. "The levels past here must be the inverse of those we've mapped."

"But your map is flawed," Jett said. "Ralph will lead us."

"He doesn't know the ship. We could pop out in the middle of Crazy territory."

"Ralph found that door, and he'll find us another. From what I've seen there couldn't be many Crazies left in their territory. They're all chasing us." Then to Ralph he said, "Find a way out, Ralph."

"Well okee-dokee then."

"Remember your promise to go home, Ralph," Jett said.

"A promise is a promise," Ralph said, still chewing the thick wad of gum. "Go straight home just like it's dinner time."

"Right," Jett said.

Ralph led the way through the mess while Jett hung back. The sailors, men, women, and children who passed looked at Jett with hope now, as if he was their leader. Jett was uncomfortable in the role, still thinking of himself as destroyer, not savior.

"They're just about on us!" Dawson said as he passed.

Then Jett spotted the black woman who created illusions. He pulled her aside and explained what he wanted her to do. He didn't know how accurate McNab's telepathics were, but Dawson's ability was crude. They would sense that Dr. Kellum's people were moving away, but they might not be accurate enough to tell which compartment they had entered.

The black woman's name was Marion; she waited with Jett, jaw set, seemingly fearless. When the last of Dr. Kellum's people made it out of the wardroom, she and Jett stood in the doorway. A few seconds later they heard the Crazies. Jett nudged Marion, and she shut her eyes, projecting her illusion.

Suddenly Jett saw himself standing by the hatch Ralph had found that led to the place with the unbreathable air. A half dozen of Dr. Kellum's people were with him, entering the green mist one by one. Jett had timed it perfectly—Marion's image of Kellum's people fleeing was still there when the Crazies risked a look around the corner. There was a shout from the Crazies, and suddenly metal fragments shot by his hiding place. Now he could see himself across the corridor, ducking and pushing the last of Dr. Kellum's people into the mist and then stepping in himself. Next there was the thunder of a dozen feet as the Crazies raced down the corridor.

Jett stood perfectly still as they crowded around the hatch with the green mist. He trusted Marion's assurance that the Crazies would see a closed hatch where he and the others waited. It worked—the Crazies clustered by the hatch with the mist. They were a ragged bunch, hair unkempt and matted, faces tattooed, sleeves cut from shirts and uniforms. Three-quarters of the Crazies were Norfolk crew, but there were a few civilians mixed in, including one middle-aged woman wearing jeans and a sweat-shirt with "World's Greatest Mom" written on it in what looked like crayon.

There was mumbling and shouting among the Crazies; no one seemed to be in charge. Then the woman in the sweatshirt shouted the others down, giving orders. Jett saw that three would go through the green mist first, and then two more groups of three in quick succession. The first group readied their weapons, two carrying crossbows. When they were ready, the first three rushed into the mist, prepared for a trap on the other side. The next three waited, counting to five, and then rushed into the mist. Only two made it through. The third got jammed in the entrance when he collided with one coming back from the other side. The returning man was coughing violently, clutching at his throat. His face and arms were blistered and his eyes were runny as if his eyeballs had liquified. Another man fell out of the mist, landing flat, his body wracked by violent spasms. Then, with a long, slow exhale, he went limp.

With a nudge from Jett, Marion turned and tiptoed away. Jett stepped back at the same time, since the closed-hatch illusion ended as soon as Marion turned. The Crazies had lost five men and were confused by the trick.

When Marion was through the other side of the mess, Jett backed across, his gun trained on the open hatch. A face appeared in the hatch and Jett fired, missing the Crazy's head by three inches. There was shouting now, and the pack was after them.

Compton had taken charge in his absence, stationing some of Dr. Kellum's people at every junction and turn they needed to make, sprinkling them like bread crumbs so Jett could find his way to the main body. At first they had passed through hatches without bothering to close or lock them, since locked hatches would give away their route to the Crazies. Now they locked each hatch they passed through and Dr. Kellum's people jammed as many as they could. Jett didn't countermand the order, however, he worried it was not only slowing pursuit but it was cutting off lines of retreat. Still, the ship seemed to have an infinite number of passages and hatches, so he let the hatches be jammed.

Ralph was leading the pack when the next attack came, Dawson shouting a warning just in time. Jett had just caught up to the rear when there were screams ahead and a fireball burst in their midst. Dr. Kellum's people broke toward Jett and he stepped aside, letting them pass. They were stopped a short distance later at a jammed hatch. Then there was pounding on the other side as the pursuing Crazies caught up. They were trapped between two enemy forces. There was a pitched battle in the front and Jett could hear the soft sputter of Peter's and Compton's guns and the clanging of crossbow bolts and metal shards skipping off metal. Every hatch along the corridor was opened in a desperate search for a way out. There was a shout when someone found an exit and the rush was on. Jett kept his gun trained on the hatch behind them. The hatch began to glow and he backed away, sweating from the heat of the red hot metal.

The door was beginning to melt so Jett backed to the hatch where Kellum's people were escaping. Compton and Peters were backing toward him from the other end, covering each other's retreat. It would be another minute before the Crazies behind them could melt a big enough hole to shoot through, so Jett turned and covered Peters and Compton while they followed Kellum's people. The compartment was long and divided into large bins. Crates and barrels were stacked everywhere, tied securely with lines. There was a connecting hatch at one end.

Jett, Peters, and Compton followed the others through the end hatch, finding themselves on the bow of the ship. Dr. Kellum's people were scattering everywhere in full retreat.

Jett looked for Ralph, spotting him a deck above near one of the gun turrets. He was opening a hatch and about to step through. Jett shouted Ralph's name and he paused, looking down at Jett.

"Don't worry, Nate. I didn't forget. I'm going home."

Before Jett could shout for him to wait, metal fragments erupted from the hatch behind him and he ducked for cover. When it was safe to look back for Ralph, it was too late. Ralph was gone. Then the Crazies came through the hatch in force.

DISCHARGED

Elizabeth's blood pressure stabilized after rising and falling unpredictably for hours. Her red blood count was down, her white count elevated, and there were high levels of lactic acid in her system. She was groggy, easily confused, and was having periodic long- and short-term memory problems. In short, she was nearly dead tired.

The doctors ordered sedation, but Elizabeth refused, and Wes agreed. Sleep prolonged by drugs could put her on the ship for ten or twelve hours and drain her even more.

Once the doctors were satisfied that her condition was stable, they released her, since there was no treatment for her condition. She left with the name of a psychiatrist in her pocket who specialized in sleep disorders. Elizabeth dropped the psychiatrist's name in a trash can in the lobby.

She rode in Wes's Explorer with the seat partially reclined, her eyes closed. Wes glanced at her regularly as he drove. Even with her eyes shut, she looked as if she desperately needed sleep. Her lids were red and puffy, her face swollen, every wrinkle accentuated. There were dark circles around her eyes and she lacked muscle tone, making her look ten years older than she was. Since having the dream Elizabeth hadn't eaten well. Every glance at her worried him more.

"Elizabeth, maybe you should stay at my place for a few days."

Elizabeth's eyes opened and a slight smile came to her lips.

"Doctor Martin, are you trying to seduce me?" she asked, smiling.

"I'm just worried."

"I was only joking. I know the way I look."

"You shouldn't be alone," Wes said.

"You're thinking of Margi, aren't you?" Elizabeth said.

"Yes," he admitted.

"So if I stay with you I won't be taking a bath alone?"

Wes felt his cheeks flush.

"Maybe you could stay with me?" Elizabeth suggested.

"I could."

They drove in silence for a way. Elizabeth shut her eyes when cars passed, as if the bright headlights were painful. After a few minutes she turned to him.

"How long do I have?"

"It depends on your dreams. If they aren't too detailed when you link, you might make it another month. I won't link you with Anita and Wanda again."

"If you did?"

"A single session could kill you."

"We started out to save Anita, remember? To find the source of the dream and stop it. If it means I have to go back into the dream, then I will."

"Ralph will come home and help us," Wes said.

"We don't know that," Elizabeth argued. "We can't wait that long anyway, or I'll be too confused to be of any help."

"I won't send you back!"

Elizabeth gave up. It was another sign of how weak she was. She had never let him win an argument before.

The only hope for getting out from between the rock and the hard place was a retarded man lost somewhere on a ship.

CAVE

Ralph searched the ship's compartments, holds, and gangways, climbing between decks, looking for the way out. He ignored the bodies in the deck and bulkheads, focussed on getting home. He was dimly aware of Dr. Kellum's ship model, but he was beyond the map now, navigating with his unique spatial sense, searching for patterns in the midst of chaos.

He was aware of shadows and sounds but encountered no one. His concentration was intense and focussed, his conscious mind blank. Like a human stealth bomber, he was undetectable by McNab's sensors.

As he entered a boiler room, an adjacent storage compartment caught his attention. Undogging the hatch, he found the compartment filled not with steamfitting gear, but green mist. He remembered watching Dr. Kellum's pole prodding the other green mist, but he didn't have the pole. Ralph also remembered something bad on the far side of that mist, something that had made one of the sailors sick. Ralph intuited danger, but remembered his promise to go home.

Home could be through this door.

Taking a deep breath, Ralph entered the mist.

Ralph was in a cave—not your standard cave. Solid rock, yes, but also electrically lit. Then he remembered Dr. Birnbaum's experiment in Mammoth Cave—that cave had lights in it.

Stepping over a floor light, he located a concrete path. It forked; he turned right on another lighted path. Overhead lights illuminated side caves, stalactites and stalagmites, and wall signs which he found unreadable. The cave widened, and he entered a small underground shopping mall featuring an information booth, a souvenir shop, and a restaurant. There were people here stacking chairs, sweeping and mopping the floors. Ralph approached a young woman emptying the cash register at the souvenir shop.

"Hihowyadoin?" Ralph said.

Surprised, and frightened by Ralph's appearance and size, she backed up a step.

"Who are you?" she asked.

"My name's Ralph, what's yours?"

"Meaghan," she said. "You shouldn't be down here. The cave is closed."

Ralph looked around, and then his arm shot out and he thumped himself on the side of the head, startling Meaghan again.

"How could I be so stupid?" Ralph said. "I gotta go home now anyhow."

Meaghan looked at Ralph with growing concern.

"Is there anyone with you? Did you get left behind?"

Ralph puckered his lips and stared into space for a few seconds.

"Nope. No one with me."

"How did you get here?" Meaghan asked.

"I came down that way, from back over there and around that way sort of," Ralph said, pointing here and there.

"Never mind," Meaghan said. "You can wait while I finish. I'll help you get home."

"Well okee-dokee then," Ralph said. Then, spotting the candy display, he said, "Got any gum?"

Meaghan handed over a package of Juicy Fruit.

"No more freebies," Meaghan said.

Ralph grinned his widest grin and ripped off the top of the package.

GUIDE

Evans didn't trust his guide. They were deep within the Norfolk, just aft of the machine shop again. Evans checked the compartment as they passed. There was no farmer inside with a broken arm, nor any bucket of metal pieces, but it was the same machine shop—Evans was sure of that. The bizarre topography of Pot of Gold meant that there were many identical machine shops. Passing the same one again and again was a sign of progress, but were they getting closer or farther from the generators?

"What level are we on now?" Evans asked.

"Level?" the sailor said, feigning ignorance.

"I won't ask again."

"Level seven, I think," the sailor said.

"Count out the levels as we go," Evans ordered.

"I haven't been to the generator level since the Crazies took it. I'm not sure I can find it."

"Then you're no use to me," Evans said.

"I'll find it. Give me a chance."

"Once I get to the generators I'll let you go," Evans lied.

A short distance later the sailor turned a corner, jumped through an open hatch, and sprinted. It was a crew berth, with hammocks hung on both sides. Concentrating on the sailor's fleeing back, Evans pushed with his mind. As if swatted by an invisible hand, the sailor was slammed onto the deck.

Evans stood over his guide, waiting for him to turn over. The sailor lay still. Evans used the toe of his silver boot to lift one side of the body. The sailor flopped back down when released. Frustrated, Evans sat on a hammock, rocking gently, waiting. If the sailor was alive, the forces inside Pot of Gold might heal him.

Evans waited, hating the quiet time. Idleness made room in his mind for recollections of when the Specials had attacked him. The details of that first mission, from its beginning at Rainbow to his final exit from Pot of Gold, were burned into his memory.

They had entered Pot of Gold in the same way that Jett's team had, but they hadn't known that their guns were useless. His power was their only weapon, and they were outnumbered and showered with metal shards, crossbow bolts, and fireballs. He was knocked senseless in the fight. When he came to, they had a knife to his throat. He didn't dare use his power. Two other members of his team were alive, and together they were led through the cruiser Norfolk to the hangar deck, then pushed through the jeering crowd gathered for their trial.

Prophet was there, acting as prosecutor, judge, and jury. The trial was short, Crazies cheering and shouting. Then came the executions. The other two went first; tied to metal poles, they were roasted alive. Even with the knife at his throat he was ready to strike out with his power before they led him to the burning stake. Then Prophet spoke directly to his mind, telling him that because he too had a gift from God, he wouldn't die. Evans's release would be a sign to the outside world that the people inside Pot of Gold were truly God's people.

With the stench of burned flesh still in his nostrils and the sounds of the screams still ringing in his ears, Evans wanted to believe Prophet. Evans told them where the exit would appear, and Prophet and his followers took him to that deck, waiting for the opening. When Dr. Lee opened an exit, Prophet motioned him forward. Raising Evans's hopes was the cruelest act of all.

"Go with God," Prophet said with a smile.

Then, just before Evans stepped into the exit, Prophet called to him.

"One more thing. Tell them what happened to the other blasphemers they sent with you."

"I will," Evans said.

"Better yet, show them!"

With that, his clothes burst into flame. As he started to scream, he was knocked into the exit. Fire couldn't be sustained inside Pot of Gold without a Special, but on the outside it burned hot and bright. Evans found himself on a metal platform in Rainbow, engulfed in flames. He had enough wits to drop and roll, but he continued to burn until a technician put out the flames with a fire extinguisher. That was only the beginning of the pain.

He suffered for months, wrapped in gauze, begging for more painkiller. But with third degree burns as bad as his, the dosage of medication necessary to stop the pain would have killed him. Later came the skin grafting, which was nearly as painful as the burning. During those months he nursed his hatred of Prophet and the Specials. Then came years of being treated as a freak or an object of pity. That too fueled his hate. When the opportunity to return to Pot of Gold came, he quickly accepted. For Evans, this wasn't about the Nimitz, it was about revenge.

The sailor stirred. Evans remained on his hammock, rocking. Finally, the sailor rolled over, his nose bloody and crooked. Seeing Evans, his face went white.

"I should kill you," Evans said.

"I can find the generators," the sailor assured him.

"Then do it."

Getting to his feet, he wiped his bloody nose with his sleeve.

"Move," Evans ordered.

The sailor led him back to the corridor, and soon they were in the routine again of walking between decks, working the sensorimotor combination that would ultimately take them to the generators.

PHONE CALL

Wes pulled into a visitor's slot at Elizabeth's condominium, then realized he was more than a visitor. Backing out, he parked in a resident's slot, taking his suitcase from the back seat. He had never stayed overnight before, and although he was coming now as a nurse, not a lover, he felt that once he stepped inside, their relationship would be different.

The door was unlocked, and Wes entered without knocking. Elizabeth kept her condominium tidy, but managed to avoid giving it the sterile feel that comes from over-organization. She had chosen warm colors—softer hues of blue, mostly—but no dominant theme. Her home was a reflection of her work and her interests. On her bookcase were pictures of family, and of women and children she had helped as a social worker. The books in the case were a mix of sociology and social work texts and self-help books, most with a feminist theme.

"Welcome, roommate," Elizabeth said from the couch.

She was sitting up, her legs covered by a quilt. Her eyes were set in dark hollows, purplish bags hanging below. Her eyelids drooped as if she was falling asleep.

"You can put your things in the office," she said.

Elizabeth used the smaller of her two bedrooms as an office, which was furnished with a desk, a leather easy chair, and a sofa. The office was tidy compared to Wes's, whose piles of old journals and photocopied articles covered his desktop, every chair, and most of the floor. There was a small stack of papers on the corner of Elizabeth's desk, a cup filled with pencils and pens, and another with paperclips. A computer sat on a side table, another pile of papers next to it. Above her desk Elizabeth had hung her diplomas, each mounted in a matching oak frame. Three mounted posters from the Mount Hood Festival of Jazz decorated the wall above the sofa. Wes's diplomas were in a cardboard box in a closet. Once, he had bought tickets to the Mount Hood Festival of Jazz, but spent the weekend in his lab debugging a program.

Elizabeth was in the bathroom when he came out, so he went to the kitchen to make a pot of coffee. The condominium was a couple of years old, but the kitchen looked brand new. The cabinets, counters, and appliances were bright white; the floor was patterned with blue flowers. Wes had never been asked to dinner here, and Elizabeth had joked about not knowing how to cook.

The refrigerator door was covered with children's drawings held in place with a rich variety of magnets. A drawing of Wes's lab with people wearing EETs was on the top layer of pictures, with Anita's uneven signature in the corner of it. Wes could identify the stick figures in the drawing by hair color and position. Elizabeth's figure had hair colored fire-engine red, his own hair was the brown of tree bark, and Monica's was black. Shamita was drawn at her station with her head bent down to her computer screen, her hair in a bun. Funniest of all were Len and Wanda, who were drawn in the background, with Wanda's oval body laying on a cot, a huge cigarette in her hand, smoke rings rising from her lips and circling Len's head. At the top of the picture was Margi, a stick figure with an EET helmet, lying on a cot.

There was a coffeemaker pushed under one of the cabinets, and after trying three cupboards Wes found a can of coffee and started a pot.

"Do you want some coffee, Elizabeth?" Wes asked, hearing her come into the living room.

Elizabeth was on the couch with her legs curled under her, the quilt over her lap, a glass of wine in her hand.

"You shouldn't drink wine," Wes told her.

"When I was twenty-three I went to visit my grandfather in the hospital," Elizabeth said. "He had called and asked my grandmother to bring him a piece of her apple pie. She made it with brown sugar. Grandmother brought the pie, but the nurses wouldn't let him eat it. They said it wouldn't be good for him. He was terribly disappointed, but we gave in and took it home with us. Grandfather died that night."

Now she leaned toward him and looked at him with some of the old fire in her eyes.

"All he wanted before he died was one more piece of grandmother's pie, and they took that last little pleasure from him. I want this glass of wine, and no one's going to stop me."

"Want me to make apple pie?" Wes asked.

"With brown sugar?" she said, smiling again.

"Sure. I hope you have a recipe. I haven't a clue about what else to put in."

"Apples."

"Oh yeah," Wes said. "Does the crust form when you cook the pie or do you make that separately?"

The phone rang and Wes answered, leaving Elizabeth to sip her wine.

"Wes, is that you?" Dr. Birnbaum asked.

"It's Doctor Birnbaum," Wes told Elizabeth. Elizabeth unfolded her legs, sitting up.

"It's Ralph," Dr. Birnbaum said. "He called. He got away and he called me."

Wes repeated the news to Elizabeth and saw the spark in her eyes again.

"Is Ralph with you?" Wes asked.

"No, you've got to go get him, Wes. I can't do it, not in this wheelchair. Please bring him home."

"Where is he?"

"In a motel near Carlsbad, New Mexico. Someone found him wandering around in the cave after it had closed."

Wes repeated the information for Elizabeth.

"Let's go get him," Elizabeth said.

Trying to stand, she swayed, then dropped back to the couch. Holding her head in her hands she breathed deep and slow.

"I'll take Len, Elizabeth. We'll bring Ralph home."

INFORMER

One of seven foundation trustees, Robert Daly had been a board member for ten years and would be board chair in two years' time, when the current chair's term ended. Daly had begun his professional life in California real estate; he had turned desert into middle-class neighborhoods, investing the profits in shopping malls, office buildings, and technology stocks. Having made his fortune, he lost interest in empire building, and like other men and women reaching middle age, counted up the years he had left in life and decided to spend them more wisely than he had his youth. Not satisfied to be remembered as a rich man, Robert Daly's ambition morphed into a desire to shape the world in his image. With his fortune valued at a half-billion dollars, Daly disengaged himself from running his various enterprises and became active in politics.

A major contributor to the Republican party, he funded the campaigns of conservative candidates and backed a variety of initiatives, including those to limit property taxes and to cut off welfare payments to illegal immigrants. For a time his political activities satisfied his need to make a difference in the world, but he was soon frustrated by the uncertainty of political influence. Candidates he helped elect were more interested in being reelected than in sticking to principles. Even his work through the initiative process was frustrated by liberal activists using the courts to block implementation of his measures. Accustomed to wielding power as the chief executive of a private corporation, he was quickly disenchanted with his country's political system and the myriad of ways in which it could be subverted.

After tasting corporate and political life and finding that neither satisfied his middle-aged needs, he floundered, looking for a new direction. That was when he was approached by the Kellum Foundation.

Daly was introduced gradually to the work of the foundation, and eventually to its shadow mission. He was attracted by the willingness of the trustees to exercise the power at their disposal. Here was a way to directly shape the future of society with immediate and measurable outcomes. When the offer to become a trustee came, Daly accepted. Two years later he moved to the Chicago headquarters to take over day-to-day operations.

It was Daly who picked Dr. Martin's grant application out of hundreds that they received each month, impressed with the boldness of his vision. When Dr. Martin's studies showed that learning could be transferred from the mind of one animal to another, Daly pushed through Dr. Martin's request to fund human research. Daly was even more eager to support Dr. Martin's studies with autistic savants.

Dr. Martin had turned to savants for two reasons. Because savants were retarded in most functions, and only showed genius in one area, Dr. Martin believed that it would be easier to blend their minds than normal ones. He also believed that by blending only the genius portions of the savants' minds together, he could create a superintellect. Dr. Martin had succeeded, but in the process, he also had released a powerful psychokinetic who had killed many people.

Dr. Martin had overreacted to the deaths, vowing never to pursue that line of research again. He had foolishly dismantled his equipment and packed it away. That was why Daly had been forced to manipulate Dr. Martin into cooperating. Now Daly found that once again one of Dr. Martin's projects had taken an unexpected turn which created the need for more direct intervention, increasing the risk to the foundation. Balancing risk against gain was the job of a trustee, and Daly was a master of the art.

Daly sat with his back to the sheet of glass that was his desktop. These days, he spent much of his time with his back to his desk. It was partly because his phone was behind him, but also because he disliked seeing his feet through his desktop. He could cover the top with a desk pad, but he knew even that practical modification of this work of "art" would upset his wife and offend his son. Instead, he sat with his back to the desk, a tumbler of tea-flavored Snapple in his hand, waiting for a phone call. When it came, he answered on the second ring, turning on the speaker phone.

"Ralph found a way out," Monica Kim said.

Daly was shocked to hear of Ralph's return. He had been getting regular reports on Dr. Martin's progress from Monica, and the project had been going well until it was complicated by Ralph's kidnapping and then his appearance in the dream. Now Ralph's miraculous return opened up new possibilities.

"Dr. Martin is going to pick him up," Monica said.

"You need to go with Dr. Martin when he meets Ralph," Daly told her. "I need to know how he got out."

"Dr. Martin took Len Chaikin. They're on their way."

Daly swirled the ice in his glass, thinking. Dr. Martin didn't know the danger he was getting into and he didn't have the skills to protect himself or Ralph. Daly had to act quickly, which would increase the risk to the foundation. Still, the potential gain continued to outweigh the risk.

"Have Dr. Birnbaum call me and ask for my help. I'll make sure they have the transportation connections they need to get there and back," Daly said. "If Ralph leads Dr. Martin to the Norfolk, you need to be with him. Can you arrange that?"

"I believe so."

"I can have Dr. Chaikin removed," Daly said.

"It won't be necessary," Monica said quickly.

"If it is necessary?" Daly probed.

"I'll call," Monica said firmly.

"See that you do."

INTERCEPT

It was Ralph who escaped from Pot of Gold," Woolman said.

Woolman had tapped Dr. Birnbaum's phone and intercepted both Ralph's call to Birnbaum and Birnbaum's call to Elizabeth Foxworth. He also knew that Dr. Martin and Dr. Chaikin were on their way to pick up Ralph.

"Remarkable," Dr. Lee said. "Were any of the others with him?"

Dr. Lee was worried. He had helped to deceive Jett and his team; they were never supposed to return. Jett and the others were called agents, but that was a euphemism for what they really were—killers.

"As far as we know, Ralph is alone," Woolman said.

Dr. Lee was relieved.

"That exit is sealed?" Woolman said.

"Yes."

Woolman had called from his Washington office, his fingers drumming on the desktop. Dr. Lee was in New Mexico at the Rainbow facility. He and Woolman had been on the phone hourly since a computer at Rainbow had detected a sudden escape from Pot of Gold. Normally there were days of warning before an escape. Since exits were hidden among the spatially distorted corridors and compartments of the Norfolk, Specials usually found them through trial and error, gradually distorting the field as they neared an exit. Aided by the time distortions inside Pot of Gold, Dr. Lee usually had the exit locations approximated, and Woolman had teams of agents ready to intercept.

"It was as if Ralph knew where to find the exit," Dr. Lee said finally, referring to the lack of field distortion before the escape.

"Is that possible?"

"Improbable," Dr. Lee said.

"So Ralph accidentally found a way out?" Woolman asked.

"Perhaps. Other Specials have. Will you be bringing Ralph in?"

"I have a team on the way. They'll pick him up at the first opportunity."

"Ralph's uniqueness is intriguing," Dr. Lee said. "If it should be necessary to perform an autopsy on him, I would like our people to do it."

"Of course," Woolman said. "You can schedule the autopsy for tomorrow afternoon.

CARLSBAD

They found Ralph at White's Motel, the only motel in White's City, which was just outside the entrance to Carlsbad Cavern National Park. Wes had been honestly glad to see him until he began pumping his hand, reminding Wes of Ralph's habits. Then, during the brief trip to the cavern to see where Ralph had come from, Ralph had talked incessantly. After finding nothing in the cave, they checked out of the motel. The desk clerk handed Wes a bill for the room, long distance calls, and the general store where Ralph had run a tab buying ice cream, Icees, gum, and candy. They were now headed north to the airport, where the Kellum Foundation jet was waiting.

"Nice threads, Ralph," Len said over his shoulder to Ralph in the back seat. "You look like an astronaut."

"Thanks, Len. They gived it to me."

"Who?" Wes asked.

"Nate did. He gave me gum, too. Got any gum, Wes?"

Remembering Ralph's love of gum, Wes had come prepared. As he drove, Len handed Ralph a pack of sugar-free bubble gum. Ralph had his head between the front seats, swinging it from side to side as he talked.

"This is the stuff that's not supposed to rot your teeth, isn't it, Len?"

"Wes bought it," Len said. "I would have gotten you the kind with real sugar."

"I like both kinds, but the sugar kind lasts longer."

"We have a lot of gum, Ralph," Wes said. "If it loses its flavor I'll give you another piece." Then, remembering another of Ralph's habits, he said, "If you need to get rid of a piece of gum I'll give you a tissue."

"You wouldn't put your gum under the seat, would you?" Len said.

Ralph puckered his lips and glanced away, trying to look innocent. "Not me, Len. I wouldn't put my gum under the seat."

"Good, because that's where I'm keeping mine."

Len laughed at his own joke, and Ralph grinned, his fleshy lips stretching wide.

"Are you sure you took us back to the spot where you found yourself in the cave?"

"Sure I'm sure," Ralph said. "Except before it was different. There was this green light shaped kind of like my mother's mirror. You know, a long circle."

"An oval," Wes suggested.

"I guess so," Ralph said. "Anyways, that's where I comed from."

Ralph had an uncanny sense of direction, and if he said that this was where he had come from, it was, but then where was the green oval now? What had created it? Why had it disappeared? Where did it lead? According to Ralph, he came from a ship and there were other people on the ship. Where was this ship?

"Tell me about the people who took you to the ship, Ralph," Wes said.

"There was Nate, and Karla, and Jim, and Robin and Billy and me."

"Nate's the one that gave you those clothes?" Wes probed.

"Yeah. Everybody got some. We all looked the same. Except Billy's got kind of ruined 'cause something bad happened to Billy."

"What?" Wes asked.

"He gots burned up."

"He died?" Len asked.

"I think so, but I dunno for sure. Robin got burned, too, one time and he didn't die."

"Robin had scars?" Wes asked.

"Lots," Ralph said.

Ralph's account confirmed details from Elizabeth's dream visits.

"Was there fighting on the ship?" Wes asked.

"Yeah. There are these bad people—Crazies. They were fighting with us. I wanted to talk to them so they wouldn't be mad, but they wouldn't let me."

Wes drove, listening to Ralph describe the fighting, piecing together a picture of two factions battling each other with makeshift weapons and psi powers. Wes had seen a psychokinetic in action, throwing objects with his mind and nearly killing Len and him. He had also heard of the ability of some to generate heat with their minds, and some who could muster a mild electric charge, but nothing to match the levels Ralph described.

Len continued to probe for details, Wes listening to Ralph's description of the strange environment of the ship. He needed information to find the source of the dream and stop it, and save Elizabeth and Anita.

It was pitch dark now, the road ahead straight and empty. He turned the headlights on high beam, illuminating the road far into the distance. In his rearview mirror he saw the lights of a car coming up behind.

"Then Nate stuck his finger in it and got lectrocuted."

Ralph was talking about the man named Nate getting shocked, reminding Wes of what happened to Elizabeth.

"He was shocked?" Len asked.

"Real bad. He was shaking and twitching on the ground."

The lights from the car behind were bright now. As he reached to change the angle of the mirror, the car pulled into the left lane, passing. Wes slowed, making it easier for the driver to pass. The car pulled parallel, then matched speed with Wes.

"What's this about?" Len said, leaning down so he could see out of Wes's window. "He's got a gun!"

Wes turned and saw a black van next to them, a man with a gun leaning out of the window. The man mouthed "pull over." Wes jammed on his brakes, and the van shot ahead. The van driver was quick, hitting his own brakes. Hand over hand, Wes cranked the wheel, trying to make a U-turn. The shoulder was too soft; Wes had to stop, back up, then turn again. The van couldn't match their turning radius, but it had a better driver who didn't bother to turn. Instead he put the van in reverse, tires squealing as he raced backwards, passing Wes, then parking crossways in the road.

Gun in hand, the man jumped out and fired two shots into the passenger door. Len gasped, then clutched his leg.

"I'm shot," Len said.

"Does it hurt bad?" Ralph asked.

Wes looked, but it was too dark to see the wound. When he looked up, the gun was pointed at him. Wes's engine was running, with the car in forward gear; the man with the gun was standing just to the right, aiming his gun through the front windshield. Wes estimated his chances of gunning it and knocking the man down, or at least spoiling his aim. He agonized over his choice, too analytical to be good in emergencies.

Then the man with the gun was distracted, looking past the car into the sky. A few seconds later Wes heard the thumping sound of a helicopter. The man with the gun hesitated, but then came toward the driver's door, gun still trained on Wes. Wes put up his hands. Just as the man reached the car door, the ground around him erupted with a dozen tiny dust geysers. A black helicopter roared overhead, a man leaning out with a machine gun. The helicopter turned to come back for another pass while the man who attacked them ran to his van.

Wes stomped the throttle, tires spinning and spewing gravel. Then they were racing down the highway, the engine whining, the transmission in passing gear. The helicopter passed over, chasing the van. Wes heard the automatic rifle fire as the helicopter strafed the van. In his rearview mirror he saw the van racing in the opposite direction, the helicopter circling above. He could see flashes of gunfire from the helicopter even after the van had disappeared over a hill.

"Len, how bad is it?" Wes asked.

"I'll live," Len said.

"Does it hurt?" Ralph asked again.

"Yes," Len said through gritted teeth.

"Want me to put a Band-aid on it?" Ralph said. "Sometimes it makes it feel better."

"Later," Len said. "What was that all about?"

"Those men in the van might be connected to whoever kidnapped Ralph. I don't know about the helicopter," Wes said.

Holding his leg, Len leaned against the car window, eyes closed.

"I'll get you to a hospital, Len."

"It's not bad, but there's something stuck in my leg."

"I was in the hospital once," Ralph said. "When I got out they borrowed me a lectric wheelchair. Maybe you could get one, Len? I could show you how to drive it."

They raced down the highway, Len holding his injured leg, Ralph prattling on, Wes alternating between worrying about Elizabeth and worrying about Len, and wondering how to find the dream ship.

THE LOST

With Jett and Compton providing cover fire in the rear, and Peters protecting Dr. Kellum in the lead, they fought the Crazies to a stalemate. Then they retreated, winding through the Norfolk to Dr. Kellum's levels of the ship. They were ambushed twice and had many wounded, but had bloodied the Crazies as well; finally the attacks had stopped. Both sides pulled back to let their wounded heal. Kellum's people were gathered in the hangar, guards posted at all the entrances, Dawson sensing with his telepathic ability for the Crazies. Jett circulated, checking the survivors, seeing who was able to fight. There were many wounded; some cut, some burned, some with the deep puncture wounds from crossbow bolts. All were healing rapidly.

It was as if Pot of Gold had a memory of the condition they were in when they first arrived and tried to keep their bodies in that state. Only severe trauma couldn't be overcome. But what about decay? What would happen to the bodies of the dead? Jett knew that Kellum had a graveyard on one level. Did the bodies simply lie under the soil, forever maintained by the field?

Jett found Peters and Compton at one end of the hangar, sitting on a spare pontoon for one of the biplanes.

"They don't work," Jett said, tapping Compton's hip unit. "I tested mine. Touching the field nearly killed me."

Compton swore, then released the catch, dropping the belt.

"Dr. Lee and I are gonna have to have a little talk when we get back," Peters said, then clucked his tongue.

"Evans got out of Pot of Gold on his first mission," Compton reminded them.

"Woolman had Lee open a door from Rainbow," Jett said. "The hip units were supposed to make that unnecessary. Woolman isn't going to let us out of here if he can help it. Not after he double-crossed us."

"If Specials get out, then we can get out," Compton said.

"There are exits," Jett said. "But once they're used, they seal them at Rainbow. If we do find one, we need to go through it together."

"That's the trick, isn't it?" Peters said. "Finding one."

"Ralph found at least three doors," Jett said. "We only got to test one of them."

"So where is Ralph?" Peters said.

"He may be gone," Jett said. "He went looking for a way home."

"So we'll have to find them ourselves," Compton said.

She said it confidently, and Peters winked agreement.

Dr. Kellum pushed his way through the crowd in the hangar, coming straight to Jett.

"We have a problem," Dr. Kellum said.

Jett's underreactive nervous system responded, and he felt a touch of amusement. He could think of a dozen problems, each worse than the other.

"The man who came with you, the one with the scars?" Dr. Kellum said.

"Evans," Jett said.

"He's going to destroy the generators."

They had come to find the Nimitz, but if the carrier wasn't inside Pot of Gold, they were to destroy the generators. Now they were trapped inside Pot of Gold and couldn't destroy it until they had a way out.

"How do you know Evans is alive?" Compton asked.

"He attacked two of my people. He made one lead him to the generators."

"He doesn't know the hip unit doesn't work," Compton said.

"He doesn't care if it works," Peters said. "He came to kill everyone in Pot of Gold and he doesn't care if he dies doing it."

"If he destroys the generators, how long will we have?" Jett asked Kellum.

"Hours at most."

Jett now had two objectives. He needed to find a way out of Pot of Gold, and he needed to stop Evans. No one knew where the other doors were that Ralph had found. Dr. Kellum had been in Pot of Gold for fifty years and had not found them. That would take time, but Evans was heading to the generators and would destroy them. Between his special power and his gun, Evans was formidable, and there was a chance he would succeed.

"We need to split up," Jett said. "Compton and I and a few of your people will try to stop Evans. You take Peters and the rest and try to find the doors Ralph mentioned."

"We know where they're not," Dr. Kellum said. "We'll search the levels between here and Crazy territory. There must be branches we're missing."

"We'll find our way back to here, but you'll have to set up a relay so we can find you," Jett said. "I want to take one of your telepathics with us."

"Take Dawson, he's the best," Dr. Kellum said.

A runner went for Dawson, and Jett studied the sailor's walk as he came. He still had a bit of a limp, but his leg was well healed.

Dr. Kellum shook Jett's hand, wishing him luck. Peters winked at Jett, then followed Dr. Kellum and his people. Kellum's group numbered about seventy, and there were other pockets of his people in hiding who they would pick up on the way.

Jett took just four men besides Dawson and Compton. He refused Dr. Kellum's Specials, instead taking two sailors armed with crossbows, one armed with a spear, and a Hispanic civilian named Roberto. Roberto had wandered into Pot of Gold while playing hide-and-seek with a nephew in the dunes of a Florida beach. He carried a homemade machete and handled it proficiently. With one of the sailors in the lead, Jett and the others set out to save what Jett had come to destroy.

HOMECOMING

You don't look so good, Elizabeth," Ralph said as soon as he saw her. "You want I should get you a laxative or something? I had the chocolate kind once. It looks like a Hershey bar but it tastes yucky."

"It's so good to see you," Elizabeth said, tears of joy coming to her eyes. From her couch, where she lay covered with a quilt, Elizabeth reached out, and Ralph leaned down accepting the hug.

Wes had been gone for a only a day, but seeing Elizabeth again had been a shock.

"We called Doctor Birnbaum on the way back," Wes said before she could ask.

Ralph sat with Elizabeth and talked while Wes fixed dinner. Wes lived alone and usually cooked for one. There were only three of them, so he up-sized his spaghetti recipe. He added prepackaged salad, and biscuits made from a mix he found in one of Elizabeth's cabinets.

Elizabeth ate little, but Ralph wolfed his food down when he wasn't talking. He slurped up long strands of spaghetti, leaving tomato-sauce tracks on his chin. His talk wandered from stories of weight lifting with "Nate" to the design on Elizabeth's plates—which were decorated with fruit. Slowly they pieced together Ralph's story, from when he was kidnapped until he walked through a green fog and into Carlsbad Caverns. Wes finished Ralph's narrative by recounting the incident on the highway to the airport. After dinner, Ralph found the Cartoon Network on Elizabeth's television and zoned out. Elizabeth sat at the kitchen table while Wes loaded the dishwasher.

"It's time to let me go," Elizabeth said.

She meant "let me die."

Wes kept his back to her, scraping plates into the garbage disposal. His eyes were tearing.

"I can't give up, Elizabeth," Wes said.

"You have to, Wes. Whatever is going on is real. It's not a dream and it's dangerous. People are dying."

"We only need to find Dawson. He's the link to you and Anita. If I can get to him, maybe I can stop this."

"I don't want anyone dying to save me. It's too late."

"What about Anita?"

"Anita can't be saved, either," Elizabeth said.

Wes had never seen Elizabeth this way—exhausted and beaten. The dream was sucking the life out of her and there was little left to take. He continued working, wiping the countertops and table.

"Promise me you'll stop looking for the ship?" Elizabeth said.

"I can't."

Elizabeth's chin sank to her chest.

"I guess there's no point in arguing," Elizabeth said. "We don't know how to get to wherever it is Ralph went to."

Her speech was slow and slurred. It reminded Wes of Margi's speech just before she died.

"Ralph said the place they left from was in a desert, and he returned in New Mexico," Wes said. "Doctor Birnbaum thinks we might start by locating all the secret military bases in the Southwest."

"If they're secret bases, then how will we find them?"

"Doctor Birnbaum says there are groups that keep track of military movements and locate secret operations. He'll contact them on the Internet."

"Even if you find where they took Ralph, they'll deny everything."

"We don't know that for sure," Wes said. "Whatever is going on may be legitimate and explainable."

Elizabeth shook her head. "I'm going to lie down."

Wes made sure she got to her room without falling. Elizabeth sat on the bed, rested for a second, and then rolled to her side. Wes covered her with a quilt and reached for the light.

"Leave the light on," she whispered.

He finished in the kitchen and then poured Ralph a glass of root beer and himself a glass of white wine. He put the glass on the table nearest Ralph, who sat cross-legged on the floor directly in front of the television.

"Thanks, Wes," Ralph said.

The Jetsons were on. It was one of the few cartoons Wes recognized, although since meeting Ralph his knowledge of popular culture had grown significantly. His own childhood had been spent in libraries.

The phone rang just as Jetson was being fired by his boss. Dr. Birnbaum was on the line.

"I may have something for you," Dr. Birnbaum said.

"You found where Ralph was taken?"

"Not exactly. There are at least twenty-seven government installations in the Southwest that are not acknowledged by any government branch. There was no way to narrow down the list based on what Ralph told you. Instead, I contacted our friend on the Internet who gave us the information about the Philadelphia Project. I'm still convinced that's the most likely connection."

Wes wasn't convinced, but he had no better ideas.

"He suggested there is a link between certain disappearances and the ship Ralph visited."

"Disappearances?" Wes probed.

"Yes. I downloaded some articles from a file he directed me to. They're the kind of stories you see in grocery-store tabloids—someone walking down the street suddenly disappearing and never being found again, things like that."

"What's the connection?" Wes asked.

"Think of what Ralph said. One second he was on the ship from the dream and the next second he finds himself in a cave in New Mexico."

"I don't understand," Wes admitted.

"Think of it in reverse. What if Ralph was walking through the cave and suddenly disappeared?"

"It would sound just like a tabloid story," Wes admitted.

"Exactly," Birnbaum said, excitement in his voice.

"But we searched the cave and didn't find anything like what Ralph described."

"No, but that might be because the passages are one-way. Ralph came from the ship to the cave. We need to find a route that goes in the other direction, to the ship."

"How?"

"If there are such paths to the ship, then anyone who stumbles into one might disappear just as quickly as Ralph appeared. I have a dozen articles describing such incidents going back twenty years."

"All from the Southwest?" Wes asked.

"From all over the country—one in Canada. I tried plotting them, but there's no discernible pattern. Then my Internet friend sent me an article frrm a Las Vegas newspaper. It's about a Hispanic Presbyterian church there that bought property near the outskirts of town. The minister was walking around the property when he suddenly disappeared. There were three witnesses who confirmed he vanished. The entire congregation turned out to search the lot, but they never found him."

"You think there's a passage to the ship?" Wes said.

"Yes. It happened only three days ago, Wes. We don't know how stable these passages are. If it's there, it might not last long. You must leave tonight. The Kellum Foundation jet is still at the Eugene airport. Mr. Daly is leaving it at our disposal."

Events were moving too fast, and Wes didn't want to leave Elizabeth in order to run off on a wild goose chase.

"But they searched the area and found nothing. Why would I have better luck?" Wes argued.

"Because you have Ralph."

DOOR

Wes wanted to buy Ralph new clothes, but Dr. Birnbaum had insisted that they leave immediately. So Ralph was still wearing his silver suit and boots when they returned to the airport. The Kellum Foundation jet was waiting where they had left it, refueled and ready to whisk them to Las Vegas. Ralph reintroduced himself to the flight crew, even though Wes doubted that anyone would forget a large retarded man dressed like an astronaut. Monica did her best to keep Ralph distracted on the drive to the airport, and away from Wes.

The Kellum Foundation jet seated a dozen people; a separate area served as a small conference room. The interior was decorated in the foundation colors of gold and royal blue. The carpet was blue with gold fleur-de-lis, the seats gold with blue accents. Wes and Ralph sat next to each other, with Monica in the opposite seat facing them. Wes watched impatiently while Ralph fumbled with his seat belt, then pushed Ralph's hands out of the way, leaned over him, and snapped it shut.

"Thanks, Wes. Mine's kinda hard to do. But I remember how to undo it."

Before Wes could stop him, Ralph pulled on the release and the seat belt was loose again.

"Oops!" Ralph said. "I can fix it in a jiff."

Ralph fumbled with the seat belt again, finally sliding the tongue into the right slot. The seat belt latched with a satisfying click.

"See, I told you I could do it."

Once they reached cruising altitude and the seat belt sign went off, Ralph was out of his seat and in the aisle, his head barely clearing the ceiling of the jet. The flight attendant had been amused by Ralph on the trip north from New Mexico, and actually seemed happy to be flying with him again. When Ralph finished with the attendant, he got into the cockpit and worked the pilots, who also greeted him like a long-lost friend. Ralph was like a joke that everyone in the world got, except Wes. Eventually Ralph remembered the free snacks and the refrigerator filled with sodas, and busied himself sampling everything.

Despite Wes's irritation with Ralph, a deeper part of Wes liked him, but he wasn't someone with whom he could share his worries about Elizabeth. Monica was there too, sitting across from Wes, but he didn't consider her a friend. She had been too eager to risk Elizabeth's life by keeping her in the dream, and her reaction to Len's injury was peculiar. She was more interested in the van and the helicopter than Len's wound. Wes wished Len was with him, or Shamita. They had been the closest to him before he met Elizabeth. But Len was injured, and Shamita was needed at the lab in case they found the ship.

Wes had refused to leave Elizabeth alone. And Elizabeth had stubbornly refused to have Shamita, Len, or Wanda as roommates. Only when Anita's mother offered to have Elizabeth stay with her, had Elizabeth agreed. Wes had dropped her off on the way to the airport, helping her inside and to the living room couch. Looking nearly as haggard as Elizabeth, Anita sat beside her holding her hand.

"I'll be back as soon as I can," Wes said to Anita's mother.

"She's welcome here. She tried to help Anita and now she's got the dream too."

With no one to talk to, Wes reclined his seat and closed his eyes. He drifted off to sleep, waking when the engines changed pitch for the descent to Las Vegas.

There was a rental car waiting for them, arranged by the Kellum Foundation; inside they found a map marked with the location of the property where the pastor had disappeared.

"How can they know all this?" Wes asked as Monica climbed into the passenger side and Ralph settled in the back seat.

"I spoke with Mr. Daly," Monica said. "He wanted to help us as much as he could."

As far as Wes knew, Dr. Birnbaum had handled the arrangements with the Kellum Foundation; and it was disquieting that Monica was on a speaking basis with one of the trustees.

It was early morning, and the traffic was thick as workers hurried to their jobs. Slowly they worked their way to the outskirts of town where subdivisions spread across the desert. Eventually the subdivisions thinned, and soon there were open patches of desert and many constructions sites. They found the empty lot where the church was to be built, pulling over behind a blue Dodge pickup. There was a fish symbol on the tailgate of the truck. At the edge of the lot was a sign reading "Future Home of New Westminster Presbyterian Church—In Your Neighborhood For You!"

Ralph was out first, slamming his door, waking a man sleeping in the pickup. The man got out and joined them by the sign. Ralph intercepted him, shaking his hand. The man studied Ralph's peculiar clothes.

"Hihowyadoin. My name's Ralph and this here's Wes and this here's Monica. What's your name?"

The man was much shorter than Ralph, but just as broad. He had black hair and a thin mustache. He looked Hispanic, but when he spoke it was without a trace of an accent.

"I'm Miguel Lopez. I'm the associate pastor of New Westminster Church."

"How did you know to meet us here?" Wes asked.

"I got a call. Someone named Daly asked me if I'd come over and tell you where Pastor Rivera disappeared. He wasn't sure when you would arrive, so I came over and spent the night in my truck. I didn't want to miss you."

"He shouldn't have gotten your hopes up," Wes said.

"Anything you can do will be appreciated. We've been praying for the pastor—and Mr. Daly's call came in the middle of our prayer vigil. Maybe it's God's answer, maybe it isn't."

"We'll do what we can," Monica said.

It was the kind of reassurance Elizabeth would have given. Not a promise to find their missing pastor, just a promise to try.

"Can you show us where you last saw the pastor?" Wes said to Lopez.

Lopez looked into the field for a second and then into the distance at a housing project on the other side of the lot, as if he was using the project as a marker.

"Follow me," he said.

He led them a third of the way into the lot and then stopped.

"It was right about here," Lopez said. "He was pacing along here, showing some of us how much of the lot the building footprint would take up. We were having doubts about whether the lot was going to be big enough. We wanted to have enough room for parking and a playground. We run a day care and preschool during the week."

"Can you describe exactly what happened?" Monica asked.

"He was walking back and forth, pacing and counting his steps, and suddenly he just disappeared—vanished right in front of us."

"Was there a green glow when he did?" Wes asked.

"I didn't see one," Lopez said.

The vegetation on the property was sparse—dark green or gray in color—and had been well trampled by dozens of criss-crossing searchers.

"Did you try following his footprints?" Monica asked.

"Follow them where?" Lopez said, indicating the flat land. "We looked for a well, or sink hole, or anything he could have fallen into, but there's nothing anywhere in the field."

Wes had no ideas for finding the pastor, but Elizabeth's gaunt face haunted him, and so he tried the absurd. He began to pace as if he was using his stride to measure the perimeter of the building. Monica joined him, walking a different path but mimicking his movements. Ralph watched, chewing a wad of gum, his face blank.

"We tried that," Lopez said. "We even got out the plans and marked length and width and all the ins and outs of the plan. We walked it off, over and over. We never found him."

Wes felt silly, but he kept walking, trying to think like a pastor who was proud of his new church building but worried that the lot they had purchased was too small. Monica gave up before Wes, going to stand by Lopez and Ralph. Wes kept trying, fearful that giving up would condemn Elizabeth to death. Eventually he had no hope left. Then he thought of Ralph.

"Ralph, we're trying to find a way to the ship," Wes said.

Ralph smiled, his loose lips spreading wide while his jaws started mashing the wad of gum between his molars at a rapid clip.

"Is that what you was doing? I thought you lost something. I would a helped ya look, but I didn't cause I thought it was a contact lens. I found one for Mrs. Binbam once, but I stepped on it first and it wasn't so good after that."

"We're looking for a way to the ship, Ralph. Can you help us find one?" Wes asked.

"I dunno, Wes. I might could. I'm kinda thirsty, though."

"If you find a way I'll buy you a Slurpee."

"Medium?" Ralph asked.

"Yes," Wes agreed.

"Well okee-dokee then," Ralph said.

Ralph walked out toward Wes and then walked to and fro, head down, his face blank. Wes stood beside Lopez and Monica, letting Ralph have the run of the field.

"Ralph's a little different," Lopez said tactfully.

"Educable mentally retarded," Wes said.

Wes could imagine what Lopez was thinking. He had met them at the field with renewed hope, knowing that a scientist was coming to examine the field where his pastor had disappeared. But the scientist had been no help and had turned the investigation over to a mentally retarded man in a silver suit who was being paid in Slurpees.

Ralph walking aimlessly, had no better luck. Wes was about to give up when Ralph stopped and stared straight ahead as if fixed on something in the distance. Then Ralph reversed himself, walking here and there just as he had before. Finally, he turned and walked directly toward Wes.

"I found it," Ralph said.

"Found what?" Wes asked him.

"The way to the ship, Wes. You gots to buy me a Slurpee."

"There's nothing there, Ralph," Wes protested.

"Sure it's there, Wes, but you can't see it from here."

Wes looked across the flat field. None of the vegetation was more then a foot high.

"Can you point to it?" Monica suggested.

Ralph raised his hand, pointed his finger, and then said, "It's down this way, and then that way, and then this way, and then that way, that way, then that way and then that way . . ."

With every "that way," Ralph's finger twisted to a new direction.

"Maybe it would be easier if you showed us," Monica said.

Ralph folded his arms across his chest and leaned back, pelvis thrust forward, shoulders back. It was his serious thinking posture.

"I dunno, I'm getting kinda thirsty."

"Show us and I'll buy you a Slurpee today and a rootbeer float tomorrow."

Ralph snapped upright, his face one big smile from chin to hairline.

"It's a deal, and a deal's a deal! Follow me."

Monica walked behind Ralph while Wes paralleled Ralph until he turned sharply left and then a few yards later made a similar move. Wes cut across the angle, easily keeping up with Ralph, who was walking twice Wes's speed. When Ralph saw what Wes was doing he stopped and put his hands on his hips, puckered his lips, and scolded him.

"You can't get there that way."

"I'm with you, Ralph," Wes protested.

His lips still puckered, Ralph wrinkled his brow as if he was thinking deep thoughts. Then he spoke like a patient kindergarten teacher.

"It's like follow the leader, Wes. I'm the leader and you have to follow. Let's do it again, but this time we'll hold hands."

"I'm not going to—" Wes sputtered.

"Play along," Monica said. "What have we got to lose?"

Ralph reversed his meandering pattern and then came straight to Wes, Monica following.

"Okay, now let's hold hands," Ralph said.

Ralph reached for Wes's hand, but Wes stepped behind Monica, letting her take Ralph's hand; then he took hers. Ralph led the way, walking straight for the distance and then turning a sharp right. Monica followed Ralph as precisely as she could, stepping exactly to the farthest point Ralph stepped before turning. Wes made a reasonable effort to copy Ralph, feeling foolish as they meandered through the lot.

Lopez remained where he was, watching intently. Wes wondered if Lopez was seeing any similarity to the pattern his pastor had walked.

"Do you see it now?" Ralph said suddenly.

"There is something," Monica said.

Wes's heart skipped a beat and he caught his breath. Trying to stay in line, he looked past Monica and Ralph. Ralph's broad shoulders blocked most of the view, but Wes could see a greenish glow. Realizing that Ralph had done it, he tried to stop their march. Only he and Monica were to go to the ship if they found a way.

"Wait, Ralph," Wes said.

"We're almost there," Ralph said, trudging ahead.

Before Wes could shout again, Ralph made a sharp left turn and disappeared into the green glow, pulling Monica and Wes with him.

VANISHED

Mr. Daly, this is Miguel Lopez."

"Something's happened?" Daly said into the receiver.

Daly started a digital recorder, checking the display to be sure the conversation was encoding. Lopez might know a route into Pot of Gold.

"It was just like before with Pastor Rivera. Those people you sent, the man and woman and that other guy, they just vanished."

Daly turned, sliding to the edge of his chair and leaning on the glass surface of his desk. He could see his feet tucked under his chair, the toes of his shoes pressed into the plush carpet as if he were ready to leap to his feet.

"Tell me how they did it."

"They asked me to show them where Pastor Rivera disappeared and then they started walking back and forth just like the pastor did. They tried for a long time but then gave up."

"Doctor Martin didn't find anything?" Daly said.

"No. The woman didn't either. That's when they asked the retarded man if he could do it."

"His name is Ralph."

"Yes, Ralph. He walked back and forth just like they did except after a

while he said he found it. Then he made them hold hands and follow him
and then they walked back and forth until they vanished, just like Pastor
Rivera."

"Ralph too?" Daly asked.

"All of them."

"Did you try following their path?"

"Yes, but it was too complicated to remember. I must have tried fifty
variations before I gave up."

Daly sighed with disappointment. Ralph had found the aperture either
because of his unique directional sense or because he could home in on
dimensional openings. Without Ralph there was little chance of stumbling
across the route in. There was movement below, and through the desk he
saw his feet come out from under his chair. He was relaxing, his best hope
gone. Leaning back, he considered his options.

He could use the foundation's resources to find someone else with
Ralph's location sense, but there was no one like Ralph in the foundation's
extensive records of people with unique abilities. Without Ralph, Daly
couldn't send reinforcements. But at least it wasn't a total loss; he had succeeded in getting Monica inside.

ELIZABETH'S LINK

Elizabeth was dreaming with her eyes open. She was on the ship and staring at something she couldn't quite see, but she knew it was horrible. She was in an empty compartment with hammocks hung from the walls. Without the link to the other dreamers the scene lacked detail. Some hammocks hung without support, floating in the air in defiance of gravity. Texture and color were missing, but it wasn't the lack of detail that bothered her. There was something cold and pervasive, like the chill from a plunge in a winter lake, that caused her to shiver with dread. There was death in that room, and the man she linked with was in the middle of it.

Anita came in then, distracting her. While the scenes on the ship continued, Elizabeth focussed on Anita and the real world. Elizabeth was lying on Anita's mother's bed. The room was decorated in pink, the quilt covered with bouquets of roses. The headboard, bed tables, and dresser were white wicker. Everything else in the room was selected to match the decor—it looked as if it could grace the cover of *Better Homes and Gardens*.

Anita sat on the edge of the bed, wearing a pink sweatshirt covered with small bunnies hopping in all directions. Elizabeth could see the little girl's own exhaustion, understanding now how draining the ship dream was.

"You're there, aren't you, Elizabeth?" Anita asked. "You're on the ship."

"Yes."

"Is something bad happening?" Anita asked.

"Yes, but I can't see it."

"Good," Anita said, and then lay next to her, head on her shoulder.

A phone rang in the living room, and then Anita's mother came in, handing the phone to Elizabeth. Dr. Birnbaum was on the line.

"It worked, Elizabeth. They're inside—they're there," Birnbaum said.

Elizabeth sat up, the image of the ship still with her, but pushed now to a corner of her mind.

"They found a way to wherever Ralph came from?" Elizabeth asked.

"I think so."

Elizabeth was afraid and hopeful at the same time. If they could stop the dreams, then Anita and she would be saved, but to stop them Wes and Monica would have to put themselves in danger. Terrible things were happening on the ship.

"Tell them not to go," Elizabeth said.

Elizabeth's mind was fuzzy from lack of real sleep and distracted by the ship images still running in the background.

"But they have gone, Elizabeth," Dr. Birnbaum said. "They disappeared just like the pastor."

"All of them? Ralph too?"

"Yes."

Groggy and distracted by the images tucked away in the corner of her mind, Elizabeth couldn't concentrate. She had been afraid that they would find what they were looking for, and hadn't wanted Wes and Monica to go in the first place. Now those who were dear to her were in that nightmare world.

"Don't worry, Elizabeth. Ralph found a way out once and he can do it again."

Elizabeth thanked Dr. Birnbaum and asked him to call if he heard anything else. Then she handed the phone back to Anita's mother, who waited expectantly.

"They may have found a way to the ship in Anita's dream. It means they might be able to stop the dream, but it also means they are in danger. We need to know what is going on. We might be able to help them in some way."

"You want to dream with Anita again?" Anita's mother said.

"If there was another way . . ." Elizabeth said.

"Anita, go get yourself a snack. There are chocolate chip cookies in the jar."

Reluctantly Anita climbed off the bed and left. When she was gone, her mother sat at the end of the bed, running her hand across the rose-covered bedspread, smoothing out wrinkles. Anita's mother was meticulous and tender. Watching her daughter slowly deteriorate was painful for her.

"Anita is going to die, isn't she?"

Elizabeth hesitated. The truth was cruel, but Elizabeth knew it was time to be brutally honest.

"Yes," Elizabeth said softly. "Unless the dream can be stopped she will die."

"You're dying too, aren't you?"

"Yes. I don't have much time left. Not as much time as Anita."

"Every time you share Anita's dream it makes you worse, and now you have the dream too."

"Whatever it is about Anita and Wanda—and Margi—that makes them receive the dream was latent in me. By sharing the dream we activated the receiving part of my brain. Every time we share the dream I become more sensitive. I dream about the ship even when I'm awake now."

Anita's mother was a strong woman who had explored every avenue to help her daughter. She was also a realist, knowing when the battle was nearing an end.

"Are we shortening Anita's life when you blend the dreams?"

"I don't think so. Wanda isn't physically affected by the dream at all, and I'm particularly sensitive. Anita falls somewhere between the two extremes. If sharing the dream is accelerating her decline, it's a small effect."

"It doesn't matter," Anita's mother said.

Her face softened, sadness settling in.

"Her slow death is slow torture for me. A quick death would be kinder for both of us."

Then her face hardened again as she controlled her grief.

"Anita is still frightened by the scarred man she saw on the ship, and the people in walls and other terrible things. The dream is bad enough for her alone, but when you share the dream with her it becomes a nightmare. I'm willing to let her help, but not if she has to see those things again."

"It may be possible to keep her from seeing details on the ship. I'm a strong receiver now, so we might be able to set the parameters so that she helps receive but doesn't perceive the dream."

Satisfied, Anita's mother stood.

"I'll ask Anita if she wants to help."

When she was gone, Elizabeth picked up the phone and punched in Shamita's number to tell her to prepare the lab. As she listened to the ringing, she realized that the ship dream was still running in a corner of her mind, and it was growing, threatening to take over her consciousness. One way or another, with or without the other dreamers, she would soon be back on the ship.

CAPTURED

U h-oh!" Ralph said. "We're not supposed to be here."

Wes and Monica looked around in wonder. One minute they had been walking in a field on the outskirts of Las Vegas, and the next they found themselves standing in a compartment—a ship's compartment. The door they had come through was open, and there was no sign of the green glow. They were in a control room with old-fashioned equipment—radios, radar, sonar, Wes guessed.

"A radio room?" Wes asked.

"Fire control center," Monica said confidently. Then, pointing through the windows, she said, "They directed the fire of the five- and eight-inch guns from here. With later designs they moved fire control below decks. This was too exposed."

Surprised by her detailed knowledge of warships, Wes's suspicions grew. He stepped to the windows that ran the width of one wall and saw the bow of the ship stretched out below. Three turrets were mounted there, one in front of the other. Each turret had three large gun barrels pointed at the bow.

"This is incredible," Wes said. "How is it possible?"

Wes stepped back through the door he thought they had come through and found himself in a chart room. There was a large flat table in the middle and racks along one wall filled with rolled charts.

"Flag plot," Monica said as he came out.

"We're not getting home that way," Wes said. Then to Ralph, he said, "Can you find another way back?"

Ralph folded his arms and leaned back, looking serious, his lips puckered.

"I'll buy you an ice-cream if you do," Monica offered.

"Chocolate dip?" Ralph countered.

"A large one," Monica said.

"Well okee-dokee, then," Ralph said. "It's a deal and a deal's a deal. Let's go."

"Not yet, Ralph," Wes said. "We need to find the man called Dawson. Can you take us to him?"

"We gots to get out of here," Ralph said, starting to walk. "This is where the not so nice people live."

"The Crazies?" Wes probed, remembering the term from Ralph's disjointed description of his experiences.

"They're not so nice. I could talk to them if you want. Sometimes if you talk real nice to people they're not so bad any more."

"Let's go straight to Dawson," Wes said.

"That's a good idea," Ralph agreed.

Ralph led them through the chart room and outside, climbing down a series of ladders to the deck below. Wes continued to be amazed by what he saw—it was a World War II–vintage warship, in perfect condition. Fascinated by the ship, he and Monica had trouble resisting the urge to explore. But Ralph left no time for side trips, setting a brisk pace.

As they climbed down a ladder to the first gun deck level, Wes found himself staring through the rungs at a human face protruding from the steel of the superstructure. Startled, he jumped the rest of the way, landing with a loud thump.

"Don't be scared, Wes. He won't hurt you," Ralph reassured him.

"I'm not scared," Wes lied.

"There's lots more like him, but there's no use talking to them cause they don't say nothing."

"Let's go," Wes said, eyes on the face in the wall.

Monica studied the face, too, reaching behind the ladder to touch the skin where it met the wall.

"It's warm, like he's alive," Monica said.

Ralph took them through a dark hatch that logically should have taken them toward midship, but they found themselves outside. Ralph didn't slow, seemingly used to the peculiar time-and-space–twisting geometry of the ship. Wes and Monica drifted toward the rail.

"Slow down a second," Monica said to Ralph.

Ralph stopped to lecture them.

"We should keep going, Monica," Ralph said.

"Just a quick look," Monica said.

Wes and Monica looked over the rail, still struck by the impossibility of this ship in the desert. Just as the dreamers had described, there was desert running a hundred yards from the ship and ending in an opaque wall. Wes looked up and saw nothing above. Looking toward the stern, he saw one of the seaplanes mounted on the stern, and more big guns pointed aft. Then he saw four men emerge from behind the catapult. The biggest man was dressed in jeans, denim jacket, and boots. His hair was long and black. The three men behind him were sailors, two carrying spears and one a crossbow.

"We gotta go, Wes," Ralph said. "The big one's name is Mr. Cobb and he can hurt ya."

Wes believed Ralph. Cobb's every move was menacing and his eyes were two coals that burned bright despite their blackness.

They only made a few steps when more men and two women came from the bow, cutting off their escape. They backed under a turret, mounted midships, the twin barrels of the guns above them. Seeing no escape along the deck, Wes pulled the others toward a hatch next to the gun.

"That's not the way, Wes," Ralph protested.

"Hurry," Wes said.

Monica ran ahead while Wes pulled Ralph toward the hatch. Just as Monica opened the hatch, she was lit up with tiny lightning bolts. She fell to the ground, writhing and twitching. The air crackled with the high-pitched buzz of electric current, and the air smelled of ozone. Wes held Ralph back.

"Stop it!" Wes shouted. "You're killing her!"

Cobb turned to Wes. Wes felt the man's insanity and saw it in the slow way he moved. Then Cobb brought his hands up, his fingers extended and spread wide like a magician casting a spell.

"Hihowyadoin?" Ralph said, extending his hand.

Sparks flew from Cobb's fingers as if he were a human Jacob's ladder, the bright blue arcs enveloping Ralph. Ralph collapsed, his body convulsing on the deck. Wes pleaded with Cobb, but the electrocution continued. Desperate, Wes jumped over Ralph, throwing himself into the electrical storm.

Wes was being electrocuted. He lost muscle control and crashed to the deck. His heart, losing the steady rhythm it had kept since the womb, now beat erratically. His eyes teared, his body begged for oxygen, but he couldn't breathe. His heart felt as if it was coming apart in his chest.

"That's enough, Cobb," a woman said.

But it wasn't enough for Cobb, and the current continued to flow. Wes writhed in pain, rolling across the deck, slamming against the superstructure. Suddenly the pain decreased, the steel grounding him. Wes forced the muscles in his arms to move, pressing his palms against the metal and letting the current flow into the ship. It was still torture, but he was dying more slowly now.

"I said stop it, Cobb!" the woman commanded. "Prophet wants them alive."

As Wes slipped toward the blackness of unconsciousness, an invisible force threw Cobb across the deck. When he hit, he rolled ten feet before crashing into other Crazies.

Gasping for breath, Wes rolled to his back, hands pressing his chest in a vain attempt to restore a normal rhythm. Slowly, his heart regained its beat and muscle control began to return. Ralph leaned over him.

"Hurts, don't it?" Ralph said.

A woman looked down on him now. She was dressed in blue slacks and a powder blue blouse with an unusual cut. The shoulders were wide, giving her the look of a football lineman. Her hair was shoulder length and curled up around the bottom—a style popular in the forties. The woman looked him over with compassion.

"Can you walk?" she asked.

Wes tried various muscle groups, rocking from side to side, flexing his arms and legs.

"I need another minute," he told her.

"Thirty seconds," the woman said.

"Hihowyadoin?" Ralph said, extending his hand.

The woman smiled at Ralph and took his hand, letting Ralph pump hers vigorously.

"I'm Ralph and this here's Wes, and that's Monica. What's your name?"

"Gertrude, but everyone calls me Gertie."

"Nice to meet you, Gertie," Ralph said. "Got any gum?"

"No," Gertie said.

"Any place around here to get a Slurpee, or an Icee. I can drink a Slushee but I don't like them too good."

"I don't know what those things are, but we don't have them here," Gertie said.

"Ice cream?" Ralph asked.

"We don't eat here, Ralph," Gertie said. "We're immortal."

"Cool," Ralph said, clearly not understanding. "Well, we gots to be going now. Nice meeting ya."

With Ralph's help, Wes got to his feet, but he wobbled, barely controlling his legs. Wes saw Cobb coming up behind Ralph.

"You're coming with us," Gertie said.

Cobb reached for Ralph, placing his hand on his shoulder. He was six inches taller than Ralph and his hand was massive. Ralph started to turn, but Cobb's fingers tightened on him. Wes could see Cobb's fingers whiten.

"If you zap him I'll knock you into the desert," Gertie threatened.

Cobb was going to hurt Ralph, but not with his power. His massive paw shook from the pressure of his shoulder pinch. Ralph's face lost only a bit of its genial look as the hand squeezed his shoulder. Then Ralph reached across with his left hand and put it on top of Cobb's. Ralph's hand squeezed, and suddenly Cobb gasped.

"Don't you zap him," Gertie warned.

To the amazement of the Crazies gathered around, Ralph lifted Cobb's hand from his shoulder, turned, and then holding Cobb's hand with his left, put his right hand in the man's quivering palm and began to pump it.

"Nice to meet ya," Ralph said.

"Damn, he's strong," someone said from the back.

Cobb tore his hand free, glaring malevolently with his wild eyes. Then he looked at the other Crazies, daring them to make another comment. All looked away.

"Prophet wants them, Cobb. You don't touch them."

Gertie turned to Wes and the others.

"He won't hurt you if you stay close to me," Gertie said.

Gertie ordered their hands tied.

"We're looking for a man named Dawson," Wes said.

"I know him," Gertie said. "He's a heretic. When we get him we're going to burn him."

With their hands secured, she led off, Ralph following immediately, Monica next, and then Wes. Wes thought about what Gertie had said about wanting to kill Dawson. The harsh reality was that Dawson's death was the only sure way to save Elizabeth and Anita.

RETURN TO THE NORFOLK

It was nearly midnight when they arrived at the lab. Shamita and Len had the equipment powered up, the liquid nitrogen lines pressurized, and the CPU near superconducting temperatures. Following checklists, they made sure all components were operational and communicating with the consoles. Shamita hurried to Elizabeth as soon as she came in, taking her arm from Anita's mother and helping her to a cot.

"Elizabeth, you don't have the strength for this," Shamita said. "We can integrate without you. I'll go into the dream."

"No!" Elizabeth said emphatically. "You might be susceptible to the dream, too. I have nothing to lose."

Len came over, limping, holding one of the EET helmets. He was unshaven, his hair was greasy, and he looked as if he had slept in his clothes.

"You look terrible," Elizabeth said.

"Look who's talking," Len answered, smiling. "It's my new plan to get Wanda to stop smoking. I don't shower until she gives up the nicotine habit."

Elizabeth smiled, remembering the little war between Len and Wanda.

"She's a tough old lady, Len," Elizabeth said. "She won't crack."

"If it doesn't work I still have one more trick up my sleeve," Len said, then lost his smile.

"Maybe Shamita's right," Len said seriously. "You shouldn't do this. Let me meld with the others."

"I can't stop the dream, Len. I can see the ship right now."

Closing her eyes, Elizabeth let the dream expand out from the corner of her mind.

"I'm walking through the ship and I'm afraid. More afraid than I've ever been."

"It's not you, Elizabeth," Shamita said.

"I know. I haven't lost my sense of self yet, but the dream is taking over my waking mind, too. Nothing can stop it now, and I can feel that Wes and Ralph are in terrible danger."

"But what can you do?" Len asked.

"I can help them get home again," Elizabeth said.

They could refuse to help her, but soon she would have no consciousness left, only the dream, and then the accumulating waste products in her brain would kill her.

Len pushed the helmet onto Elizabeth and adjusted it until Shamita signalled that the reception was clear. Elizabeth was sticking the monitor leads to her own chest and temples, so Len helped Anita up onto her cot and into her helmet.

"Elizabeth said Anita wouldn't have to see the people in the dream," Anita's mother said.

"I only need a little more reception sensitivity," Elizabeth said. "I'm getting the basic images and feelings without the others."

"We'll try using you as the primary matrix and patch Anita and Wanda in," Shamita said. "Anita's sensitivity will make it hard to keep her out entirely, but we should be able to hold her reception to normal level."

"She won't see the scarred man or the people in the walls?" Anita's mother asked.

"It should be her normal dream," Shamita said.

Satisfied, she kissed her daughter on the forehead, pulled a blanket over her, and said good night. Wanda came in as Anita's mother left, a cigarette hanging from the corner of her mouth.

"You're late," Len said, following her to her cot.

"I was playing bingo, if it's any of your business," Wanda said. "You paged me right in the middle of the blackout game for the big jackpot."

Len pushed the helmet onto her head, trying to keep his face away from the cigarette smoke trail.

"Did you win?" Len asked as he worked with the helmet.

"Hell, no," Wanda said. "I'm here, aren't I?"

Shamita signalled good reception, but Len stayed close to Wanda, leaning until he was almost touching her.

"Len, did you lose your deodorant?" Wanda asked.

"Oh, do I smell bad?"

Wanda looked at him stone-faced for a second and then burst out laughing.

"Oh, I get it, Len," Wanda said, trying to control her laughter. "You stop washing your armpits and I'm supposed to beg for mercy and give up smoking?"

Wanda's laugh dissolved into a coughing fit. When that finished, she started laughing again.

"This is it?" Wanda said, barely controlling her laugh. "This is the best you could do? Ha! You're pathetic, Len. I almost feel sorry enough for you to give up smoking out of pity—almost."

"Wanda, we need you to relax," Shamita said.

Still chuckling, Wanda closed her eyes, resting her head on the pillow.

"The cigarette, Wanda?" Len said, holding out his hand.

"Forgot I still had it," Wanda said, taking the cigarette from the corner of her mouth and handing it to Len.

Len dropped the cigarette on the floor and ground it out with a violent twisting of his heel. His face was red as he walked to his console.

"I didn't want it to go this far, Wanda, but you've left me no choice," he said.

"Tell me you don't have another pathetic plan to force me to stop smoking?"

"Trust me, Wanda, you don't want to push me any farther."

With one last chuckle Wanda said, "Bring it on, Len. Whatever you can dish out I can take."

That exchange was the last thing Elizabeth heard as the dream expanded to fill her consciousness. Unlike before, the details filled in slowly; the dream pieced together as Anita and Wanda were integrated into her consciousness. She was on the ship now, walking down a corridor as the featureless walls took on detail; pipes ran the length of the ceiling, a red alarm bell appeared on her left. Now she could hear the sound of feet on metal, and then there were people. She was following a sailor carrying a spear, and in front of him was one of the people in a silver suit, his gun in his hand. Farther ahead was a man in civilian clothes carrying a crude machete. There were others behind her; she turned, seeing the woman who had held her captive before—Compton was her name. There were also two more sailors, each carrying a crossbow. Elizabeth looked around her to make sure Anita wasn't with her before she spoke.

"Wait," Elizabeth said.

The others jumped at the volume of her voice, turning on her angrily. Jett came to her, speaking softly.

"Are they coming?" Jett asked.

"Who? I mean, I'm not Dawson, I'm Elizabeth."

"Elizabeth, was the integration successful? Did we manage to keep Anita out of the dream?" Shamita asked.

"Anita's not with me," Elizabeth assured Shamita. "Shamita, I can't talk now."

The man looked perplexed, and then he understood.

"You're the social worker."

"Elizabeth Foxworth. I came for Ralph before."

"Keep your voice low," he whispered back. "I don't need a social worker right now, I need Dawson."

Elizabeth felt the Dawson part of her mind stir, his feelings blending with hers. Their two minds were slowly merging into one mind, and the Dawson part of her wanted to help the man called Jett.

"I'm looking for three people who came to the ship," Elizabeth whispered. "Ralph is one of them."

"Ralph's back? How?" Jett wanted to know.

"He found a way in."

"If Ralph is back, he might be our ticket out of here," Compton said.

"But we'll need time," Jett said. "We have to stop Evans."

Jett turned to Elizabeth.

"I need Dawson," Jett said.

"He's here with me."

"Get Dawson, now!" Jett insisted, putting his gun under her chin.

It was an empty threat. Still, the gun triggered a visceral response. At the same time, a feeling bubbled up from deep in her mind. Dawson's consciousness was screaming a warning.

"Someone's coming," Elizabeth said.

Jett spun around, waving to the man with the machete who was farthest down the corridor. The warning came too late. Three men with crossbows came around the corner and fired. Jett threw himself on Elizabeth, knocking her to the deck, a bolt passing just over his shoulder. One of the sailors behind Elizabeth took a bolt in the throat and fell, making wet gurgling sounds as he lay on the ground. Their men returned fire over Jett's prostrate body, then reloaded, stepping into the crossbow stirrups and pulling on the cables that served as bowstrings. Using the fallen sailor as cover, Compton opened fire. Jett ordered retreat, then came up firing, another bolt whizzing past his ear. Jett and Compton drove the archer back around the corner.

As Elizabeth ran for cover, Jett came up on one knee, gun aimed down the corridor. The man with the machete retreated, head low. Jett fired a couple of rounds at the corner as the man passed, then followed him, walking backward. When they were all safe around the corner Jett whispered to the man with the machete.

"Roberto, how close are we to the generators?"

Roberto exchanged signals with one of the sailors and then held up two fingers. The sailor nodded agreement.

"Two levels away," Roberto said.

"Is there another way to the generators? Could Evans have gotten past them on another route?"

"The closer two levels are together, the more ways they are connected," Roberto said. "It's like if you want to go from Miami to New York you must head north on the interstate, but when you get to the city limits there are dozens of routes to Manhattan."

"Then find us another route," Jett said.

Roberto led them up to the deck above, but ducked as soon as his eyes cleared the top. The deck rang from a shower of metal. Objects shot through the stairwell over Roberto's head, ricocheting off the wall, sending Elizabeth and the others ducking for cover. Roberto jumped down.

"Not that way," Roberto said.

Then they heard a deep voice that seemed to come from all parts of the ship, as if it was the voice of the ship.

"There is no escape," the voice said.

The Dawson part of Elizabeth cowered in terror.

"It's McNab," Roberto said.

"The one called Prophet?" Jett asked.

"He speaks in your head," Roberto said.

"Telepathy?" Elizabeth asked.

"You should know, Dawson, you taught me all this stuff."

"Dawson's connected," one of the sailors explained. "He's got someone from the other side."

"Bad timing," Roberto said.

Roberto turned to Jett and Compton, holding out his hand.

"Give me your guns," he told them.

Instantly, Compton's gun was in his face.

"Easy, Compton," Jett said. "Why do you want our guns?"

"Prophet can get into your mind. He can take control. Make you move just like a puppet. Worse, he can change you, make you believe different than you ever have. That's why the Crazies follow him. He took hold of their minds and he made them believe in him."

"Then why aren't all of you following him?" Jett asked.

"He can't get to everyone," Roberto said. "He's tried many times with me. I've felt him in my head poking around, looking for a handle on me, but he never found one. Not these guys either. We don't know about you and her. You've got to give us those guns until we know he can't get to you."

"Surrender," the voice boomed in Elizabeth's head. *"Surrender and the worthy shall join us. You are surrounded. There is no escape."*

"Maybe if we talked with them," Elizabeth said.

"You don't talk to Prophet. If he can't control you, he calls you a heretic and they burn you."

As Roberto spoke, Elizabeth saw that Compton's face was blank. Then her gun arm swung toward Jett. The Dawson part of Elizabeth took control and she shouted a warning.

Roberto and Jett moved at the same time, Roberto lunging for the gun arm, Jett twisting, slapping at the weapon. The gun fired as Roberto hit Compton. Jett took the bullet, grunting as he fell; then Compton's gun fired again, the second round narrowly missing Jett. Roberto was on her then, pinning her to the floor while the sailors circled, looking for ways to help. Then the Dawson part of Elizabeth's mind shouted another warning.

Men with crossbows appeared and fired. Their two sailors took bolts in the chests and fell, one clutching at the shaft, screaming. The other dropped silently, dead before he hit the ground. Elizabeth turned to run, but more men were coming down the stairs and around the corner. She froze, putting her hands in the air, frozen in fear. Jett was on the ground bleeding from a wound in his side. Roberto was still wrestling Compton for the gun, but now men surrounded them, pulling Roberto off. The men began to disarm Compton, trying to release the belt that held her pack and gun.

"Let her keep her weapon. She is one of the faithful now."

Compton stood, shaking her short hair from her face, and held her gun on Jett as his gun and pack were taken away. Then the men parted, and another man came slowly through. He was barrel-chested, with blond hair cropped short over an oval, puffy face. He wore the stripes of a chief petty officer.

"*I am Prophet*," he said without opening his mouth.

His voice was loud and clear in Elizabeth's mind, and it terrified the part of her that was Dawson.

NIMITZ

Prophet led the column through the Norfolk. Elizabeth and the other captives walked in the middle of the line, hands tied behind their backs. They were viciously shoved whenever they lagged. Roberto and the wounded sailor were first, Roberto's arm around the sailor's waist. One of the Crazies had pulled the crossbow bolt from the sailor's chest by putting his foot on the sailor and giving the bolt a vicious yank. Jett was next in line, and Elizabeth last. Compton was directly behind her, acting as if she had been one of the Crazies all her life. Elizabeth tried reasoning with her, but the only reply she received was a crack on the head with the barrel of Compton's gun. In a matter of seconds, Prophet had reached inside Compton's mind and turned her against Jett and the others. Elizabeth knew that her host, Dawson, was resistant to Prophet, or he would have been turned long ago. She didn't know about herself. Would she end up being manipulated into worshipping a self-appointed prophet of God?

Finally, they were led outside on the port side of the Norfolk and pushed toward the stern. As they cleared midships, Elizabeth saw something new; the Dawson part of her reacted, too. The Norfolk had a sister ship on this level, and it was massive.

Directly astern of the Norfolk was an aircraft carrier that towered above the cruiser. At least twice the size of the Norfolk, the massive ship was lined up directly behind as if it was chasing the smaller ship across the desert. Jett was ahead of Elizabeth and stopped, staring at the ship. Elizabeth, in Dawson's body, stood to one side of Jett, and shoulder to shoulder they gaped in awe at the giant war machine.

"It's the Nimitz," Jett said.

Elizabeth's mind flashed back to something Dr. Birnbaum said—there had been rumors on the Internet about something happening to the Nimitz. Seeing the great ship here frightened her in a new way. Supercarriers were the greatest war machines on the planet, and only something with cosmic power could snatch one from the ocean and deliver it here.

Their view of the Nimitz was obscured by part of the Norfolk's superstructure and by the cranes and catapults on the stern. Still, they could see aircraft parked on the deck. They were fighters mostly, but also other specialty aircraft—two with elliptical radar domes—and helicopters. Elizabeth felt like a country bumpkin seeing a city for the first time, staring up at the skyscrapers. The Dawson part of her shared the feeling, intensifying it.

Compton shoved Jett from behind to get them moving again, pushing him after the other Crazies who were moving toward the stern of the Norfolk, following Prophet.

"It's the Nimitz, Compton. It's what we came for. Can't you snap out of it?"

"Move or I'll hurt you," Compton said, her tone emotionless.

"Prophet wouldn't like that," Jett said.

Compton dropped her gun to Jett's knee.

"I said I'll hurt you, not kill you," Compton said.

Jett didn't move, daring Compton to shoot.

"Let's go," Elizabeth said to Jett through Dawson's body.

Jett didn't move.

"This isn't the time or the place," Elizabeth said.

Jett nodded, then he followed Roberto, who was still supporting the wounded sailor.

Ahead, Elizabeth could see that a rope bridge had been rigged from the Norfolk to the Nimitz. The bridge sloped steeply from the stern of the Norfolk to the flight deck of the carrier. It was a flimsy-looking contraption, essentially four cables drawn tight between the Norfolk's cranes and two towers erected on the flight deck of the Nimitz. Ropes were woven around the cables, partially enclosing the sides of the bridge. Planks made up the bottom. People were crossing it now, coming from the Nimitz to the Norfolk, and Elizabeth could see more people on the flight deck. The

Crazies seemed to have moved their base of operations from the Norfolk to the Nimitz. Above the bridge was another cable, one end strung from higher on the superstructure of the Norfolk and the other end attaching somewhere on the flight control island on the starboard side of the Nimitz's flight deck.

Elizabeth studied the Nimitz. Held perfectly balanced on its keel by the strange forces that had brought it here, the carrier was fully exposed. She could see the twin anchors pulled up tight to the ship, the sharp curves of the hull, and the protruding sponson which supported the runway angling across the flight deck. Then she noticed a man hanging by his hands from the flight deck, held by a rope around each wrist. After seeing the first man, she could see others, a half dozen of them hung across the piece of the bow that was visible.

As they neared the stern, Elizabeth spotted something in the desert below. Jett saw it too, drifting toward the rail. Two large machines sat on the desert floor, each shaped like a snail's shell, cables running from them. Compton saw Jett's interest and ordered him away from the side. Jett complied, but his eyes busily took in details of the machines in the desert, the bridge, and the placement of guards.

As they approached the bridge they were turned inboard and pushed through a hatch just forward of the catapults. They climbed down to the ship's hangar. The hangar was by far the largest open space below decks on the Norfolk. Around its perimeter were repair facilities, parts storage, and barrels of oil and grease. The overhead hatch was open, and cables and hooks from the crane dangled above as if it had recently been used to lower something. Twenty men and women were gathered in the hangar. They were dirty, wearing homemade jewelry, decorated with tattoos, and brandishing weapons. They parted for Prophet like the Red Sea for Moses.

As Elizabeth and the others were led to the center of the group, she realized that three men here were different. All three lacked the jewelry and tattoos of the Crazies, two of them wearing green jersies, the third a khaki uniform. Elizabeth guessed that the men were from the Nimitz. They stood by what looked like pieces of aircraft.

"All finished?" Prophet asked.

"Yes, sir," the sailor in khakis said.

"Excellent."

Prophet waved Elizabeth and the others forward. Roberto still helped the wounded sailor, whose breath was even and regular now, even with the bloody hole in his chest.

"I want you to see this," Prophet said with his mouth closed, his voice reverberating in their minds.

They were pushed forward until they stood face to face with Prophet.

"Do you know what these are, Nathan?"

Prophet was talking to Jett like a father to his child, calling him by his first name.

The devices were large silver cylinders set in metal cages. Three black boxes were fixed below the cylinders, thick coils of wiring running from box to box and to the cylinder. Covering the cylinder were smaller devices that looked as if they were made out of plastic, two wires running from each.

"Well, Layton," Jett began.

Prophet was shorter than Jett by three inches, but he was powerfully built with thick arms. He was also quick-tempered and fast; his right hand slapped Jett across the face before Jett could react.

"You will call me Prophet," Prophet said directly to their minds. Then, with his voice, he said, "I ceased to be Layton McNab when God called us to this place and anointed me his Prophet."

"You ceased being Layton McNab when you lost your mind," Jett said.

Prophet struck with his left hand, knocking Jett back a step. The man's face was flushed, his lips tight. He was determined to bend Jett to his will, and Jett would rather die than bend.

"Not the time or the place," Elizabeth said to Jett.

Jett spit blood from his mouth.

"You tell me when and where," Jett said to Elizabeth.

Jett had been briefed on the Nimitz's arsenal. He knew what Prophet had spread out on the deck.

"You've removed the thermonuclear warheads from two Tomahawk cruise missiles," Jett said.

"That's right, Nathan. Of course, I don't understand exactly what makes them work—something about the atoms banging into each other. We didn't have these when we fought the Nazis but I heard the Japs got a taste of a couple of these babies. I understand they pack as much explosive power as a thousand-plane raid."

Prophet smiled, revealing yellow teeth discolored by years of chewing tobacco.

"Know what?" Prophet continued. "We just set one of these off!"

Prophet chuckled, and his people laughed with him.

"I know what you're thinking—really, I do," Prophet said, chuckling at his own joke, the Crazies joining in.

"You're thinking that if one of these warheads has been detonated, then why haven't we all been blown to pieces?"

Prophet turned slowly, dramatically, building suspense.

"We are here because God himself holds the atoms in the warhead tight in his protective hand, just like he holds us in his hand."

Prophet held his hand out, slowly closing his fingers and clenching them tight as he spoke. The Crazies mumbled approval, some whispering "Amen."

"And when the time comes—God's time—he will release his mighty grip and the world will feel his wrath."

With his arm still outstretched, Prophet flicked his fingers out, opening his fist. His face was red, his jaw set, his voice loud and firm. Then his lips curved into a smile. In seconds he had gone from maniacal to whimsical.

"Like I said, one of these bombs has been detonated, but you know, I can't exactly remember which one."

Prophet turned slowly, showing his smile to his followers.

"One of them is going to be sent home, but since I can't remember which is which I'll just have to guess."

His followers laughed, enjoying his game.

"Eeny, meeny, miny, mo," Prophet said. "Which one back to earth should go?"

Prophet pointed back and forth between the warheads as he spoke, enjoying the captives' discomfort.

"Do you know one potato, two potato, three potato, four?" Jett said suddenly. "Five potato, six potato, seven potato, more."

The Crazies were stunned into silence by Jett's audacity. Prophet kept his smile, but his eyes stared hard at Jett. Elizabeth cringed, thinking Jett foolish to taunt a madman.

"Another good one is bubble gum, bubble gum, in a dish, how many pieces do you wish?" Jett said.

Prophet lost his smile, his stare cold and hard.

Quiet!" Prophet boomed in their heads.

His game spoiled, Prophet was red with fury.

"Bring the bomb," Prophet ordered. "And bring them!"

Crazies dragged Elizabeth and the other captives across the hangar. The warheads were both on dollies, and one was pushed ahead of them toward an inboard hatch.

"Let's see what's in here." Prophet said, smiling again.

Prophet opened the hatch a crack, peeking inside, then turned his head to them with an expression of mock surprise.

"What could it be?" Prophet said.

Pulling the hatch open, Prophet stepped back, revealing a glowing green mist.

"I wonder where this leads?" Prophet said.

Prophet's eyes bored in on Jett, waiting for a reaction. He got none.

With a quick hand motion from Prophet, the warhead was rolled to the hatch. When they lifted the front wheels of the dolly over the lip of the hatch, Jett tensed. Elizabeth stiffened, too. If Prophet had managed to detonate the warhead, once it reentered the world it would be released from the forces that kept it from going off.

"The scroll!" Prophet commanded.

A Crazy with long, dangling copper earrings made out of hammered shell casings stepped forward, holding out a paper roll tied with a ribbon. Prophet put the scroll inside the metal framework. Then he raised his hands toward the sky and spoke directly to their minds.

"To glorify you," Prophet said.

At his signal, the dolly with the warhead was pushed into the green mist. Closing and latching the hatch, Prophet looked pleased with himself.

"It's time for you to be judged for your sins," Prophet said. "Take them to the Nimitz."

At the mention of judgment, excitement rippled through the Crazies. Prophet led off, Crazies falling in behind him like a palace guard. Elizabeth and the others were pushed after Prophet, guards in front and behind. Compton kept behind them, gun trained on their backs. Their path led them up to the deck of the Norfolk and to the stern, where the makeshift bridge connected them to the flight deck of the Nimitz.

Two could walk side by side on the bridge, but it would be tight; the Crazies crossed single file, spaced ten feet apart. The bridge creaked and groaned with each additional weight, swaying and bouncing with the movement of the Crazies. Roberto and the wounded sailor were the first of the captives onto the bridge. Then Jett motioned Elizabeth forward.

Pausing at the edge of the bridge, Elizabeth studied the planking, which was made up of a variety of wood and metal pieces. The sides were of rope strung between the upper and lower cables. The ropes merely outlined the sides of the rickety and steeply sloped bridge, hinting at safety but not promising it. With her hands tied behind her, Elizabeth couldn't hold the cables for support.

Growing more confident as she crossed, Elizabeth looked around. The men farthest ahead appeared to be climbing a ladder to the deck of the Nimitz. In the desert below she could see the shell-shaped machines.

Cables trailed from them, one running back into the Norfolk while two others stretched out in either direction, running all the way to the opaque walls that marked the border of this world.

As the bridge's incline increased, Elizabeth concentrated careful that each foot was squarely on a support. Risking only quick glances now, she saw the huge anchors, each bigger than a car, and then the hanging men strung along the sides of the ship. They all wore modern uniforms; she guessed that they were Nimitz crew survivors who were resistant to Prophet. With another glance, she saw movement. The sailors were alive, twisting in agony, pulling up with their arms, and trying to ease their breathing.

The deck was near now, and Elizabeth concentrated on the climb. She reached the flight deck, where the planking ended and makeshift stairs led down. A crowd of Crazies was waiting for her. Like the other Crazies she had seen, they were a rag-tag collection, mostly sailors, with a few civilian men and women sprinkled among them. They wore ragged clothes and bizarre jewelry, and their bodies were decorated with tattoos. Among them she saw the unadorned bodies of the Nimitz's crew, who were acting as is if they had always been Prophet's followers.

Now on the deck, she could see that the Nimitz was badly damaged. The planes parked on the stern were scorched; the paint was blistered and blackened, the canopies opaque and bubbled as if they had been exposed to extreme heat. The deck of the ship was blackened too. And the crew of the Nimitz had suffered the same fate as crew on the Norfolk. Pieces of bodies protruded from the flight deck in places—half a man here, head and shoulders there, just an arm farther down the deck. But while the men on the Norfolk looked whole and healthy, the Nimitz crew that had merged with the ship were burned and blackened. Instinctively, Elizabeth looked for Anita, making sure that the little girl wasn't seeing this new ugliness.

Whatever had happened to the Nimitz, happened in the middle of flight operations. Three arresting wires were still stretched across the runway, ready to be snagged by the tail hook of a landing jet. An F-14 was just off the other end of the runway, as if the disaster had struck just as it cleared the runway for the next plane. The fighter's exterior was burnt black like the other planes.'

The deck was vast; on acres of steel, the island on the starboard side of the ship was the only protruding structure. Gathered at the stern was a large throng of Crazies, who were milling about and generating crowd noise like fans filling a football stadium. More Crazies were coming across the bridge from the Norfolk, wild-eyed with excitement, hurrying toward the stern.

Elizabeth, Jett, Roberto, and the wounded sailor were surrounded by armed Crazies. Compton kept her gun on Jett, even with his hands tied. The Crazies were waiting silently, looking down the deck toward the stern. Then came the booming of a crude drum.

"It's time," one of the Crazies said, motioning with his spear.

"This might be the time and the place," Elizabeth said to Jett.

Jett looked at Compton, who still had her gun on his back.

"Not yet," Jett said.

Elizabeth didn't know if there would be another opportunity. She feared suffering in Dawson's body, not only for her sake but for Dawson's, too. They shared enough consciousness for her to know that he came from a large, boisterous family which he missed dearly, and that he was a brave man who had volunteered to fight for his country. Elizabeth also feared for Anita, who would die unless they could find a way to stop the dream.

As the drumming from the stern fell into a steady beat, their guards took up positions in front and behind, marching to the rhythm. Despite the wild appearance of the Crazies, their procession was formal and solemn. The crowd ahead jeered.

The captives were led to the edge of the crowd, which refused to part. Guards pushed men and women aside to make room. As they plunged into the mob, it reformed around them, swallowing them like a malevolent amoeba. The guards kept them moving but made no attempt to protect them from the mob. They were jabbed and prodded by surly men and women who cursed them. Elizabeth realized that, like the scourging of Jesus, the abuse from the crowd was part of the judgment ritual. Dawson's body was more rugged than Elizabeth's and absorbed blows she knew her body could not. A vicious kick to her knee collapsed her leg, and Elizabeth fell. Peals of laughter rippled through the Crazies. A blow came from the tangle of legs, kicking her in the side. Defensively, she rolled into a ball and took the next kick to her kidneys, her back arching with the spasm of pain.

"You're gonna burn now, Dawson," a man shouted.

"A little taste of hell before you go," another said and then laughed.

Others shouted insults and cursed the body Elizabeth occupied, and whose pain she felt as if it were her own.

"Elizabeth, this is Shamita. Can you understand me?"

"Yes, Shamita," Elizabeth mumbled.

"Your vital signs are dangerously high. What is happening?"

"Don't bring me out," Elizabeth said. "I haven't found them yet."

"I'm worried," Sharnita said.

"I'll be fine," Elizabeth lied.

"What's he saying?" someone above her asked.

"He's out of his head," another shouted.

"He's faking," another said. "Prophet will see right through it."

Then she was pulled roughly to her feet. She found herself facing an angry woman whose eyes were dark with hate.

"It's because of you my Johnny is dead," the woman said, then spat in Elizabeth's face.

"It wasn't me," Elizabeth said.

Before Elizabeth could explain, the woman kicked Elizabeth in the groin. Elizabeth had been hit there before, but as a woman. Now she understood why men were so vulnerable to a blow between their legs. The pain was paralyzing. Her knees buckled, but hands kept her from falling. She had an urge to put her hands between her legs, as if touch could lessen the pain, but with her hands tied she could only squirm and moan, each motion and sound sending cackles of glee through the mob.

"Kick him again, Lucy," a man shouted.

Lucy was taking aim when a guard stepped between them, proving that there were limits to the crowd's abuse. Pain still wracked Elizabeth's body, broadcasting from her groin through her midsection. She couldn't walk without support. Slowly the pain subsided and she could stand erect again. Ahead, she could see a metal platform built on the stern of the ship. Mounted on the back of the platform was a large cross. A podium sat in the middle. In front of the platform were chairs and benches arranged in a semicircle. The Crazies had been using this part of the Nimitz for a church. Then Prophet sprang to the platform and shouted to the crowd.

"Bring the heretics forward!"

Robbed of her revenge, Lucy stepped up to Elizabeth, putting her lips close to her ear.

"Prophet promised to roast you slowly," Lucy said. "He promised me you would die screaming. We're going to start at the bottom and burn your toes off and then your feet. We're going to blacken every bit of skin on your body, and I'm going to personally roast these," she said, jamming her hand into Elizabeth's groin.

The squeeze revived the pain, and Elizabeth nearly collapsed. Lucy's obscene hold elicited chuckles from the crowd.

"We're bringing you out, Elizabeth," Shamita said.

"No," Elizabeth said, at the same time wishing that the pain would end.

"I'm dissolving the integration," Shamita said.

"I want to help," Elizabeth protested.

Pushed through the crowd, she found herself next to Jett at the base of the platform. She and the others were pushed to their knees. Roberto was next to Compton, and the wounded sailor was on the far end, the blood on his shirt now crusted. Prophet strutted on the platform, arms in the air like a politician on election night. His face had the rugged look of a boxer who has stopped too many punches with his face. His hair formed a gray fringe around a shiny scalp. He looked fifty, but moved and talked with the energy of a younger man.

"Elizabeth, can you hear me?" Shamita said in Elizabeth's head.

"Yes," Elizabeth said.

Now Prophet came to the edge of the platform and thrust out his hand, offering it to Compton. Taking his hand, Compton stepped up on the stage. Standing next to Prophet, she beamed at him as if he were a god.

"She came to us from the outside world to do us harm," Prophet said, touching the gun in Compton's holster. "Like Eve in the Garden of Eden, she came to destroy the paradise God has given mankind, to ruin God's plan for his chosen people. But we won't disobey God again. We won't listen to the serpent. We won't turn our back on the God who has given us eternal life again!"

The crowd erupted in cheers and shouts of affirmation. When they quieted, Elizabeth heard Shamita again.

"Elizabeth, are you still in the dream?"

"Yes. I'm on a different ship. There's a crowd of people," Elizabeth said. A slap on the head and a hissed, "Shut up," made her cringe.

"Something has gone wrong," Shamita said. *"We've dissolved the integration. You should be back with us."*

With mounting horror Elizabeth realized that she and Dawson were now permanently linked. They would live out their lives fused as one person until death parted them.

"This one was saved because she heard the voice of God calling to her and she answered," Prophet shouted.

Prophet's arm was around Compton, who was giddy. Her face was as bright as her silver suit.

"But these would not listen to God's Prophet," Prophet shouted from his pulpit, indicating the kneeling captives. "These turned their back on God and the gift of his salvation."

"Elizabeth, I don't know what to do," Shamita said. *"I can't get you back."*

"God punishes those who turn their back on him with everlasting fire. Can we do any less?"

"No!" came the shouts of the crowd.

"Wanda is separate and awake," Shamita continued, *"but we can't wake Anita. The only step left is to disconnect from you. I don't think it will make a difference, but we have to try. Once we do, we lose contact."*

Shamita's voice in her head had been a security blanket for Elizabeth, as had been the knowledge that she could go back to her world at any time. Now she was losing both of those.

"What is God's punishment for unbelievers?" Prophet roared.

"Burning!" the crowd returned like a Greek Chorus.

"I'm disconnecting you now, Elizabeth."

"What should we do with these heretics?" Prophet shouted.

"Burn them!" the crowd shouted in reply.

"Elizabeth, I'm afraid," a child's voice said.

Elizabeth felt a touch on her arm and looked down. Anita was there, eyes open wide, face white with fear. Gone was the pretty dress with the bunnies on the front, as was the perfectly combed and curled hair. The Anita who was with her now wore overalls and her hair in pigtails, and was missing her two front teeth. This Anita's face was haggard, her eyes baggy and sunken, her lips trembling.

"Hold me," Anita begged, leaning against Elizabeth.

Elizabeth struggled with the cord that tied her hands.

"Burn them!" the crowd shouted around her.

GENERATORS

They were close to the generators now. His guide's behavior had changed. The sailor was more cautious now, never speaking, moving more slowly as they worked their way through the bowels of the Norfolk. Four times Evans and his guide had hidden as Crazies passed. Most of their close calls had been brief; the Crazies had been hurrying to some destination. Once, they had been forced to hide in a storeroom near the mess, among crates of canned fruit, while Crazies milled around. Finally, someone had hurried in, shouting, "There's going to be a trial!"

The Crazies stampeded from the mess then, and once again Evans and the guide crept through the corridors. Emerging out onto the deck, they were shocked to see the Nimitz directly astern of the Norfolk.

"I've never seen such a ship!" the guide whispered.

Evans wavered for a second, enough of the agent left in him to remember his mission—but the Nimitz had never really been his goal. He had come for revenge, and if that meant destroying the Nimitz as well, it couldn't be helped.

The Crazies were gathered on the stern, lining up single file to cross a bridge built to the Nimitz, so it was easy to slip along the deck, keeping under the gun turrets, and then descend below decks again near the bow.

Finally, his guide led him down to a small compartment where he whispered, "This has got to be the level."

"The generators?" Evans replied softly.

"It's through these compartments," the sailor said, pointing.

They were on the lowest deck of the ship, just past a series of powder magazines, and just outside the first of two boiler rooms. If there weren't any space-bending tricks on this level, there should be an engine room and two more boiler rooms past that.

"You'll never make it," his guide said.

"We made it this far," Evans told him.

The sailor shook his head.

"I just hope I get to see you die before they get me."

"Then you better be lucky, because you go first," Evans said, shoving the sailor into the first boiler room.

Evans hung back, letting his guide get a small lead—small enough so that he couldn't sprint away. The sailor paused inside, eyes busy. The room was filled with two massive oil-fired boilers and what looked like miles of pipe. There was an infinite number of places where guards might be hiding. When no crossbow bolts whistled out from dark crevices, the sailor took a deep breath and inched deeper into the compartment. Evans stepped in behind, keeping close. Suddenly there was a loud thump, and his guide flew toward him as if lifted by an invisible hand. Whatever force held him in the air quickly expended, and he fell to the ground, tumbling over and then rolling into a bulkhead. He lay still, his neck broken.

Evans jumped back through the hatch and flattened against the bulkhead. Then, reaching inside himself for his own power, he stoked the furnace that was its source until he felt his full strength. Listening for movement, he waited, keeping his power at full. When he heard footsteps, he leaned around the corner, letting go a wide push. Five people were emerging from hiding. His power knocked them down like tenpins. He jumped in before they could get up, his weapon firing.

His Teflon bullets found three of them, killing two sailors and a woman dressed in hip-huggers and a polyester blouse. One man managed to fire his crossbow, but his aim was spoiled by fear. Evans killed him just before he himself was struck by another invisible blow from the last man—the Special.

The Special hit him hard; his face felt as if it had been struck with a board. Evans rolled with the blow, coming up running, then flattening against a boiler before he could be hit again. Quickly he recharged his own power, then leaned out and pushed, catching the Special as he was sneaking closer. Evans fired and the Special rolled instinctively. Evans's bullets stitched along behind him. With a wider compartment, the Special might have made it, but in the equipment-packed boiler room he ran out of space. He slammed against a control wheel, Evans's bullets ripping through his shoulders and back.

Evans waited, listening. Would there have been only five guards? With Crazies out searching for Jett and the others, and the trial underway, they might have spread themselves too thin. If so, it was a mistake he was ready to exploit.

He worked through the next boiler room slowly, unchallenged. An engine room was next. He paused outside, listening. He heard nothing. Time was on the side of any guards hidden inside. Soon someone would find the dead guide, or the guards Evans had killed. Once the alarm went out they would forget their trial and he would be overwhelmed.

He risked a quick glance, snapping his head back from the open hatch and then picturing what he saw. There was nothing but the steam generators. Now he leaned around the corner and studied the open hatch at the other end—no movement. Pulling his head back, he took a deep breath, dropped into a crouch, and stepped in. He moved quickly, ready to shoot at the slightest movement. It took only a few seconds to travel the distance to the bulkhead by the next compartment, but it was high-risk and exhilarating.

Now flat against the bulkhead by the hatch, Evans readied himself for the next move. He took another quick look around the corner, then flattened back. The field generators were there, two dome-shaped tandem machines about six feet high. The boilers had been removed to make room for the generators, but the piping and fittings for the boilers still filled part of the space. He had seen no one.

He planned his next move. The best cover was to his left, behind a row of pipes that ran from where one of the boilers had stood to near the bulkhead, and then turned forty-five degrees, disappearing into the ceiling. There would be a passage between the pipes and the bulkhead. He would begin there, working through the room, sweeping it clear of any guards. With a deep breath, he jumped through the hatch and sprinted left. Two bolts whistled from above. He dove, the bolts passing high. Flat on the ground, he spotted two men on steam pipes near the ceiling. Both men were getting up, moving to new positions. He killed the slowest with a shot between the shoulder blades.

Behind him there was movement; he turned to see a sailor charging with a spear. Evans's first shot punctured his stomach and the second his chest; he dropped a few feet away, the spear clattering across the deck. The man was still alive, but dying. Evans ignored him, hurrying to cover behind another rack of pipes closer to the generators. If the sailor with the spear had made his move sooner, it would have been a better ambush.

There was at least one more hidden man ready to die to protect the generators. Evans hoped their fanaticism would work to his advantage. If he got close to the generators, they would panic and get reckless. With his superior weapons he would make short work of them.

Evans found the passage between the bulkhead and the pipe racks and worked his way along it. He finally came to a space in the plumbing that led straight to the twin electromagnetic generators. Sitting on square bases bolted to the deck, the generators looked like giant hand grenades mounted lengthwise. Between them sat an enclosed metal box connected with heavy cabling to both generators. Someone had chopped through the cables. Other cables ran from the electromagnetic generators to their power source. These cables had been cut too. Still, the twin generators hummed, generating the force that kept Pot of Gold in existence. Boldly, Evans trotted toward the closest generator.

TRIAL

Cobb shoved Wes from behind at the slightest provocation, making his back sore from shoulder to shoulder. No matter how close he walked to those in front, Cobb found reasons to punch him. Hesitate at a ladder and *Thump!* in the back. Turn a corner too wide and *Thump!* again. Slow to keep from running into Monica and *Thump!* It was petty torture designed to provoke him, so Wes took the abuse stoically.

Travel through the ship was confusing, and Wes soon gave up memorizing their route, counting on Ralph to know the way out. Ralph walked with Gertie, chattering away, telling her about Wes and Elizabeth and Dr. Birnbaum. Gertie listened, amused. Eventually, they emerged from the ship near the biplanes. In the desert behind the Norfolk was an aircraft carrier. It was twice the size of the Norfolk, and judging from the ship's size and the aircraft on its flight deck, Wes guessed that it was a supercarrier. Then he remembered Dr. Birnbaum saying there were rumors about something happening to the USS Nimitz. Now Wes knew that the Nimitz had been hijacked to this neverland.

A primitive rope bridge had been rigged between the Norfolk and Nimitz, and Wes and the others were dragged to it. Guards crossed first, then Monica and Gertie. Next it was Ralph's turn. Fascinated by the bridge, Ralph watched how the others crossed. The bridge swayed and bounced, and those crossing matched their rhythm to that of the bridge. When Ralph's turn came, he started to cross with the same stride he used when walking to the 7-Eleven. After just three steps he was out of rhythm and fell against the side.

"Help him," Wes pleaded. "He can't do it with his hands tied."

Gertie came back, taking one of Ralph's arms, steadying him.

"Thanks, Gertie. It's harder than it looks, isn't it?" Ralph said.

"It is, Ralph," Gertie said. "Maybe we should hold each other up while we cross?"

"Okee-dokee with me, Gertie," Ralph said.

Thump! Cobb hit Wes. Stepping up, Wes started across, matching the rhythm of the bridge. Wes was slow, and a gap opened between him and Ralph and Gertie. Cobb kept his distance now, having his own difficulties with the bridge.

As he crossed, Wes saw another set of cables rigged above the bridge to one side. Ahead, on the carrier, he could see that the cables were attached to a pulley system and a winch. Below in the desert he could see two machines with cables leading from them. Ahead was a heartbreaking sight. There were men hung from the deck of the Nimitz, decorating the ship's perimeter like bizarre Christmas ornaments.

Once they were across, they were held on the flight deck while Gertie ordered a man to run ahead. Wes could see a crowd and a man on a platform at the far end of the carrier. Behind the man was a large cross. The crowd cheered occasionally, and when Gertie's runner reached the platform the people turned as one and looked down the deck at Wes and the others. Then they cheered, sending chills down Wes's spine. A drum boomed, and the guards fell into a double column, marching in rhythm with the drum. Gertie walked in front of the captives and Cobb behind. They marched past bodies of sailors embedded in the deck to the waiting crowd.

Kicks, blows, and curses were heaped on them as they passed through. All around Wes were angry, tattooed faces, spitting and cursing. A fist caught him on the side of the head and he stumbled and fell. Quickly he curled up to make himself less vulnerable. Wes took a dozen kicks before the abuse stopped. He was hauled to his feet by Cobb and pushed after the others. Bound and abused by the mob, Wes felt like an aristocrat being led to the guillotine.

Monica received the same treatment and took it stoically. Ralph, however, repeated "Hihowyadoin" to everyone he passed; the people stared at the peculiar man, many smiling and responding.

The platform was near now, and Wes could see a man standing center stage, wearing the uniform of a chief petty officer. It was Prophet. A woman in a silver suit stood next to him, her hand resting on a holstered gun. She was wearing a suit like Ralph's, and Wes recognized her from the sketches Dr. Birnbaum had made of Ralph's kidnappers.

"This day is rich with the Lord's blessings," Prophet said.

Then Prophet's voice sounded in Wes's head.

"My name is Prophet. Come forward and be judged."

As if everyone in the room had heard, the crowd erupted with screams of affirmation. The captives were shoved forward, Gertie clearing a path and Cobb following.

"Well done, Gertie," Prophet said. "Well done, John."

Gertie smiled at Prophet's compliment, and Cobb nodded his head.

Pushed to the base of the platform, Wes could see others kneeling with their hands tied. One was a wounded sailor, another a Hispanic man. There was one man in a silver suit; when he turned, Wes recognized him as the other of Ralph's kidnappers. The last man was young and wore his brown hair oiled, neatly parted, and combed to the side. He wore a blue shirt with cut-off sleeves, and his eyes widened in recognition when he saw Wes.

"Hi Nate, hi Roger," Ralph said. "I'd shake your hand but I can't on account of mine being tied up. You too?"

Then Ralph looked up to the woman on the platform.

"Hi Karla. Whatcha doin up there? Are you gonna sing a song or something? Can I get on the stage too?"

The man staring at Wes tried to stand.

"Wes, it's me!"

Wes realized that it was Elizabeth in the body of Roger Dawson. He surged forward, but was shoved down next to the man in the silver suit. Once on his knees, he leaned out so that he could see the body that held the woman he loved.

"Elizabeth, what are you doing here?"

"I came to help, but I can't get back. Anita's here too and she's terrified."

"Dissolve the integration," Wes said.

"It was dissolved," Elizabeth said.

Shocked, Wes tried to understand what had happened. Elizabeth was still in the dream even without the integration, so she no longer needed to join with Anita and Wanda in order to be receptive. But why was Anita there? Somehow, by linking their minds, Wes had strengthened both the link to Dawson and the link between Anita and Elizabeth. Now Elizabeth and Anita were like two radios tuned to the same frequency; what one received, the other also received. Wes thought furiously for a solution. He could think of only one. If they increased the voltage of the signals that suppressed neural activity, and broadcast widely, they would create an electrical storm. The effect would imitate electroshock therapy and probably trigger a seizure, but it could temporarily suppress Elizabeth's reception faculties.

"Tell Len and Shamita to try scrambling your entire cortex," Wes said.

The man in the silver suit between Wes and Elizabeth took in the exchange, his face passive.

"What?" Elizabeth said.

"I said—" Wes was cuffed from behind, his ear stinging from the blow.

"Scramble the cortex," the man in the silver suit repeated.

Then Prophet glanced at the man in the silver suit and nodded to Cobb. The air crackled behind the man and his hair stood on end. Cobb struck him, and he writhed on the deck as a hundred sparks danced over his body.

"Stop it," Elizabeth screamed through Dawson's body.

The punishment continued.

"You shouldn't do that, it hurts," Ralph said to Cobb.

Ralph started to rise, and Cobb turned on him, the air crackling around Ralph and then erupting in the bright blue of electric light. Ralph convulsed, but made no sound.

"*Enough,*" Prophet's voice sounded in Wes's head.

Cobb stopped immediately, and Ralph suddenly relaxed, his head hanging limp.

"That hurts worser than anything," Ralph said.

"Jett, are you all right?" Elizabeth said.

Wes looked down at the man Elizabeth called Jett. He was struggling back to his knees. He moved slowly, but confidently. Jett gave a quick nod, assuring him that he wasn't badly injured.

"*Now, if we have everyone's complete attention, I will continue,*" Prophet said.

"You're a ventrilkist, aren't you?" Ralph said. "Your lips don't move, but I can hear you talking."

Prophet focussed on Ralph, and Cobb moved behind him.

"*I speak with the voice of God,*" Prophet said. "*Just as God speaks directly to our hearts, I speak directly to your mind. But it is not only the gift of god-*

talking that God has entrusted to me. I can look deep into a person's soul and know whether Jesus is in their heart."

The crowd erupted into shouted "Amens" and started praising God as if they were at a Pentecostal camp meeting.

"Sadly, your friends have turned their backs on the gift God has given us—the gift of eternal life," Prophet said, switching to voice. "I ask you—no, I beg you—to repent and accept God's gift. Be like this one," he said, holding out his hand to the woman on the stage wearing the silver suit. "She opened her heart to God's servant and she was put on the right path. Now she will live forever in this joyous fellowship."

Now Prophet stepped in front of Monica, closed his eyes, and leaned his head back. Monica's face was taut with fear, and then her eyes went wide and her mouth opened in surprise. After a moment of concentration Prophet opened his eyes and shook his head sadly.

"This one will not obey God."

"Burn her!" the crowd shouted.

Next Prophet stepped in front of Wes, again closing his eyes. Instantly, Wes could feel him in his mind, rifling his memories, feeling his thoughts and emotions. Wes felt as if he was being sexually molested, and he was sickened by the personal intrusion. Memories were triggered randomly, flashing through Wes's head in a confusing buzz. His childhood was there, his first day of school, a spanking he'd received, being teased for being a nerd, high school graduation, scholarship offers coming in the mail—his entire life flickered past, all his personal memories exposed for a stranger. Worse was Prophet's manipulation of his emotions. Wes had always tightly controlled these, but Prophet unlocked Pandora's box, releasing Wes's feelings. He was flooded with one emotion after another.

Wes was at the mercy of Prophet, who pulled memories and emotions from him at will. He was suddenly a sad little child standing at the edge of the playground watching the other boys choose up sides for baseball, knowing he would never be asked. Then he was a happy teenager crossing the auditorium stage for his diploma a year before his peers. The next instant he was terrified, seeing Len lying in a bloody pile after his chest had been crushed by a psychokinetic whom Wes had accidentally created—Prophet dwelled on this memory. Then Elizabeth was in his mind's eye, and Prophet was sharing the lust Wes felt for her but kept buried. Memories of kissing her, holding her and touching her filled him, his body responding as if she were in his arms now. In their link, he felt Prophet's own lust for Elizabeth. But Prophet had sampled the wrong memory, and

Wes fought Prophet's presence with a flurry of angry emotions: disgust, rage, and hate flooded him, pushing on Prophet's intruding mind, cornering it, and battering it into a smaller and smaller space.

Realizing his mistake, Prophet retreated from the Elizabeth memories and reached for loyalty and devotion, pulling them from Wes's emotional pool with images of his father and mother, teachers who had mentored him, and a grandfather who had doted on him; all of these Prophet tried to attach to his own image. Wes knew that if he succeeded, Wes would become a devoted follower. Wes resisted, closing his eyes and nurturing the hate that came from Prophet's psychic molestation of Elizabeth.

"*Give in and live,*" Prophet said in Wes's mind.

"Never," Wes thought back.

"*Then die,*" Prophet said, and released Wes, who recoiled as if he had been physically struck.

"This one has chosen the fire over life," Prophet said.

"Burn him!" the crowd roared.

Prophet gave Wes a thin smile and then stepped to Ralph and repeated his routine.

"Stop that, it tickles," Ralph said suddenly.

Prophet opened his eyes and studied Ralph, puzzled. Then he closed his eyes and probed again.

"You're going to make me laugh," Ralph said, smiling broadly.

Prophet squatted on the stage, looking at Ralph quizzically. With his fringe of graying hair and his chestnut-brown eyes, Prophet looked fatherly, and spoke kindly.

"You have a most unusual mind, Ralph," Prophet said.

"Thanks," Ralph said as if he had been complimented.

"This one has turned his back on God's gift, too."

"Burn him!" the crowd shouted.

Now Prophet raised his hands, quieting the crowd on the deck of the carrier. Prophet waited for complete silence. Then he spoke to the captives, but in a voice loud enough for all those gathered on the deck to hear.

"You could have joined our fellowship, but you turned your back on God and the mission God has given us—the mission we are about to undertake."

The crowd murmured excitedly, but then quieted without Prophet's urging, anxious to hear his words.

"God brought us here and gave us eternal life so that we would prepare ourselves to serve him as his chosen people. He established a covenant with us just as he did with Abraham, and freed us from hunger, disease, and death, and gave to us abilities like those spiritual beings who share heaven with God. But just like with the children of Israel, there were those who were weak, who denied God, and we drove them from our fellowship. Then the world sent its agents—people like you—to destroy us, and we repulsed them as well, becoming stronger in our faithfulness, trusting God that he would make his plan clear to us.

"Only when the heretic Kellum came to us with his plan to destroy this world God created for us, did God reveal his final plan for us. Kellum wanted us to go back to the world to resume our sinful ways, but God wanted more for us. So we let Kellum build his machines, and when I saw what they could do I knew God was pleased with us and ready to make his chosen a mighty people again. God brought this ship's weapons to us so that we might return to the world and build a new Israel."

Cheers erupted from the crowd.

"Set my people free!"

The crowed roared approval, shaking their medieval weapons in the air. They wouldn't be quieted now and continued to shout praises at Prophet. Walking up and down the platform, Prophet fed off their adulation. His ego finally satiated, he quieted them by raising his arms above his head and bringing them down slowly. Prophet played his flock like an organ, using arm motions to stir them up and quiet them down.

"They will shut down their machine that traps us in here, or they will be punished with the nuclear fire of their own evil creation."

Wes was horrified by what he was hearing. The madman on the platform had access to the Nimitz's nuclear weapons and was threatening to use them against the world. Wes didn't doubt that he would carry out his threat.

"When we have finished moving the rest of the nuclear weapons to the Norfolk, we will be ready to return to the world."

Again the crowd erupted in deafening roars of approval. Prophet quieted his flock with another dramatic arm motion. Then he strutted across his stage, looking down at his kneeling captives.

"Before we can finish God's work, we must once again purify his flock."

"Burn them!" the Crazies shouted.

With a dramatic turn and a point he stopped in front of the wounded sailor.

"Bring that one," Prophet said.

Even half conscious the sailor knew what was coming, and struggled vainly as he was dragged roughly up onto the stage. A metal post was brought to the platform and fitted into a hole. Then the sailor was tied to the post.

"Mr. Rust, do God's work," Prophet said.

"Burn him, burn him, burn him!" the crowd chanted.

A bearded man in a brown leisure suit climbed onto the stage. He wore a cruel smile, clearly enjoying his work. Wes struggled against his bonds to no avail. Even if he broke free, he was powerless to stop what was about to happen. With the crowd shouting encouragement Rust bowed his head, his chin nearly touching his chest. Instantly, Wes could feel the heat. Then the air around the sailor began to glow.

"Don't look, Anita," Elizabeth said with Dawson's voice.

The sailor was panting and begging for mercy, his face beaded with sweat. Suddenly his pants burst into flame and the screaming began. The mob erupted in cheers and applause as the flames licked up the legs of the sailor. The agony of the sailor chilled Wes's blood, and his eyes teared in sympathy. The sailor was hoarse by the time the flames reached his waist, his throat producing only scratchy wails. Suddenly he collapsed, unconscious. Weak from blood loss, he died before the torture was over.

Rust stopped abruptly, the flames dying quickly, leaving the sailor's flesh and clothes smoldering. The flames couldn't be sustained without Rust's psi influence. The crowd booed and shouted their disappointment. Prophet stepped back to the center of the stage.

"This is my fault," Prophet shouted. "I should have given the life-sustaining field a chance to heal him, but I was loathe to waste God's gift of healing on one condemned to the fire."

"It was right," a woman shouted from the mob. Others shouted agreement.

"Never mind, we have others who will suffer God's full punishment," Prophet said.

Now Prophet walked slowly in front of the kneeling captives.

"Who shall go next?" Prophet said. "Roberto, who has refused God many times before? How many of the faithful have you killed, Roberto?"

The Hispanic man glared defiantly. Prophet moved on to Monica.

"Perhaps Monica should go next. Ladies before gentlemen?"

"Burn the Jap," a sailor shouted.

"I'm not Japanese, I'm Korean-American," Monica protested.

"The newcomers tell me we went to war with the Koreans," Prophet said.

"That was North Korea," Monica said. "I was born in America."

"It doesn't matter what you are. The wars with the Germans, the Japanese, the Koreans—those are of the old world. Evil against evil, heretic against heretic. Here, the war is between the followers of God and the followers of Satan."

Then Prophet turned to Ralph.

"Ralph has a simple mind, but still I cannot reach him. It's a shame, but he is strong and will last a long time in the fire."

"It's not nice to hurt people," Ralph said.

Ignoring Ralph, Prophet stopped in front of Wes.

"Perhaps this one. I thought you would join us, Dr. Wes Martin, but you are too full of yourself to make room for God."

Then Prophet moved on to Jett.

"Nathan Jett, professional killer. God would have even you in his flock, but you refuse him."

"I refuse *you*, Layton McNab, not God," Jett said.

Prophet's face flushed.

"Here I speak for God," he said with grand arm gestures.

"Here you play God," Jett said.

Teeth clenched, face purple, Prophet broadcast widely so that all heard. *"Blasphemy will be punished."*

Sparks arced from Cobb's fingers into Jett's back, knocking him to the ground where he squirmed silently like a worm on a hot sidewalk. After a minute of torture, Prophet ordered Cobb to stop. Immediately, Jett relaxed, his face serene, inscrutable.

"Has the evil one given you anything else to say?" Prophet said.

Jett's mouth opened, but Ralph spoke first.

"I don't think it's a good idea to say anything, Nate."

"Out of the mouths of babes," Prophet said. "Take his advice or taste Cobb's gift again."

"Electrocution or fire? If that's my choice, I'll take electrocution," Jett said.

Prophet reddened, angry at the way Jett knew his thoughts. Prophet did want to burn him. Slowly, his smug grin returned.

"You will be saved for last," Prophet said. "We'll see what kind of tongue you have after you've seen the flesh cooked from the bones of your friends."

"I have no friends," Jett said.

The woman in the silver suit stepped next to Prophet.

"He's right. He has no feelings for anyone."

"I've seen his heart," Prophet said. "He loves Ralph."

The woman in the silver suit looked surprised, while Ralph beamed.

"Ralph reminds him of his brother," Prophet said. "His brother Jason killed himself, didn't he, Nathan? You saw your brother's mangled body, and it made you cry. Now you'll watch Ralph die and we'll see if there's enough humanity left in you to muster another tear."

Jett started to speak, but Prophet hushed him.

"If you say another word I'll have your tongue cut out."

Jett kept silent, and Prophet smiled in satisfaction. Then Prophet turned to Dawson.

"Roger, I honestly hoped you would never be brought before me. We were friends."

"I'm not Roger," Elizabeth protested.

"I know what you are, demon. You have possessed him and turned him against his best friend, and his savior."

"I'm not a demon, I'm a social worker."

"What's the difference?" Prophet said, the mob laughing. "I have decided. The sooner we cleanse our fellowship, the sooner we can finish transferring the bombs."

Taking center stage again, Prophet raised his arms and assumed a low and pretentious voice.

"Roger Dawson, we send you to the fire to purify you of the demon that has possessed you. May God have mercy on your soul."

Dawson was dragged to his feet.

"No!" Wes shouted. "Elizabeth!"

"Anita, get away from me," Elizabeth shouted.

Wes knew that wasn't possible. What Elizabeth saw and felt, Anita would, too.

The smoldering carcass of the first victim was dragged away, and the man who was part Dawson and part Elizabeth was tied to the stake. Then Prophet raised his hands to quiet the mob.

"Mr. Rust, make this temple pure again."

With a smile, Rust stepped forward, and the air around Dawson's body began to glow.

ACID BOMB

Evans reached the nearest of the twin generators safely and squatted behind it, looking and listening. It was a game of hide and seek. Even with two of the Norfolk's boilers removed, the compartment was still filled with piping. There were many hiding places. The guards knew that he was after the generators, and they would protect them with their lives.

Evans's pack had two compartments. The bottom held the compressed air canisters that powered his gun. The top portion of the pack was detachable; he released the catches, pulling it free. He was unzipping the top when he heard the attack. Evans lunged left, a spear creasing his side. He fumbled for his gun as the Crazy pulled the spear back, ready to plunge it into his chest. Evans kicked at the spear. The sailor hesitated, waiting for the clear path to a vital organ. The two-second delay was all Evans needed. Three quick shots struck chest, neck, and jaw; the Crazy collapsed in a heap.

Evans felt his side, his hand coming away sticky with blood. It wasn't a fatal wound and would heal quickly in Pot of Gold. He worked quickly now, extracting the bomb and pulling the three red safety rings which extracted three long red plastic strips. The detonators could now strike their targets. Evans peeled the protective plastic sheet from the bottom of the bomb, put one foot on the base of the generator, and stood, placing the bomb on the top. He pulled two more rings, releasing the catalyst that would mix with the liquid and cement the bomb to the generator.

Movement in the pipes across from him caught his eye, and Evans ducked. A sniper was taking position high on a rack of pipes across from the generators. Now Evans would be exposed when he finished triggering the bomb. It couldn't be helped. He stood, pulled out a metal rod from the side of the bomb, gave it a half twist, and then rammed it in, hearing the satisfying sound of glass breaking. He pulled the second rod and repeated the procedure. There was only one step left.

An explosive device could not detonate within Pot of Gold, so Dr. Lee had created acid bombs which two of the team members carried. The bombs were glued to the casing of the generators; when the glass vials inside were crushed, the liquid contents would mix to create an acid which would eat through the metal casing of the generator, destroying the coils inside. Since it was the resonance created by two generators that sustained the time-and-space distortion, only one had to be destroyed to collapse the field. Now Evans reached up to the bomb one more time to remove the coated plate that kept the acid from the generator. Once pulled, nothing could stop the acid.

As Evans stood, the sniper fired. The bolt from the crossbow glanced off the top of the generator and caromed into the air. Evans fired three rounds to pin the sniper down; then he heard noises. Crazies were coming, and they were coming in force.

CONFRONTATION

Roast him slowly," a woman shouted from the crowd.

"Very slowly, Mr. Rust, very slowly," Prophet said.

Dawson's body, with Elizabeth's consciousness, was tied to a stake on a platform. A crowd of Crazies was gathered in a semicircle in front of the platform to watch the execution. Wes and the other captives were on their knees, waiting their turn. Elizabeth struggled at her bonds with Dawson's strength, but couldn't free her hands. The pyrokinetic, Rust, dressed in his leisure suit, approached slowly, head down, concentrating on Dawson's feet.

The crowd murmured in anticipation. Under Rust's pyrokinetic influence, heat waves formed around Dawson's feet. Rust brought the temperature up slowly, hoping to maximize Dawson's pain. Wes doubted that Elizabeth and Anita, weakened by the lack of normal dreaming, could survive that level of agony. Even if they did, the psychological trauma of being burned alive could do irreparable harm.

Dawson was panting now, ready to scream as his trouser legs heated toward combustion point, the skin underneath already searing. Helpless and desperate, Wes pleaded for mercy, but his voice was lost in the cheering of the crowd.

Suddenly there was a commotion in the back. The crowd noise changed from joy to worried babbling. Prophet held up a hand, stopping Rust. Dawson's breaths were rapid and deep, as if he were hyperventilating. Dawson stared at his legs, holding perfectly still, as if to keep the superheated cloth from touching his skin.

There was shouting from down the flight deck. Prophet held out his arms, quieting the crowd.

"They're after the generators!"

The news spread quickly through the crowd. The edge of the mob was already flowing toward the Norfolk when the word reached the platform. There was panic in the air. Prophet started from the stage, pushing Rust in front of him.

"Cobb, guard the heretics!" Prophet ordered.

Then Prophet pointed at men close to Cobb, ordering them to stay behind, too. Reluctantly, four sailors remained, eyes on the retreating mob. Unhappy about being left behind, Cobb stared after Prophet like a faithful dog ordered to stay by its master. The bridge was a bottleneck; but those Crazies who were crowded at Nimitz's stern parted for Prophet.

Once Prophet was out of sight, Cobb checked the captives' bonds, then joined the other guards who were standing down the deck where they could see more of the Norfolk.

Wes tried twisting his wrists, testing the cords. There was very little wiggle room, let alone enough to slip his hands out. Wes saw Jett watching him.

"Let's sit back to back," Wes suggested. "Maybe I can untie your ropes."

"It won't work," Jett said. "They'll notice."

"Maybe we can find something to rub the ropes against and cut them."

"Not enough time," Jett said.

"We've got to try something," Wes said, looking at Dawson hanging limp, still tied to the post.

Wes had never met anyone harder to read than Jett. He showed no fear, not even concern. Jett turned toward the stage and said in a soft voice, "Now's the time and the place, Elizabeth." Then he turned to Ralph, who was staring at the deck, his face blank.

"Hey, Ralph," Jett said.

Ralph looked up, his generous lips folding into a smile.

"Got any gum?" Jett said.

Now Ralph's smile widened, and he said, "Nope, not even that pink stuff."

"Not that gum that stinks!"

"Pee-yew," Ralph and Jett said together.

"We've got to get loose," Wes said, frustrated.

"Want to have a contest, Ralph?" Jett asked.

"Sure."

"First one to break the ropes tying their hands wins a pack of gum," Jett said.

"Do they gots to share?" Ralph asked, looking serious.

"Nope," Jett said. "But if I win I'll share with you."

"And if I win I'll share with you," Ralph said, smiling. "Who gets to say go?"

"Let's have Doctor Martin say it," Jett said.

"Sure. Wes is fair, aren't you, Wes?"

"Shut up over there!" one of the guards shouted, pointing a spear in their direction.

When the guard turned back to the Norfolk, Wes whispered, "Go, now."

"You gots to say ready-set first, Wes. That's how it's done."

"I said shut up!" the guard ordered.

Wes froze when Cobb glanced at them, but then relaxed when he looked away again. One of the other guards looked their way, then started toward them.

"We should wait," Wes said.

"Do it now," Jett said firmly.

With another glance at the approaching guard, Wes said "Ready, set, go!"

"What's going on?" the guard said.

The guard was now halfway to the captives.

Ralph's shoulders tightened and shook, and his face reddened. Jett's arms and shoulders were quivering, too. Suddenly there was a "snap," and Ralph pulled his hands free.

"I win," Ralph said at a near shout, waving his arms in the air, ropes still around his wrists.

"Untie me," the other captives said at once.

"One of them is loose," the guard shouted, rushing at Ralph with his spear.

Still tied, Wes could only shout a warning to Ralph, who stared dumbly at the approaching weapon. What happened next came in a rapid-fire blur.

The other guards came rushing down the deck, leaving Cobb, who followed slowly, confident in his special power. Just before the guard with the spear reached Ralph, Jett jumped to his feet, his hands already free. Intercepting the guard's lunge, he grabbed the spear, head-butting the guard at the same time, breaking his nose and weakening his grip. Jett wrested the spear from the guard's hands and jammed the blunt end into his solar plexus; the guard crumpled, his nose bleeding.

"Hold him, Ralph!" Jett ordered. "So he won't hurt anyone."

"Okee-dokee, Nate," Ralph said, wrapping his arms around the guard. "Got a nosebleed? Try putting your head back," Ralph said as he held the sailor firmly.

"Roberto, turn around," Jett shouted.

Jett was swinging the spear by the shaft before the Hispanic man was fully turned, his roped wrists extended. The spear struck and was pulled away in a flash; then Jett spun to face the onrushing guards, tossing the spear up and back and catching it midshaft with his arm cocked. The motion was fluid and precise. Without hesitation, Jett threw the spear at a guard who was aiming a crossbow at him. Both men launched at the same time, but only Jett had the reflexes to throw and then dodge. The spear buried itself low in the guard's abdomen while his bolt passed over Jett's shoulder, flying past Dawson's limp body. Eyes wide, the guard dropped his crossbow and stared in shock at the protruding shaft. A small red stain surrounded the entry point, but then, under the weight of the sagging spear's shaft, the tip of the spear was forced upward, slicing toward his sternum. With a gasp the guard grabbed the shaft, but it was too late. The blood flowed freely now from the fatal wound, and he collapsed to his knees, then fell onto his side with a sob.

Ignoring Cobb's approach, Jett charged the two other guards who wielded knives. Still tied, Wes was helpless and could only watch as Jett took on the guards. Then Roberto broke free, scrambling to his feet and running to the speared guard. He picked up the crossbow. Stepping into the stirrup, he drew the bow, cocked it, then nocked another bolt.

Having seen Jett in action, the other guards hesitated, wielding their knives defensively, jockeying for position. One guard saw Roberto with the crossbow; he broke and ran toward the bridge. Roberto tracked the running man with his weapon, loosing the bolt before he was more than a few yards down the deck. The shaft struck just under the guard's right shoulder blade, nearly disappearing into the body cavity. The guard took one last step and collapsed. Unnerved now, the last guard turned to flee, but Jett spun, sweeping his leg into the guard, knocking his feet into a tangle. Then Jett was on him and with two quick blows to the neck, came up with the guard's knife and tossed it to Roberto.

"Free the others," Jett ordered.

"Cobb?" Roberto protested, cocking the crossbow again.

"You'll never get a shot off," Jett shouted. "Get the others out."

Cobb's arm was extended toward Roberto; his long black hair was splayed out around his head, and his fingertips were sparking. Roberto flattened behind a row of chairs just as a ragged spark shot from Cobb's fingers as if he were a human electric eel. Wes saw that Cobb's hair fell to his shoulders after the discharge. In his black boots and denims, he looked like a Hell's Angel. Then his hair began to rise from his shoulders, his electric power building.

Wes heard Roberto slithering along the deck, using the rows of chairs for cover. He came up behind Wes, slitting the ropes in one smooth motion. Wes wanted to run to Elizabeth, but climbing up on the stage would make him an easy target. He saw Jett maneuvering himself between Cobb and the stage, deliberately stepping into harm's way. Wes knew that Jett had no chance on his own against Cobb, and moved to help.

"Give me the crossbow," Wes ordered.

Roberto hesitated, looking at Jett and then at Dawson.

"I'll help delay Cobb while you cut him free," Wes said.

"I only need a few seconds—then get away from him. He can knock you on your ass with a flick of his finger."

Nodding, Wes took the bow, feeling awkward as he fit his hand to the trigger and brought the bow up level. Made entirely of steel, the bow was heavy and powerful looking. Wes realized that he didn't have the quiver so he wouldn't be reloading, but from the look of the crosspiece, he doubted that he could draw the bow anyway.

With the unfamiliar weapon in hand, Wes turned to the confrontation taking place a few yards away. Locked eye to eye, Cobb advanced slowly on Jett, his arms spread wide, his fingertips crackling and sparking like fourth of July sparklers. Jett stood perfectly still, letting Cobb get closer, showing no fear. He wasn't going to run; he was going to take the monster's attack, sacrificing himself to save the others.

With Cobb and Jett intent on each other, Wes felt invisible, and decided to move to a better position. He couldn't risk hitting Jett with the unfamiliar crossbow. Wes took only a few steps before Cobb's arm swung toward him and five jagged streaks of light shot from his finger tips. The high voltage fired every nerve ending in Wes's body and he convulsed, muscles taut. He fell to the deck, his body trembling.

Raising his head, Wes saw Jett holding his ground, letting Cobb come within a few feet of him. While Cobb was engaged with Jett, Roberto sprinted across the stage to Dawson, cut him down, and threw him over his shoulder.

"Do you need help?"

It was Monica, crawling toward Wes from behind.

"I'm okay. Help Roberto get Elizabeth-Dawson out of here."

Wes turned back just as Cobb struck. Arms spread wide as if ready to hug Jett, Cobb threw sparks which arced from every fingertip into Jett, spreading along his arms and shoulders. Flashes of electric light cracked and hissed—the peculiar thunder of miniature lightning bolts. Wes hurt for the man who sagged under the assault but had the strength to keep standing.

"Let's go," Roberto shouted as he and Monica dragged Dawson past Wes, down the deck, and toward the island. To Wes's relief, Dawson was awake. Wes rolled over and got up on his knees. He could follow the others, but he wouldn't leave Jett.

Wes lifted the crossbow again, his arms still weak, the bow swaying so badly that Jett was as much at risk as Cobb. Fearing that Jett couldn't take much more, he steadied the bow and pulled the trigger. The bolt buried in Cobb's thigh. The big man had been mute before, but now he roared like a wounded animal. Cobb grabbed his injured leg, interrupting his electrocution of Jett. Jett was free. Wes struggled to his feet and toward him. To his surprise, Jett was coming to him, reaching out, offering Wes support.

"How could you take that?" Wes asked.

"I wouldn't have lasted much longer," Jett said. "I'm not ready for him yet."

Closing his eyes and concentrating, Jett held out his hand, spreading his fingers wide. Tiny sparks crackled in the spaces.

"Whatever he is, I'm becoming," Jett said.

"Can I let him go now, Nate?" Ralph said, arms still wrapped around the guard.

Jett turned to answer, but then Cobb stood again, arms held straight in front of him, pointing at Roberto and Monica, who were hurrying down the deck with Dawson. An electric bolt enveloped the group, and they collapsed in a heap. Then Cobb turned with a limp, striking Wes and Jett. Wes fell, but Jett stood his ground, taking the charge. When Cobb finished his discharge, he turned back to Roberto and the others, preparing another charge. Jett dropped down next to Wes.

"I'm not ready," Jett said. "He's got ten times the power I have."

Now Wes heard the electric crackle as Cobb attacked the others—Elizabeth, he remembered, he's attacking Elizabeth and Anita.

"The best we can do is spread out," Jett said. "I'll last the longest, so I'll rush him. Keep on the opposite side of him from the others. You'll never get across to the Norfolk, so head for the island and find another way off the ship."

The electric crackle stopped. Cobb was turning his attention back to Wes and Jett.

"Get away from me," Jett commanded, pushing Wes.

"Take your shoes off," Wes said suddenly.

"What?" Jett said.

"Ground yourself," Wes said.

Understanding instantly, Jett sat, fumbling with the laces on his silver boots. Wes could see Cobb's arms pointing in their direction now. To give Jett more time, Wes stood and ran. Cobb followed him with his arms, the lightning flowing from his fingertips, dancing toward Wes. Wes went down hard, laying flat, face and hands pressed against the deck, current flowing through him. Then he saw Jett spring up and sprint toward Cobb, bare feet pounding across the flight deck.

MELT DOWN

Evans could tell from the vibrations of the deck that a large number of reinforcements were coming. For now, he was safe behind one of the shell-shaped generators, but he couldn't finish triggering the acid bomb without standing and exposing himself to the snipers. It was a risk he had to take.

He stood, reaching for the last plate. He heard the whoosh of the crossbow bolt a second before it pierced his hand. The pain paralyzed him for a few seconds, giving the archer a chance to reload. Before Evans could recover from the shock, another bolt came from behind, creasing his shoulder and glancing off his collar bone.

Evans collapsed, turning as he did, firing blindly, searching for the archer. He spotted him cocking his weapon. Evans fired, his bullets stitching a line across the archer's body from knee to shoulder.

Sitting again, his back to the generator, Evans dropped his gun and reached for the bloody tip of the bolt protruding from his hand. It was a piece of steel tubing sharpened at one end. Grasping the shaft, Evans pulled the bolt from his hand. The pain was excruciating, but it reduced to a throb when the steel was out.

Steadying himself against the generator, gun in his good hand, Evans bobbed up and then ducked down. It worked. The sniper's shot passed over his head, clattering onto the deck behind. Reaching over the generator, Evans fired six rounds in random directions. Suddenly there was the sputter of another of Dr. Lee's special weapons, and Teflon bullets ricocheted off the top of the generator.

"You don't want to destroy the generator," a woman shouted.

Evans recognized Compton's voice.

"Dr. Lee lied to us, Evans," Compton shouted. "The hip units don't work. There's no way out, not unless we follow Prophet."

Evans looked down at his unit; the green ready light still glowed.

"Why should I believe you?" Evans asked.

"Jett tried it. He couldn't get through the field."

Compton's voice was closer now.

"I don't believe you," Evans said. "Prophet got to you."

"It's the truth," Compton said, closer again.

"I want to hear it from Jett," Evans said.

"He's dead," Compton said. "I'm in command now, and I'm saying there's no way out of here without Prophet."

Evans believed her. He had never trusted Woolman, but neither did he care if he got back. Prophet had killed him long ago, so it didn't matter if the hip unit worked or not. He had no life to go back to.

Reaching around the generator, he fired a few rounds, trying to catch them by surprise. Compton fired back, and Evans hunkered down behind the steel of the generator. Then he felt Prophet in his mind, feeling around, touching his thoughts.

"Do you know who this is?"

"I know," Evans said.

"Listen to your shipmate. She's giving you the gospel."

"You burned me," Evans said. "You turned me into a monster."

"You were a monster long before we touched you with the cleansing fire. You came to kill; the Devil's wolf among the lambs of God. Do unto others as you would have others do unto you, it says in the Bible. If we had treated you as you treated us, we would have killed you. But we showed you the mercy you would have denied us. We left you your life so you would have a chance to repent and to carry the message of salvation to the world."

"You left me nothing but pain. Now I'm going to destroy your little kingdom," Evans said.

"You don't want to destroy the generator. You don't want to hurt us!"

Prophet was in his mind, poking into places he had no business going, setting off sensations and memories, creating a swirling cerebral storm. Through the buzz, Evans realized that he had to act soon if he was going to succeed. He stood, keeping his head low; his back ached, his hand throbbed. He could feel Prophet in his head, pulling on his feelings, trying to create loyalty where there had been none before.

"The serpent beguiled Eve, and she ate of the tree of knowledge. Then Eve beguiled Adam and he, too, ate. Don't play the role of the serpent, Robin. The serpent of the Garden lies in the center of the lake of fire and he is calling to you. Don't listen to him. God has given us the gift of eternal life, an eternity to prepare ourselves to return to the world. We are nearly ready, Robin, and God has given us the means to build a new Christian nation that none will dare attack. We have their superweapons, Robin, and they shall be the rock on which we build this new nation. Join us, Robin, answer God's call."

Evans slapped his injured hand against the side of the generator, the pain helping to shut out Prophet's seductive voice. Then he concentrated, summoning his special power, hoping that Prophet was too full of himself to sense what was coming.

"No matter how far we stray, God always gives us choices, Robin. He gave the world Jesus, and they rejected him. Now you have to choose between the lake of fire and eternal life in God's service. You don't want to hurt us, Robin! You don't want to destroy the generators!"

"Like hell I don't!" Evans said.

Standing, Evans released his power, sending an invisible wall over the top of the generator. Compton was there—her legs were knocked out from under her, her shots fired wild. Two bolts and a spear were launched, sailing over his head. Dropping his gun to dangle from the connecting cable, Evans grabbed the plastic plate in his good hand, braced his foot against the generator, and yanked the plate from the bomb, releasing the acid.

In a few minutes Pot of Gold would lose its protective field.

ESCAPE

Cobb was formidable—a large man with long greasy hair, coal black eyes, and arms as thick as Wes's thighs. Silhouetted against the opaque nothingness of the edge of this strange world, he had an overpowering physical presence even without his ability to generate electricity. Cobb generated a charge that paralyzed first and then killed. Standing near the stern of the Nimitz, Cobb was singlehandedly keeping the captives from escaping. Monica, Roberto, and Elizabeth in Dawson's body were lying on the deck, knocked down by a charge from Cobb. Ralph was behind Wes, still holding one of the guards, while the bodies of the other guards were scattered on the deck. Wes was taking Cobb's torture now; he was being slowly electrocuted. His only hope was Nathan Jett, who was up and running toward Cobb.

Cobb broke off his attack when Jett started his barefoot charge across the deck. Still wracked with pain, Wes watched Cobb bring his arms around toward Jett. Cobb weighed fifty pounds more than Jett, but he was fast, too. He swung his arms around and released another charge at Jett. Sparks arced between the deck and Jett's bare feet as he ran and rammed the bear-sized man at full speed. The two of them went down, enveloped in a crackling light show as bright as arc welding.

Wes hurried to check on the others. Roberto and Monica were dazed, just getting muscle control back. Elizabeth, in Dawson's body, was awake.

"Elizabeth? Are you still here?" Wes said.

"Yes, Wes," Elizabeth replied with Dawson's voice.

"Are you hurt?"

"My legs are burned," she said. "Anita's are, too. What I felt, she felt. She's in shock."

"We've got to get out of here," Monica said, urging the others on.

Jett and Cobb were locked in an electric brawl, Jett keeping his body tight against Cobb's. Electricity discharged from their entwined bodies in all directions. Roberto and Wes were anxious to help, but found no way to penetrate the electric barrage.

"Let's get Ralph," Wes said.

"Can I let him go now?" Ralph asked as they approached. "He said he would be good."

"Where's the gun?" Roberto demanded.

"I don't know," the guard said, his eyes darting from face to face.

Roberto pressed his knife against the man's throat, the tip drawing a drop of blood.

"It's in the captain's quarters," the guard said.

"Show us, then we let you go," Roberto told him.

Ralph released the man to Roberto, who turned him around and held the knife to his kidney.

"Show me where the gun is," Roberto said.

The Crazy led Roberto toward the island on the starboard side of the ship.

"Nate's in trouble, Wes," Ralph said. "We gots to help him."

Ralph started forward, but Wes held him back.

"There's nothing we can do, Ralph."

Jett and Cobb were locked so tight that the close body blows and head butts did little damage. Each man struggled to get a choke hold on the other, but both were experienced and blocked each other's moves.

Suddenly there was a loud crack as Cobb and Jett were separated, Jett landing on his back, Cobb on his knees. Now, with three feet between them, Cobb could use his power effectively. Jett rolled, trying to touch his bare feet to the deck before he took the charge. Cobb respected Jett's abilities by now, and wasn't going to give Jett the time. Cobb's hands were up and the charge was starting to flow into Jett.

Wes spotted the crossbow he had dropped. There was no time to find the bolts, so in desperation he threw the weapon at Cobb. Seeing the weapon coming, Cobb deflected it with a flick of his hand. In that moment Jett kicked Cobb in the face; his bare foot landed with a loud smack. Stunned, Cobb swung reflexively, forgetting to use his power. Jett's next blow came from a fist to the side of Cobb's face. Cobb reeled. Now Jett's blows rained fast and furious. Cobb could do little but protect his face while he tried to stand. Jett circled, pounding first one kidney and then the other. Dizzy from pain, Cobb staggered to his feet and reached out, sending arcs of electricity randomly. Jett stood his ground, pounding away at the kidneys, taking occasional jolts with only a grimace. Then, taking a kick to the back of his knee, Cobb was down again, and Jett was on his back, arm snaking around his neck. Wes knew how the fight would end now. Ralph and Anita didn't need to see it.

"Ralph, take us where Roberto went," Wes said, pointing toward the island.

"Okee-dokee, Wes," Ralph said.

Ralph helped Monica support Dawson, putting his arm around his waist and lifting.

Wes saw that the fight was over; Jett was walking away slowly from Cobb's body.

"We were a good match," Jett said.

"They're coming!" Monica shouted.

Two Crazies were coming off the bridge, looking down the deck. Soon they were shouting toward the Norfolk. They hurried to a hatch leading into the island, but suddenly it opened by itself. Roberto was inside, holding Jett's weapon. Jett took the pieces one at a time, reassembling the weapon as they hurried into the bowels of the supercarrier.

"Where's the guard?" Wes asked Roberto.

"He promised to count to a thousand before he comes out of the captain's cabin," Roberto said, struggling to keep a straight face.

"I can count to a hundred," Ralph said.

"I'm feeling something," Elizabeth said.

Then Elizabeth bent as if listening to someone shorter than her.

"Anita feels it too. The ones you have been fighting—the Crazies—are sad and frightened. Something terrible has happened to them."

Jett stopped Elizabeth.

"Is it about the generators?" Jett asked.

"Yes. I'm not sure what it means, but it's something about a generator."

"It means this place isn't going to exist much longer."

Then there were voices and the sound of heavy footsteps—the Crazies were coming. The Nimitz had been pulled into Pot of Gold, not had the time and space distorting field created around her, like the Norfolk, so the interior of the ship connected and flowed in a logical way. But even here body parts protruded from bulkheads and decks, as on the Norfolk. Having seen many of these body-part statues, they moved past them quickly, no longer horrified by the sight. Wes, however, noticed something new. The Norfolk's crew statues were all male and all white, while on the Nimitz there was diversity, with African-Americans, Asian-Americans, and women suffering the same fate.

Jett led them now, setting a fast pace. As on the Norfolk, there was a utilitarian feel to the ship, the emphasis being on function and survivability, not aesthetics. Bulkheads were painted in muted grays and greens, and every compartment had a clear function. Storage, equipment, bunks, repair, conference, and mess passed in a blur; Wes barely had time to glance into the compartments as they rushed after Jett. Unlike on the Norfolk, here there was equipment that would have seemed impossible to the World War II sailors. One large compartment, labelled "Print Room," was filled with copiers and computers, suggesting a sophisticated print-making capability. Another room was equipped like a home theater, with a large-screen television, a VCR, and a rack of videocassettes.

They passed through a ready room decorated with the squadron insignia of lightning bolts and a rising sun. A bulletin board covered with papers made up half of one wall, a blackboard the other half. Pilots' names were written on another wall, with yellow and green stickers grading the pilots' performance. A VCR and TV were mounted in one corner; the TV screen was glowing, the speaker issuing a steady hiss.

They hurried through rows of high-backed chairs, out the other side, and deeper into the ship. In the next corridor they came to a dentist's office, complete with dental chair and drills, and an x-ray machine. Beyond that was the clinic. The Nimitz had all the features and functions of an American city.

Running from the sounds of pursuit, they emerged into a hangar. It was a vast space, four stories high, filled with planes and equipment. With wings folded, F-14s, A-10s and other aircraft were scattered throughout the hangar. Most of the jets were parked, but others were undergoing maintenance, some with engines disassembled. Yellow lines painted on the deck marked spaces kept open for walking. In the middle of the largest open space they found three cruise missiles, which had been brought out of the nuclear storage vault deep in the Nimitz. One of the missiles was disassembled, the work having been interrupted by the trial.

Jett rushed past the missiles to one of the elevators used to raise the planes to the flight deck. From the elevator they could see the opaque wall that marked the edge of this world. Forward, they could see the Norfolk. Above them hung some of the crucified crew of the Nimitz, still writhing in agony, unable to die. Ropes and cables hung from the elevator, and two rope ladders led to the desert below.

"Cut everything but this rope and that ladder to the desert floor," Jett ordered.

Roberto hacked the ropes, Jett firing his weapon to cut through the cables. One by one the lines were severed, leaving only one ladder and one rope.

"Down the ladder," Jett ordered. "I'll hold them off until you're down."

Without another word Jett ran back the way they had come.

"Monica, you go first," Wes said. "Then Ralph, Roberto, and Dawson. Help the person above you."

Wes had arranged the order of descent in such a way as to help clumsy Ralph and the injured Dawson. Monica climbed down ten feet and then waited as Ralph awkwardly turned around and squatted, not sure how to coordinate his movements to get onto the ladder. Wes held one of his arms steadying him.

"I can do it, Wes. I'm not a baby you know," Ralph complained.

Wes ignored him, holding Ralph's arm until he was two rungs down. Monica was below, helping Ralph descend. Jett's gun sputtered in the back of the hangar, followed by shouts of alarm. The Crazies had arrived. Wes followed the others onto the rope ladder, trusting Jett to find a way to escape.

Ralph set the pace down the ladder, Monica staying close below him, the others backed up above Ralph. Jett's gun was still firing in the hangar bay above, although they heard less and less of the fighting.

The hull of the carrier curved inward, and they were soon dangling in space, feeling helpless and exposed. Wes could see no one in the desert below; when he looked forward toward the Norfolk, he saw no one there, either. With painful slowness, Ralph lowered himself slowly to the desert floor, Monica holding him as he stepped gingerly off the ladder.

"See, I told ya I could do it," Ralph announced.

With Ralph safely down, Roberto and Dawson descended quickly, Wes following, relieved to be within safe jumping distance, and then to feel his feet on the ground. There was no sign of Jett.

Roberto led now, moving along the hull toward the Norfolk. Wes herded the others after him, feeling safe under the curving hull even though it looked as if the great ship could tip over on them at any second.

A whirring noise above caught Wes's attention. Jett was sliding down the rope he had ordered to be left dangling. Once on the ground he disentangled from the rope, then aimed his weapon up the side of the ship. Wes expected him to cut the rope and the ladder at the top near the elevator, but instead he fired just below the curve of the ship, the bullets smacking into the hull. Only a few rounds missed, and Jett quickly cut the ladder and the rope, leaving the end dangling forty feet in the air.

Jett caught up just as crossbow bolts rained down, impacting behind and ahead of Jett, who ducked under the hull.

"Let's move," he said.

Glancing behind, Wes saw Crazies reaching the severed end of the ladder. One hung precariously from the rope while others slid down from above. Those on the bottom of the ladder shouted at those above, and they began reversing the climb. Those on the rope, however, were hanging on for dear life, since the climb up was infinitely harder than the climb down. Then the lowest man on the rope slipped, hitting the desert with a solid thud. Still alive, he rolled on the ground holding a broken leg.

The machines Wes had seen from the rope bridge were ahead, and as he and the others came out from under the curve of the hull they could see Crazies crossing from the Norfolk to the Nimitz. A Crazy on the bridge spotted them, alerting the others. Seconds later they were under fire; they took cover behind one of the machines.

"We should make a run for it," Roberto said. "If they get archers lined up on that bridge, we're done for."

"Can you cut the cables on the bridge with your gun?" Wes asked.

"Not at this range, but there's another way."

Jett released the catch on the belt holding his pack. He pulled the pack halfway around to the front, then opened the top and took out a cylinder attached to a thick plate, with three red rings along one side and two on the top. There was a plastic sheet on the bottom which Jett tore away, revealing a ring of putty. Rotating his pack to his back again, Jett stood, slapping the device on top of the machine behind which they were hiding.

"What are you doing?" Roberto said.

"If I understood Doctor Kellum right, these machines are keeping the Nimitz here. If we can shut one of them down, we can send the Nimitz back where it came from."

"A bomb won't work in here," Roberto said.

"It's acid. It will eat through an inch of steel." Jett tapped the flimsy casing of the device. "This won't even slow it down."

Now Jett pulled each of the three red rings, extracting long plastic strips. Then he pulled two more rings, and finally he pulled a metal rod out from the side of the bomb, gave it a half twist, and rammed it in. Wes heard the sound of glass breaking. Men with crossbows were gathering on the bridge and now fired a volley down at them. Jett ducked, the bolts caroming off the machine. Jett returned fire. The bridge was too far for his weapon to do significant damage, but the Crazies ducked anyway.

He pulled a second rod from the other end of the bomb and jammed it in, too; this was followed by the sound of more glass breaking. Finally, Jett pulled a flat piece of plastic from the bottom.

"That's it," Jett said. "Time to go. I'll cover you."

With a yank from Roberto and a push from Wes they had Ralph up and hurrying across the desert. As Wes stepped away from the cover of their machine he could see that it was beginning to smoke.

Jett followed, firing his weapon. The Crazies fired intermittently while dodging Jett's rounds, which spoiled their aim. Smoke was pouring from the machine now, and the Crazies noticed, shouting and pointing. They hurried to the cover of the Norfolk's hull and out of the line of fire from the bridge.

"What's going to happen?" Wes asked.

"Dr. Kellum said those machines pulled the Nimitz through the force field to this place. One machine can't keep it here, so the Nimitz should go back to where it came from."

"Then shouldn't we be on it?" Wes asked.

"Coming through that electric field the first time killed most of the crew. Even if we survived the trip back, the electric charge will blow the fuel tanks on the planes and detonate the munitions. The ship will be an inferno."

"What about the nuclear weapons?" Wes asked.

"The ones we passed in the hangar were intact and safe, but they've got one on the Norfolk they claim to have fired. If Dr. Kellum is right about the effect of this place, then it could go critical if it ever gets back home."

Now there was a loud hum. The machine was coming apart from the inside, vibrating violently, threatening to tear loose from its mounting. The hum stopped abruptly, followed by a grinding noise and a sudden violent spasm. Then the machine was still. The Crazies watched, faces frozen, unable to believe what had happened.

"Look!" Jett said.

Following the direction his finger pointed past the stern of the Nimitz, Wes could see that the opaque force field was moving toward the Nimitz's stern. It hit the stern with a flash and a deafening crackle. The Crazies on the

Nimitz stampeded, rushing for the rope bridge, fighting each other at the entrance, piling up, creating a human dam. Those on the bridge ran for the Norfolk, but their out-of-step running caused the bridge to vibrate and sway; they stumbled and fell, struggled to their feet, and fell again.

The field swept the length of the carrier with a circle of light. Around the circumference the field was clear, and Wes could see ocean and blue skies. It was a way home that no one could survive. The field caught up with the Crazies piled up at the entrance to the footbridge, electrocuting them. When the field hit the cables holding the bridge, the electric charge was conducted through the cable supports, knocking Crazies off their feet. Two fell from the bridge, dropping silently to the desert, stunned by the electric charge. The field kept coming, swallowing pieces of the bridge. Wes and the others backed away, not sure if the field would stop. With another flash of light, the field finished reshaping, and when it did, the cables connecting the bridge with the Nimitz were severed, the bridge collapsing and dumping unconscious bodies into the desert. Just before the last of the field regained its opaqueness, Wes glimpsed the Nimitz back in the Atlantic, its decks on fire, its planes exploding.

COLLAPSE

Evans ducked behind the generator as soon as he had pulled the last plate free from the acid bomb. Retrieving his gun, he hunkered down behind the generator, ignoring the barrage of bullets, bolts, and spears. It was done. They would die now. Knowing that, some of the hate left him, taking his energy with it. He felt his wounds throbbing now. He was ready to die, but with his mission accomplished he found he wanted more. He wanted to watch them die.

Reaching over the generator, Evans fired a few rounds and then retreated back down the narrow space between the racks of pipe. Aware of movement to the left, he flicked his wrist, firing across his body into the pipes. There was movement to the right; he fired again, driving a Crazy with a spear back under cover. Then a woman stepped in front of him. She was dressed in blue slacks and a blue blouse, her hair neatly combed and curled. Then, as if he had been swatted by a giant hand, he was knocked to the deck. She was psychokinetic and powerful.

Evans came up with a psi strike of his own, but she countered and blocked his blow. Evans concentrated, using every trick he'd learned to maximize his power, but he couldn't break her. She was half his weight at best, and in a normal fight he would have broken her neck in a few seconds. Physical mass didn't matter now. It was her power against his, but she had the advantage of time. He had to kill her fast.

Summoning every bit of his psychokinetic strength, he put it into one last all-or-nothing burst of power. It wasn't enough. She recoiled with shock but quickly recovered. She was stronger. With a blow of her own, she knocked him to the deck. His head felt as if it had imploded, and his vision was blurred. Blood ran from his nose across his lips. Then there were hands on him, holding him. The woman who had beaten him came, wiping a drop of blood from her own nose.

He tried summoning his power again, but got nothing but pain in response and more blood from his nose.

"Should we bag him, Gertie?" one of the men holding him asked.

"No. I broke him," she said.

Evans knew it was true. Something had burst in his brain. His power was gone. Would this place restore his power? He wouldn't live long enough to find out.

They stripped him of his weapon and tied his hands, taking him to Prophet. Ordered to sit, hands tied behind his back, Evans watched from the deck as Prophet tried to pry the bomb from the generator. It had a soft seal designed to conform to the curved surface of the generator and space-age glue that made a joint stronger than a weld; Prophet had no chance of removing the bomb. After several minutes of work he threw his crowbar to the deck in frustration.

"Use the gun," he said to Compton. "Blow it off of there."

Compton fired round after useless round into the bomb casing. Dr. Lee's guns didn't have the power to pierce the metal. Dr. Lee had also added a soft outer coating made up of layered Kevlar. Frustrated, Prophet jerked the gun from Compton's hands, stretching it to the length of its cable and then firing another six rounds into the bomb casing. Accomplishing nothing, Prophet screamed for someone to bring him an axe. Three men ran from the room.

Two axes were brought. Prophet took one, swinging with all his might. The casing dented, but the soft outer layer absorbed much of the blow. With three more swings Prophet shredded the outer layer, reaching the metal case. But after a half dozen blows the casing was merely dented. Then a sailor pushed through the crowd with a hacksaw. Wisely, Prophet stepped aside and let the machinist's mate go to work. The mate sawed feverishly. When exhaustion slowed him, Prophet ordered another to take his place. Lee's alloy was hard, but the hacksaw had created a noticeable groove. Evans worried that they might find a way to save the generator.

There was a commotion in the back, and a sailor pushed through the crowd, hurrying to Prophet.

"The Nimitz is gone, sir. The heretics escaped and destroyed the desert generators."

Prophet launched into a swearing fit, frightening his followers, who backed away defensively. Evans smiled at Prophet's rage. When Prophet regained his composure, he shoved the sailor with the hacksaw away and took a turn, sawing frantically. A man in shorts and a tie-dyed tee-shirt knelt, watching the blade.

"We're almost through," the man said suddenly.

Prophet picked up the pace. He sawed recklessly, repeatedly losing his place in the groove and resetting it. Suddenly, a brown cloud spouted from the bomb. The man in the tie-dyed shirt caught a facefull, sucking the brown gas into his lungs. Coughing, he clutched at his throat and collapsed. Prophet was coughing, too, as were others near the bomb. As the cloud expanded, it touched Evans, and he felt the vapor react with his good skin, burning him lightly. The mob backed away, dragging with them those doubled up in coughing fits, and leaving Evans behind. Only when Prophet had recovered and the gas had dissipated did they return, approaching the bomb cautiously.

Suddenly there was a change in the sound of the generator. The mob froze, all eyes on the generator, all ears listening to the machine. The generator began to vibrate, and emitted a hum which varied in pitch from high to low. The vibrations increased, the generator moving in its heavy steel mounting. Then, with the sound of grinding metal, the generator seized up and went silent, leaving only the hum of its twin. Suddenly, Evans's skin prickled and his hair stood on end. His back crackled as the static discharged into the pipe that he was leaning against. For a long minute no one moved or spoke. Eternal life had just been snatched away from the Crazies.

Evans enjoyed the moment—Prophet's fantasy destroyed by Evans's acid bomb.

"It's over, Prophet," Evans said. "Your little kingdom is doomed."

Face blood-stained, hands tied, his power gone, Evans still felt victorious.

Prophet still had his Special ability, but he was as broken as Evans. The kingdom he dominated was doomed. Then Prophet's head came up, his eyes bright.

"Dr. Kellum can repair the generator," he said.

The mob murmured agreement.

"We can still fulfill God's plan and build a new Israel," Prophet declared.

"Ralph found a way out before," Compton said. "If he does it again, Kellum could get away."

"Spread out. Search every level. Kill the rest of the heretics, but bring Dr. Kellum to me alive."

As the mob rushed for the exists, Rust stepped forward.

"Do you want me to finish the purification?" Rust said.

Evans recognized the leisure suit and the neatly trimmed beard of Rust. He was the Special who had set him on fire the first time Evans had entered Pot of Gold.

"There's no time," Prophet said.

Evans felt a twinge of hope. If they left him behind to go chasing after Kellum, he might escape. Then, through blurry eyes, he saw Prophet pick up the axe. He closed his eyes, regretting that he wouldn't see the last act of the play, but knowing how it would end. The last thing he heard was the whoosh of the axe blade as it cut through the air.

SITE VISIT

Dr. Lee waited nervously in his office for Woolman's arrival. The director of the Office of Special Projects seldom visited Rainbow, and then only for routine inspections. Today's visit was different. Woolman's phone call demanding Dr. Lee's presence at Rainbow had been curt and hostile. Dr. Lee didn't know what to expect.

They had detected another escape from Pot of Gold and notified Woolman according to routine. Finding the Special was not Dr. Lee's responsibility, so Woolman couldn't blame him if that had gone wrong. The other possible reason for Woolman's visit was the recent reconfiguration of Pot of Gold's field, but the change had happened after Woolman's phone call and the director couldn't know about it yet. While Dr. Lee waited, he studied the data spread on his desk. Something remarkable was happening to Pot of Gold.

The phone rang. It was a guard announcing Woolman's arrival. Too nervous to sit, Dr. Lee stood, fidgeting until his boss appeared. Woolman's normally pudgy face was tightened rock hard, and his bald head was shiny with perspiration. Woolman came into Dr. Lee's tiny office, slammed the door with a flick of his hand, and glared at Dr. Lee across the desk. Dr. Lee decided to take the offensive.

"I was going to call you," he said. "We've had an unexpected event. Pot of Gold has reshaped itself."

Dr. Lee's words came out in a rush of nearly incoherent babbling, but Woolman understood. His face softened slightly and he looked puzzled. Dr. Lee had knocked him off guard.

"What does that mean?"

"As you remember, the field configuration fluctuated in the months before the Nimitz disappeared and then assumed the ovoid shape at the same time that the ship vanished. I assumed that was because the inhabitants of Pot of Gold had found a way to alter the field and pull the Nimitz inside. However, since we have received a negative signal from Jett's team, and nothing else, it suggests that the Nimitz isn't inside Pot of Gold as we feared. The reversion of the field to its original shape suggests that the ovoid shape was a temporary aberration, perhaps caused by an external force—sunspots for example."

Dr. Lee ended with a nervous smile.

"The Nimitz is inside," Woolman said flatly. "That escape you detected wasn't a Special, it was a nuclear warhead from the Nimitz's arsenal, and the warhead was armed. A note came with it from Prophet. He's ordering us to shut down our containment field or the next bomb he sends out will detonate."

Dr. Lee lost his smile.

"We must send in troops," Dr. Lee said.

"If we do, they'll send out a ten-megaton thermonuclear warhead."

"But we sealed that gap when we detected the escape," Dr. Lee said.

"If they got one through, they can do it again," Woolman said. "The CIA is breathing down my neck over this. They want to know how my agents could miss something as large as a supercarrier in a place as small as Pot of Gold, and why anything or anyone is ever allowed to get out. They want to know why there wasn't a permanent solution to Pot of Gold before the Specials inside became a nuclear power."

All of the CIA's questions were unreasonable, but Dr. Lee wasn't foolish enough to argue. There had been no permanent solution to Pot of Gold because there was no way to eliminate that little pocket in the fabric of the universe as long as its field was intact. They had tried crushing it with Rainbow's field, but without knowing the resonant frequencies that had created Pot of Gold in the first place, they couldn't duplicate the power; and the only two people who knew those frequencies were Albert Einstein, who took the secret to his grave, and Walter Kellum, who was trapped inside.

"They're making me the fall guy, and I'm not going down alone. You're responsible for keeping Pot of Gold locked up tight, not me. I've never yet failed to catch one of those bastards you let escape, and I've lost many good agents doing it. Now they've got nuclear weapons and it's a new ball game. I want to know what you're going to do about it."

"What can I do that I haven't done?"

"You can seal it up once and for all. Forget the Nimitz. She can stay where she is as long as her nuclear weapons stay with her."

Dr. Lee wanted to protest: teams of scientists had tried and failed for twenty years to find a way to permanently seal Pot of Gold; but nothing rational would satisfy Woolman today.

Then the alarms went off.

Alert beepers sounded all over the lab, giving Dr. Lee an excuse to escape from his office. Hurrying to a monitoring station, he scanned the consoles, looking to see if the field had reconfigured again. He knew from the commotion that something catastrophic had occurred. Technicians jabbered excitedly, pointing at monitors. Dr. Lee recognized what had happened immediately. Pot of Gold's field had collapsed.

"Call up the field topography," he ordered.

"What's going on?" Woolman demanded.

Ignoring Woolman, Dr. Lee studied the three-dimensional picture that normally represented Pot of Gold's energy field; but now the only field on the screen was Rainbow's. As he watched, the bubble displayed on the screen was redrawn, the scrolling readout at the bottom indicating a one-percent decrease in size.

"Give me a projection of how long until zero field." Dr. Lee said.

Algorithms based on every conceivable contingency were programmed into the computer, but it took the technician a few tries to access the unfamiliar program. Once displayed, it took Dr. Lee only a few seconds to soak in the data.

"Your agents succeeded," Dr. Lee said. "Pot of Gold has lost its field and it is collapsing."

"How long?" Woolman said crisply.

"It will be gone by morning."

Woolman thought through the implications. Collapsing Pot of Gold had long been the goal, since it would exterminate the threat of the Specials once and for all. But with the Nimitz inside, it was a riskier proposition.

"There's no way to stop it now?" Woolman asked.

"No."

"Can you speed it up?"

"Increasing the power of our field has never had any effect, except to seal exits," Dr. Lee said patiently.

Dr. Lee had explained this many times to Woolman. Certain resonant frequencies were needed to create a dimensional rift, but once it existed, it sustained itself. Neither Dr. Lee nor his predecessors had been able to discover the frequencies of the original Philadelphia Experiment. The field they created around Pot of Gold's field wasn't self-sustaining, and wasn't capable of creating dimensional rifts. It could only seal exits.

"Imagine opening a window," Dr. Lee explained. "Once the window is open, you can place a stick in the sill, and the stick will keep the window open. It doesn't have to be a very large stick to hold the window up—a dowel the size of a pencil will do. While you could replace the dowel with a two-by-four, the extra thickness isn't necessary."

"Don't patronize me," Woolman said gruffly. "So, if the stick has been removed, why won't the window close?"

"The window is closing, but slowly, and we have no way to push it closed. It's all happening according to physical laws we don't understand. We are monitoring the collapse and should gather a great deal of data."

"I'll put our agents on alert," Woolman said, heading toward Dr. Lee's office.

Dr. Lee was relieved to have Woolman out of his hair so that he could concentrate on what was happening to Pot of Gold. The supercomputer at Rainbow had run thousands of simulations of what would happen to time and space when the field collapsed. Many of them projected the creation of multiple new exits as time and space curved through the corridors of the ship. What wasn't clear from the modelling was where those exits would lead.

After an hour of refining the time projections on field collapse, Dr. Lee took his new estimates to Woolman. The director was sitting in Dr. Lee's desk chair, fingers drumming on the desk top. Dr. Lee sat in the visitor's chair and presented his time table. Woolman was indifferent, distracted.

"If there is an escape during the collapse, is there any way to remotely determine whether the escapees are Specials or from the team we sent in?" Woolman asked.

Dr. Lee understood Woolman's concern. Jett and his team were more dangerous than Specials.

"There's no way to tell them apart except by visual inspection."

"It's going to be a long night," Woolman said.

"But the last one," Dr. Lee responded.

ALERT

Robert Daly studied his son's latest creation with dismay. It was a credenza, and like the desk his son had created, it was made of glass and bronze. Each corner of the rectangular structure was held together with twisted brass tubing, each unique, each uglier than the last. The brass continued along the joints of the credenza, holding the pieces of glass together. The large brass corners meant that the credenza couldn't be pushed flat against a wall like his old one, and it now protruded into his Chicago office. Even more annoying was the fact that it was made of glass. Nothing could be kept inside the piece of art without being seen. The reports that had been removed from his old credenza were stacked on the floor, and Daly wondered where his wife and son expected him to store them. One piece of furniture at a time, his wife and son were slowly turning his office into a museum of modern art. He detested modern art.

His secretary buzzed and then forwarded a call from New Mexico. This was the second call from New Mexico in the last few hours. The foundation monitored activity at Rainbow from a secret facility just outside Rainbow's perimeter, intercepting scrambled satellite communications and cellular-phone calls. Also, because the field was imperfect at bending light, they were able to indirectly monitor the electromagnetic field.

Victor Munoz, one of the young Ph.D.'s hired to work the facility, was on the line and very excited.

"There is movement in the field again," Munoz blurted out. "Something is happening."

"Is it reshaping again?" Daly asked calmly.

"No, sir. It's constricting," Munoz said.

Daly understood the implications of a constricting field. Ever since the government had discovered the effect of the field on the men inside, it had tried to destroy the Norfolk and its little separate pocket of space-time. Finally, the government had succeeded, and would kill Dr. Kellum, the Norfolk's crew, and its own people. Daly wondered about the Nimitz, since his intelligence indicated that the government did not want to destroy Pot of Gold with the carrier and its nuclear weapons inside.

"How long will the field last?" Daly asked.

"If the shrinkage remains constant it won't last more than twelve hours."

Daly knew that time in Pot of Gold was perceived differently, and that those inside would live out the last dozen hours of Pot of Gold in what would feel like a couple of hours, or even minutes. He felt responsible for those he had manipulated into entering the Norfolk's universe, and especially for Monica Kim—but he didn't feel guilty. Rescuing Dr. Kellum had long been a goal of the foundation. What was happening to the Norfolk was tragic, but out of that tragedy would come the possibility of instantaneous travel from point to point, and even to other worlds. The secret was locked inside the Norfolk with Dr. Kellum, and if it cost lives to recover him, those deaths would be more than compensated for by the new technologies. Now, however, it looked as if they would lose both the technological secrets and those he had sent inside.

"What do you want me to do?" Munoz asked.

"Monitor the field until it is gone. Record everything, no matter how trivial."

Pot of Gold was doomed, but the game wasn't over. Ralph was the wild card in the deck. He had escaped from Pot of Gold before. If he did, the Office of Special Projects would intercept him and anyone with him. Daly hung up on Munoz and asked his secretary to get the foundation's security chief on the line.

NORFOLK'S SCREAM

Roberto set a reckless pace through the Norfolk, gambling that the Crazies were behind them. Through Dawson's body, Elizabeth sensed the desperation and anger of the Crazies, as if the ship itself was vibrating with it, telegraphing the message of their insane desperation to every level. When Roberto led them through the wardroom and outside, they understood the Crazies' fear. The nothingness that was the edge of their world was getting noticeably closer. Moving like the minute hand of a clock, too slow to be perceived, the opaque wall of force was creeping toward the Norfolk.

As they climbed through the superstructure toward the conning tower, a sailor stepped from a gun emplacement and fell into step, talking to Roberto.

"The field's collapsing," the worried sailor announced.

"The generators are dead," Roberto said.

The sailor's face paled.

"What are we going to do, Dawson?" the sailor said, falling back to walk with Elizabeth. "Without the generators—man-oh-man we're so dead."

"We'll find a way out," Elizabeth said through Dawson's body.

"Is Anita still with you?" Wes asked.

"Yes," Elizabeth said. "She's a strong little girl, but I don't know how much more she can take. Her body is exhausted, and a person can only operate at a crisis level for so long."

Wes knew that everything Elizabeth said about Anita applied to her, too.

"Have Shamita and Len reestablished contact?"

"No," Elizabeth said.

It was a race now to find a way off of the ship before the Crazies caught them or the field collapsed. As Roberto and Ralph led them through combinations that took them to new levels of the ship, they picked up more sailors left behind to guide Jett and his people. As the group grew, their pace slowed.

Jett moved forward to walk with Ralph.

"When we get out of here, let's go get some gum," Jett said.

"How about that pink stuff?" Ralph said, a smile spreading from ear to ear.

"Not that stuff that stinks?" Jett said, smiling back.

"Pee-yew!" the men said together, Ralph snorting and grinning.

It wasn't funny, and Wes couldn't understand why Jett was playing along with Ralph.

"Jealous?" Elizabeth said.

It was Dawson's deep voice, but the taunting tone was familiar to Wes.

"Of course not," Wes said.

Now they came out on deck again and were horrified to see the opaque wall within arm's reach of the railing.

"How much further?" Jett called to Roberto.

"Soon," Roberto shouted over his shoulder.

"Are we going to make it?" Elizabeth asked Jett.

"We have a chance," Jett said evenly. "I'm betting on my friend Ralph to find us a way out of here."

"I'll do my best, Nate," Ralph said.

"Well okee-dokee then," Jett said.

Ralph snorted, smiling wide enough to show his wisdom teeth.

Wes frowned, concerned that Jett was using Ralph.

"I can feel something," Elizabeth said.

Jett was instantly business, gun in his hand.

"Crazies?" Jett asked.

"I don't think so. There are a lot of people ahead."

They found seventy or eighty people gathered. The group was a mix of sailors, civilian women, and children, all dressed in a bizarre variety of clothes representing the last five decades. As Jett moved to the lead, the people parted for him, looking to him with hopeful faces. Jett ignored them, heading directly to a middle-aged man peering over the side of the ship and hanging onto his glasses to keep from losing them. When he saw Jett, he looked relieved.

"We found three new levels and dozens of new branches," the man announced.

"But no exits," Jett finished for him.

"I have scouts out now, but we have very little time."

Wes stared at the man who was speaking with Jett, recognizing him from somewhere. He was balding, with what little hair he had spread thin across his scalp. As he struggled to recognize him, Monica pushed her way through.

"Doctor Walter Kellum," Monica said, holding out her hand. "I've been sent to bring you home."

Then Wes recognized him. Walter Kellum had died fifty years before. A confidant of Einstein, he had participated in early theoretical work on the atom bomb before splitting off to work on another classified weapon system. He had died mysteriously during the Second World War; his estate endowed the foundation. Now all the pieces came together. The Philadelphia Experiment, the Kellum Foundation's involvement, and his own role. Monica had brought the dreamers to Wes in order to manipulate him into helping to find Dr. Kellum.

"You were sent?" Kellum asked, confused.

"The trustees—" Monica began.

"Can the foundation get us out?" Jett asked, cutting her off.

"No, we'll have to get out on our own," Monica said, looking to Ralph.

Jett turned to Ralph, who smiled broadly.

"Find us a way out," Jett said.

"I don't know, Nate," Ralph began.

"For a banana split," Jett said.

"Well okee-dokee then," Ralph said. Then, to Dr. Kellum, he said, "Do you gots your ship with the spaghetti in it?"

Kellum shouted orders, and the ship model was brought forward.

"Can I hold it? I won't break it or nothing, I promise."

Dr. Kellum handed it over to Ralph who held it like a newborn baby while he stared into the maze of wires. Instantly, his face went blank.

Suddenly there was an ear-piercing scream. Wes clapped his hands over his ears to stop the pain. Then the Norfolk shuddered, sending those on deck stumbling and grabbing each other to keep from falling.

"The field is touching the ship!" someone shouted when the nerve-wracking scream had died down.

Wes could feel the ship vibrating from the pressure of the collapsing field. Jett stepped to Ralph, touching his arm.

"Ralph, we're out of time. Take your best shot."

Ralph's eyes came to life again and his grin returned.

"For a banana split?" he said. "Follow me."

Wes watched amazed as eighty people fell in behind Ralph, trusting their lives to him. Wes followed, too, as confident in Ralph as he had ever been in anyone.

BYSTANDERS

"Let's go back in," Len said.

"We can't help," Shamita argued. "There's no point."

"I want to know what's happening."

"They're dying," Shamita said. "Does it really matter how?"

Shamita was standing by Anita's cot, stroking the unconscious girl's hair. Anita's respiration was rapid, her blood pressure and heart rate falling. Her body had fought the good fight, but now it was wearing out. Len stood by Elizabeth's cot, noticing that her red hair had lost its normal sheen. Her face was gaunt, the skin baggy under her eyes. Like Anita's, her vital signs had peaked an hour earlier, her blood pressure high rising enough to cause a stroke if there been any weaknesses in her vessel walls. Her sympathetic nervous system was in overdrive, adrenaline flooding her circulatory system. With no blood sugars to metabolize, and the sugar reserves in her liver exhausted, Elizabeth's body had defaulted to metabolizing proteins—Elizabeth's body was digesting itself.

Studying Elizabeth's haggard face, Len agreed silently with Shamita. It didn't matter how they died, only that they would.

"It matters a whole hell of a lot how you die," Wanda said suddenly, as if she read Len's mind.

Wanda was sitting on her cot, legs dangling, cigarette hanging from the corner of her mouth.

"Your friend Elizabeth is trying to save that little girl and her friends, and that's what I call death with dignity," Wanda said. "I'd take her death over mine any day of the week and twice on Sunday."

Shamita started to speak, but Wanda talked over her.

"Know how I'm going to die? Alone in a nursing home, being cared for by strangers. Dying alone, without friends or family, that's a terrible death. Take the advice of an old woman and be there with your friend when it happens."

Shamita stroked Anita's hair another minute, thinking.

"I'll begin the integration," she said.

"Anita's mother should be here," Len said.

As Len walked to the door, he pointed at Wanda.

"If you're such a smart old lady, then why are you still smoking?"

"Because it annoys the hell out of people like you," Wanda said. "Ha!"

RALPH'S LEAD

Ralph stopped suddenly, and Elizabeth ran into him. Instantly, there was a traffic jam spreading back through the compartment they had just left. They had just made another of the space-bending connections that characterized the interior of the Norfolk, leaving the deck near midships, and entering the superstructure just behind one of the gun emplacements. Now they found themselves in a long corridor lined with crew berths.

"What's wrong?" Jett asked Ralph.

"It's the same only different," he replied.

"This must be one of the new levels," Kellum said, holding the ship map out to Ralph. "The scouts found this line branched, and went here and here," he added pointing inside the model.

Ralph took the ship model and stared at the multicolored wire strung through its interior, his face blank, his lips puckered.

Elizabeth looked down at Anita, who now resembled one of the stick figures in her drawings. The little girl had suffered so much, personally and empathically, that she had repressed all feeling and was nearly catatonic.

Breaking his trance, Ralph said, "I'll be right back."

Jett started after him, but Elizabeth held him back.

"We've trusted him this far," she said.

Jett stayed, his hand resting on his gun, his eyes on Ralph.

Ralph walked left down the corridor that normally led through crew berths and below the aft eight-inch gun emplacement, ending at the hangar. Jett paced restlessly while he was gone. A minute later Ralph was back, walking past them and down the narrow corridor in the other direction. This time Ralph took longer. Just when Jett was ready to go after him, there was another high-pitched scream of metal buckling under enormous pressure, and the ship shuddered again, hard enough to stagger them and elicit cries from the crowd.

When the noise stopped and the vibrations died, Elizabeth realized that the ship was tilting.

"We're listing to starboard," Kellum said. "It was the ship's symmetry that allowed the poles to orient forward and aft, keeping the ship perfectly balanced on her keel. If we're listing, it means part of the hull has been crushed, distorting the lines of force."

"Does that give us more time, or less time?" Jett said, cutting to the real issue.

"Less, but even worse, it means some passages may be impassable."

"Okee-dokee, let's go," Ralph said, coming back with a big grin and motioning them toward the stern.

"Go, go, go," Jett shouted, hurrying everyone after Ralph.

Elizabeth was horrified to see the corridor ahead filled with body parts. Arms protruded from bulkheads with hands clenched, legs hung from the deck above so low that they had to duck to pass. A half man in the deck forced the crowd to flow around him the way a mountain stream flows around a rock. There were more body parts here than in any other corridor she had seen.

"I want to go home," Anita told Elizabeth. She was still invisible to everyone but her.

"We're trying, Anita. Remember, this is just a dream and it will be over soon."

"It's not a dream. It's real."

"Yes. It's real," Elizabeth admitted.

Elizabeth held Anita's hand. Ralph led with Kellum right behind, cradling his model ship in his arms like a mother holds her baby. Monica kept no more than a step or two behind Dr. Kellum at all times, eyes busy, body alert, moving much like Jett and Peters.

Elizabeth and Wes were in the lead group, too, along with Jett and

Roberto and a half-dozen armed men who flanked them whenever there was room. Peters was in the rear with another armed group. The women and children had gathered in the middle.

Suddenly someone shouted from the rear, and the message was carried forward.

"Crazies coming," a relay yelled.

Kellum immediately turned to Elizabeth, seeing her as Dawson.

"Do you feel them, Dawson? Where are they?"

Elizabeth closed her eyes, giving more of herself over to the Dawson part. She could feel the anger and the desperation of the Crazies, and the one common thought they all shared.

"They're coming for you, Dr. Kellum," she said.

"Are they close?" Jett demanded.

"I can feel them everywhere," Elizabeth said.

"They must be behind us," Wes said.

"We have to keep moving. Go, Ralph," Jett shouted.

The ship vibrated constantly now, its tilt noticeably worse. Like a squad of marines infiltrating hostile territory, they hurried, staying close to one another, checking every berth and compartment they passed.

A flash of light announced the attack; that was followed by panicky screams and shouting. The sputter of Peters's gun sounded over the grunts and groans of hand-to-hand combat. Armed men rushed to the rear as the women herded the children forward, jamming the corridor.

Jett took charge, telling a third of the men to guard Ralph and Dr. Kellum at the point and ordering the rest into side compartments so that the women and children could get through. Once the corridor cleared, he sent reinforcements to the rear, and then positioned the rest of the men in hatches to leave the central corridor free for retreat. Kellum had three powerful Specials in his group; a fire thrower, the old woman who created illusions, and a psychokinetic. Jett held these in reserve.

"Elizabeth, can you hear me?" Shamita said.

"Yes, Shamita," Elizabeth said.

"Tell them to try shutting down your entire cortex," Wes said from behind her. "Block all higher functions. Anita, too."

"We'll be unconscious," Elizabeth said.

"Yes."

"But we'll still be linked to this body—to Dawson."

"It might break the link."

"But if the link isn't broken, then what happens to this man?" Elizabeth said.

Elizabeth sensed that Wes was holding something back. His love for her was distorting his thinking, causing him to overlook Dawson.

"Will Dawson be unconscious?" Elizabeth asked gently.

"It's likely," Wes said. "It may cause a seizure."

"He would be defenseless, Wes. He could be killed."

"Elizabeth, someone has to die to break the connection," Wes said bluntly. "The cruel fact is that if Dawson dies, you and Anita are saved."

"There must be another way," Elizabeth said.

"There isn't."

"Can we just scramble Anita? She doesn't need to go through this."

"Your minds are working as one. I don't know if it would work."

Elizabeth weighed the risks against the benefits, and spoke to Shamita and Len.

"Shamita, if you can hear me, I want you to set it up so you can block all of Anita's higher cerebral functions."

"Len and I considered that, Elizabeth, but it won't eliminate the connection, just mask it."

"What are you doing, Elizabeth?" Anita said. "I'm afraid."

Elizabeth looked down at the little girl, regretting that she hadn't included her in the decision.

"If the dream gets bad, Anita, Shamita and Len will make it go away."

"Make it go away now," Anita said.

"If we do it now, someone might get hurt," Elizabeth explained.

"Do it soon?" Anita pleaded.

"Set it up, Shamita," Elizabeth said, "but don't block Anita until I tell you."

Ralph stopped at a compartment, everyone backing up behind him. Inside there was green mist.

"Looky there, everybody," Ralph said. "I found one."

Word of Ralph's find spread down the column.

"We need to test it," Kellum said.

"No time," Jett said, stepping toward the compartment.

Roberto stopped Jett.

"I'll go," he said. "They need you more than they need me."

Jett agreed, knowing that he was right. Roberto probed the mist with a spear, pushing it in as far as he could. It was intact when he retracted it. Taking a deep breath, Roberto stepped into the mist.

"Want I should show you the other one?" Ralph asked.

"Is it near?" Jett said.

"Just down there," Ralph told him.

"Just down there, or down there, and there and there," Jett said, making multiple hand motions.

"Just down there," Ralph said with a point.

Jett looked at the mist, reluctant to leave their possible salvation.

"Elizabeth," Jett said to the Dawson body. "Can you feel the Crazies?"

Elizabeth closed her eyes and probed the corner of her mind where the Dawson consciousness was hiding.

"I feel them everywhere."

"Would you and Wes go with Ralph? See if there is another way out."

Wes went with Elizabeth, four armed men following. The sounds of fighting could be heard as the rear guard fought a delaying action. The corridor was packed around the green mist, other people spilling down the corridor in both directions.

"It's not far, Elizabeth," Ralph was saying. "Lots of the pieces of spaghetti in Walter's model come together here."

The corridor ended at another hatch which Elizabeth recognized as usually leading to the hangar deck. Ralph opened it slowly. The hangar was where it should be. They stepped in, studying the interior—there were three frozen men just inside. Further in, many partial bodies decorated the interior. Ralph had said something about map lines coming together on this level and Elizabeth thought it might explain why there were more bodies. Above them, the hatch was open a few feet, and Elizabeth could see the Norfolk's crane.

Ralph crossed the hangar, the others following. Directly opposite, Ralph opened a hatch, revealing a short corridor ending in another hatch. There were two hatches on either side of the corridor.

"Something's not right," Ralph said in a sing-song voice. "It shouldn't be like this."

Ralph stepped to the first hatch on the right and opened it, revealing another green aperture.

"Well okee-dokee then. If there's one here, then there's got to be another one there," Ralph said with a nod of his head down the corridor.

"We need to test it," Elizabeth said.

Taking a spear from a guard, Wes poked it into the mist and then retracted it; the shaft and the metal tip came out pitted and sour-smelling.

"Sulfuric acid," Wes said.

Disappointed, Elizabeth looked back toward Jett's group. She shook her head and then mouthed, "There's another door."

Jett gave her the okay sign. Then there was a commotion as Roberto emerged, healthy and alert.

"That's the way home," Wes said.

Elizabeth studied the reactions of Jett's group. The celebration ended quickly.

"Something is wrong," Elizabeth said. "Ralph, you better take us to the next door."

The guards watched Jett, hoping for a recall signal, while Elizabeth and Wes followed Ralph. Suddenly, a fireball came from above, engulfing two of their men. Then came the battle cries of the attacking Crazies.

Elizabeth and Wes each grabbed one of Ralph's arms, pulling him toward the nearest compartment, fumbling the hatch open, and climbing inside.

"This isn't the way, Elizabeth," Ralph complained.

It was full of crates, and there was no other exit. Pushing Ralph between two stacks of supplies, Elizabeth and Wes took positions on either side of the hatch, the sounds of battle raging outside.

ENDGAME

Rainbow was essentially a high-tech prison, not a research facility. The only experimentation done there during the fifty years of its existence had involved finding ways to destroy Pot of Gold. Most of the technical staff spent their time monitoring an energy field that changed very little. Until recently, the only breaks in the monotony were the unpredictable escapes of the Specials. Now the work was anything but dull.

Beginning just before the disappearance of the Nimitz, Pot of Gold's field reconfigured three times, exciting the underutilized staff. Then there had been the insertion of the agents, and finally Woolman's arrival. Now Rainbow's staff was energized by a mix of excitement and nervous tension. Mental cobwebs created by years of dull routine were swept away by frenzied activity and the anticipation of how the game they had started would play out. Dr. Lee shared the excitement, but understood the risks as well.

With the latest printouts, he returned to his office, finding Woolman on the phone, his fingers drumming as he listened intently. Woolman hung up as Dr. Lee came in.

"They found the Nimitz. She's in the same longitude and latitude as where she disappeared."

"What about her nuclear weapons?" Dr. Lee asked. "Have they been accounted for?"

Woolman shook his head.

"They can't get on board. She's on fire, and there have been numerous secondary explosions. The flight deck has buckled and she's listing to port. She's going to be a total loss. They're recommending to the President that she be sunk before the reactor is breached."

"Then there's no way to know if they have any more of her nuclear warheads?"

"No," Woolman said.

In his mind, Dr. Lee ran through the various computer simulations of the collapse of Pot of Gold. They were all highly speculative, but in most, the computer concluded that the mass of the Norfolk would be pushed out of Pot of Gold. What wasn't clear was where that mass would go.

A technician knocked on the door frame, asking Dr. Lee to return to the monitoring stations. Woolman followed Dr. Lee to a monitor displaying a three-dimensional representation of Pot of Gold's field. Dr. Lee studied the map in amazement. Not one of the thousand simulations of field collapse had predicted what was actually taking place.

"What does it mean?" Woolman asked.

"The field has lost its spherical shape—far exceeding normal fluctuation parameters. None of our simulations predicted this."

"Will the field collapse or not?" Woolman said.

"There is nothing to keep it open," Dr. Lee said evasively.

"Then what's the problem?" Woolman wanted to know.

"I don't know that it's a problem, but you can see the field is reforming into a cylinder—a cigar shape. The field is stretched between two poles. There seems to be a great deal of dynamic tension."

"Meaning what?" Woolman said.

"What happens when you stretch a rubber band as wide as it will go?" Dr. Lee hinted.

"It slips out of your fingers and snaps back," Woolman replied.

"Or it breaks," Lee said.

"Will the field collapse before the band breaks?" Woolman asked, picking up on the analogy.

"I don't have any data to base such a projection on," Lee said. "But there is another concern. One of those poles is Rainbow."

CRUSHED

Jett and Dr. Kellum waited anxiously outside the portal Ralph had found; Kellum's people backed up behind them down the corridor. Wes and Elizabeth had gone ahead with Ralph to find a second door, but there was little time left. The ship was being crushed by the collapsing field, and Prophet and his cult were in pursuit, skirmishing with the rear guard. Suddenly, the green mist shimmered, and Roberto stepped back through.

"Is it a way home?" Dr. Kellum demanded immediately.

"No."

"But you were there a long time," Kellum said.

"Yeah, but it's like nowhere I've ever been. It's a weird damn maze."

"It has to be home," Monica said. "You could breathe the air."

"It's a place full of green doors like this one. There must be hundreds of them, maybe thousands."

"It's a nexus," Dr. Kellum said. "A focal point where the holes in time and space converge."

"We'll never find our way through it," Roberto said.

Jett hesitated only a second, wanting this to be the door home, but trusting Roberto.

"The other door!" Jett had time to say before there was a flash and a scream.

"Surrender Doctor Kellum, or you'll all die," Prophet's voice sounded.

"Get to the other door," Jett shouted.

Jett took three steps before Crazies poured around the corner, rushing them en masse. The Crazies in front carried a two-piece metal shield that they fitted together and held in front of them, filling the corridor. Jett's Teflon slugs couldn't penetrate the shield. Jett adapted, firing at their feet, wounding one Crazy. The man stumbled, releasing the shield, but another stepped into his place. The slow advance continued, but now the men holding the shield crouched, keeping their feet and heads covered.

Kellum's telekinetic came forward and with a stare sent a wall of force into the metal shield, knocking the Crazies down. Jett fired over the shield. Then a fireball streaked toward them. Jett flattened against the bulkhead, and Kellum's last powerful telekinetic took the fireball in the chest. Engulfed in flames, he ran into those behind, burning those he touched. The flames extinguished quickly, but the damage was done, and he collapsed.

The air filled with spears and crossbow bolts, Jett taking cover behind one of the frozen men protruding from a bulkhead. The man's left leg and arm were buried in the bulkhead, his face frozen in perpetual surprise. Jett could feel the warmth of the frozen man, and realized that he was alive. More crossbows were fired, and both sides took casualties. A bolt buried itself in the back of the frozen man that Jett was using for cover. Pressed against the man's chest, Jett felt a muscle spasm. The man's lips had been set in an oval, but as Jett watched, the lips opened wider, more of the teeth showing. Another fireball shot past, and Jett, pulled back into the battle, opened fire again. The shield was back up, protecting the attackers.

"Rush them," Jett yelled, leading the way.

At full speed, he hit the shield with his shoulder. The advanced stopped briefly as the Crazies behind adjusted their footing, recovering from the blow. Then more men hit the shield, filling every space in the narrow corridor, pushing with all their might. Slowly, with the shield moving backwards, they won the brute-force contest. Then reinforcements hit the other side and they reached a stalemate.

Jett called for someone to take his place, and when his niche was filled, he fired high over the shield, bullets ricocheting into those on the other side. Then the shield was moving again, pushing the Crazies toward the hangar.

"What do we do when we reach the hangar?" Roberto said, coming to stand next to Jett.

"Ralph's somewhere straight ahead. We drive them into the hangar and to the left, and we take out anyone to the right. Then we get our people across to Ralph."

There were compartments along the corridor; Jett had ordered the hatches closed. Suddenly, a hatch opened and they were flanked. Hacking and stabbing, the Crazies attacked the men holding the shield. Jett jumped into the space left by the wounded men. If the shield fell, fireballs would devastate their ranks.

Armed with an axe, a Crazy broke through, charging Jett. Jett turned and raised his body. The axe blade cut into his pack, impacting the nitrogen canisters that powered his weapon. The gas vented explosively, spraying the attacker with supercold compressed gas. With his last round, Jett punched a hole in his attacker's heart.

Roberto was hacking with his machete, keeping more Crazies from getting through the compartment. Jett grabbed the axe of the man he had just killed and joined the assault, the Crazies giving way under their combined blows.

"Hold the shield," Jett shouted over the melee.

Men squeezed past them to the shield, filling the spaces and stopping the advance of the Crazies. Jett and Roberto's attack was bloody, but effective. The chopping and slicing disabled the attackers and drove them back into the compartment. Once through the hatch, the Crazies broke and ran, leaving three bleeding men in and around the door.

"*Give us Dr. Kellum and you will live,*" Prophet's voice rang again.

They were winning the shoving match with the shield, pushing the Crazies back toward the hangar. Jett was suspicious. It was too easy, too steady.

"Doctor Kellum, keep them pushing the shield back," Jett ordered. "Roberto, grab a couple of men and follow me."

Jett opened the hatch through which the Crazies had attacked. The compartment was clear except for the bodies of dead men. Jett led Roberto and two men in, shedding his useless gun. The compartment was filled with hammocks strung from the bulkheads. There was another hatch at the far side, connecting with another crew compartment. On the far side of that compartment the watertight door was closed. As Jett stepped through to the second compartment, two Crazies swung down from hammocks, armed with lengths of pipe.

Jett blocked the first blow with the axe handle, then pushed the attacker away just in time to fend off the blow of the second attacker. He backed through the hatch, stumbling deliberately, suckering his attacker through. Roberto buried his machete into the Crazy's midsection. The other Crazy fled, Jett catching him just as he reached the far hatch. He killed him with one swing.

Jett dragged the body to the side. Picking up one of the Crazies' pipe weapons, he handed it to a sailor and motioned for him to go first.

Roberto released the latches with a nerve-wracking squeal, then pulled the door open. The shouts of fighting men were loud on the other side. With a sign from Jett, the sailor jumped through, swinging his weapon left while Jett moved right. Two guards were caught by surprise and died.

They found themselves in the hangar; behind it, the Crazies were massed. They moved stealthily, creeping up behind a life-jacket bin. Peeking over the top, Jett could see Prophet directing the battle. Six armed men stood with Prophet, who wore one of Dr. Lee's special guns. Jett was right about the shoving match with the shield. Prophet's men were giving way to Kellum's people, while others stood ready on either side of the spot where the corridor connected to the hangar. They were ready to ambush Kellum's people. As one of Prophet's converts, Compton was part of the trap, ready with her weapon.

Jett signalled the others that there were seven men to deal with. Roberto expected a clever plan, but the only way was to rush Prophet and try to close the distance before Prophet shot them. Jett was ready to lead the charge when the Norfolk changed everything.

It started with a vibration that built to a violent shudder—men were staggering on the deck. Then there was an ear-splitting metal shriek as if the ship were being torn in half; at the same time, the ship tilted. Jett and his men were thrown against a bulkhead. For the first time in his life, Jett was afraid. He protected his head to keep from being knocked unconscious as the ship shuddered violently.

A few seconds of calm followed, then the bulkhead he was leaning against bulged. The ship vibrated again, accompanied by a hideous grinding sound. Suddenly, a beam tore through the bulkhead, slamming into the deck just in front of Jett's face. Then the ship stabilized again. Jett's heart was pounding, and his throat was dry. A few days ago, the slightest emotion had intrigued him, but now he hated the way fear immobilized him. Regaining emotional control, he got to his feet.

"It's now or never."

Climbing over the beam, Jett was ready to rush Prophet, but Prophet had seen them.

Jett and Prophet locked eyes.

"Who can stand against us if God is on our side?" Prophet transmitted.

"God doesn't take sides," Jett said.

The ship shuddered again, but without the junkyard scream of crumpling metal. Then Jett's vision blurred, and Prophet and his men seemed to waver as if Jett were looking at them through desert heat. The death spasms of the ship had quelled the battle, and now the moaning could be heard.

Low and pitiful, the human sound came from all around them, as if the ship's suffering had been given voice. The frozen men were unthawing, beginning to move. Those living on the Norfolk had long ago learned to ignore the men buried in the bulkheads or frozen in corridors as if they were fixtures. Now those men couldn't be ignored. They were moving and making sounds—the sounds of suffering.

The different moments in time that created the multiple levels of the ship were collapsing back into one time stream. The men who had merged with the steel of the ship were beginning to flow with time again, entering their present.

Individual voices could be heard now, pleas for help. It was a bizarre and horrifying sight as the partial bodies around them came to life. Everyone was transfixed by it—everyone but Jett. Jett charged.

He was only a few yards from Prophet when he sensed the attack. Prophet was slow with the unfamiliar gun, bringing it up too late. Jett bent, hitting Prophet's arm with his shoulder, driving it back against his rib cage. Prophet went down hard, but rolled at the same time, trying to throw Jett off. Jett clawed at Prophet's gun arm, but Prophet was an experienced bar brawler. With a full-body heave and a quick duck, Jett was thrown off. Then Prophet brought the gun around.

Jett was shot, the slug penetrating his chest and glancing off a rib. It wasn't a killing wound, but Prophet's next shot would kill him. On the sharply tilted deck, it was an uphill run to Prophet. As Jett took his first step, Roberto and his other men attacked. With a two-armed swing of his machete, Roberto sliced a guard's stomach. The wounded guard staggered into Prophet, spoiling his aim. Before Prophet could react, Roberto severed the cable connecting the gun to the gas canisters. The cable whipped violently, spraying liquid nitrogen and slapping at Prophet. Jett knew the gun held one last pellet in a charged chamber, but Prophet didn't. Jett hit him waist high.

Prophet cracked him on the skull with the weapon, proving that he didn't know it was still loaded. It was a brawl now, and Prophet was formidable and brutal. Head butts, bites, and scratches came fast and furious. As they grappled, Jett judged his opponent's strengths and mapped his moves. A minute into the fight Jett knew the outcome. Prophet wasn't a good match. With a quick spin, Jett maneuvered himself behind Prophet, his left arm snaking around his neck, the crook of his arm pinching Prophet's throat. Thirty seconds later Prophet's arms stopped clawing at Jett's head and his legs began to twitch. Hearing a sharp intake of air, Jett loosened his choke hold slightly. There was a thin line between death and anoxia, and Jett had Prophet walking that line.

With Prophet under control, he looked to see Roberto and two surviving sailors fighting to keep reinforcements away from Jett. Releasing his grip briefly, he retrieved the gun and pressed it to Prophet's head, dragging him to his feet at the same time.

"Stop or I'll kill him," Jett shouted.

Prophet stirred, and Jett tightened the choke hold, then tapped on Prophet's skull with the gun. The fighting around them stopped. Slowly, word of Prophet's capture spread, and the battle in the hangar ended. But when the sounds of battle died, the chilling pleas and moans of those trapped in the bulkheads could be heard clearly again. Those in the hangar moved away from the bulkheads, keeping out of reach of the disembodied arms which clutched randomly.

"The cable is cut, the gun won't work," Prophet broadcast. *"Kill them."*

"I'll kill him," Jett said, looking for Compton.

"He's bluffing," Prophet repeated.

Prophet's men advanced; Roberto and his men were ready to defend. Jett let Prophet's men take two more steps, then pulled the gun from Prophet's head and shot one of the advancing Crazies. Then the gun was at Prophet's head again.

"Take another step and your god is dead," Jett said.

Prophet didn't broadcast now, uncertain of how the weapon worked.

"Clear the way," Jett ordered. "Call off the attack."

He pushed Prophet forward, and the Crazies parted.

"Give us Kellum," Prophet said.

"He's no use to you now," Jett said. "The ship is doomed."

"It's not too late," Prophet said. *"Doctor Kellum can repair the generator."*

As Jett and Prophet moved forward, the Crazies stepped aside, watching for an opportunity. Jett moved slowly over the sloped deck, making sure of each step. Soon he could see where the Crazies had prepared their ambush. The shield was lying in the hangar, Kellum's men having pushed it all the way down the corridor. Dead and wounded men lay everywhere, the injured adding to the moans coming from the bulkheads. Jett realized that if the war continued much longer, there would be no one left to escape. Then the rest of the Crazies parted, and he saw the shine of Compton's fire suit. Eyes busy, she quickly appraised the situation, her eyes coming to rest on the severed gun cable. Then she smiled and raised her gun.

TRAPPED

The battle raged on outside the storeroom where Elizabeth, Wes, and Ralph had taken cover. Elizabeth could still see Anita standing next to her, arms wrapped around her leg. Elizabeth smiled reassuringly, but wondered if the little girl saw her as the Elizabeth she had first met, or the Elizabeth nearly dead from dream deprivation.

Suddenly the Norfolk let out a death scream as metal buckled and a portion of the superstructure collapsed. Most of the crates were tied down, but a stack broke free, tumbling to the deck. The ship rumbled and shuddered, tilting as it did. A bulkhead buckled, folding inward, rivets popping off with the velocity of bullets. The compartment was folding in on itself, leaving little room to stand. The vibrations continued, but the structural collapse slowed. When the ship was stable again, Elizabeth leaned out and saw the backs of armed Crazies. Flattening back, she signalled Wes to be quiet.

"What did you see, Elizabeth?" Ralph said in his best whisper.

Putting her fingers to her lips, she shushed Ralph, who mimicked the signal.

"We know you're in there," a voice shouted from the corridor.

Elizabeth and Wes exchanged looks, neither moving.

"Come out or we'll force you out," the voice demanded.

"Want I should go out and talk to them?" Ralph said.

Elizabeth shushed Ralph again.

Then a fireball shot through the hatch, setting a crate on fire. The fire quickly died to a smolder, the room filling with acrid smoke. Elizabeth's eyes teared and she suppressed a cough. Ralph, coughing loudly, came out of his hiding place rubbing his eyes.

"I can't see so good," he said, his face tear-streaked.

Wes pulled Ralph flat against the bulkhead just as another fireball struck and more smoke boiled up from the crates. The room was thick with smoke now and the heat was becoming unbearable. Blinded, lungs filling with smoke, they felt helpless.

"We're coming out," Elizabeth shouted.

Wes went first, hands in the air. Ralph followed, and then Elizabeth, coughing to clear her lungs. Anita, invisible to all but Elizabeth, went with her, coughing as well; the little girl was experiencing everything that Dawson did. They were surrounded by guards with spears and clubs. When Elizabeth's eyes cleared, she saw Rust, the man who had tried to burn her on the Nimitz. Rust smiled cruelly.

"We've got some unfinished business, Dawson," Rust said.

"You shouldn't oughta hurt people," Ralph told him.

Rust smiled at Ralph, then held his hands out, face concentrating. The air around Ralph began to glow.

"Leave him alone," Elizabeth pleaded.

"He's harmless," Wes said.

Rust's smile broadened, and Elizabeth realized that the more they begged him to spare Ralph, the more he would enjoy torturing him.

"It sure is hot in here," Ralph said. "Are you making it hot?"

"Please stop," Wes said.

"Leave him alone, Rust!" a woman ordered.

The Crazy named Gertie pushed through the guards.

"I don't take orders from you," Rust said.

With a look from Gertie, Rust was knocked to the deck. He came up with hands extended, as if ready to burn her, but she held her ground, staring him down.

"They've got Prophet!" someone yelled from the hangar.

Rust hurried past Gertie to the hangar.

"Take them," Gertie ordered the guards.

Elizabeth and the others were pushed toward the hangar. The sounds of battle were gone, replaced by the sounds of suffering. The hangar was filled with men and women, many wounded, many dead. There was debris everywhere. The deck was tilted at a sharp angle, the bulkheads were crumpled, the hatch above had folded in. Most horrifying of all were the bodies in the decks and bulkheads which had come alive. In the midst of this hell was Jett, his gun to Prophet's head, advancing through the wreckage. Then Elizabeth saw Compton step forward, bringing her gun to bear on Jett.

"You're bluffing," Compton said.

"This ship is doomed. Our only hope is a door out of here," Jett said.

"Doctor Kellum can repair the generator," Prophet broadcast.

Elizabeth could feel a hidden level to Prophet's message. He was calming their fears and bolstering their loyalty at the same time.

"He's insane," Jett said. "You don't have to die with him. Come with us."

"With the cable cut you only have one round left, Jett," Compton said.

"He used that shot," Prophet said, understanding now and reaching for the arm around his neck.

Roberto lifted his machete to Prophet's face, and he stopped struggling. Compton advanced, other Crazies circling, closing in. Then Jett dropped his gun and held out his hand.

"I killed Cobb!" he shouted. "I have his power!"

The spaces between Jett's fingers sparkled with electric light. Prophet's flock stopped their advance, afraid of Jett's power. Then Compton shouted for Gertie.

When Gertie left them, Rust smiled at Elizabeth malevolently. Without Gertie to protect them, Rust would burn them at the slightest provocation. Elizabeth's hand twitched, and she looked down to see Anita shivering uncontrollably. Anita was staring at a half man protruding from the deck, pleading for help.

"Shamita, are you ready with Anita?" Elizabeth asked.

"Yes. Len says her heart rate and BP are spiking. We've called for an ambulance. Anita's mother's with her. Elizabeth, the same thing is happening to you."

Elizabeth didn't feel the weakness of her own body because her immediate sensations were from Dawson's.

"Separate them," Compton ordered Gertie, pointing at Jett and Prophet.

With a hard stare, Gertie knocked Prophet and Jett into a crumpled bulkhead. Jett's grip was broken by the blow, and Prophet wrestled himself free. Then the Norfolk collapsed again.

The deck of the hangar rose with a sharp peak running its length. Bodies tumbled from both sides of the crest, Jett and Prophet disappearing on the far side. Elizabeth tumbled backwards. The guards and Rust forgot their captives, fighting to survive. Above them, Elizabeth could see the remains of the hatch, and just beyond it the opaque field. Then there was a sound above, and men and women scrambled for cover as the crane from the stern crashed into the hangar, burying the half man whom Anita had been staring at.

The ship vibrated constantly now, the sounds of crumpling steel everywhere. The war was over; everyone was scrambling to save their lives. Dr. Kellum appeared across the hangar with Monica and Peters.

"This way!" Dr. Kellum shouted. "There's a way out here! This way!"

Dropping their weapons, former enemies struggled together through the wreckage toward Kellum and past him down the collapsing corridor. Then Jett appeared without Prophet, climbing over the crest in the dock.

"Ralph's other door," Jett shouted, "what about the other door?"

"Ralph," Elizabeth shouted. "Is the other door close?"

"Sure," Ralph said, getting to his feet. "It's this-a-way." He pointed back down the corridor.

Before Ralph could move, one of the biplanes crashed into the hangar. Jett disappeared behind the wreckage. When the plane settled, Elizabeth could see Jett pinned under a piece of the wing. Roberto rushed to him, clearing the smaller pieces of debris. He tried to lift the weight from Jett, but couldn't free him. Panicky men and women rushed past, ignoring Roberto's pleas for help. Then Ralph pushed past Elizabeth, climbing through the wreckage toward Jett.

"Ralph, there's no time," Wes shouted.

"I'll be right back," Ralph said.

Wes started after him, but was driven back when Norfolk's second biplane was jammed into the hangar. Now they were cut off from Ralph. Four Crazies were trapped under the new wreckage, one of them Rust. Wes and Elizabeth worked to free the trapped men. One was dead, his skull crushed, but the others were alive.

"Help me first!" Rust ordered.

The catapult had come with the second biplane, its latticework now a twisted mass of steel and many of its joints broken. The bulk of the framework was over Rust, so they started with the nearest man. The first Crazy came out easily, thanking them.

"Help me or you'll burn," Rust ordered.

The rescued sailor looked at Rust nervously, but helped Elizabeth and Wes to free the second man. With Wes and Elizabeth lifting, they barely managed to take enough pressure off the trapped man to drag him clear.

With a broken leg, he couldn't help lift the wreckage. Rust was impaled by a piece of the steel latticework, his side soaked in blood. They tried a lift; Rust screamed when they moved the steel an inch, and then passed out. Seeing the piece of steel protruding from his side, Elizabeth knew that they wouldn't be able to drag him out like the others. Rust would need to be cut free, and that would take time they didn't have.

Elizabeth looked back in the hangar for Ralph. He was with Roberto, his hands under the wreckage pinning Jett's legs, his muscles straining. The wing was still connected to the fuselage, and as Ralph lifted, Roberto pulling Jett from underneath, the entire airplane moved. Jett flexed one leg, then the other, and then stood.

"Kill the heretics. Only when this place is cleansed of their impure thoughts will God restore our paradise."

Prophet was still alive.

The Crazy helping them with Rust turned like a zombie, unable to resist the commands of his master. He reached for Elizabeth. The Crazy with the broken leg wrapped his arms around Wes's legs. Elizabeth slapped his hand away. The Crazy reached for her again. Remembering that she had the power of Dawson's body, she made a fist and swung with all of Dawson's might. She hit the Crazy just below the cheekbone. He reeled from the blow. Picking up a loose piece of steel, she hit him in the side. The sailor tried to rise. Prophet was still manipulating him.

"Stay down," Elizabeth said.

Ribs broken, breathing ragged, the Crazy struggled to get up. Elizabeth struck again, catching him squarely on the back of his head. This time he stayed down. Elizabeth turned to help Wes, but he had already freed himself by striking the Crazy's broken leg. Now Elizabeth looked back for Ralph.

Ralph was with Roberto and Jett, and was surrounded by the remaining Crazies, who were all answering the commands of Prophet. Compton was there, too, gun in hand.

"Kill them," Prophet broadcast.

Prophet was climbing through the wreckage, one arm hanging limp. The man who had declared himself ruler of the kingdom of Pot of Gold was a pathetic figure, but he was still in control of his flock. With another command from Prophet, Compton's arm stretched out, gun pointed at Jett's head.

LAST CHANCE

"*Kill Nathan Jett!*" Prophet projected.

With Prophet broadcasting thought commands to kill him, and Compton's gun pointed at his head, Jett knew that he was going to die. He had never feared anything, not even death, but now he found he did care. He had changed since meeting Ralph. It saddened him to know that Ralph would die—he hadn't felt sad since his brother's death.

A flash of silver behind Compton caught Jett's eye. Peters was taking aim. Gertie caught the movement, and the psychokinetic struck, flinging Peters against the wreckage next to Jett. Peters collapsed in a limp pile. The distraction over, Compton again pointed her gun at Jett. Her hand was shaking and her jaw was set. She was trying to resist Prophet.

"*Kill him!*" Prophet ordered.

There was no one to save them now except the Norfolk, which was in its death throes. With a mighty twist, the bulkheads bowed out and the deck rippled, knocking the survivors down like bowling pins. When the ship settled again, what had been a bulkhead was the deck, and a crevice ran the width of the ship. Jett shouted above the din.

"Ralph, hold Gertie so she won't hurt anyone."

Ralph got to his feet, holding out his arms to steady himself.

"I don't want to hurt you," Gertie said. "Stay where you are."

"I don't want to hurt you, too," Ralph replied.

She stared at Ralph, pushing with her mind. To her surprise, debris behind him clattered across the deck. Trying again, she knocked one of the Crazies from her feet. Ralph came on. Quickly, she picked up a three-foot piece of pipe, tossed it in the air, and pushed it psychokinetically. Ralph was almost on her, deflecting the pipe with his arm.

"Ow!" Ralph exclaimed.

Then Ralph wrapped Gertie in a bear hug.

"Tell me if I squeeze you too tight," Ralph said. "I squoze a bird too hard one time and it kinda died."

Gertie struggled in his arms, but had no hope of breaking free.

Compton had gone down hard when the ship twisted; now a stream of blood was running down her face. Jett had time to limp to her before she recovered her senses. He wielded a piece of steel for the knockout blow. Compton was quick, and rolled away from the blow. Jett adjusted his aim, bringing the piece of steel down low on her back, puncturing one of the nitrogen cylinders. Her pack inflated and burst, the spray of liquid nitrogen creating a cloud of ice particles. Before the ice cloud dissipated, she was up in a low crouch.

Jett feigned a swing, watching her countermove. She was fast. He moved in, and she brought a leg to his head so fast he barely had time to block it. He counter-punched, his fist finding a rock-hard stomach. The deck was moving beneath them now, rising as if to crush them against the electric field coming from above. Compton attacked furiously with blinding kicks and punches. He took them, surprised by her power. If they had fought on level ground, she would have been a better match, but she stumbled, feet tangling in debris, and Jett caught her jaw with a right fist. Stunned, she dropped her guard, and he pummeled her head.

Seeing Compton go down, Prophet charged Jett from behind. With a one hundred and eighty-degree turn, Roberto swung with his machete, catching Prophet in the midsection and stopping his mental broadcasts once and for all. Without Prophet's manipulation, those advancing on Jett stopped, faces blank. With another shudder from the Norfolk they panicked.

"This way!" Dr. Kellum shouted again from the corridor where Roberto had found the nexus.

Only Dr. Kellum's face was visible. The corridor was nearly filled with wreckage, except for a hole at the bottom through which Kellum was shouting.

Roberto herded the last survivors toward Kellum. Elizabeth and Wes were trapped behind the wreckage of a biplane on the other side of what was left of the hangar.

"What about the other door?" Jett shouted to them across the chasm.

"We never found it," Wes shouted back.

"Climb through to me," Jett shouted.

"There's no way," Wes said.

"Take Ralph and go," Elizabeth shouted from Dawson's body.

The ship continued to twist slowly; by now, the original decks and bulkheads nearly unrecognizable.

"Take care of Ralph," Wes called.

"Like I would a brother," Jett shouted back.

Jett turned away and then stopped, stepping back to the blockage and shouting to Wes and Elizabeth.

"There's a nuclear warhead in here somewhere," he told them. "If you make it out, get away as fast as you can."

"You can let Gertie go now, Ralph," Jett said.

Gertie turned on Jett as soon as Ralph released her, but she was uncertain, not angry.

"Come with us?" Jett said.

After a glance at Prophet's body, she nodded, then turned and climbed over the wreckage toward the hole where Dr. Kellum continued to call. Compton was only half conscious. Even though she had tried to kill Wes, she was still part of his team. Helping her to her feet, he wrapped his arm around her waist. The left side of her face was swelling, her left eye merely a purple slit. She spoke through a split lip.

"I want a rematch."

"Anytime," Jett said.

Gertie climbed like a mountain goat, but Ralph was clumsy and slow. They were walking bent over by the time they reached the opening, with no more than five feet of headroom left in the hangar. Jett supported Compton up the climb, shoving Ralph into the opening behind Gertie.

"I can do it myself, Wes," Ralph protested.

Compton went next, crawling behind Ralph and pushing gently on his bottom to keep him moving. Jett climbed in last. It was a tunnel through twisted steel. Halfway through he found Peters. He was punctured in several places, pinned in the wreckage like a butterfly in a collection. He still wore his weapon, but there was no time to retrieve it.

Jett continued through, pulled the last few feet by Monica and Roberto. What had been a corridor was now a steel tunnel ending in the green glow of the door that Ralph had found. Holes that had been compartment doors were all along the tunnel, some below, some above. There were the body parts of frozen men here too, but none moved now. Gertie was ahead of them, maneuvering through the slowly twisting tunnel toward the green light. Monica helped Dr. Kellum, and Roberto helped Compton. Jett took Ralph's arm.

"I can do it myself, you know," Ralph protested.

"I know, Ralph, but is it okay if I hang on to you to keep my balance?" Jett said.

"Okee-dokee, Nate," Ralph said.

They reached the green glow without losing Ralph. Kellum and Monica stepped in as they arrived.

"A maze of these doors?" Jett said to Roberto.

"Hundreds, maybe thousands," Roberto said, his face creased with worry. Then, with a smile, he said, "They've got to lead somewhere."

He took Compton's arm and disappeared into the mist.

"Want I should go get Wes and Elizabeth?" Ralph said.

"No, Ralph."

"I wouldn't get lost or anything," Ralph said.

"I know," Wes told him. "It's time to go."

"And when ya gotta go, ya gotta," Ralph said.

"And I really gots to go," Jett and Ralph said together.

Then, arm in arm, they stepped into the green mist.

WRECKAGE

The ship was being crushed and twisted by a force beyond Wes's comprehension. If he and Elizabeth were to survive, they would have to find Ralph's other exit without him. Wes wanted to leave the wounded Crazies behind, but Elizabeth was already helping the one she had clubbed, getting him to his feet. In Dawson's body she was stronger than Wes, and held the man up with little strain. Wes struggled to get the man with the broken leg over his shoulder in a fireman's lift. When they were both ready, supporting or carrying semiconscious men, they started down what was left of the corridor. There was a green glow at the end of the corridor, but no way to know where it led. The Norfolk continued to twist and elongate; what precious little headroom remained was fast disappearing.

"Don't leave me," Rust shouted from behind.

Wes turned slowly, causing the wounded man over his shoulder to whimper. Rust was conscious again, his face pressed between the steel beams that held him.

"We can't get you free," Wes said.

"You're not leaving me here!" Rust shouted.

"There's nothing I can do," Wes said.

Elizabeth started forward again, supporting the injured sailor. Suddenly the air in front of Rust glowed and a fireball streaked toward Elizabeth. Wes's warning came too late. Elizabeth and the sailor burst into flame.

"Scramble Anita!" Elizabeth screamed as she fell, rolling to put out the flames. "Shamita, scramble Anita!"

Wes dropped his man and ran to Elizabeth, beating the flames with his hands. Dawson's clothes were blackened from the waist to the head and nearly indistinguishable from the burned skin around his neck. Blisters covered most of the left side of his face. When the flames were out, Wes checked the sailor Elizabeth had been helping, feeling his smoldering body for a pulse. He was dead.

"Wes, don't let Dawson die to save me," Elizabeth said through blistered lips.

With a flash, Rust launched another fireball, striking the man Wes had been helping. The sailor writhed on the ground and Rust hit him again. Soon he lay still.

"Help me or you'll burn," Rust said.

"Shamita said my body is almost gone," Elizabeth said. "You can't save me, but you can save Dawson. He has a wife, and brothers and a sister. He's a brave man, Wes, a good man. I have no more right to live than he does."

Then Dawson's face contorted with pain; pain that Elizabeth was feeling too.

"This is your last chance," Rust said.

"I'm coming."

Wes hurried back to Rust and looked at the steel that held him. It was impossible for one man to move.

"Maybe if I use a lever," Wes said.

Rust watched him warily.

"You need to get me free before you try to lift again," Rust said.

Leaning forward, Wes looked behind Rust, trying to see where the steel piercing his body attached.

"I can't see," Wes said. "I need to reach behind you."

"Carefully," Rust said.

Wes reached into the ruined latticework of the catapult, moving slowly. Then, extending two fingers, he rammed them into Rust's left eye. Rust screamed, striking blindly at Wes and then clamping his hands over his ruined eye.

Bent nearly in half, Wes hurried down what was left of the passage, careful not to fall into one of the open hatches that were twisted into the deck. Taking Elizabeth by the arms, he dragged her toward the green light.

Rust was incoherent now, his angry screams blending into the cacophony of metal being contorted. Then the steel that held Rust lifted and he became part of the mass forming the tunnel. Rust hung from above now, still alive. His head moved slowly back and forth, searching for Wes. When he locked on Wes, a fireball materialized, rocketing toward him and Elizabeth. Wes ducked, and the fireball disappeared into the green glow. Now Wes crawled, dragging the body that held his Elizabeth. Rust fired again, his fireball hitting the side of the shrinking corridor and coming apart in a shower of candle-sized flames.

More fireballs were launched, impacting around Wes, spraying him with embers and singeing his skin. Then the structure holding Rust twisted sharply, and with a last scream the Special was pressed into the steel mosaic making up the top of the collapsing passage, his crushed body indistinguishable from the other debris.

Wes reached the green mist and paused, not knowing what waited on the other side. It didn't matter. It was the end of this world. The remaining passage was just big enough to crawl through. Gathering his strength, Wes dragged Dawson's unconscious body into the mist.

ERUPTION

Absorbed by the remarkable contortions of the field, Dr. Lee and his technicians were slow to notice the alert signal indicating a breakout. When they did, they realized that the hole in the field was in their own backyard.

"What's going on?" Woolman demanded, hovering at Dr. Lee's shoulder.

Dr. Lee ignored Woolman. They had monitored the changing shape of the field and its slow collapse. Slowly it had assumed a cigar shape with each end of the cigar representing a magnetic pole. One pole terminated near Rainbow. The other pole couldn't be detected locally, nor by the agency's Keyhole spy satellite.

"Patch in the cameras," Dr. Lee ordered.

A dozen security cameras monitored the compound day and night. Now it was nearly dawn and the sky was glowing in the east, but the desert was still steeped in darkness, and the cameras could distinguish little. Every thirty seconds the image switched to a view from a new camera. Finally camera eight was called up, and in one corner of the monitor Dr. Lee saw a small fire.

"Zoom in," he ordered.

The camera moved clumsily, but soon the fire was in the middle of the screen. A small patch of sage was burning. Opposite the fire was a soft green glow, like the light from a television in a dark room. Then a figure appeared, a silhouette in the green light. He was dragging a body.

"We have a breakout," Woolman said.

Woolman turned to an agent who acted as his bodyguard.

"Take a team and pick them up. No exceptions, no matter who it is!"

The agent nodded once, understanding that Woolman's orders meant that anyone escaping from Pot of Gold was to be killed, even if it was one of their agents. Woolman had carefully prepared his people for the possibility of having to kill their own with a cover story about Jett and the others having been turned into Specials.

"We'll have them in a few minutes," Woolman said. "Now close that opening so no one else gets out."

"There's nothing we can do," Dr. Lee said. "But Pot of Gold is still collapsing."

"There are no other breakouts?" Woolman asked anxiously.

"No other breakouts."

Dr. Lee turned his attention to the tube-shaped field displayed before him, wondering what form the final collapse would take. Then the computer-generated model representing the field reshaped again, the center of the tube flattening first and then collapsing toward both ends. The final sealing of Pot of Gold was coming from the inside out, and half of what was left of the Norfolk was coming toward them.

A technician shouted for Dr. Lee's attention. The fact that the young woman was seated against the far wall indicated that her function was of secondary importance. In fact, so peripheral was her station that Dr. Lee couldn't remember what it was for.

"We have incoming aircraft," the young woman said.

Then Dr. Lee remembered that Rainbow monitored air traffic over the facility. Rainbow hid itself by pretending to be an abandoned military facility, but the airspace over the military reserve was still restricted.

"What?" Dr. Lee said, having difficulty shifting his attention from the collapse of Pot of Gold. "Are they yours?" he asked Woolman.

"No," Woolman said. "Number and type of aircraft?"

"Two. Judging by signature and speed I'd say they are helicopters," said the technician. Then, after another look at her radar screen, she said, "They just dropped below our radar."

Woolman pulled his cell phone from his pocket and punched the number pad.

"I want air cover over Rainbow, and I want it now," he ordered.

PILE UP

Wes found himself in a desert just like the one that had surrounded the Norfolk, a green oval still glowing behind him. There were lights from a building a short distance away, but he had to rest before he could hope to lift Dawson's body again. It was dawn, and the sun was just peeking above the horizon, driving the shadows slowly back to their daytime hideaways. Elizabeth moaned through Dawson's body, reminding Wes of her last words. She wanted this man saved, and Wes would honor her request if at all possible.

Without the field to nurture him, Wes found his weakness lingering. He had come to depend on the quick recovery from exhaustion he had experienced on the Nimitz and the Norfolk. But Dawson needed immediate medical attention, and there wasn't time for Wes to recover his full strength.

Studying Dawson's wounds in the dim light, Wes realized that there was no way to carry him without aggravating his injuries. Wes squatted, sliding his hands under his body. Then he heard an engine.

A van was coming from the buildings in the distance. It raced across the desert at a reckless pace. Wes's heart sank when he realized that the van was identical to the one that had attacked them in New Mexico. There was nowhere to run, and he wouldn't leave Dawson and Elizabeth, so he stood between the injured man and the approaching van.

Then there was a screech behind him, and Wes turned to see a mass emerging from the green mist. What was left of the cruiser Norfolk was coming home.

Wes dragged Dawson's body away from the aperture. The metal was pouring from the opening now, piling up and tumbling toward him. He heaved Dawson to his shoulder, feeling a sharp stabbing pain in his back. Dawson gasped as his baked flesh was torn. Wes staggered away from the emerging mass, angling away from the metal and the van. Dawson moaned with every step.

The steel of the Norfolk piled up behind them, only to be pushed away by more emerging from inside. The mass was so great that the ground shook as tons of compressed steel poured into the desert with the sound of a nonstop auto wreck.

The van had stopped; men were hanging out the doors, looking at the spectacle in the desert. Wes continued walking away, his legs as well as his back hurting now as he hurried deeper into the desert. Looking back over his shoulder at the growing mound, Wes remembered Jett's warning. There was a nuclear warhead somewhere in that mass, and it could be live. Wes jogged, quickly using up his energy reserves. Finally, exhausted, he collapsed to his knees, first laying Dawson down as gently as he could. Dawson was unconscious, the pain too much for him to bear. Wes was glad, because it meant that Elizabeth and Anita were unconscious, too.

The van was coming again. It would be over soon; the men in the van would make sure that they never told their tale. Wes lifted Dawson's head and cradled it in his lap, stroking the man's hair. Still unconscious, Elizabeth wouldn't know that he was holding her when the end came, but he held her just the same.

The steel was being expelled toward the buildings in the distance. The sound was painfully loud, and mixed with the clanging and screeching was a sound like fingernails on a blackboard. It was this cacophony that hid the sound of the approaching helicopters.

The sun was nearly over the horizon now, and the helicopters came out of the sun, skimming over the desert, flying recklessly low. There were two of them, both black like the one that had rescued them in New Mexico. One helicopter veered toward the van, the other coming toward Wes and Dawson.

A door opened in the helicopter approaching the van and the barrel of a machine gun protruded. The gun fired, the slugs stitching across the desert toward the van, then across it; the side windows shattered. The van swerved, tilting up on two wheels, and came to a stop, slamming back to the earth. The helicopter roared past the van, turned in a tight circle, and headed back, strafing the van again. Wes saw no movement in the van, but the gunner continued to fire. In the distance Wes saw two more vans coming across the desert.

The thump of the helicopter rotors and the explosive sputter of the machine gun could hardly be distinguished from the racket created by the expulsion of the Norfolk. Wes watched the second helicopter approach and land as if it were a silent movie. He covered Dawson's head with his body as the helicopter landed and its backwash scoured them with a miniature sandstorm. Wes opened his eyes to see two men running toward them. Both were dressed in black flight suits; both wore black helmets with dark visors.

"I'm Doctor Wes Martin," Wes tried to explain as they reached him, but they ignored him.

One man lifted Dawson over his shoulder, the second helped Wes. They hurried to the helicopter and were helped inside. Wes sat with Dawson's head in his lap, stroking Dawson's hair but seeing Elizabeth. Then the helicopter lifted off and the door was closed. The last thing Wes saw was the twisted remains of the cruiser Norfolk still pouring into the desert.

Remembering the nuclear warhead, Wes pulled one of the helicopter's crew down to him and put his lips to the side of the man's head, shouting so that he could be heard inside the helmet.

"There may be a live nuclear warhead in that wreckage. It could go off!"

Leaving Wes and Dawson, the crewman hurried forward to the cockpit. Abruptly, the angle of the helicopter changed, the ship climbing as the pitch of its engines shifted. The pilot was racing for cover.

The man Wes had warned came back, taking off his helmet and squatting next to Wes, shouting so that he could be heard. He was a young man, maybe thirty, with a short military cut to his hair, but wearing no military or civilian insignia.

"How big of a warhead is it? How many kilotons?"

"I don't know," Wes said. "I think it came from the aircraft carrier Nimitz."

That meant something to the man, and he nodded.

"How long do we have?"

"Minutes, at best," Wes guessed.

With that, the crewman returned to the cockpit to talk with the pilot and copilot. The discussion was animated; the crew was deciding on a course of action. A minute later the crewman returned, talking to the man who had carried Dawson. Together they opened the side door, sliding it wide. Wes could see the other helicopter, and behind that the remains of the Norfolk still piling up in the desert. In the sky above the wreckage he could see specks. There were helicopters in pursuit.

Suddenly the helicopter rose sharply, climbing so steeply that Wes had to brace himself to keep from falling over. The climb continued, the crewmen by the door hanging on with one hand, and one of the men leaning out, watching the pursuit behind them. After a minute of climbing, the helicopter dove just as steeply, angling toward the ground in a reckless descent. Wes could see the rocky side of a mountain flash by the door as they levelled out. They were flying low through a mountain pass.

The helicopter maneuvered sharply, negotiating the pass. After a few minutes it went into a steep descent, the sound of the rotors echoing off the canyon walls. Suddenly Wes's stomach fluttered the way it did in elevators. Then, with a thump, they were on the ground. The engines shut down, and the thump of the rotors slowed. Looking outside, Wes saw the other helicopter land. The crew were frenetic now, shouting to each other, disconnecting wiring, preparing the helicopter to survive the electromagnetic pulse of a nuclear blast. One of the crewmen was boosted to the roof of the helicopter, and Wes could hear him working on the engine above.

They were in a canyon, its steep stone walls only fifty yards from the helicopter. Then there was a bright flash, as if a thousand strobe lights had gone off; the crewman slid off the roof and dove inside as soon as he hit the ground. As Wes bent to cover Dawson, the sound of the nuclear explosion reached their canyon. The shock wave would be right behind.

LAST CALL

Robert Daly's wife and son had struck again, coming to his Chicago office and replacing the pole lamp that had matched his original office furniture with one of his son's creations. It was made of bronze tubing and glass, of course, the tubing holding together the tall glass structure that ended in a glass ball. There were no light bulbs that Daly could see; instead, the whole structure glowed with a soft light as if filled with neon gas. The strangest thing about the lamp, however, was that he liked it. In fact, it was a beautiful piece, both aesthetically pleasing and functional at the same time. He was sure that his son could make a business out of such creations if he would mass-produce them, lowering the cost per unit. Daly was equally sure his son would never go "commercial" with his art—not as long as his father continued to support him.

His phone sounded, and he answered his secretary's buzz.

"Doctor Martin is calling for you," she said.

"Put him through," Daly said. "Hello, Doctor Martin. How is Ms. Fox-worth?"

"She's still unconscious," Dr. Martin said.

"What about the little girl and the man you brought back with you?"

"No change, I'm afraid. Mr. Dawson suffered cardiac arrest, and by the time your people revived him he had suffered anoxia. There was brain damage and he's comatose."

"I'm sorry to hear that. I would have liked to talk to him," Daly said.

"Anita is semiconscious—she seems to be stable, but incoherent most of the time."

"Are Mr. Dawson and Ms. Foxworth still linked?"

"Yes. Anita was psychically linked with Mr. Dawson before I integrated their minds. Then, when I linked the dreamers together, Anita's connection to Dawson was strengthened. Elizabeth apparently had a powerful latent ability that was released when I integrated her mind with the others. Eventually, her and Dawson's minds fused."

"What about the other woman?"

"Wanda? She doesn't dream of the ship anymore—in fact, she doesn't dream at all. Mr. Dawson is broadcasting the equivalent of white noise and that's all Wanda picks up."

"There's no way to break the link?" Daly asked.

"It's possible if the psychological trauma of what happened to them—being burned and seeing all that death—is so great that their coma is a defense mechanism. I doubt it. I believe Dawson is the key. He's the transmitter, and Anita, Wanda, and Elizabeth are the receivers. Until he stops transmitting, Elizabeth and Anita will share his coma."

"I see," Daly said. "It must have been hard for you, knowing that by saving Mr. Dawson you were condemning Elizabeth and Anita."

"I hoped we could find a solution."

"A way they all could live?" Daly said.

"Yes."

They were silent for a minute, Daly thinking about the problem and possible solutions.

"Doctor Martin, the foundation is extending your grant for another year. We are very interested in your work with schizophrenics and your theory that they may be receiving alien psychic transmissions. Your recent experiences make your theory even more credible."

"I'm taking a leave from the university. I'm going to care for Elizabeth."

"I understand. The grant will be available when you are ready."

"One more thing, Mr. Daly. The government is claiming that the explosion in New Mexico was caused by terrorists smuggling a nuclear weapon into the country."

"Yes."

"But it's a lie. The weapon came from the aircraft carrier Nimitz."

"And you want to tell the world what really happened?" Daly said.

"Yes. The sinking of the Nimitz, the Philadelphia Experiment, the men and women trapped there by their own government, the nuclear explosion, everything. The people have a right to know."

As a trustee of the Kellum Foundation, Daly had a more practical view of people's rights. He and the other trustees had determined that the most good would come from supporting the government's cover story. The foundation's sociometric projections suggested that the most likely outcomes of the government's story would be increased border security, including a wall between Mexico and the U.S., and more coastal patrols. The end result of that would be a sharp decline in illegal immigration, drug smuggling, and unemployment among the primarily Hispanic populations of the border states. The benefits of an improved standard of living would be passed on to their children, moving much of the Southwest Hispanic community into the middle class. Two other outcomes would be unnecessary increases in the defense budget, and a continuation of conservative dominance of the political parties, both acceptable to the foundation.

"Doctor Martin, I understand your frustration, but you and the others are safe only as long as you don't tell your story. No one will believe you anyway. You have no proof."

"So they get away with it?"

"Not everyone. Some of the key players were at ground zero in New Mexico, and many more up the chain of command have been fired or reassigned. If it helps you keep faith in our government, you should know that very few officials actually knew the whole story of what happened in Philadelphia in 1943. Even fewer knew that the crew of the Norfolk were still alive."

"Then, what's to prevent it from happening again?"

"The only one who could duplicate the Philadelphia Experiment for certain was Doctor Kellum. Besides, the intelligence agencies are afraid of the powers they unleashed—both the physical and the psychic. They're not anxious to pursue that line of research."

Daly didn't add that the foundation was very interested in continuing the research into resonant magnetic fields, and had two projects already underway.

"Then it's over," Dr. Martin said.

"Except for your people," Daly said.

There was nothing more to say except goodbye. When Dr. Martin hung up, Daly rocked back in his chair, putting his feet up on his glass desk, and staring at the glow of his son's lamp. Dr. Martin had called him with no agenda—only an empty threat to blow the whistle on the government's cover-up, and to update him on Elizabeth and Anita's conditions. Daly knew Dr. Martin was too smart to go public with what he knew about the loss of the Nimitz and the New Mexico disaster. The real reason for the call had to be read between the lines. Dr. Martin had made it clear that Elizabeth and Anita could not recover as long as they were linked to Roger Dawson, who could linger in a coma for years and was unlikely ever to regain consciousness.

The solution to Dr. Martin's problem was obvious. Buzzing his secretary, Daly asked her once again to get the director of security on the phone.

AWAKENING

Len was late the day Elizabeth woke up. Wanda, Shamita, and Wes were there, and Anita came from her hospital room wearing a pink robe and bunny slippers. For three days Elizabeth's brain waves had made steady progress from abnormal delta to normal alpha rhythms. She had begun to respond to sounds and touch the day before, and her eyelids had fluttered frequently as if she was trying to open them. She woke briefly in the morning, but by the time Wes arrived she was asleep again. Everyone except Len was gathered around her bed when she woke the second time that day.

The others greeted her warmly as if she were back from a long trip. Too emotional for words, Wes let the others talk first and express their relief.

"I was afraid I waited too long to call the ambulance," Shamita said.

"I'm all right," Elizabeth assured her.

Elizabeth held out her hand for Anita, who took it, stepping close. Anita's eyes were dark circles still, her cheeks hollows, and her arms and legs stick thin. She had no body fat, but was eating well, quickly gaining back weight.

"How are you, Anita?" Elizabeth asked.

"Good. Know what I dreamed about last night? Bunnies," Anita said with a toothless smile.

Then she held up her foot so that Anita could see her bunny slippers.

"Doctor Martin gave me these. Aren't they neat?"

"I'm happy for you," Elizabeth said. "Did I wait too long to get you out of the dream? What do you remember?"

"I remember being burned a little," Anita said sadly, then quickly added, "I dreamed about going to school yesterday."

"I'm happy for you, Anita. What about you, Wanda? What are your dreams?"

"Last night I dreamed I was playing bingo. To tell you the truth, I haven't dreamed about anything but that ship in so long, I kind of miss it."

Now Elizabeth reached out for Wes.

"What happened to Roger Dawson?" she asked.

"He was badly burned. His heart stopped, and by the time he was revived there was brain damage. He died a few days ago."

Wes avoided Elizabeth's eyes when he told her of Dawson, and she knew there was more to tell, but that this wasn't the time to hear it.

"What about Ralph and Monica, Jett, and Dr. Kellum, and all the others?" Elizabeth asked.

"We've heard nothing," Wes said. "No one knows where they've gone. I called Dr. Birnbaum, about Ralph."

Nothing was said now; they were all saddened by the loss of Ralph and Monica, but Wes and Elizabeth were also saddened by the loss of so many others they had met. Then Elizabeth realized who was missing.

"Len?" she said abruptly. "He was shot. Is he all right?"

"He's fine," Wes said. "He should be here."

"He's afraid of me," Wanda said.

Wanda held up a pack of Lucky Strikes.

"He's supposed to take me to the airport. I aim to smoke the whole pack before we get there. Ha!"

There was a tap on the door frame—it was Len.

"Good to see you awake," Len said from the hallway.

"Come in so I can see you," Elizabeth said.

"Okay, but just for a second. I'm all set to drive Wanda to the airport."

As Len stepped into the room, the air was filled with an overpowering stew of perfumes and colognes mixed with other unidentifiable smells.

"Len, you stink," Anita said.

"I couldn't stink," Len said. "I'm wearing Brut, Old Spice, British Sterling, and some of every other old cologne I could find."

"Get back in the hall," Wes said.

"I'm only here long enough to pick up Wanda," Len said.

"What are those things around your neck?" Elizabeth asked.

"Car air fresheners," Len said, holding up the Christmas tree–shaped pieces of cardboard. "I've got fresh pine, cinnamon, and lemon-lime."

"Get out of here, Len, you're going to put Elizabeth back in a coma," Shamita said, holding her nose.

"Time to go, Wanda," Len said cheerfully.

"It's a good try, Lenny," Wanda said. "But it's only a few minutes to the airport."

"I booked you out of Portland so you don't have to make that extra connection. It's two and a half hours from here," Len said.

Wanda glowered at Len, cigarettes still clutched in her hand.

"And I've been on an all-bean diet for three days," Len said.

Then Wanda cracked, laughing loud and long, and ending with a deep cough. When she stopped coughing, she held out her cigarettes. Len took them triumphantly.

"But you take a shower before we go," Wanda said.

"The cologne's on my clothes. I have a change in the car."

"You're all right, Lenny," Wanda said.

Holding her nose with one hand, she looped her other arm through his as they walked into the hall.

When Wes looked back at Elizabeth, her eyes were closed, her breathing deep and slow. He leaned close, watching her eyelids, seeing that her eyes were moving rapidly back and forth under the lids.

"Sweet dreams," Wes said, then kissed her on the forehead.

EPILOGUE

Nine months later

Luther Simpson's pickup sped along the rural Kansas road, anticipating every turn, hill, and gully as if it had a mind of its own. After forty years of driving the road, Luther needed only a small part of his conscious mind to guide the truck, even in the dark. Singing along with the country music coming from the radio, he was thinking about getting a cold beer out of the fridge when he got home and sitting down with his wife, Carolyn, to watch a little TV.

Luther passed the turn for the Connors' farm, knowing now that he was ten miles from home. The Connors hadn't owned the farm for fifteen years, but it would always be the Connors' farm to Luther and the others who were Kansas born and raised.

Another couple of miles, and he crested another small rise and saw a green glow in the distance—something that didn't belong. It was the wrong color for fire, and there had never been lights there. He judged that the glow was coming from Bill Miller's wheat field.

Another rise, and he saw the strange glow again. He marked the direction, confirming that it was in Miller's field. Another rise, and the green glow was gone. Luther searched for the glow at every turn and rise, but never saw it again. After a couple of miles he judged that he was near where he'd seen the light, and stopped on the road, getting out into the cool spring night air. Climbing into the back of his pickup, he scanned the field, seeing nothing—no glow, no burned ground. Climbing back in, he started the engine, turned the radio back on, and promised himself to give Bill a call in the morning.

With his headlights on high beam, he shifted through the gears, picking up speed. Speed limits were speed suggestions to Luther, and he routinely exceeded them on roads as familiar as this one. Then his headlights picked out a figure walking along the side of the road. It was a big man with a funny gait, wearing a shiny pair of coveralls. He had long, sloping strides and swung his arms in wide arcs. Wherever he was going, he was going in a hurry, but the strange thing was that there was noplace to go unless you lived nearby, and Luther was sure he had never seen the man before.

Slowing, Luther pulled up alongside and looked him over. His shiny coveralls were dirty, with many rips and tears, and the sleeves had been torn off. Luther honked, and the man stopped. When Luther rolled down his passenger window the man came over and leaned his head in. He had a large mouth with thick lips, and a heavy brow. To Luther, he looked retarded.

"Hihowyadoin?" the man said so fast that Luther could barely pick out the words. At the same time, he put his hand through the open window. "My name's Ralph, what's yours?"

"Luther," he said, smiling reflexively in response to the man's big grin and shaking his hand, feeling a powerful grip. "Where are you going, Ralph?"

"Home."

"Do you live near here?"

Ralph pulled his head out of the truck and looked around, then put his head back in.

"I dunno," he said. "I live that way, but I'm not so good at figuring how far it is."

"Are you staying with someone near here? Maybe the Millers or the Sweenys?"

"I don't think so," Ralph said.

"Then where did you come from?"

"Back that-a-way," Ralph said.

Using hand motions, he pointed back and forth.

"Then that way, and that way, then that way, then that way. It took a long time to find the way."

Luther decided that Ralph wasn't smart enough to explain himself.

"My wife made an apple pie this morning, Ralph. What would you say to coming home and having a piece with me?"

"With ice cream on top?" Ralph asked with a big smile.

"Got a gallon of vanilla in the freezer."

"Well okee-dokee then," Ralph said, climbing into the truck.

Giving the truck gas, Luther shifted through the gears. Carolyn was in for a surprise, but she was a people person, and he knew she would love Ralph. Suddenly, Ralph's hand shot out and he thumped himself on the side of the head.

"How could I be so stupid?" Ralph said.

"What's the matter?" Luther asked.

"I forgot my friends. Can they come, too?"

"Friends?" Luther said, stopping the truck.

Looking through the rear window, Luther saw people coming out of Bill Miller's wheat field. A big man in a silver suit like Ralph's led the way, and behind him came a ragged looking mix of sailors and civilians. There were two dozen on the road now and still more coming through the wheat.

"Hope you got lots of pie," Ralph said.